The Wild Irish Rose

Jody Clark & Jessie Taylor

ISBN-10: 0998086428
ISBN-13: 978-0-9980864-2-2

DEDICATION

For the endless support of our friends and family.

&

For all the small towns and the people who live there.

&

For all the dark things that held the light…

ACKNOWLEDGMENTS

* Front cover photo of Maine sign by Christian Burris
* Back cover photo of Maine drive-in by Nicole Champagne
* All chapter titles & lyrics used by permission of Chris Trapper

* A very special thanks to Chris Trapper & The Push Stars *

When I sat down to write my 4th screenplay, I didn't have a clue what I wanted to write about. At the time, I was listening to a lot of Chris Trapper and his former band The Push Stars. Not only did I find myself hitting repeat on a few of their songs, but those same songs began to create distinctive scenes in my head. At that point, I came up with the storyline, characters, and the dialogue. I then decided to use a handful of Chris' songs to help facilitate the story.

When I finished, I knew I needed to get Chris' permission and blessing before I attempted to search for a director or the financing. I sent him a random social media message and asked if he would give the screenplay a read, and not only did he read it, but he loved it. We have since become good friends and he has been a huge supporter of mine. Even though it's a small-scale movie, it's been a long, tiresome process searching for the proper financing. So, like the rest of my screenplays, I decided to turn "The Wild Irish Rose" into a novel just to *get the story out there*.

Foreword

Writing, in its purest form, is a beautiful tool. While I have made a good living off songwriting for nearly two decades now, I realize that my greatest thrills have been the rare moments when someone was actually inspired by my work.

About a decade ago a young writer approached me and said some of my songs had inspired him to write a screenplay. At the time I was maybe a little jaded to what the talent level of someone who was inspired by my work might be. But for some reason, this seemed different because of the determination and enthusiasm this particular writer conveyed. It seemed to say he meant business, or in the least, believed in his work a lot.

I was curious to read it, and when I did, my instincts were correct: his characters came to life, their conflicts became my conflicts, and as I turned each page I couldn't wait to see what happened next. In truth, I forgot I had anything to do with the process because to me, his story was better than my song.

And now, the screenplay blossoming into a novel is just the sort of thing that gets me excited. How a few simple songs became a small town filled with characters rich with longing, desire and broken dreams, I'll never know, but either way, I am happy to be along for the ride.

- Chris Trapper

1
Boston Girl

"But I always ended up by myself
With the blues in my heart
And my love on the shelf"

Sometimes, the longer you stay away from home, the harder it is to return. It's been nearly seven years since Emily McLoughlin has been home. To her, home wasn't just a mailing address, it was more of a feeling — one of security, comfort, and belonging. It was a lack of all those things that began the stirrings of homesickness in Emily that she would soon no longer be able to deny.

As Emily rode the T through Boston, she let her soft green eyes fall on a small child sitting in its mother's lap a few seats away. The child, not more than 18 months old, stared curiously back at her while the mother stared distractedly out the window.

The little girl looked at Emily with large serious eyes, the way children do when they are sizing up adults. She was reading Emily's well-made-up face for a sign of emotion but found only a blank surface, so she continued to regard her cautiously.

It felt refreshing to be studied through innocent eyes, thought Emily. A small smile tugged at the corner of her lips, which she always kept painted the color of merlot wine.

The toddler caught Emily's smile and was delighted at the gleam of light her small movement created across one of her many piercings. Emily watched the child studying all the many trinkets that decorated her earlobes and lips. She smiled again and shook her head to dazzle the child further.

This small gesture was enough for the little girl to determine that even though Emily looked quite different, she was not a threat. The toddler opened her mouth in an expression of joy and smiled back at Emily as she threw her chubby arms up in a gesture of enthusiasm. Her charm was not wasted on Emily.

"Hi, beautiful," said Emily.

The remark drew the attention of the well-dressed thirty-something year old mother who cast a defensive look at Emily. The woman's eyes settled on Emily's oxblood red Doc Martin boots, which were laced tightly over her ripped black fishnets stockings. The woman's look of distain increased as her gaze reached Emily's short black and red plaid skirt and tattered Ramones t-shirt, which she wore beneath and soft leather jacket. Emily fidgeted nervously with one of her piercings and chanced a smile at the toddler's mother.

The woman looked at her in disgust and turned her baby in her lap out of Emily's view. She picked up her three hundred dollar Gucci purse and moved it from the outside of the seat to a location secured between her body and the side of the subway train.

Typical rich bitch, thought Emily. She was used to the judgmental stares by now. It was times like these that she actually looked forward to getting inside the walls of the club. At least there, she received lingering looks of appreciation instead of disapproving glares.

A snicker from a few seats back distracted her, and she became acutely aware she was the subject of amusement from a group of young men behind her. She cast an annoyed look over her shoulder at the group of young college boys. They were all sporting Red Sox baseball hats and jerseys.

One of them gave her a wide-toothed, greasy smile. He let his eyes wander slowly from her face to her ample chest and didn't bother hiding his growing excitement at what he found there. In an attempt to distract herself from their hushed tones and muffled snickers, she pulled on one of the magenta streaks she had dyed into her dark brown hair.

"Are you going to work or are you… getting off?" one of the boys asked in her direction.

The other two chuckled in appreciation.

"I bet she wants to *get off* with me at the next stop," added another.

Emily felt her cheeks grow hot as she fumbled around in her purse for her ear buds. In her experience, assholes like this usually settled down if she could just manage to ignore them long enough.

Just then, she felt one of them grab a lock of her hair. He stroked it softly through his fingers and leaned close to her ear.

"What do you say there, sweetheart?" he asked now inches from her face.

"I say being a dick won't make yours bigger," Emily growled fiercely.

The smile fell from his face when he realized he had misjudged her. He quickly held up two hands and began to back off slowly. The others had grown equally somber.

"Take it easy there, beautiful. We were just messing around with you," he tried to assure her.

Emily glared at him through fiery eyes as she watched him return to his seat. The others regarded her with surprise as if they had attempted to pet a dog they mistook as friendly, only to find it snapping and snarling at their fingertips.

The train came to a stop, and without taking her eyes off them, Emily got up to leave. As she approached the door, Emily caught the toddler out of the corner of her eye peeking at her over her mother's shoulder.

Once she was on the sidewalk and briskly walking toward her

destination, she was able to shake off the tension from her train ride. The air was starting to take on the crispness of fall, and the subtle change in the air made her think of happier times. She let her mind travel back to a time when she and her little sister, Lily, would rake leaves up into a big pile in their backyard and take turns jumping into them. Lily would laugh as Emily made it rain leaves on top of her head until she was wearing a colorful crown of red and golden hues. It seemed like a lifetime ago.

A black and white photo displayed in one of the storefront windows brought Emily out of her reverie. She paused a moment to admire the light the photographer had caught shimmering in the darkness of a raven's wing.

Even dark things are capable of holding light, she thought and smiled at the irony. This obviously didn't apply to her. There was no light in her darkness. She lost that a long time ago. She shook her head and pushed the thought from her mind.

Despite her self-degradation, she worked up enough courage to enter the store. The walls were filled with photos of bridges, boats, baseball players, old churches and graveyards; anything and everything one might find in Boston. She felt a flutter of excitement in her chest as she looked at all the images captured so perfectly. Each one stirred a different emotion in her. She paused at each to appreciate its energy.

Remembering that she had to be somewhere, she pulled her eyes off the exhibits long enough to seek out an employee. In the back of the store she found an area with a desk. Invoices were scattered across one side and a cash register on the other.

As Emily approached, a tall, slender blonde wearing a form fitting black dress stepped out from behind a wall.

"Can I help you?" she asked in a kind voice.

Emily had a hard time making eye contact. She always had a hard time with eye contact. Her gaze darted from the desk, to the wall, to the woman, and then landed firmly on the floor.

"I…"

Emily forced her eyes back to the woman, who stood waiting patiently.

"Well, I was wondering…"

Emily's gaze was drawn to a photo of the Park Street church lit up at night. The photo made her feel small, like she was being judged. She imagined her mother sitting on a throne next to God Himself looking down at her in disgust.

"I have some photos. I have a lot of photos actually."

The woman smiled warmly waiting for Emily to finish.

"I just thought…"

Emily's eyes darted around nervously while avoiding the Park Street Church photo. She took a deep breath and looked the woman in the eyes.

"I was wondering if you'd like to display a couple here in your store?"

Understanding clicked brightly behind the woman's intelligent gray eyes.

"If you have a business card you'd like to leave, I'd be happy to look at your website," she answered professionally.

Emily felt her battleship sink down to the pit of her stomach. She didn't have either. Embarrassed, she fidgeted anxiously with thin metal bracelets on her wrists.

"Oh right," said Emily. "How stupid of me. I don't have a card to give you, and I'm kind of still working on my website."

The woman's posture tensed just slightly enough for Emily to notice.

"Oh, I see. Well, please stop by again."

Emily knew that she was being politely dismissed. She could feel her cheeks growing hot with embarrassment.

"Ok, thanks."

Emily turned quickly and headed for the door. On her way out, she didn't look at any of the art work. Instead, she held her eyes steady on the exit and the city streets beyond.

***

The red neon sign on the side of the brick building flashed *Live Exotic Dancers* below the assuming name of The Red Garter. Emily took a sharp right and headed down the alley where she found the back door.

The first person she saw on her way to the dressing room was one of the bouncers, Charlie. He greeted her with a genuine smile. She liked Charlie. He was one of the few bouncers there that actually looked out for the girls and took his job seriously. He was a lot like the big brother she never had.

"Hey Charlie! How's your little boy doing?"

"Oh, staying out of trouble for the most part. Although, we did have to have a serious talk with him yesterday about the importance of wearing pants outside the house. That little shit just hates wearing clothes. The minute the Misses wasn't looking, he stripped down to nothing and took off outside."

"He didn't learn it from me, I swear!" Emily said.

They both laughed at her joke as he clapped her on the back.

"Good one, Em!"

In the dressing room, Emily found Chloe and Amanda getting ready for the next show.

Chloe stood in front of a full-length mirror admiring her perky breasts and shifting them around inside her hot pink bikini top. Even Emily stopped to appreciate them as they rolled around like two firm oversized marbles on her chest.

Amanda was perched at one of the makeup dressers applying powder to her already too-bronzed face. When she caught Emily's pale reflection and sunken eyes in the background of her mirror, she turned a concerned face toward her.

"Jesus, Emily! You look like shit. Late night?" she asked.

"Just the usual. You know, arguing with Eric all night," Emily sighed.

With this, Chloe also turned her attention to Emily.

"Why are you even still with him?" she asked for the hundredth time. "He was a jerk when you met him and he's a jerk now…"

"And when he wakes up tomorrow, he's still going to be a jerk," Amanda finished.

"I know. I guess I just always thought I could…"

"Change him?" Amanda finished once again. "Trust me on this one, once an asshole, always an asshole. That's my motto. Just remember, if you ever decide to see the light, there's always a place for you at my apartment."

Emily was distracted by the vibration of her cell phone in her coat pocket. She anxiously fished it out and looked at it.

"Let me guess. The asshole himself?" said Chloe

The lines of worry pulled the corners of her brows together in concentration.

"No, it's not Eric. It's my Aunt Kay in Seattle. She's been leaving messages for two weeks now. She says it's important, but I'm sure it's just her annual pitch to get me to move out to Seattle with her and my uncle."

Both Amanda and Chloe shot her a look that suggested she take the call. Emily relented, then tucked a strand of her dark streaked hair behind one of her heavily studded earlobes and brought the phone to her ear.

"Hey Aunt Kay. Sorry I haven't called you back, I'm actually at work right now. Can I call you back in the… What?"

Chloe and Amanda watched as Emily quickly walked to the quietest part of the dressing room away from the sounds of the DJ announcing the next dancer. Concern and sadness were evident in her voice as she continued the conversation in hushed tones.

Chloe and Amanda strained to hear anything that might indicate the reason for Emily's concern, but all they could hear was the DJ's voice talking over the fading music of AC/DC's "Shook Me All Night Long".

"Give it up for the lovely Lexus. If you want Lexus to continue to *shake you all night long*, she'll be giving private dances in the VIP room. So make sure you pay her a visit, and guys, don't forget to whip it out... your wallets that is. Now, welcome to the stage the sexy, scintillating Savannah!"

Hearing her cue, Amanda shot one last concerned look over her shoulder at Emily before she headed out toward the stage. A moment later, Emily ended her phone call and walked back over to Chloe.

"Is everything ok, Em?"

"Lily is in the hospital again. Her cancer is back."

"Oh my God, sweetie, I am so sorry! Her and your mom are still way up Maine?"

Emily nodded solemnly.

"You're gonna go see her this time, right?"

Emily sighed heavily and shrugged her shoulders as she cast her eyes to the floor. She hadn't been a very good sister to Lily in recent years. She wondered if too much time had passed for her to start now. The last time she saw Lily face to face was when she left home seven years ago.

She didn't want to talk about it; not with Chloe, not with anyone. Emily walked out to the bar and distracted herself by watching the bartender, Leah, skillfully pour ten shots of Fire Ball whiskey for a group of young jocks sitting at a nearby table.

Emily thought she'd have no problem finishing all ten herself if she had gotten the news a few weeks ago. Leah alerted the waitress that the shots were ready to be served. She then approached Emily.

"Hey Em, Diet Coke?"

Emily pulled her eyes from the group as they happily chimed their shot glasses together above their heads. She was unable to look away until they had thrown the shots back in unison with one swift jerk of their chins.

"Um, yeah. Diet Coke," Emily answered distractedly.

Leah slid a tall glass of ice and soda over to Emily and quickly disappeared to the other end of the bar where two new patrons had appeared.

Emily watched Amanda dance on stage and smiled as her friend moved with grace and ease toward the pole at the center of the stage. She started with elegant little pirouettes around the steel then effortlessly moved into more complicated positions like the Chinese flag and the extended Frodo. Soon, Amanda's skin began to shine with the gleam of exertion, making her toned muscles more prominent. Her straight blond hair twirled around her like a dancer's skirt caught in the breeze. Dazzled by her beauty and skill, Emily felt her mood begin to lighten. Most of the time, the club made it easy to forget the unpleasant aspects of life.

Emily recalled meeting Amanda and Chloe three years ago when she started at the club. They took her under their wings and showed her all the ins and outs of the trade and taught her all the strenuous moves of dancing.

Over the years, Emily had seen dozens of girls come and go. Each of them had their own reasons for dancing on the stage. The majority of them were single mothers just trying to survive. Others used the job as a means to pay their way through college.

Then there were the girls like her. The ones that lived for the attention, the free drinks, and the hazardous lifestyle that often came along with the job. There was never a shortage of men or drugs willing to make you forget your nightmares for a night.

Something had shifted in her this past year though. Emily

contributed part of the change in her to Chloe and Amanda. They had also recently experienced a change in lifestyles and were trying to get out of the addicting routine of living day to day, line to line, and place to place. They wanted something more stable, and they made difficult changes to obtain a more secure lifestyle.

Chloe stopped turning tricks on the side and lost the abusive men in her life. She now used her free time to take classes at a community college outside of Boston. She even turned Emily on to a couple of photography classes there.

Amanda started going to AA so she could be sober for her little girl that hadn't known a real mother since she was born. Now, instead of spending her days getting wasted, Amanda spent time playing with her four year old and taking her to see family members she'd never known before.

Amanda had been Emily's closest friend over the past few years. Their bond was first established over their fondness for hard drugs and hard men. Amanda had a tendency to be a little more extreme in her habits, and Emily watched as it started to control her life.

One night, Emily got a call from the hospital informing her Amanda had been in a car accident. When they had asked Amanda who to call, Emily was the only name she gave. Later, Emily learned that Amanda had run her vehicle off the road into a ditch after leaving a coke party. Luckily, her injuries were limited to a small cut on her forehead and a bad concussion.

Emily stepped in and took care of Sarah, Amanda's little girl, while Amanda recovered. The accident was a blessing of sorts because it had shaken Amanda up enough to start making some life changes. Seeing Amanda gather the strength to turn herself around not only impressed Emily, but it inspired her to do the same.

The growing aroma of sickly sweet beer and cigarettes snapped Emily back from her memory. Before Emily felt his hand on her shoulder, she smelled the man behind her. This gave her the opportunity to brace herself for the encounter. She turned to face the forty-something year old man that swayed unsteadily on his feet behind her.

"So listen, sweetheart, what are your thoughts on going back to my place later? I'll make it worth your while," he slurred into her face.

Emily swiped his hand from her shoulder and attempted to ignore him. The man took it as sign to pull a wad of money from his wallet to assure her that he could pay. He swayed forward and backward as he fumbled clumsily through his wallet and presented her with a handful of wet crumbled bills.

"I'm a dancer. And that's ALL I do!" Emily retorted hotly.

Normally, a bouncer would have already been at her side. She looked anxiously around for Charlie.

"Dancer, stripper… whore, it's all the same thing," the man argued with a shrug of one shoulder.

He stuffed the bills back in his wallet and moved closer to her. She backed up against the bar in an effort to move away from him. Undeterred, he reached down and cupped her ass beneath her skirt, giving it a firm squeeze and pulled her closer to him.

Instinctively, Emily grabbed her drink off the bar and threw it in his face. He squeezed his eyes shut against the onslaught of sticky soda and ice. Emily stepped back as ice bounced off his face and scattered noisily across the bar top.

An instant later, one of the other bouncers was at their side and had the guy by the arm. Emily watched the bouncer roughly escort the man out of the club. Little rivers created by the ice melting on her chest traveled rapidly down her torso, but it did little to cool her temper.

Emily was too upset to notice Amanda watching her with concern from her upside down position on the stage pole. She was also too upset to hear Leah call out to her as she stormed back to the dressing room to collect her things. And she was certainly too upset to hear her manager threaten to fire her if she walked out the door.

2

Big Mistake

"Turn out the party lights, they mean nothing to me tonight
'Cause I want to change my life, if I could
Fill up my heart with love, sweep out under the rug
Empty out all the drugs, all for good"

The subway was busier than it had been an hour ago when she traveled into work. Most of the passengers were wearing Red Sox memorabilia, and the realization dawned on her that there must be a game tonight.

Emily blinked back tears and swallowed a hot lump that kept rising in her throat. She thought about how ridiculous it was for people to spend hundreds of dollars to sit in undersized century old seats to watch grown overpaid men play a stupid game. What did they care anyways? Most of them were probably all over-privileged little college kids that had Mommy and Daddy pay their way for everything, she thought.

She let her eyes settle on a couple in their mid-twenties sitting across from her. The man sported a Big Papi jersey and a crew cut. He watched his girlfriend with adoring eyes as she pulled her long straight blonde ponytail through the hole in her pink Sox baseball cap. Emily fought the urge to vomit. You couldn't pay me enough to dress like that, she thought.

Emily didn't feel guilty being so judgmental about all the people that surrounded her, for she knew they were doing the same thing when they looked at her. She was sure the only thing people saw was a jaded, heavily pierced and tattooed girl who loved to dress in all black. She was sure the words druggie, loser, and slut were used as well.

Sadly, she recalled the one and only time she went to a Red Sox game and the one guy that maybe saw something more in her. It was just over four years ago with a boy named Brian. She met him at the coffee shop she used to work at.

Each morning he would come in and order the same thing; black coffee and a sesame seed bagel. At some point, he became so predictable that she would have his order ready for him at 7:45 each morning. He would always appear within minutes and looked impressed that she had remembered his order.

She could tell that he found her attractive. He would always drop his eyes quickly to the floor if she caught him looking at her. He would then look up and smile sheepishly at her, knowing he'd been caught admiring the view. Sometimes, he would hesitate a moment or two after he had paid for his order, struggling with something more to say. Usually he just threw a generous tip in the Styrofoam cup and awkwardly told her not to spend it on something to make her more beautiful because that wasn't possible.

Over the course of a few months, as he gained the courage to stay and talk to her longer, she learned that he was a student at Northeastern. She also learned one of his favorite classes was photography. She mentioned to him that she had always wanted to learn more about it but could never afford the classes.

Brian saw his opening and finally asked her out. He offered to take her to a Sox game and maybe give her some photography pointers. He definitely wasn't her type, but she found herself saying yes before even thinking it through.

He picked her up from work one afternoon and started their date by taking her to a photography exhibit at the Museum of Fine Arts.

She marveled at all the different styles and subjects while Brian pointed out some artists that he liked. He took the time to explain to her the different lenses and settings that could be used to capture various affects.

Afterwards, they grabbed lunch at a cozy little café and strolled around Boston Commons. Brian told her about his family, his various hobbies, and his favorite friends. Emily didn't really have any of those things, so she just listened intently to Brian talk about his.

When he suggested they take a ride on the Duck Boat, Emily hesitated. Emily always thought it was just a stupid tourist attraction for mindless people that couldn't think of a better way to spend their money. Whenever it had been spotted in the past, Emily and her present company never missed the opportunity to make fun of it and the people aboard. But when Emily saw the hopeful look in Brian's eyes as he awaited her response, she didn't have the heart to let him down.

As they boarded the boat, Emily prayed she wouldn't see anyone that could recognize her. Ironically, within moments after the tour began, her embarrassment turned to excitement. To her surprise, there were many photo opportunities all around her.

She quickly pulled out her camera and began taking shots. Brian was impressed at some of the angles that she got and showed her how to adjust her lens settings to capture different light and sharpness. When she looked at her pictures, she beamed with satisfaction.

Even the Red Sox game had pleasantly taken her by surprise. It was like another small world hidden behind the walls. She really didn't care so much for the game and the players as much as she did about the setting and the crowd. The whole environment hummed with an energy and excitement that was infectious.

When the Sox made a dramatic ninth inning comeback, the crowd jumped to their feet. The roar of the cheers erupting around her shook her to the core. She grabbed her camera and zoomed in on a little nine year old boy. His face was lit up with the joy of Christmas morning. It was clearly his first game as well. She snapped a shot of him cheering excitedly.

The date ended a little after midnight. As Brian walked her towards an apartment, where she slept on the couch, he tried to engage her in conversation. Emily was suddenly quiet.

"I feel like all we've talked about was me all day," he laughed. "So, do you have any brothers or sisters?" Brian asked.

Emily hesitated and stuttered, "I… I, have a younger sister. Her name is Lily."

"Ah, so you're a big sister, huh?"

"Not really," she shrugged.

Brian frowned. He didn't seem to understand.

"Do you see each other often?"

"No."

"That's too bad. Why not?"

"I don't know. Life just gets in the way I guess," Emily answered with another shrug.

"Life gets in the way of family?" Brian asked incredulously. "When was the last time you saw her?"

Emily hadn't liked the way the conversation was going. She squirmed inside her leather jacket. Clearly, he didn't get it. How could an all-American boy like him understand a piece of trash like her anyway, she thought?

Brian sensed that she was getting uncomfortable, so he dropped the subject. They walked on in silence. When they reached her door, he told her he had a good time and would like to take her out again. Emily shifted nervously in her shoes, but then she found herself looking at his mouth. Her anxiety was suddenly replaced with yearning. She forced her eyes away quickly and found he was looking happily into her eyes. That had made her smile. There was something about him that made her forget herself.

He reached down and touched her cheek. The gesture startled her. She hadn't expected it, but his touch was soothing and warm. She found herself leaning into it just a bit.

He took her chin in his hand and drew her mouth up to his. The kiss was warm and lingering, and she braced herself for the placement of his other hand. She expected to find it wandering presumptuously toward her ass, or maybe he'd even think he could get a touch of her breast. Instead, he had put his hand firmly on her hip and pulled her gently closer. Then, for just a moment, she stopped thinking and just let herself become lost in the kiss.

When he pulled away, she blinked up at him a little star dazed.

"Good night, Emily."

With that, he turned casually and walked down the concrete stairs. He glanced back to smile at her one more time and waited for her to get inside safely.

She was confused by this. He hadn't groped her, or asked to come inside, and now he waited to see her through the safety of her doorway? She stood there, not knowing what to do, before she finally turned and went inside.

When the door closed between them, the reality of the day started to set in. She had actually met a decent guy that was into her. That alone, put her completely out of her comfort zone. She knew how to behave with jerks that only wanted one thing, but she had never been with anyone that might actually be interested in getting to know her. She knew she didn't have anything to offer him. He was smarter and warmer than she could ever be. She was just an empty shell with a black hollow soul — a "bad seed" as her mother once put it. If she let it continue, she would inevitably disappoint him just like she disappointed all the important people in her life.

This thought sent a wave of anxiety rushing through her blood and into her lungs. She forced herself to take some slow, deep breaths before walking up to the second floor apartment.

She found her roommates inside sitting in a cloud of bong smoke and a ring of scattered beer cans. One of their friends was bent over the coffee table snorting a line off a mirror. She found this scene comforting and joined them. She wanted to forget Brian and go back to a scene that felt familiar. Screw Brian, she thought, just before twisting open the cap of a Colt 45. The rest of the night was lost in a haze.

After that, she avoided his phone calls and stopped making an effort to have his order ready for him each morning at the coffee shop. When he came in, she greeted him with the same casual indifferent tone she used on all the other customers.

It didn't take him long to get the message. His visits became fewer and further between until eventually he stopped coming in altogether. She was both relieved and disappointed when she realized that she would never see him again.

The screeching sounds of the subway train braking pulled her out of her thoughts long enough to realize it was her stop. She wasn't sure at what point she started crying, but she quickly swiped the tears from her cheeks. The gesture left a trail of smudged mascara across her face, and she stepped onto the sidewalk with raccoon eyes.

When she reached the small one bedroom apartment she shared with her boyfriend, Eric, she hoped he would be home. She just wanted someone to hold her and tell her everything would be ok. She realized she might be shooting for the stars on that one, but she let herself be hopeful anyway.

When she walked through the door, she saw that Eric had a couple of friends over. They were sitting around the living room playing video games and smoking pot. Reality always had a way of disappointing her.

The red bandana wrapped around Eric's forehead did little to contain his jet black hair, which spiked out wildly in various directions. He wore a black Misfits t-shirt with the sleeves ripped off. It not only exposed his white wiry arms, but it also provided a sidelong view of the snake tattoo that spiraled up his torso and onto his chest. His bright red Telecaster guitar leaned between his legs, which were clad in black ripped jeans.

"Babe! You're home early!" Eric greeted her as he sucked a hit through a long glass pipe.

"Can't I ever just come home to some peace and quiet? Just once?" Emily remarked.

"What? The band had rehearsal tonight. We're just blowing off some steam before we do our second take. Besides, you're home early, remember?"

Troy grinned excitedly at Emily through his heavily studded lips. He swept his long blonde bangs out of his face with a practiced fling of his chin.

"Hey Emily, how about a drink?" Troy asked, holding up a Budweiser.

"I'm all set," Emily said.

"Nah, I meant mine is empty. Why don't you get me one?"

The guys laughed at Emily's expense. Andrew slapped Troy on the back, congratulating him on his brilliant wit.

Emily pulled off her jacket, exposing two arms of ink. Her right bicep was wrapped with a scene of a pin-up girl. The brunette girl straddled an upright bottle, which was labeled *dreams*. Surrounding her was a cloud of swirling purple smoke as she cast a defiant look over her shoulder. The pin-up was wearing nothing but a pair of silky purple panties, merlot lipstick, and a pair of red heels. Thorny roses emerged from both above and below the swirling purple smoke. The vines led up Emily's shoulder to where a stork carried a baby away into the clouds. On her left arm was a barren and withering black tree with orange smoke spiraling behind it. Hidden in the tree's black, twisted branches were the initials of her family members.

Emily flung her jacket down on the back of the couch and huffed in exasperation. She started to walk out of the room but Eric stopped her.

"Come on Em, don't be like that. Take a hit and you'll feel better."

A part of her wanted desperately to take a hit. A long, deep hit that would allow her to escape from her reality. Instead, she relented and shook her head no. Emily walked over and sat on the arm of the sofa next to Eric and rested a hand on his shoulder. Maybe if he saw her up close, he would see that she had a rough day.

Eric started coughing and hacking out a big cloud of smoke. His body shuddered violently and shook her hand from his shoulder. He then looked at her and started laughing.

"Ahh, I forgot. You don't *do* that stuff anymore." Eric turned to his friends to explain further. "Emily thinks she doesn't want to drink *or* smoke anymore. She says she's gonna clean up her act. She thinks she's gonna be a famous photographer and shit."

Emily *was* trying to clean herself up, and she really *did* want to do something with her photography, but hearing Eric say it out loud, the way he did, made her stomach turn. Part of her thought she was just kidding herself, and that maybe this shitty lifestyle was all she was good for. The other part of her, the angry part, wanted to punch Eric in the throat.

"So let me get this straight," began Andrew, "you don't drink or smoke anymore, but you have no problem grinding your ass on some horny stranger's lap?"

All three guys chuckled.

Andrew stroked his purple Mohawk and spread his leather-clad legs as if to invite her over. When she didn't budge and just glared at him angrily, he presented her with a ten dollar bill.

"What kind of boner bounce will this get me?" Andrew smiled.

Too exhausted, Emily looked to Eric for support.

"Hey, come on Andrew," said Eric. "You know better than that."

Emily was only slightly appeased until she heard Eric finish his statement.

"She's gonna need at least a twenty spot to do that. Right. babe?"

Emily looked at all of them in disgust and got off the arm of the couch. Without another word, she disappeared into the bedroom.

Emily's eyes immediately settled on a 5 x 7 framed picture. It was of her and Lily at the ages of eleven and five. They were wearing dresses and laughing under the maple tree in their backyard in Braintree. It stabbed at Emily's heart.

She hated there was something that existed in this world that could touch her heart. She struggled against a moment of self-loathing, abolishing herself for failing the one good thing in her life. Lily. How could she have left her behind?

In that moment, Emily was clear on what she had to do. She needed to go up Maine to see her sister, and in turn, she knew she needed to confront her mother. The thought of that confrontation sent a sick feeling to the pit of her stomach. Emily also knew she needed to leave this apartment... and Eric — for good.

Although it seemed like a spur of the moment decision to leave him, the truth was, it had been brewing for weeks... months. Looking back, Emily always knew what a no-good boyfriend Eric was, but it wasn't until she finally stopped drinking and drugging a few weeks earlier that she fully realized what a low-life, selfish jerk he truly was.

Emily whirled around the bedroom, franticly tossing various clothing into a beaten up old suitcase. After a handful of items, she looked around to find nothing left of herself; no trinkets, no souvenirs, no sentimental gifts. Nothing.

She went to the closet and retrieved her camera and lens. The last thing she grabbed was the photo of her little sister. She intended to nestle it securely on top of her packed bag, but instead, she clutched it to her chest.

The loud screeching sound of Eric's amplified guitar sounded from the living room. The excited muffle of voices followed. Emily found her ear buds and quickly plugged her ear with music from her playlist.

By looking at her, one might expect her musical taste would be more on the dark and sad side or perhaps on the dark and angry side. Either way, one would assume it to be dark.

While there were plenty of those types of bands in her playlist, her musical taste was actually quite varied: from Goth, to heavy metal, to cheesy 80's music, and even some old school hip hop. (Emily was secretly a huge fan of the Beastie Boys.)

Tonight, however, she turned to the softer and calmer tones of The Cranberries. As the lead singer Dolores O'Riordan attempted to soothe Emily with her ballad "I Will Always", Emily contemplated leaving right then and there. She placed her packed suitcase and a tattered backpack on the bed and stared at it for a long moment but ultimately decided against it.

If Eric saw her walking out with all of her stuff, there would surely be a confrontation. Of course, he would probably beg her to stay; sweet talk her the way he always did when they would fight. Eric was a giant douchebag, for sure, but somehow he had the ability to say the right things at the right time to convince her otherwise.

Another reason Emily didn't chance leaving yet, was what if he *didn't* beg her to stay? What if he didn't even bother to sweet talk her? Both scenarios were equally depressing to her. She decided to stash her bags under the bed and crash for the night. With the picture frame still clutched tightly in her hand, Emily fell onto the bed and curled into a ball. She looked again at the photo and thought, *sometimes you have to accept things can never go back to the way they used to be.* She had it all planned out, tomorrow morning she'd wake up bright and early and leave unnoticed and unbothered.

That night, images flooded the darkened corners of her mind, reminding her there was another life - another reality that was possible for her to reach once more.

When the morning light hit her eyes through the half opened blinds of the bedroom window, she found herself looking at the photograph of her and Lily that she had fallen asleep holding.

She rubbed at the stiffness that covered her eyes and cheeks and realized she had been crying in her sleep again. How clever the body was to release the emotions it was denied during the day amidst the wee hours of the night when nobody was looking.

From the time her head hit the pillow last night until she opened her eyes, Emily's mind had come up with a plan — a master plan. She knew she didn't have a job anymore, but she knew that was a good thing. Emily didn't know what she'd do for work once she got back into town, but she knew she wanted something less degrading, something less naked. Sadly, she knew whatever that new job was, it would also be *less* money. However, at this point in her life, it wasn't about the money, it was about changing her life for the better. It was about being the girl she always wanted to be, but for whatever reason, she wasn't.

She had already taken care of her shitty dead-end job, and now she was about to take care of her shitty dead-end relationship, or "relationshit" as Chloe not-so-affectionately referred to it. Once out of the apartment, she'd head straight for the bus station and purchase a ticket to Maine; to whatever God forsaken hick town her mother had moved to a few years earlier.

Emily knew she needed to be there for her baby sister, but she also knew she needed to make amends with her mother. The latter one made her feel like she was about to jump off a cliff without knowing what was at the bottom. At least she had established a social media relationship with Lily when they reconnected on Facebook about a year ago. Emily hadn't seen or spoken a word to her mother in nearly seven years.

As Emily sat up in bed, she looked down at her rumpled clothes from the previous night. Her first order of business would be to put on something a bit more conservative for her mother's sake. She hated the thought of dressing up just to please people. She glanced at her club outfit from last night and also knew she hated the thought of undressing just to please people.

Emily searched through her clothes and came up with a happy medium. She would still dress in all black, but it would be a conservative black. Reluctantly, she also removed some of her piercings, but only some, she told herself. She then put on a fresh coat of her favorite merlot colored lipstick. That one was non-negotiable.

She pulled the ear buds from her ears and found the distant sounds of snoring coming from the living room. She approached the bedroom door and peered cautiously out to see if anyone was awake.

She saw no movement in the sea of discarded beer bottles, empty pizza boxes and strewn band equipment. Deeming it safe, she tiptoed back to the bedroom closet and fished around in the back of the top shelf until she found a certain shoe box she knew would contain her emergency stash of funds.

After a moment of riffling through the contents of the box, she felt certain there should have been more. She stuffed the handful of fifty and one hundred dollar bills in her backpack then searched frantically for the remaining bills, which she felt must have fallen out on the shelf. Finding none, she deducted that Eric must have discovered her stash and helped himself.

"Fucking asshole!" Emily muttered and threw the empty shoe box against the wall.

Taking one last glance around the empty bedroom, Emily grabbed the framed photo off the bed and placed it carefully on top of her packed bag.

As she eased in a cat-like motion out the bedroom door, she was careful not to step on various body parts that lay scattered across the floor. As she stepped over one tattooed arm after another, Emily felt like she was walking through a mine field. One wrong step could cause an explosion, she told herself as she navigated carefully around another embodied combat boot.

Once in the safety of the threshold, Emily cast a long sorrowful look at the life she was leaving. Although she knew there was nothing left for her there, she felt naked without the cover of her sweet blissful ignorance. She knew what lay in front of her was far more terrifying but possibly far more rewarding. As she quietly closed the door behind her, she felt maybe for the first time in a very long time she was moving in the right direction.

3
Faded and Jaded

*"I hope I don't stay this way faded and jaded
And followed by second-hand smoke."*

Emily stood in line at the bus station nervously adjusting the straps on the Nikkon camera she wore around her neck. She flipped through some of the last photos she had taken of Amanda and her daughter. Emily knew once she turned her phone back on there'd probably be multiple texts and missed calls from Amanda and Chloe. She might not always show it, but she was appreciative of their concern and for their friendship.

Just as she had predicted, with a push of a button her phone lit up with a handful of texts and voicemails from her friends. Emily started to text Amanda but decided on an actual phone call. After three unanswered rings, Emily assumed, due to the early hour, Amanda was probably sleeping or was spending time with her daughter. When it came to her mother-daughter time, Amanda never had her phone on. Emily loved that about her friend.

After the fifth ring, Amanda's recorded voice chimed through the phone indicating, *Life is short so say what you need to say.* Emily debated on hanging up, but decided there was wisdom in Amanda's message after all.

"Hey, Amanda, it's Emily. I'm sorry I didn't return your messages last night, and I'm sorry I stormed out of the club the way I did. I don't think I can take that shit anymore. I'm at the bus station right now. I'm headed to Maine to see Lily… and my mother. Anyway, I shouldn't be gone too long, but I was kinda hoping when I get back I could take you up on that offer. You know, me moving in with you? Let's just say the club wasn't the only thing I quit last night. You girls were right, Eric is never gonna change. Once an asshole, always an asshole."

The woman in front of Emily at the bus station ticket window was finishing up her transaction, so Emily wrapped up her message quickly.

"I gotta go, but I will give you a call later. Bye."

Emily ended the call and stepped up to the window. The middle-aged woman looked like she was trying to count the piercings on Emily's face for a little diversity in her day. Emily watched mildly amused as the clerk's eyes darted from her eyebrow, to her nose, to her lip and then finally to her ears.

"Eighteen," Emily said.

When clerk gave Emily the deer in headlights look, she added, "Piercings. I have eighteen in case you were wondering."

A light bulb went on behind the woman's dull brown eyes. She cracked a smile at Emily.

"Yeah, I guess I was. I only counted ten though."

"I took some out, and I also have a few others," Emily said with a shy smirk.

"Oh. Oh I see! Well what can I do for you?"

"I need to get to Maine. Pine Ridge, Maine to be exact."

Again, Emily found herself looking at bewilderment on the woman's face.

"Where?"

Emily smirked despite herself.

"Yeah, my thoughts exactly."

***

Even with her private window seat and the distraction of the scenery that went by, Emily still felt a little uncomfortable. She pulled at the collar of her black lace button up blouse and tugged at the hem of her black pencil skirt. The heel of her ankle boot swayed to the beat of a Chris Trapper song playing on her iPod. Although Emily listened to a wide variety of music, the acoustic and melodic storytelling style of Chris Trapper was a far cry from what you'd expect a dressed-all-in-black girl would be listening to.

She had actually gotten into his music by complete accident. A few months earlier, she was out with Chloe at a little club over in Somerville where Chris happened to be playing that night. Emily was mesmerized by his relatable, heart-on-his-sleeve songs and lyrics. Over the ensuing months, she found herself downloading a ton of his songs, including ones with his old band The Push Stars.

"I hope I don't stay this way, faded and jaded and followed by second-hand smoke…" sang Chris Trapper.

Although she had heard the song many times before, the lyrics hit her as if it were the first time she had ever heard them. The words resonated deep within her to a place she always tried to deny existed – a place where she cared what happened to her. She skipped the song and listened to Cake singing about a girl with a short skirt and a long jacket instead.

The bus climbed the rising slope of an enormous green arched bridge marking the transition from New Hampshire to Maine. Large cranes lined the water's edge and a massive cargo boat passed below.

A sign greeted her on the other side of the bridge, simply stating:

"Welcome to Maine - The Way Life Should Be"

Emily snorted out loud.

An elderly woman sitting across the aisle from her looked at her with startled concern.

That sign is so fucking ironic, Emily thought. She quickly grabbed her camera and snapped a shot of the sign. She couldn't imagine *any* life that waited for her in Maine, never mind one that promised a better way of living.

This was Emily's first trip to Maine. Besides her brief stay with her aunt and uncle out in the Berkshires in western Massachusetts, she hadn't really been anywhere. There was that one time she went to Rhode Island for a weekend, but that was to dance at a huge bachelor party, and the memories of that night and trip were foggy at best. Just as well, she thought.

As the bus rolled up Interstate 95 and through the York tolls, Emily racked her brain for anywhere else she had traveled. Sadly, she had to go all the way back to when she was eleven and Lily was five. Emily's step-father took all of them to the White Mountains in New Hampshire. She didn't remember the actual mountains that much, but she remembered the two little amusement parks they went to: Storyland and Santa's Village.

Emily found herself smiling out the bus window at the memory of her and Lily getting their picture taken with the cheesy, mechanical Itsy Bitsy Spider. She also remembered them riding in the pumpkin carriage heading towards Cinderella's castle. Lily was so excited. They both were.

When "Pictures of You" by The Cure came on her iPod, she cranked up the volume. It was one of Emily's favorite songs. The lyrics didn't make her think of old boyfriends or past relationships, but instead, it simply reminded her of her childhood; of memories long since gone… of the good times that were no more.

As Robert Smith's melancholic voice cut through her heart, she was reminded of another place she had visited. This one was back before Lily was born; back when it was just her and her mother.

Emily's Grampa took her, her mom, and her aunt Kay to Cape Cod for three days. It was Emily's first trip to a real beach. She remembered how soft and hot the sand felt on her tiny feet. Her Grampa had helped her build what she had deemed *the coolest sand castle ever.*

She didn't know it would be the last time she would go to the beach with her Grampa. He died the following winter from a heart attack. Emily's mother had tried explaining that Grampa had gone to heaven, but Emily didn't understand fully what heaven was. She only understood it was so far away and that she'd never see her Grampa again.

She understood now what heaven was, but she knew she'd never go where Grampa went. Only good people were granted entrance heaven her mother had told her. Sinners went to hell. She was a sinner. She wasn't always though.

Emily remembered a time when her mother still thought she was good enough for heaven. She thought of the countless cartwheel contests she had with her mom and Aunt Kay. She was only four, and it seemed like a lifetime ago, but that trip was one of her favorite memories. That was back when her mother was fun… and back when Emily was innocent and less jaded.

When the sad Cure song ended, and when her nostalgic memories faded, Emily found herself wiping tears from her darkened eyes. She shut off her iPod and self-consciously glanced around to see if anyone was witnessing her pathetic display of emotion. Luckily, no one was. Everyone was either sleeping or had their faces planted on their phones.

The sight of this reminded her to check her own phone. There were two texts: one from Chloe and the other from Amanda. Chloe's text read: *You're doing the right thing, Em! See you soon.* Chloe ended her text with a red heart emoji.

Amanda's text read: *Everything is gonna work out with Lily and your mother. I just know it! Your bedroom is ready and waiting when you come back. Love you!* Amanda ended hers with triple red hearts.

Those were the only two texts. There was nothing at all from Eric. Emily wasn't sure how she felt about that. He was probably still passed out drunk, she justified.

The bus came to a halt in Portland. It was there that almost 75% of the people exited. While the bus was stopped, Emily got off and raided a vending machine for some much needed food. It had been almost twenty-four hours since she had anything to eat. When the bus left the station and continued north, Emily's thoughts returned to Eric.

Emily met Eric when she had just started dancing at the club. Not only was Eric a regular at the Red Garter, he was the resident drug dealer for a lot of the girls. His wise-ass, carefree attitude fit Emily perfectly. Eric was also in a band. A fast-talking bad boy in a band with drug connections was just what Emily was looking for.

She knew he could supply her with what she was looking for at the time — a lapse in memory. Those days, she woke up to forget. He gave her an out. He supplied the drugs, the scene, the music, and a place to retreat. Emily thought that was what happiness was — forgetting.

Lately though, she woke up curious about the things she tried so hard to forget, wondering, hoping if they might be worth remembering. She was a lost soul searching through the rubble of the junkyard life she had created, looking for something salvageable.

With her ear buds reinserted, and her iPod turned on, Emily closed her eyes and got lost in Tori Amos' "Winter". Her thoughts again turned to her mother. She hadn't seen her in nearly seven years. She hadn't talked to her on the phone or even sent her a Christmas card. She knew seeing her mother while visiting Lily was inevitable, and the thought made her stomach turn inside out. She wondered if her mother would even recognize her now, and if she did, would she even acknowledge her.

Emily tried to imagine what they would say to each other.

Awkward small talk was the best case scenario she could muster. They hadn't exactly had a warm relationship before their falling out, and it went from lukewarm to ice cold when she left.

All the anger she felt toward her mother had lost its edge over the years. All that remained now was simmering disappointment, which sat largely ignored on the back burner of her heart.

She looked at the screen shot she had taken of Maine's welcome sign and snorted again. Yeah, right, the way life should be, she thought bitterly. Everyone should be so lucky as to have a sickly sister and an emotionally hollowed mother. The picture would serve as a good laugh when she got back to Boston.

Emily began to notice the traffic thinning as the two lane highway, lined heavily with trees that blocked any other possible view, rolled on. The larger SUVs and fresh-off-the-lot sedans became further and fewer between. They were replaced by Chevy pickup trucks and rust colored classics, most of which probably qualified as antiques but were still being driven for practical purposes.

Emily snapped a picture of a Moose Crossing sign. She knew she must be getting close. She'd never seen a moose, but she smiled as she remembered a story her mother once told her about a moose.

Her Grampa had taken her mom and Aunt Kay on a camping trip to Maine. They had been traveling in a Volkswagen bug. They never saw the moose in the road. They only saw its legs as its body towered above the sight of the windshield. Grampa slammed on the brakes but not quick enough. Their car became lodged directly under the moose's body.

Her mother and Aunt had been terrified. Apparently, the moose was equally terrified because it got so upset it shit itself. As the nuggets of turd rained over the windshield of the VW bug, her Grampa instinctively turned on the wipers. Of course, that only made matters worse by smearing the hot steamy turds all across their line of sight.

There was nothing left for them to do but wait for the moose to dislodge itself from the top of their vehicle. Her mother said it took about ten minutes of awkward shuffling on the moose's part before it figured out what the hell was up and how to free itself from the situation.

In the end, both the moose and the VW bug had escaped relatively unscathed. Emily always wondered if that story was actually true or if it was just exaggerated for her amusement. She also sadly wondered if she'd ever have a story like that to tell. So far, nothing in her life really felt worth sharing.

As the bus passed an eighteen wheeler hauling logs, Emily made eye contact with the heavily bearded trucker driver. She smiled and pumped her elbow up and down in the window. She remembered her Grampa had taught her it was the universal sign for truckers to blow their horn. She wondered if Maine was still in touch enough with the outside world for the sign to work here.

To her surprise, the trucker gave her a wide-toothed grin and blasted his horn for her. She couldn't help being quite pleased with herself as she leaned back in her seat and smiled.

When the bus reached Waterville, the driver announced that it was the last stop. Emily and two other passengers were the only ones left on the bus. As two men clad in plaid and Carhartts exited the bus, Emily lingered behind so she could talk to the driver.

"Excuse me, but did you say this was the last stop?" she asked.

"A-yah."

"A-what?"

"'Tis," confirmed the driver again with a nod this time.

"Well, what bus do I take to get to Pine Ridge then?"

"Pine Ridge?" the driver asked with an incredulous huff.

Emily nodded.

"That's about an hour west of here. You'll have to take a smaller local bus for that, darlin.'"

"A smaller… local bus?" Emily repeated.

The bus driver was now looking at her with superior impatience.

Emily just rolled her eyes and got off the bus. She'd figure it out. She didn't need help from some inarticulate moron, she thought.

4
Look What The Wind Blew In

*"I always keep in mind that where you end up is where you are
And if you live to regret and you cannot forget
You won't get very far"*

Pine Ridge, Maine – otherwise known as the town that time forgot. The town's Main Street was set up like most small New England towns, with storefronts dotting either side of the narrow street. Sadly, like most small towns this far up Maine, most of the storefronts were rundown with For Lease signs in their windows.

At the top of Main Street stood a simple wooden church with its white paint chipped and faded. Its dark steeple was a sharp contrast against the crisp blue autumn sky. On the opposite end of the street sat a nostalgic looking general store.

The front porch of the store was lined with old water barrels filled with merchandise and patio furniture. A giant stuffed black bear wearing a bright red scarf stood on his hind legs beside the front wooden double doors. A pile of newspapers were stacked neatly between his feet.

One would think that the giant, looming black bear would be the porch's centerpiece, but the true focal point of the porch was the rustic wooden bench at the far end; more specifically, the three elderly men who sat upon the bench.

Max, Gus, and Harold were quintessential old Mainers.

Max sat with his thumbs hooked under the straps of his bright red suspenders, pulling them slightly off his plaid shirt as if trying to create leverage against his own body weight. A closer look would reveal his mouth was working steadily on something small curled on the inside of his tongue. His white beard was long enough to start forming curls at the tips, and they danced about on his jaw while he continued to manipulate the contents of his mouth.

Gus sat between Max and Harold and wore an old leather aviator pilot hat with a pair of goggles strapped through a loop on either side the hat. Under a long unruly beard, his face was heavily lined with tanned wrinkles, which gave his skin the appearance of well-worn leather. Over the years, the vest had become too small to button up, but he stubbornly refused to eliminate it from his wardrobe, so he wore it unbuttoned over his denim shirt. His deep set brown eyes, the same color of the leather straps of his goggles, were fixed on Max.

Harold sat on the far end of the bench with his arms folded over his broad chest. His blue eyes shone deeply with the degree of wit and wisdom that only old age can bring. His gray hair was kept neatly pinned under a straw fedora. A baby blue ribbon wrapped around the base of his cap matched the shade of his eyes to a tee. It also matched his short sleeve plaid button up shirt. A corncob pipe could be seen poking out of the left breast pocket. Unlike, the other two, Harold's face was clean shaven. Harold's attention was also fixed on Max.

Suddenly, Max tilted his head back at a drastic angle and launched something from between his lips. He released his suspenders as he leaned back proudly in his seat. All three men stared at a pile of sunflower seeds that was gathered on the porch floor in front of them.

"That one nearly hit the railing!" Max exclaimed.

The other two nodded solemnly. Gus took the package of seeds that had been tucked between him and Max. He carefully began to search the package for a seed that offered the best shape and size for optimum spitting distance.

"I can beat it," he said confidently.

Amidst their seed spitting contest, the three old Mainers' attention was drawn to a small blue bus rumbling up Main Street. The writing on the side read: Lakeview Retirement Home.

"Uh oh, Gus, looks like they're finally coming to take you away!" said Harold as he elbowed his friend.

Gus set the package of seeds aside and finished his can of Moxie soda before responding.

"Retirement home my ass! I'd rather kiss the Angel of Death than be put in that place!"

The bus came to a stop at a faded wooden bench across from the general store. After the cloud of dust from the bus settled, the old men fixed their eyes upon the stranger that had just entered town.

"Well Christ on a cracker! Here's your chance Gus! There she is, the Angel of Death!" exclaimed Max as he pointed to Emily, who stood looking bewildered at her new environment.

It was apparent that none of them had ever seen a woman quite like Emily before; maybe on TV, but not live in person smack dab in the middle of Pine Ridge. Normally, new folks were a welcomed curiosity in town, but this one had a troubled look about her. The men eyed her warily.

Clad in her black attire, Emily stood in direct contrast to all the small, colored storefronts that lined the narrow main street of town. The sun shone brightly, and a light September breeze rustled the trees that were neatly planted along the sidewalks.

A young boy, no older than six, whizzed past her on his bike. She stepped to the side to avoid getting caught in the path of his dirt bike. She looked around for his parents and was surprised to see him unsupervised.

What kind of place is this where children run the streets without anyone to watch over them, Emily thought? She pulled her long black trench coat closer to her body and fixed her eyes on a faded sign that read: Corbin's General Store. It doesn't get much more general than that, she thought. She suspected the building itself used to be a private residence at one time.

The corner of her lip curled in amusement as she looked at an advertisement in the front window which stated: Beer & Ammunition Sold Here. That's a winning combination, Emily thought.

As Emily continued to scan the general store's front porch, her eyes became fixed on the three old men. None of them had enough manners to pretend not to stare. Instead, they all gawked as she crossed Main Street towards them. Emily ignored their stares and gaping mouths as she approached the store. She was used to people staring, but what she wasn't used to was the silence that blanketed the town. There were no loud voices, no sirens, and no obnoxious honking of horns and rush of traffic.

"Jiminy Crickets!" said Gus as his dark eyes focused on Emily. "Grab your crucifixes! She's coming this way!"

As she approached, the men stared shamelessly.

"Jesus, what happened to her face?" asked Max.

"That's her face?" asked Harold. "I thought it was a dart board!"

"You better watch it Harold," said Gus. "She's probably a witch come to cast a spell on your store."

Max watched as this dressed-all-in-black, multi-pierced stranger moved towards them. "She looks like she just walked outta a Stephen King book," said Max wide-eyed.

The town was quiet, too quiet. The eerie silence mixed with the three creepy old men staring at her caused Emily to mumble to herself, "It's like I just walked into a fuckin' Stephen King book."

The men shuffled nervously in their seats as Emily climbed the three wide wooden stairs of the porch. She figured since she had the attention of three locals, she'd ask for directions.

"Um, I'm looking for Maple Street?"

"Oh? That's up past the Wilson Farm," Max answered.

"No, Max," said Gus. "That's Maple Lane."

"No, no!" said Harold. "That's Maple Road. I live on Maple Lane."

"Are you sure?" asked Gus. "Because this morning you forgot your dentures."

"I think I know what road I live on!" argued Harold.

It was obvious that she was getting nowhere fast with the three stooges, so she decided to try her luck inside. Without excusing herself, she headed for the opened entrance doors.

The aroma of candles and spices hit Emily as soon as she stepped through the old wooden double doors. A giant rack of jerky was prominently displayed at the front of the store. A handwritten sign above the rack boasted the jerky was made locally. There were dozens of flavors and types ranging from wild boar to ostrich to alligator. There was even a Moxie flavored jerky.

Small round tables filled with other locally made items like jams, candles, and sauces created a pathway to the free standing shelves at the back of the store. These shelves contained more everyday items like canned goods, boxed meals, and household supplies.

A coffee station with a few small tables was set up on the left wall just beyond the cash register. A case displaying freshly baked goods sat beneath the coffee station. The appeal of coffee was too great to resist and Emily took a step toward the station.

The wide wooden planks of the worn floorboards creaked and groaned loudly under her feet, causing her to pause with uncertainty. She wasn't used to floors that sounded like they were going to fall out beneath her when she walked on them.

She glanced over her shoulder and wondered if she should turn back. She could still hear the old men bantering outside.

"Speaking of Maple Street, I have a mean hankering for pancakes with maple syrup," said Max.

Harold started to suggest waffles instead, but Emily shifted her attention back to the store where she caught movement from the corner of her eye. A woman inside the store had just approached the register. She stood with her back to Emily, finishing her transaction at the counter.

The store clerk, and owner, Joan Corbin, gave Emily a warm smile and she handed the woman at the counter a brown paper bag. Her smile was so warm and genuine Emily actually found herself smiling back at the woman. Emily's smile quickly faded, however, when she heard her bid her current customer off.

"Good to see you again, Susan," Joan chimed.

Emily's face dropped and she braced herself. It couldn't be her mother, Emily told herself. It had to be a different Susan. She wrestled with conflicting emotions of excitement and fear. Before she could settle on either one, the woman turned around, and Emily found herself face to face with her mother.

"Hi… Mom," Emily quietly said, trying to keep her voice neutral.

"What are you doing here?" said Susan in complete shock.

Susan took a step back to regard her daughter. Emily shifted uncomfortably in her shoes under her mother's scrutiny.

"Aunt Kay called me yesterday. She told me that Lily wasn't doing so well again."

"When will my sister learn to mind her own business?" Susan said more to herself than to Emily.

Emily's neutral tone faded. "What are you talking about? Lily is her niece… and my sister. I think that qualifies as our business too."

Joan shifted her sharp blue eyes to a shelf behind the counter and began to rearrange the items there that didn't need adjusting. Aware their conversation was within ear shot, Susan lowered her voice.

"You have to be kidding me. You haven't seen your sister in years. What's the sense of showing your face now? She'll just be upset when you disappear again. Trust me, she'll be better off if you just leave now."

Emily didn't bother trying to hide the hurt and anger in her voice this time.

"You mean, you'll be better off, right? I knew seeing you again would be a bad idea, but I'm here for Lily. Not you!"

"I see you haven't changed a bit. You're still every much of a sassy little brat as you ever were."

Emily chuckled sarcastically at her mother's comment and sneered viciously at her.

Eager to end the unpleasant reunion with her daughter, Susan called out her good-byes to Joan.

"See you later, Joan. You might want to keep the doors closed. Now that things are cooling off, you never know what the wind will blow in."

"Take care, Susan," Joan called after her, but she was already at the door.

Before Susan stepped out onto the porch, she looked back over her shoulder at Emily.

"She's been through a lot you know… we both have," Susan said. "Don't think you're going to waltz back into her life again. The church and I are the only family she needs now."

Her mother's words struck like daggers on the soft spot the guilt had left on her heart. She knew she had deserted her little sister when she needed her most. She'd never be able to take that back, but she was here now, and she was trying to do the right thing. Masking her true emotions by rolling her eyes dramatically, Emily shot back what she hoped was an equally hurtful response.

"You're so good at driving people away, you really should have opened a taxi cab company. It's no wonder Steve left you."

By the look on Susan's face, Emily could tell her remark was as damaging as she had intended. Somehow, it didn't feel as good as she imagined it would though. She immediately regretted it, but before she could take it back, her mother turned and left.

"Shit!" Emily muttered to herself.

Outside on the porch, Susan took a moment to collect her composure. She hadn't meant to come across so harshly, but her first impulse was protecting Lily. She was so fragile right now, even the smallest stress could set back her recovery, never mind seeing her misfit sister for the first time in seven years. Susan took a deep breath and shook her head as she headed to her vehicle.

Through the store window, Emily watched her mother walk away. This was absolutely not how she had intended their initial conversation to go. She wasn't expecting sunshine and smiles, but she certainly didn't think her hurtful sarcasm would rear its ugly head so soon.

"Shit," she mumbled again as she thought to herself, "I didn't even get to find out what hospital Lily is in."

After taking a few steps down the sidewalk, Susan stopped cold. Part of her wanted to turn around and go back into the store and wrap her arms around her first born daughter. It had been so long, she couldn't even remember the last time she hugged her. Susan knew she played an equal part in their disconnection all those years ago. But sadly, for both of them, like most of us in life, the longer you wait to apologize, the harder it becomes. And now, after seven long years of silence, it was definitely easier to resort to sarcasm and bitterness.

Hoping she hadn't heard the entire conversation, Emily turned to face Joan. By the sympathetic look she saw on Joan's face, she knew she wasn't so lucky. Joan tucked a strand of her long white hair behind her ear then straightened the white apron that she wore over her pastel blue plaid shirt.

"I'm really sorry about Lily," Joan said. "She's always a ray of sunshine whenever she comes into the store. I think it's great that you've come to visit her."

Joan's kind remark had caught Emily off guard.

"Where you end up, is where you are," Emily mumbled sarcastically.

"Excuse me?" asked Joan.

"Never mind," Emily said, avoiding eye contact with Joan.

"Oh, alright," Joan said. "Is there something I can help you with?"

"Umm…" Emily began. "Umm, you don't happen to know what hospital Lily is in, do you?"

The fact she had to ask a complete stranger where her own sister was, made the guilt she carried ten times heavier. If Joan was surprised that Emily didn't know which hospital Lily was in, she didn't show it.

"She's over in Grafton Falls. It's about thirty minutes northwest of here."

"Oh."

Emily's face grew a little more sullen. How stupid of her to assume the hospital would be here in Pine Ridge.

"Please tell me there's another way to get to the hospital other than that smelly old blue bus?" Emily remarked.

Joan grimaced, obviously familiar with the bus.

"I'll tell you what, my son Ryan is headed out that way to run some errands. I'll have him give you a lift."

Immediately uncomfortable with the idea, Emily shifted nervously in her chunky heels.

"Oh, no. That's ok. I couldn't. I don't wanna be a …"

"Oh nonsense," Joan interrupted.

Just then, Ryan stepped through a storage room located behind the counter. He wore a navy blue L.L. Bean sweatshirt, jeans and a Red Sox hat.

"Ryan, this is…"

Realizing Joan hadn't gotten Emily's name, she was forced to stop and look apologetically at Emily. Although Emily was a bit hurt that her mother had obviously never mentioned her before, she was quick to fill in the information for Joan.

"Emily," she said with a polite nod.

Ryan smiled at her, creating a dimple above his strong jaw line. Emily observed he had the same striking shade of blue eyes as his mother. Instead of returning his smile, she cast her eyes to the floor.

"Right, Emily," Joan said. "Emily is Ms. McLoughlin's daughter. I need you to give her a ride to Grafton Falls so she can visit her sister."

Ryan's eyes danced with amusement as he noted the only color Emily wore were the dark red streaks in her hair. At least her piercings gave a little contrast to all that black, thought Ryan.

He went to a school with a girl that had Emily's look. She was always drawing weird images of sad cats and talked to herself a lot. He wasn't surprised when she dropped out her senior year.

"Oh, I didn't realize Ms. McLoughlin had another daughter," Ryan said.

"Apparently neither does she," Emily added.

She pulled her cell phone from her pocket and frowned when she saw that she didn't have any service. She spun in a wide circle with the phone held out in front of her.

"Is there someplace I can go that I can get service?" Emily asked.

"Yeah, in my truck after we get to the edge of town. Anything before that is kind of hit or miss," Ryan said. "Come on, let's go."

Ryan steered Emily toward the exit and told his mother they'd be back in a few hours.

Outside, Ryan paused at an old Chevy pickup painted pine needle green. The word 'Heartbeat' was painted on the bottom right corner of a rusted tailgate. A thick layer of mud was caked and splattered along the side panels.

"This is it," Ryan announced and motioned Emily to the

passenger door.

"Of course it is," Emily replied sarcastically. "Leave it to my mother to move to East Bumfuck."

Ryan raised an eyebrow at her harsh assessment of his hometown but said nothing. In truth, he might have used that exact phrase once or twice to describe Pine Ridge. He climbed into his truck and waited for Emily to join him.

Emily hesitated, but the thought of riding the blue bus again edged her forward. She pulled on the handle but nothing happened. She tried again and pulled harder, but the door wouldn't budge. Assuming it was locked, she waited for Ryan to unlock it for her. Instead, he reached out and popped the door open from the inside.

"I forgot to tell you, you have to really pull up hard on the door handle or it won't open."

He watched in guilty amusement as Emily sized up the climb she would have to make to get into the cab. She put one thickly soled heel on the cab floor and tried to balance herself against the door. She hopped on one foot trying to get the momentum to lift her body up into the cab. The door slipped behind her and she stumbled back, catching herself just before she landed in a puddle of mud. Ryan smirked. She had obviously never ridden in a truck before.

"Grab the Oh Shit handle and pull yourself up," he instructed her.

"The what?" Emily asked.

Ryan nodded to the handle above her head.

"Oh." Emily said as she found the handle. "Shit."

If she could pull herself up a pole, she could certainly handle this, Emily thought, and grabbed hold of the handle. In one smooth motion, she pulled herself up into the cab. Once inside, she happily bounced around on the seat until she shuffled her body into a comfortable position. To her surprise, she found that her feet didn't touch the floor, but that didn't really bother her. What bothered her was the entertained look on Ryan's face.

"First time in a truck, huh?"

"Boy, you're a quick study. Not much gets by you, does it?" Emily jeered.

Not bothering to wait for his response, Emily started to reach over her shoulder for the seat belt, but Ryan stopped her.

"Not that one. That one doesn't work. I put in another one behind that one."

Sure enough, there were two sets of seat belts attached to the cab wall. Emily grabbed the other one and attempted to fasten it. Ryan watched her struggle with it for longer than he should have. Normally, he would have offered his help by now, but Emily's sarcastic demeanor didn't make it easy to be accommodating. Finally, he couldn't watch any longer.

"Do you want me to get that for you?"

"No, I can get it. I just can't understand why this thing doesn't click!" she huffed.

Luckily, one of Ryan's better traits was patience. He leaned back and watched her continue. She was actually kind of pretty when she was concentrating, he thought.

Finally, Emily dropped the metal buckle with an exasperated sigh.

"What the fuck is wrong with this thing??" she demanded.

Ryan calmly leaned over and secured her buckle with one quick jerk of his hand. As he leaned in close, Emily noted he didn't smell of beer and cigarettes like most men she knew. Instead, he carried the same sweet aroma of the general store.

"Is this thing even safe?" Emily asked.

"Of course it is. What truck is safer than one with two sets of seat belts for every passenger?" Ryan chided.

Emily pushed back against her seat with a huff and pushed her hair out of her eyes.

They drove on in silence for several miles. Emily quickly noticed there were no chain restaurants or convenience stores along the way.

The only thing Emily saw were large New Englander style homes, rolling fields, and dilapidated old barns. These reoccurring structures were only broken by the occasional gas station.

Emily gasped in surprise then started snickering as they passed a woman pumping gas. She was wearing yoga pants, hair curlers, and a camouflaged tee-shirt.

"What's so funny?" Ryan asked.

"I can't believe anyone would actually go out in public like that!" Emily exclaimed.

"Like what? You mean the curlers?" Ryan asked.

"Um yeah, and those pants!" Emily cried.

"What's wrong with her pants?" Ryan asked.

He liked woman in yoga pants.

Emily scrunched up her face in revulsion.

"I don't *do* yoga pants, that's all," Emily stated, and then added quietly, "and neither should she."

Ryan shook his head. Emily could possibly be the rudest woman he ever met. He decided to politely change the subject.

"So, have you ever been to Pine Ridge before?" Ryan asked.

"I've never been anywhere in Maine before," Emily answered. "How anyone can choose to live up here in the sticks is beyond me. No offense."

Ryan grimaced and chose to ignore her comment.

"Where are you from?" he asked.

"I'm originally from Braintree, Mass, but I've been living in Boston for a while now."

"Ahhh, a Masshole, huh?" Ryan joked.

Emily scowled at him.

"No offense," he added with a smile.

Emily was more annoyed by the fact his blue eyes also smiled at her. Of course he would make fun of her, she thought. It was clear to her that he obviously thought he was better than her.

"Hey, I'm just kidding," Ryan continued. "I love Boston. I was actually there for a Sox game last summer."

"There's more to Boston than the stupid Red Sox, ya know?" Emily sneered.

Ryan gripped the steering wheel tighter. I've met icicles warmer than this girl, he thought. Her hostility and sarcasm baffled him. As he gazed at her many piercings, he thought, I better keep a safe distance or I could end up hooked at the end of one of those things.

He began to wonder if driving the rest of the way in silence would be more enjoyable than continuing a conversation with her. He tried the radio, but after turning the dial a few times, he got nothing but commercials, country music, or gospel programs. He decided to make one last attempt at conversation.

"So what do you do in Boston?" he asked.

"What's with all the questions? You writing a book or something?" Emily responded with a look of distain.

Ryan shook his head in frustration. He was going to have a talk with his mother about volunteering him for taxi service when he got back home. At this rate it was going to be a very long ride to Grafton Falls, he thought. Quite frankly, he was perplexed that Emily didn't appreciate his attempt at polite conversation. After all, he was doing *her* a favor.

The winding country road finally left the houses and farms behind and started to run alongside a small river. On the far edge of the riverbanks were some old brick buildings. Many of their thin glass windows were broken. The sloped wooden roofs were sagged and caved in the middle. Seeing them lay dark and vacant always made Ryan feel a little depressed.

"When those old paper mills were in their prime, Pine Ridge had a population nearly triple what it is now. It didn't always used to be such a quiet town." Ryan explained.

"Triple, huh?" Emily asked feigning interest. "So that must have put the population up to almost sixty people or so?"

Growing used to her sarcasm and lack of manners, Ryan ignored her and continued.

"Supposedly, a few years ago, there was talk of L.L. Bean buying them, but I guess the deal must have fallen through."

Emily rolled her heavily painted eyes. She wondered why he couldn't take a hint. She was so anxious and nervous about seeing Lily, she couldn't think about conversation even if she wanted – and she certainly couldn't imagine ever wanting to with Ryan.

"Do you always talk this much?" she asked.

Ryan wanted to ask her if she was always so charming, but he thought better of it. He just resigned to driving the rest of the way in silence and let himself get lost in the scenery of the rolling fields and towering trees. Occasionally, he stole a glance in Emily's direction to find her with a serene look on her face as she also took in the rustic landscape.

He was slightly relieved when they finally pulled into the hospital parking lot. Usually, he found interacting with women came easily, but this one definitely wasn't like any he had met before.

As Emily sized up the enormous building, she felt her stomach tighten. She wished she didn't have to go in alone. She didn't want to ask Ryan to come in with her though. She was sure he couldn't wait to get rid of her.

"Thanks for the ride," Emily said.

"It was my pleasure," Ryan lied.

Emily opened the truck door with a loud creak and a clunk. She looked down at the ground measuring the distance she needed to cover. She swung her legs over the edge of the seat and debated the best way to exit the truck without breaking an ankle. She tested by stretching her foot out toward the pavement. She decided it was too far for that approach so she brought it back up and started to recalculate. She scooted a little closer to the edge.

Ryan stifled a snicker, but it didn't go unnoticed by Emily who shot a hot glare over her shoulder at him.

"Just jump."

"I was planning on it!" Emily retorted.

She actually wasn't planning on it, but it seemed like a better option than slithering down the side like a snake, which was going to be her next approach. She launched herself out of the cab and landed gracefully on her feet. Once she hit the ground, she adjusted her skirt and flipped her hair over her shoulder.

"I have a few errands to run in town," Ryan said, "but I'll be back to pick you up. No hurry, of course. Take your time with your sister."

"Thanks," she said.

"Anytime," Ryan answered as he backed the truck up.

Yeah, anytime I feel like torturing myself with your presence, Ryan thought as he drove away. He really didn't understand her. Never in his twenty-eight years had he been met with such hostility from the opposite sex. He was doing Emily a favor, the least she could have done was feign politeness. Feeling a bit self-conscious, Ryan pulled open the front of his sweatshirt and took a whiff of himself. Nope, all good there, he thought.

5
Still In Me

"No matter how far I go
Or what beautiful face I see
Or how many miles between
You're still in me"

Emily stood in the doorway of room 217, peering in at the small figure sleeping under the blankets. When she saw the bald head and bony fingers curled around the edge of the blanket, she double checked the numbers outside the door to make sure she had the right room. Lily's blonde locks and her full rosy cheeks had been replaced by spiky patches of stubble and sunken cheek bones.

Still thinking there had to be some kind of mistake, she crept silently closer to the bed to get a better look at the unfortunate soul it held. When she got within reaching distance and saw the telltale beauty mark above the corner of Lily's mouth, her breath caught in her throat.

Emily started to back up. She wanted to be there for her sister but hadn't been prepared to see her laying there looking like a completely wasted version of her former self. When had it gotten so bad? Emily tried to remember the last time she spoke with Lily on Facebook. Was it early September? No, she remembered it was a week or two before Lily started her senior year. August? Had it really been that long? Emily was known to go weeks without checking Facebook, but still, she should have at least reached out to see how Lily's big senior year was going. She cursed herself for ignoring her aunt's messages the past couple of weeks.

"Such a selfish little bitch," she mumbled at herself.

Emily started to wonder if she was strong enough for this but quickly realized that statement was equally as selfish. This wasn't about her, it was about Lily.

Just then, Lily's long dark lashes began to flutter open. Emily stood still in silence as she watched Lily blink the sleep from her baby blue eyes. When she looked at Emily, her eyes seemed to be too large for her head.

"Emily!! I knew you'd come see me! I just knew it!"

Even though they had started to reconnect on Facebook a year earlier, this was the first time she had actually heard Lily's voice in seven years.

Lily's voice sounded older than she remembered, but it also seemed smaller and weaker. Lily pulled her thin arms from beneath the blanket and reached out to her sister. Emily felt her heart shatter and land at her feet.

Before she knew it, she had her sister wrapped up in her arms and she was blinking back tears. Emily noted with concern that she could feel Lily's ribs through the thin hospital gown. Lily pulled back and regarded her sister with wide curious eyes.

Her eyes moved over Emily's face and her black attire.

"You look beautiful, Em." Lily whispered.

"Aw, thanks, kiddo," Emily replied.

Lily's eyes then settled in wonder at the piercings that lined Emily's face and ears.

"Whoa. Mom didn't even want me to get my ears pierced *once*," said Lily in awe.

Emily smiled. It was good to see the cancer hadn't taken her humor.

"Have you seen her?" Lily asked cautiously.

"Seen who?"

"Mom."

"Oh, yeah."

"How did that go?" Lily asked hopefully.

"It could have gone better," Emily answered. "Whatever. Some things never change I guess."

"I'm sorry I haven't messaged you in a while," said Lily.

"Lily, you totally don't need to apologize for that."

"As soon as I started getting sick again, Mom took my cell phone and laptop away. She said she read somewhere that they can give off harmful radiation that might impede my recovery."

Both girls giggled and rolled their eyes at each other.

Emily continued to smile and said, "Do you remember the…"

"Five foot rule?" they both said together and giggled again.

Their mother's silly neuroses went way back. When the girls were younger, one of her rules was everyone needed to be at least five feet away from the microwave while it was in use.

"Remember we used to freak her out by only standing two feet away?" said Emily.

"While wearing tin foil hats," giggled Lily.

"The look on her face was priceless," Emily added and joined her sister in giggling. Lily's giggling turned into uncontrollable coughing.

"You okay?" Emily asked with a serious look.

When her coughing finally subsided, Lily looked into Emily's eyes and smiled.

"I'm better than okay now that you're here. I've just missed you so much, Em."

"I've missed you too, Lily Pad."

"Aww, I haven't heard you call me that since forever."

Lily's eyes swelled up with tears. She blinked and released one glittering tear down her pale freckled cheek.

"I remember I started calling you that when you were going

through your frog phase. Remember that stuffed frog I bought you for your fourth birthday? You used to bring that thing everywhere with you. What was his name again?"

"Tony," answered Lily as she smiled widely and lifted her pillow revealing the same frog. She held it up for her sister to inspect. The frog showed the stress of a long term relationship with an owner that loved it every day of the week. Its belly was starting to split at the seams, and its coat, once soft and plush, was now matted and balding in some places. Worst of all, it had lost one of its shiny black eyes.

Emily put her hand to her mouth.

"What happened to him?" Emily laughed.

Lily seemed to not understand what Emily was talking about and turned the frog around to inspect it herself. To her, it was just as adorable as the day she had pulled it from the polka dot wrapped box Emily had put it in. Looking at it again, she could see now why Emily might be surprised.

"I guess we both have seen better days," Lily said sadly.

She stroked the bald spot on top of the frog's head and gave him a kiss.

"Don't worry, I still love you, Tony," she whispered to the frog.

Feeling a bit silly for considering the frog's emotional state, Lily was quick to shift the conversation back to her sister.

"I'm assuming Aunt Kay called you?" Lily asked.

Still smart as a whip, Emily thought. Her sister knew better than to think for a minute their mother had called her. Lily knew the only other family member to have stayed in contact with Emily was their aunt Kay.

"Yeah, she said you weren't doing so hot," Emily whispered.

For some reason, she didn't want to say it out loud. Maybe it was because once it was said out loud it became more real.

Lily just brushed off her sister's words with a hand.

"How did you get all the way up here? Did you take a bus?"

Emily chuckled as she recalled the blue senior citizen bus and its mixed smell of vitamins and urine.

"Yeah, something like that."

"How's the… how's the… club going?"

Emily was grateful for her sister's attempt at conversation, because if it were left up to her, she wouldn't know what to say.

"It's actually not going. I quit last night."

Over the past year of reconnecting with Lily, Emily was careful what she revealed to her little sister. She had reluctantly told Lily that she worked at a strip club, but she made certain to gloss over the sordid details and poor lifestyle choices she had made over the years.

Lily sat up straighter in bed and her face brightened some. She was glad to hear her sister left that place. Lily's only knowledge of strip clubs were what she saw on TV or in the movies. She pictured a sleazy, seedy joint where drugs were prevalent and where drunk, horny men groped the dancers, not to mention, that episode of Law & Order where strippers were being targeted for murder.

Whenever Lily would voice her concern, Emily joked it off by telling her she was watching too much TV. Emily reassured Lily that the Red Garter was nothing like that. In reality though, it was exactly like that… minus the murder part.

Lily wanted to encourage her big sister that she had made the right decision without coming across as being judgmental or holier than thou.

"You should totally do something with your photography, Emily. I loved looking at all the pictures you would post online," said Lily. "I haven't seen any in a while though." she added with a frown.

Emily smiled a sad smile. Those were the types of smiles that seemed to come most easily to her.

"Are you still dating that punk rocker?" Lily asked.

"I kinda quit that last night too," Emily said quietly.

She thought Eric would be just waking up right about now. He probably wouldn't even realize she was gone for good. He'd probably just assume that she had left for work. There'd been a kind of accidental brilliance about her sudden departure.

"That's good," said Lily and then added, "I guess. I mean, he sort of sounded like a…"

Emily saved her from having to finish.

"A jerk? Idiot? Douchbag? Yeah, pick your choice from any of the above," said Emily.

Embarrassed she had brought it up, Lily cast her eyes to her lap and nodded.

"Yeah," she agreed softly.

"What can I say?" said Emily. "I'm a loser magnet."

Lily wondered if that statement included her. She really wanted her sister to like her, and she was remorseful that she had been so clingy all those years ago. She couldn't help but think that played a part in Emily leaving home.

A young nurse, with mahogany hair and a lean figure, entered the room. She looked at Emily with sincere interest which made Emily feel that she needed to explain herself.

"I'm Emily. Lily's sister," Emily offered.

"Oh? I haven't seen you here before," the nurse noted.

Her comment sent a striking stab of guilt through Emily's core. She instinctively felt herself stiffen and go on the defense.

"Well, I'm here now," Emily answered tightly.

The nurse, sensing Emily's discomfort, softened her approach.

"Well Emily, it's time for Lily's treatment. You can come back later tonight to visit again if you'd like?"

Knowing that she was being dismissed, Emily reached out to her sister again and embraced her.

"I'll be back, Lily," she said with commitment.

Lily nodded solemnly. She wasn't sure she believed her, but the idea of Emily coming back for a second visit meant the world to her.

"Where are you staying?" Lily asked.

"Relax, kiddo. You just worry about getting better. I'll figure out the rest. I always do, right?"

Lily nodded. She knew Emily was very self-reliant. Emily practically raised her alone those last couple years at home. Nobody knew better than her, that her sister could conquer the world with a plastic fork if she needed to.

"Right," Lily agreed.

Emily kissed her forehead and turned to leave.

"Oh Emily," Lily called after her. "I almost forgot to tell you, I got accepted to Boston College. We will be able to see each other all the time next year. Isn't that great news?"

Emily was stopped in her tracks by an emotion she didn't quite recognize. When she imagined having her baby sister back in her everyday life, she realized the feeling was happiness. A small smile tugged at the corner of her merlot lips.

"The best news I've heard in a long time, Lily Pad."

When she reached the door, she looked back at her sister.

"I'm really glad you're here, Emily."

Emily nodded.

"Me too kiddo. Me too."

***

Outside, Emily found Ryan's truck parked in the visitor parking lot. As she approached the truck, she watched Ryan drumming his hands on the steering wheel jamming to a song. The sound of heavy bass sent vibrations through the crisp autumn air. She immediately recognized the song. It was "Closer" by Nine Inch Nails. It used to be one of her go-to songs at the club. She was shocked and a little impressed that this Maine boy had even heard of them. Of course, Emily had absolutely no intention of letting him know she was impressed.

Remembering the trick to opening the door, she pulled up hard on the handle and gave the door a hard jerk.

"Hey," she said entering the truck.

Ryan screamed.

"You scream like a little girl," Emily chided.

"What the hell is wrong with you?" Ryan asked angrily as he turned off the song.

"Sorry, I didn't realize I would be interrupting a one man jam party in here."

She watched with satisfaction as the color flooded Ryan's cheeks. Emily climbed in easily this time, and Ryan noted she was a quick learner.

The ride back to Pine Ridge was a bit quieter, but that was only because Ryan didn't press her with polite conversational questions. Even still, he could tell Emily's mood had improved. She seemed more relaxed, and he even caught her smiling once or twice as she gazed out the window.

6
Falling Away

"I'm out imagining my greatest escape
I'm tired of being a victim in this race
Another day and I must say, I just look the other way
I go to sleep, I'm satisfied
Either fading or falling away"

Back at the store, Emily and Ryan found Harold, Max and Gus still sitting on the bench drinking Moxies.

"It's about time you got back to work," Harold said gruffly to Ryan. "This place doesn't run itself, ya know? While you were out gallivanting, a big delivery came in."

"Dad…" Ryan started, but Harold cut him off.

"Oh don't worry, son. I'm sure your sixty-six year old mother can handle it by herself. Let's just hope she doesn't throw her back out or worse yet, give herself a heart attack."

Ryan adjusted the brim of his Red Sox hat and hurried inside. He sincerely hoped that his father was just giving him a hard time and that his mother wasn't inside shuffling around heavy boxes.

Emily followed him inside, wanting nothing more than to avoid another conversation with Larry, Larry & Darrel. Besides, Lily had brought up a good point, she needed to find a place to stay. She hoped Joan would help direct her to a local motel — if such a thing existed.

Inside, they found Joan sitting at the counter reading a magazine.

She looked up and smiled affectionately at both of them.

"Did you see Lily, dear?" she asked Emily. "I bet she was glad to see her big sister, huh? How is she doing?"

Emily wasn't sure which of Joan's three questions to answer first. Fortunately, she didn't have to.

"What's with all the questions, Ma?" asked Ryan mockingly. "You writing a book or something?"

Emily smirked at Ryan's clever sarcasm. Joan, however, did not appear amused. She dropped the magazine and shot Ryan a look that clearly stated he was skating on thin ice.

Emily took the distraction as an opportunity to explore the store further. In the front corner, she found framed photography displayed on the walls. Stepping closer, she examined the different shots that captured Maine's nature scene; sunsets on the lake, a silhouette of a lone tree free-standing in a field, close-ups of loons, and even one of a moose emerging from a swamp with swamp grass tangled in its antlers.

"Are you a photographer?" Joan asked with interest when she saw Emily inspecting the art.

"No, not really," Emily answered. "Not professionally anyway."

Joan had good intuition about people and she sensed Emily was just being modest. She decided to test the waters further.

"You know what? I just picked up some old frames at the flea market. I'd love to get your opinion on them."

Before Emily could refuse, Joan grabbed her by the wrist and was leading her away to one of the back rooms.

"I'll be out back putting away the order, Ma," Ryan called out.

Ryan pushed up the sleeves of his sweatshirt and approached several stacks of boxes. After studying the label, he grabbed one off the top and turned to bring it to the appropriate destination. In the process, he nearly collided with his brother, Danny. Danny had a talent for sneaking up on people.

Danny was five years older than Ryan, but in many ways he was much younger. Danny stood with his dark hair rumpled and disheveled. He wore a Goonies Never Say Die t-shirt over his husky frame. The tee-shirt, like every shirt he wore, was consistently tucked into the waist of his jeans and secured with the same brown leather belt he wore each day. His dark brown eyes were a bit glazed as if he had just woken up from a dream.

"Jesus, Danny! You nearly made me pee my pants!" Ryan exclaimed.

If one more person snuck up on him today he would be headed for a nervous breakdown. Danny didn't move. Instead, he fixed his eyes down to the floor and began to sway from side to side nervously. The grip on the grocery bag he carried tightened and released, tightened and released. Ryan eyed the backpack strapped over his shoulders.

"Headed out to the woods, buddy?" he asked in a softer tone.

Danny made a slight nod but still didn't look up to make eye contact. He knew he had scared Ryan, and he hoped that Ryan didn't stay angry about it.

"Well, say hi to Uncle Frank for me, huh?" Ryan coaxed. "And no more trying to make me pee my pants, ok?"

One corner of Danny's mouth tipped up in a half smile. It would be funny if Ryan actually peed his pants, he thought.

Ryan grabbed Danny's shoulders gently and pulled him in for a hug. Danny brought one arm half way up and almost touched Ryan's shoulder before he went limp in his arms. When Ryan released him, Danny pointed anxiously toward the door.

"Uncle Frank wants to see me," Danny explained.

Ryan nodded and mumbled, "You're the only one he ever wants to see."

Danny stared blankly at Ryan, unaffected by his comment.

"Ya better get going then," Ryan said with a smile.

Danny stopped at the back door and looked over his shoulder with a big smile.

"I'll be back, Ryan," he said. "Don't… don't pee your pants," and with a laugh, he was off.

***

In another room, Joan pulled out some antique frames she had bought at a flea market to show Emily. Emily examined them thoughtfully and nodded. She found a simple one with wood that looked nearly rotted.

"I like this one," she said. "You could paint it white and go over the paint with a scrubbing brush to enhance the distressed look."

"Oh, I've never done anything like that before," said Joan. "You might have to show me."

"Ok," Emily agreed shyly.

"Do you plan on staying in town long?" Joan asked.

"Playing it by ear I guess," Emily answered.

She chuckled sadly at the irony, but Joan just looked at her inquisitively.

"Like the rest of my life," Emily added.

"Oh," Joan chuckled politely. "I guess most of us did that when we were your age."

Sensing her opening, Emily figured it was a good time to ask about local lodging options.

"Umm, is there like a motel or something around here? It doesn't have to be anything fancy. The cheaper the better," Emily implored. "Actually, is there some place closer to the hospital maybe?"

She felt uncomfortable asking for help. She was used to figuring everything out herself, but things didn't seem so easy to figure out here in Hicksville.

Joan's look of amusement softened to something warmer.

"There's a couple of motels in Grafton Falls, but…" Joan cringed, "but I wouldn't really recommend them to anyone."

Emily had stayed in quite a few sketchy places over the years, so Joan's warning didn't really deter her. Before Emily could inquire more about these motels, Joan presented her with another option.

"I'll tell you what, why don't you stay with us while you're in town?" Joan offered.

Emily put her hands up and backed away. There was absolutely no way she was going to stay with the Corbins. What was wrong with this lady anyways, she wondered. What kind of sick ulterior motive did she have? Or was she so pathetic looking that she evoked the sympathy of strangers? This was bullshit, Emily thought.

"Oh no, I couldn't," Emily said in a tone that encompassed stern politeness. "Just tell me the name of one of those motels and I'll be fine."

Joan read the emotions that ranged from anger, to confusion, to disbelief on Emily's face. It was clear the poor girl had never been given a break before. The thought made Joan even more determined to help her out, but she knew she'd have to handle it delicately.

"Look, most of our kids have moved out of town. It's just Ryan and our other son Danny now. We have more room than we are used to. You'd be making our house feel full again," Joan said.

Emily balked, and her eyes instinctively bolted toward the door.

"No charge of course," Joan added hopefully.

She missed having her daughters in the house. Living with her husband and two other full grown men, the house had more testosterone running through it than a football field. Another woman in the house would be a welcomed change.

Emily could see now that Joan's was sincere, but she still felt weird about it. Mrs. Corbin was a total stranger offering to help her, and without knowing her motivations, she felt uneasy about it. Maybe she was trying to unload her talkative son on her. Who knew? People were crazy, Emily thought. And who the hell was this other son she spoke of? What if he was even more talkative than Ryan?

"Um, thanks but I couldn't impose like that," said Emily. "I just wouldn't feel right."

"Oh trust me, you wouldn't be imposing. I could use the company... especially from another female. Ever since Claire and Lacey moved out, I've been outnumbered."

Despite herself, Emily cracked a smile. It had been a while since she felt wanted by a mother figure. The thought of having an older woman to talk to did hold some appeal, but still, she couldn't accept the offer. Somehow though, she didn't hear herself declining.

Sensing Emily's hesitation, Joan decided to seal the deal in the moment of silence.

"Ok, then. It's settled," Joan declared. "I'll have Ryan run you up to the house and get you settled in."

Just then, Ryan walked into the room.

"Get who settled into where?" he asked.

"I offered to let Emily stay with us while she's in town visiting her sister," Joan explained. "Why don't you take her home and get her set up in Lacey's old room?"

Ryan had to stop his jaw from hitting the floor. He absolutely couldn't believe his mother had invited Little Miss Doom and Gloom into their house. She must have completely flipped her biscuits, he thought. Ryan tried to stall to give his mother a little time to reconsider her hasty offer.

"I gotta finish taking the delivery in first," Ryan answered.

"Oh, those boxes can wait," Joan said with a dismissive wave of her hand.

Before Ryan could protest further, Joan already had another idea forming in her head. Sensing Emily's inhibition, she figured she might be more comfortable in the apartment above the garage.

"Actually, why don't *you* take Lacey's room, Ryan, and give Emily the garage apartment."

Although it was posed as a suggestion, Ryan knew it was more of an order. Was he being punished for something?

"What? My apartment??"

"Yes, it will give her more privacy," Joan said delighted with herself for thinking of the idea.

"But Ma…"

Emily felt guilty for Mrs. Corbin's suggestion, but she was right. Emily was a bit of a loner and having an apartment over the garage did hold more appeal. Still, she didn't see why Ryan should have to give up his space for her.

"I really don't mind staying at a motel, Mrs. Corbin. You don't have to go through all this trouble."

"Oh, nonsense," said Joan. "Ryan can move into the house for a bit. Right, Ryan?"

Joan gave her son a pointed look that clearly indicated there would be consequences to pay if he didn't agree with her. Ryan sighed and nodded.

"Yes, Ma."

Satisfied the situation had been resolved, she slid Emily's suitcase over to Ryan. Ryan dutifully picked up the suitcase and waited to be dismissed.

"But I don't even know how long I'll be here. It could be awhile…" Emily started.

"Stay as long as you'd like dear," said Joan.

Ryan could hardly contain himself any longer. Stay as long as you like? Was she out of her mind? He shot his mother an "are you kidding me" look, but she just smiled sweetly back at him. Knowing he was defeated, he just shook his head.

Emily caught the look and gave Ryan an apologetic shrug. She turned back to Mrs. Corbin.

"Thanks again Mrs…"

"It's Joan, and you're welcome."

As Ryan and Emily stepped onto the porch, they were greeted again by Harold and his two sidekicks. Emily wondered if they ever left.

"Workin' hard or hardly workin' there, son?" Harold asked.

"Looks like hardly workin' to me," said Max.

"You've been back for five minutes and you're already taking another break?" asked Harold.

Exasperated, Ryan threw his free hand up and opened his mouth to explain, but before he could get the words out, he was interrupted.

"Youth nowadays – no work ethic," Max said and shook his head sadly.

"I went fifty years without taking so much as a coffee break," Gus added.

Ryan rolled his eyes and indicated for Emily to go down the stairs ahead of him. Emily stopped and took her suitcase from Ryan.

"I can carry my own bag," she said.

Ryan put his hands up in a gesture of surrender.

She hiked the suitcase up and descended the stairs.

"Looks like you got an independent woman on your hands there, son," Harold remarked.

"She NOT my woman," said Ryan, and then muttered under his breath, "Thank God."

He watched Emily struggling to open the tailgate of the truck and quickly went down to help her. He anticipated another sarcastic response as he unlatched the chains on the sides for her, but she just huffed and tossed her suitcase in without a word.

Ryan wondered if Emily was always this warm with everyone or was this something special she reserved just for him? Maybe she was a man hater, he thought. He stopped to ponder this further. Was Emily a man-hating lesbian? His instincts told him it wasn't that, but maybe it did have something to do with gender. Or perhaps it was something like love at first sight in the opposite direction. He tried to think if he ever instantly disliked anyone but quickly found the answer was no. His parents taught him not to be judgmental of people, and he had already resolved to try harder to give Emily the benefit of the doubt.

She wasn't staying with her mother, so he deducted there must have been some kind of falling out there. His family had always stuck together no matter how difficult life had gotten. He couldn't imagine ever turning his back on them or vice versa. And he certainly couldn't imagine what that could do to a person if it did happen.

He wasn't exactly sure what Emily's deal was, but with her living in such close proximity, he was going to find out.

"Don't suppose you have a Dunkin Donuts in town, huh?" asked Emily.

Ryan shook his head and joked, "Believe it or not, not every place in America runs on Dunkin."

Emily didn't share in his humor and frowned deeply.

"We actually have really good coffee at the general. I could go get you one if…" Ryan started.

"I'll live," she interrupted. "I'm not staying long enough to mind," Emily told herself this as much as she did to Ryan.

"Actually," Ryan began to point out, "Pine Ridge has an ordinance that prohibits any franchises from ever coming to town. Pretty cool, huh?"

Emily didn't think that was pretty cool at all. She couldn't throw a rock from her apartment without hitting at least five different franchises.

Ryan started his truck and headed back up Main Street. He took his first right onto Maple Lane. The Corbin's house was about a half mile down the road just passed an old, rundown drive-in movie theater. The giant sign was missing quite a few letters and read: P ne R dg D ive In. One could only assume it had been closed for years.

The first driveway after the drive-in was the Corbin's. It was a long, winding dirt driveway lined with maple trees. The filtered sunlight played across Emily's eyes like a kaleidoscope. The neatly trimmed green lawn stretched out on either side.

At the top of the hill sat a large white farmhouse with a wrap-around porch. On either side of the steps were two old milk jugs repurposed into flower pots. Red carnations bloomed from the tops of both of them. Two old rockers with faded black paint stood on one side of the front door. An old metal framed porch swing creaked softly as it rocked in the breeze. In front of the door, an old dog lifted its head and attentively watched the truck approach.

When Ryan pulled up in front of the double doors of the garage, the chocolate lab got up from its resting spot on the shady porch and waddled over to greet them. Its tail thudded vigorously against Ryan's legs. When Emily jumped out of the truck, the dog's mood quickly flipped. He circled around the truck and began to bark vigorously at her.

"Riley!" Ryan yelled.

The dog paused long enough to throw a questioning look over his shoulder at Ryan and then resumed his barking. Emily stood frozen in place.

"It's ok, Emily," Ryan assured her. "He won't hurt you."

Ryan rounded the side of the truck and stood next to Emily.

"Riley, stop that!" Ryan said in a stern voice.

Riley bowed his head in submission and approached Emily, who cautiously held out her hand. Riley wagged his tail at her gesture and eagerly leaned out to sniff it. A moment later, Emily's legs were being assaulted by his happy tail whacks.

"Good boy," Ryan said, and patted Riley's head affectionately.

Ryan went around to the back of the truck and released the tailgate. He grabbed Emily's suitcase and started for the back stairs that led up to the loft apartment over the garage.

"You sure do travel light for a woman," Ryan remarked.

He really would have been shocked if he knew that within the contents of her suitcase was everything she owned. Emily stopped him and grabbed the suitcase from him.

"I told you, I can carry my own bag."

She thought of the framed photograph of her and Lily resting on the top. She wanted to be sure to keep it safe. She knew the only way to keep something you hold dear safe was to guard it yourself.

Emily followed Ryan into a small studio sized kitchenette that overlooked a spacious well-lit apartment. The afternoon sun shone through the large picture window in the front of the open concept apartment. The living room space was outlined by a small love seat and a coffee table that faced a modest entertainment center. To the right was a bedroom with a full-sized bed. The one door in the apartment stood on a kitchen wall close to the entrance. Emily assumed this is where the bathroom was located.

Ryan watched Emily look around and was bewildered by the surprise on her face.

"Not what you expected?" Ryan asked.

Emily didn't answer. Instead, she thought of the apartment she shared with Eric that was constantly littered with empty pizza boxes and beer cans. Looking around this apartment, she didn't see any clutter. In fact, it was so clean she wouldn't have guessed a guy her age occupied the space, or a guy of any age for that matter. The only evidence she saw of Ryan was a gray sweatshirt draped neatly over the back of a chair at the kitchen table.

Emily's silence made him feel uncomfortable, so Ryan found himself offering an explanation of the space.

"Once my parents realized us kids were starting to outnumber the bedrooms, they built this space up here. I think we've all taken turns up here at some point or another," said Ryan. "It's also served as a good space for guests over the years."

Emily just nodded. She suddenly felt a little homesick for her Boston apartment. Ryan kept babbling to fill the empty space her silence left.

"When I came back to town, this just seemed like the obvious choice for me."

Emily snorted. She just assumed he meant when he came back from college. "So you still live at home?" she chuckled.

Ryan looked embarrassed and then indignant.

"Technically I live in my own apartment… which just so happens to be located in my parents driveway. I might have chosen a different location, but my dad had a heart attack not long ago. I think it makes my mother feel better knowing I'm close. Neither one of them would ever ask for help around the house with the things he used to do but can't anymore. This way, they don't have to ask."

Immediately, Emily felt badly for her snarky remark. She reminded herself to try and keep her judgmental assessments to herself, at least until she got back to Boston.

Emily peered around the corner into the bedroom. She found the bed neatly made, and a spotless wooden bureau gleamed in the light that poured through a small window above the bed. It even smelled clean, she noted.

"Jesus," she whispered in awe.

"What?" Ryan asked defensively.

"I've never seen a guy's apartment look this neat and clean before… not a straight guy anyway."

Considering her own words, Emily looked at Ryan with an arched eyebrow. Before he could respond, Emily provided another explanation.

"Let me guess, your mom comes up here every couple days to do damage control and make sure you haven't let any rats in? Does she make your bed for you too?"

Ryan feigned hurt pride as he clutched his heart.

"No. I do all my own housekeeping, thank you very much! I just like things neat and uncluttered."

Emily couldn't help but smirk.

"So you like men as much as me?" she concluded.

"What?! No!" Ryan exclaimed.

He shook his head venomously and put his hands up as if to ward off her assumption about him.

"I'm as straight as they come! Like totally straight, thank you very much!" Ryan declared.

Emily laughed at his reaction. Ryan stopped breathing for a moment. The sound of her laughter was like sunlight on water. It caught him completely off guard. All he had heard from her since they met were snorts and sarcastic chuckles. He watched bemused as she wandered over to the entertainment center.

"The remote is around here somewhere," Ryan said as he scanned the apartment for it.

"It's not a big deal," said Emily. "I don't really do TV. It's nothing but reality show crap anyway."

Ryan watched Emily's attention turn to a small bookcase on the back wall.

"Feel free to borrow any of those books. I actually just got the new Stephen King…"

Before Ryan could finish, Emily interrupted, "Why would you think I like Stephen King? What, just because I look the way I do, you think I'm into dark horror shit?"

Ryan was tempted to retort with 'Um, no, I just thought you'd like Stephen King because he's a fucking great writer!' But he didn't. He held his tongue and moved on with the tour.

"The bathroom is over there. There are towels on the shelf in the closet."

He could see Emily wasn't listening to him. Instead, she was eyeing his collection of CDs that lined the bottom shelves of the entertainment unit.

"Feel free to listen to anything you find in there," Ryan offered.

Emily scoffed at him and gave a distasteful glance at the music collection without even looking closely at them.

"Ha! That's ok. I think I've had my fill of country bumpkin twang on the bus ride up, thanks."

Ryan opened his mouth to combat her comment but figured it wasn't worth it. She had already made up her mind about him. Clearly, she thought she knew everything about him, and quite frankly, he didn't see any reason to set her straight. He had never met anyone so judgmental and as critical. He decided to leave her alone with her opinions. He gave her a tight smile and turned to leave.

"Oh, in case you were wondering, those are clean sheets on the bed. I just changed them this morning."

His comment made Emily crack another smile, and she shot another suspicious look in his direction. Before she could rattle off another zinger, Ryan interjected and pointed his finger at her.

"Totally straight!" he declared again for the record.

Before she could insult his manhood again, Ryan closed the door behind him. Once the door was closed, the feeling of solitude was immediate. Emily hadn't been alone since she left Boston early that morning. Now that she was, reality came crashing down on her shoulders.

What had she done? She was hundreds of miles away from everything she knew, and she had left without so much as a word to Eric. Now she was in a town where she knew nothing and no one. She tried to shake off the anxiety that threatened to settle in around her.

Needing a distraction, she wandered closer to Ryan's music collection. She could always cheer herself up by poking jokes at the artists in his collection. She tried to guess what she might find there, running down a list in her head. There'd likely be some Brad Paisley, some Tim McGraw, and definitely some Lady Antebellum. There'd probably be some old school country icons his parents got him hooked on in there like good ole Willie Nelson or maybe some Dolly Parton.

At first glance, she shook her head in disbelief. She found many of the same artists she listened to in the collection. She even found some obscure artists that she had a hard time believing Ryan even knew existed. In fact, the only country she found was Johnny Cash, which, quite frankly, was an all-American staple in her book.

With her interest piqued, she studied the collection a little further. She was sure she could find something in there she could tease Ryan about later. When she saw the artist, her eyes lit up — The Backstreet Boys. Ah ha! Everyone had their own guilty pleasures hidden somewhere in their music collection, Emily thought.

Outside, Riley greeted Ryan again and eagerly dropped a ball at his feet. Ryan reached down and scratched Riley's ears.

"She doesn't *do* TV," Ryan informed the dog.

Riley just cocked his head and moved his eyes from Ryan's face to the ball.

"I bet she thinks she's too cool for this place, huh?" he asked Riley. "And who the heck doesn't like Stephen King?"

Riley just whined and nudged the ball closer to Ryan's feet.

Reluctantly, Ryan picked up the ball and tossed it into the yard for him. A moment later, Riley returned wagging his tail and challenged Ryan to pull the ball from his mouth. Ryan laughed and began to playfully chase the dog for the ball.

Emily sat on the love seat inside the apartment and watched Ryan and Riley play in the yard. This place was too damn Norman Rockwell to take, she thought and pulled out her phone. She wondered if reception here was on the "hit" side of "hit or miss".

She saw Eric had called and left a message. Her phone indicated she had two bars. That was probably enough to play the message, but she wasn't sure she wanted to hear it. Instead, she just stared at the name on the screen and imagined what he might have said in the message. He probably figured out she was gone and wanted to confront her about it. Would he be angry or saddened that she had finally left?

She shook her head no. She was likely giving him too much credit. He was probably just calling to ask her to bring home some pizza for him and the band. She hit play.

"Well, well, well, Em, not only did you pack your shit and leave, but I just heard you fucking quit the Red Garter too. Guess you finally met some rich old sugar daddy and ran off with him, huh? Whatever, you'll be back when you need a fix. Won't be long, I'm guessing. Later."

Emily threw the phone down on the cushion next to her. He was such an arrogant little prick, she thought. His message only confirmed she had done the right thing. It also showed her how little he thought of her and how greatly he underestimated her.

7

From The Balcony

"With so many seats to choose from, you sit where you always do
...'til you won't someday.
No more crying from the balcony. Go find your front row seat.
Don't be a stranger to the symphony. Feel your real heartbeat."

At the general store, Ryan helped his mother lock up. Gus and
Max had long since left, and Harold snored heavily on the bench.
Ryan approached him and gave his shoulder a gentle shake.

"Hey, Dad, time to go home."

Harold choked back a snore and swatted Ryan's hand away.

"Home? Can't go home until you get some work done around
here," Harold muttered in his sleep. "You didn't do a damn thing
today and now you want to go home?"

"Oh Harold, leave the boy alone," Joan said. "He's doing a fine
job running the store. Heck, word around town is he runs it better
than you did."

Harold's eyes flew open at her words, and he jolted up in his seat.
Ryan shot his mother a warning look that clearly stated she shouldn't
have said that.

"What? What! Word around town my ass!! When I ran this
place..."

Ryan mouthed the well-rehearsed line along with his father.

"... eight days a week, twenty-five hours a day!"

Ryan and his mother smiled at each other.

"Yeah, yeah, Dad, you were a regular Doctor Who redefining the time space continuum," Ryan said and extended a hand to help his father off the bench.

Harold looked at Ryan's outstretched hand with contempt, but despite wanting to get off the bench himself, he took his son's hand. His body just wasn't what it used to be before the heart attack. His knees had been bothering him for years, but after the heart attack, he didn't have enough strength left to push through the pain like he did before. Now, just getting off the bench left him winded. The doctors said it would take several months for him to get back to what he was before, but Harold was starting to have his doubts that he'd ever be the same again.

Regardless of the hard time he gave his son, Harold was grateful that Ryan took over his duties. It pained him to admit it, but he really needed the boy. He shook his head sadly as he remembered picking Ryan up out of the dirt when he had fallen off his first bike. He brushed off Ryan's hands and knees and inspected each one carefully. It seemed now the roles were reversed.

Ryan put a hand on his father's shoulder to steady him while the old man found his balance. When he gathered himself, Harold shook off Ryan's hand.

"I got it," he said gruffly.

***

As the Corbins drove up their driveway, Harold looked up at the light shining through the upstairs apartment window. He was about to lecture Ryan on the cost of electricity, but then he remembered Joan explaining to him Emily would be using the apartment while she was in town.

"I still can't believe you're letting that freak girl stay here," said Harold as he eyed the apartment suspiciously.

"And what exactly makes her a freak?" Joan asked.

Harold turned to her incredulously.

"How about the fact that she has more holes in her ears than Swiss cheese, for starters?"

"Oh hush! She's a very sweet girl!" Joan scolded.

"If she's so sweet, why isn't her mother offering her a place to stay?" Harold asked skeptically.

"Harold Corbin! It's not our place to judge other people's situations. The girl needed a place to stay, and I offered it. End of discussion," Joan stated firmly.

Harold craned his head to look out the window up at the gathering night sky. He nudged his son and exclaimed, "Look out Ryan! By the looks of the sky, I'd say she's probably already turned into a bat for the night. Better sleep with our windows closed tonight. She might be coming for us!"

Ryan couldn't help but chuckle. His old man might not be as physically healthy as he used to be, but his wit was sharper than ever.

"Enough! *Both* of you!" Joan scolded again.

Ryan stopped laughing and attempted to regain his composure. Harold, however, bared his top teeth and flapped his wrists to mimic bat wings.

In the dim light of the cab, Joan missed this silent mockery. If she had seen her husband, Harold would have earned a long heated lecture about making fun of people and setting a poor example for their son.

***

In the garage apartment, Emily unzipped her backpack and pulled out her photo album. It wasn't quite where she wanted it to be yet, but she was hoping to use it as her portfolio one day. This would have come in handy the other day at that photography store in

Boston. She set the photo album on the table and then pulled out two pads of paper. One was her sketch pad, and the other, the more tattered one, was her journal of sorts. She mainly used it to write her personal thoughts, but she also used it to jot down some of her favorite song quotes. She always wrote in it when she was sad or upset, and somehow, getting her emotions out on pages made her feel better. She swore she worked out more with pen and paper than most people did in years of therapy.

She filled three pages since listening to her message from Eric. She wanted to call him back and tell him there wasn't a sugar daddy and that no man was better than what he could offer her. She didn't though. Instead, she picked up her journal and began to write.

She wrote about the events that led up to her abrupt departure from Boston, the figurative and literal struggle it took to get to Pine Ridge and the disappointment of her mother's reaction to her arrival. She wrote about the general store and the kind people she met there and how their kindness both confused and frightened her. She wrote about how she was trying to change the way she shut down when things got difficult and how she needed to stop keeping people at arm's length, especially people who were actually trying to help her.

Emily's face beamed when she wrote about seeing her baby sister in person after nearly seven years. She loved that they were able to have a real face to face conversation rather than text to text. Sadly though, the glow fell from her face when she thought about Lily's condition. Emily learned a long time ago that most things in life weren't fair but thinking of her baby sister lying in the hospital made her heart sink.

Emily also wrote about the pull she felt inside herself to alter the direction of her life and the uncertainty she felt surrounding it. She'd been sitting watching life pass from the sidelines for too long now. She knew it was time to start being an active player in her life. She put the journal down with a sense of satisfaction. She decided she needed to wash off the day and start fresh tomorrow.

In the bathroom, she turned on the hot water and let the steam fill the small room. She stood in front of the full-length mirror and began to strip off her clothes. Removing the conservative clothes she picked out that morning to impress her mother was a relief. She felt foolish now looking at her wardrobe choice laying in a heap on the floor. She actually thought a good outfit would be enough for her mother to look at her differently. She kicked the clothes into the corner with a feeling of satisfaction.

***

After a long visit with his uncle Frank, Danny trudged up the driveway. Although he had a strange way of showing it, Uncle Frank liked when Danny would visit. Frank, like Danny, didn't want to talk much. They made good company for each other.

Danny saw the light on over the garage and quickened his pace. He wanted to see Ryan. Maybe he could sneak up on him again, and maybe this time Ryan would pee his pants for real.

As he climbed the apartment stairs, he chanted a little song in his head. "Gonna make Ryan pee his pants, pee his pants. Gonna make Ryan pee, pee, pee his pants!"

***

Inside the Corbin's farmhouse, Joan, Harold, and Ryan were gathered around the dinner table. Joan glanced nervously at the clock. It was the third time she looked at it in the last five minutes. Knowing what was troubling her, Harold tried to comfort his wife.

"Eh, quit worrying, Joan. I'm sure Danny is fine."

"He's always home for dinner," Joan said quietly.

She continued to stare at her plate but couldn't take a bite. Danny might be a full grown adult, but he was still very much a little boy and she would always worry about him.

"He just went for a walk in the woods to bring Uncle Frank some supplies, Ma," said Ryan. "It's not like he went to a rave or something."

Joan stood up and threw down her napkin.

"What if he got hurt... or lost!" she cried in an exasperated tone.

"He's not hurt, Ma. And Danny has been walking those woods for years. He knows those trails better than anyone," Ryan reassured her.

Joan grabbed Danny's plate off the table and took it to the kitchen. Harold and Ryan exchanged a hopeless deer in headlights look. A moment later, Joan returned with a glass of wine in her hand.

"Speaking of Frank, isn't it about time you paid him a visit yourself, Harold?" Joan asked.

Harold nodded. He knew his wife was right. Still, she pressed on because she was upset and sensed Harold's reluctance.

"We can't keep relying on Danny to bring supplies out to him and check on him," she added.

Joan took a large gulp of her wine and looked at the clock again.

"Really Joan, you need to stop worrying. Danny is a thirty-three year old adult for crying out loud," Harold stated.

"Don't tell me not to worry! It's my job to worry about him!"

***

Emily shut off the water and wrung out her hair. She pulled the shower curtain open and stepped out. When she turned around, she was face to face with a man wearing a Goonies Never Say Die t-shirt. Her heart leapt into her throat, and she released a made-for-Hollywood blood-curdling scream.

Danny, who had been expecting Ryan to step out of the shower, was equally surprised and also started screaming. Who was this stranger in Ryan's apartment? And why was she screaming? And why did she have metal stuck all over her body? And why, for the love of God, did she have metal stuck in her private parts??!!

He shut his eyes and covered his ears, but it was too late. He had already seen things he could never unsee. Still, he tried, maybe if he closed his eyes tight enough or screamed loud enough, he could block it all out.

***

Inside the Corbin farmhouse, the dual screaming from the apartment put an abrupt halt to the conversation at the dinner table. Harold immediately calculated what must have happened and calmly continued to chew his pork chops.

"I think Danny is home," he remarked casually.

Joan and Ryan jumped up out of their seats, and with one exchanged look, simultaneously bolted for the door. Harold just sighed and took a gulp of milk.

"I knew that girl would be trouble," he mumbled.

Within seconds, Ryan and Joan were standing in the garage apartment. They found Emily standing in the bathroom wrapped in a towel. Danny stood dumbstruck in front of her with his mouth wide open.

"What is going on here?" Joan asked anxiously.

"I'll tell you what's going on here," Emily fumed. "This perv walked in on me while I was in the shower!"

Danny cast his big brown eyes to the tiled bathroom floor. His thick, full lips were wet and trembling. His shoulders were pulled up tensely around his neck like a turtle trying to retreat from its predator.

"Oh honey, this is our son Danny," Joan explained.

"So?" Emily retorted hotly. "Does he creep on all your guests or is this just something special for my benefit?"

A low whining sound came from Danny's throat as he began to rock back and forth on his heels. Joan shot Emily a pleading look and quickly put an arm around his shoulders. She bent her head down low and said something softly into his ear.

"Danny hangs out with me at night a lot," Ryan attempted to explain. "He must have thought it was me in there. He likes to sneak up on me and scare me sometimes when I get out of the shower. He likes to scare me anytime actually. Don't you, Danny?"

Danny shot his brother a quick nervous glance and then bolted his eyes back to the floor. Ryan laughed and gave his older brother a playful nudge with his elbow.

"Don't you?"

Danny nodded and managed a small sheepish smile.

Emily didn't understand how anyone could be making jokes right now. If something like this happened back in Boston, the guy would be taken away in cuffs. That is, if somebody didn't take matters into their own hands first.

"Danny, this is Emily. She's going to be staying here for a while, okay?" Joan explained gently.

Danny looked at Emily for a split second and then shot his eyes back down to the floor. He nodded, but continued to rock back and forth then began nervously humming an 80's song. Danny resorted to this when he was feeling uncomfortable or nervous. Tonight's hum was "Down Under" by Men at Work.

"That means Ryan is going to stay in the house with you, okay?" Joan continued.

At this, Danny stopped rocking and looked up at Ryan hopefully. Ryan nodded, indicating that it was true.

"There now, how about an apology, Danny?" Joan asked. "I think you nearly scared poor Emily to death."

Danny shook his head no and started to rock back and forth

again.

"Ok, maybe later," Joan said. "Come on inside. I cooked pork chops for dinner. Are you hungry?"

Danny nodded and rubbed his stomach eagerly. With her arm still around Danny's shoulder, she gently guided him toward the door. She cast an apologetic look over her shoulder at Emily and mouthed the words, *I'm sorry* to her.

It was now clear to Emily that Danny must have some sort of disability. Still, her heart was racing and she was more than a little unnerved. As she watched Joan and Danny leave, she was acutely aware that Ryan was staring at her. She felt the heat of his gaze, and for a moment, she felt like she was on stage again.

Ryan's eyes traveled over Emily's toned arms and chest. He watched beads of water trail down her neck and disappear into the front of her towel. He let his imagination linger there for a moment but was distracted by the sound of Emily loudly clearing her throat.

"You can leave now too," she said sternly.

Ryan knew he had been caught looking a little too long and a little too intently at her. His cheeks flushed with embarrassment.

"Oh, right, sorry," he said.

He turned abruptly to leave, and a moment later, Emily heard the apartment door shut.

She quickly walked over and latched the lock tightly in place. She leaned up against the door and let out a deep sigh.

"Oh my God," she said to herself and rolled her eyes.

What had she gotten herself into? What kind of family was this? Maybe tomorrow she would go into town and look at some other accommodation options. Surely, there had to be some place a little less weird where she could stay; a bed & breakfast, or an empty boxcar or something.

She was sure Joan would understand. For now, though, she was ready to put it behind her and just relax. It had been a long day and all she really wanted was to curl up and relax.

From her bag she found a pair of soft gray yoga pants and an old tattered Cure t-shirt. Robert Smith's face peeked out at her from beneath an array of surreal flowers. Red letters above the scene read: *Disintegration*, and Emily thought it seemed ironically appropriate. She pulled them on and headed for the couch.

No sooner did she sit down, there was a soft knock at the door. Emily let out an exasperated sigh and got back up off the couch.

"For fuck's sake!" she said to the empty apartment.

She looked cautiously through the peep hole and saw Ryan standing there nervously on the stoop.

"You've got to be shitting me," Emily whispered to herself.

She pulled the door open and Ryan stood there shuffling with his hands in his pockets.

"Sorry to bother you again, but my mom wanted to know if you would like to join us for dinner," Ryan explained.

He did a quick appraisal of her attire, being sure not to cross the line this time. He noted with amusement the yoga pants that she blatantly told him earlier she would never be caught dead in. He thought about calling her out on it but decided she deserved a break.

"Tell her thank you for the offer, but I'm not hungry," Emily replied, vaguely feeling the pull of her stomach at the mention of food.

"Ok then, I'll see you tomorrow," Ryan said and turned to leave.

As Emily started to shut the door, she saw Ryan turn back around.

"Hey Emily, I really am sorry about the whole shower thing. My brother Danny really didn't mean any harm. He acts a little different because he has autism, but he really is a good guy. And he really did think that is was me in the shower. He doesn't mean any harm to anyone. Ever."

Emily felt her features soften at bit. She didn't say anything, but she nodded and managed a small smile. That was enough for Ryan to know that she understood and all would be forgiven.

"Well, if you change your mind about dinner, come on over," Ryan said.

Emily wanted to say thank you, but once again, the kindness extended to her by complete strangers left her speechless. Instead, she just nodded and closed the door. She was careful to latch the lock securely before returning to the couch.

Her stomach grumbled and complained to her loudly. She wondered why she didn't accept the invitation. Why didn't she just say - *Sure, I'd love to. I'm starving!* She knew the answer was that she simply found it easier to say the things she shouldn't say, and difficult to say the things she should. She was, in fact, quite hungry. She thought back to the granola bar she grabbed at the bus depot and realized it was the only thing she had eaten all day.

She thought again about the last thing Ryan said to her. She knew it wasn't too late to get up off the couch and take Joan up on her offer. Still, she couldn't. It didn't feel right. Her own mother couldn't even pretend to be happy to see her again so how could she take advantage of the compassion offered to her by someone else's mother? Besides, if she gave them the chance, they'd surely arrive at the same conclusion her mother had and label her a bad seed. It was safer to lay low, she thought, and plugged her ear buds in to drown out the noise in her head.

Ryan smiled as he walked back to the house. The Cure's Disintegration t-shirt she had been wearing came as a pleasant surprise. That was one of his favorite albums. He couldn't help but think maybe Emily wasn't as alien as he first thought. He tucked the information away just in case he found himself getting held off by her at arm's length in close quarters again.

The yoga pants, though, that was the funniest part. She was so quick to denounce the woman wearing those same pants earlier today. Now, there she was, wearing them herself when she thought nobody would be looking.

"I don't do yoga pants," Ryan said to himself in his most catty Emily voice.

Inside, Ryan joined the rest of his family at the dinner table. He was glad to see Danny had settled back into a more comfortable mood. He now swayed happily back and forth in front of his plate singing a song to himself.

"What's that you're singing, Danny?" Ryan asked. "You got a new song?"

Danny nodded happily.

"What is it?" Ryan asked. "Can you sing it for us?"

Without looking up from his plate, Danny started singing his song loud enough for everyone at the dinner table to hear.

"Emily got shot with a BB gun, do da, do da…"

"What the hell are you singing about?" Harold asked confused.

"I think he's talking about Emily's piercings," Ryan chuckled.

"Someone shot Emily in the nose with a BB gun, do da…" Danny confirmed.

Joan smiled sweetly at her son while Harold shook his head.

"Are you singing a song about Emily's pierced nose, Danny?" Ryan asked.

Danny nodded his head and shifted his eyes from side to side.

"And her privates," Danny added.

Cold milk shot out of Ryan's mouth and sprayed across his plate. He quickly grabbed a napkin and started coughing into it.

Joan looked up with alarm.

"Did he just say what I think he said?" she asked.

"Emily got shot in the private parts, do da, do da…" Danny sang happily.

Joan went white. Harold's thick, white eyebrows knitted together in confusion.

"What the hell are you talking about, Danny?" Harold demanded.

Danny grew quiet and fixed his eyes steadily on his plate.

Ryan recovered himself long enough to offer an explanation to his father.

"I think he means she had *it* pierced, Dad."

"It? What the hell is *it?*"

Ryan gave his father a telling look. Harold's eyes bulged from their sockets, and his eyebrows were lost momentarily under his white hair line.

"Her who-ha?? Is that what he said??!! She had her who-ha pierced?" Harold asked in disbelief.

Joan clutched the edge of the table to stop herself from fainting.

"Oh dear Lord," she whispered as she searched for inner strength.

"I told you she was a freak!" Harold declared.

"Settle down everyone. It's not that big of a deal. Lots of girls are doing it now. You could say it's a bit of a trend nowadays," Ryan explained.

Joan reached for her glass of wine and took a large gulp.

"You mean there are others?" Harold practically shouted. "She's in a God-damn who-ha piercing cult for Christ sake!"

Realizing anything more he said would only make matters worse, Ryan looked to his mother for help. Joan, however, was lost under a tilted wine glass.

Danny looked at Ryan and smiled happily through a mouthful of mashed potatoes. They all finished their meal in silence.

8
Avalanche

"We are the ones who are never afraid
We need no rehearsal to dance.
We're well aware this may be our last chance
So bring on the avalanche"

The next morning, Emily awoke to the sunlight hitting her face. Living in an apartment in the city, surrounded by other apartment buildings, Emily never saw sunlight in her window. So despite being an early hour, she welcomed the warm beam of light awakening her.

As she got out of bed and stretched her legs, she realized she hadn't slept that well in a long time. There had been no loud band music coursing through the night or wild obnoxious drunken laughter from the next room to interrupt her sleep.

She wondered again about Eric and hoped some part of him might miss her by now. Movement from out the window interrupted her thoughts. She looked just in time to see Danny disappearing into the woods.

"Where the hell is he going?" Emily wondered out loud.

***

Harold, Max, and Gus sat on their bench on the general store's porch. This morning they were engaged in a lively conversation about the highlights of old age.

"The last time I felt truly happy was when Margery brought home hemorrhoid ointment for me," said Gus.

Harold and Max nodded thoughtfully.

"The last time I felt happy was when I told my AARP representative to go to hell," said Harold.

Just then, Emily came strolling around the corner.

"Speaking of hell…" said Max, and nodded in Emily's direction.

She was dressed in tight black jeans and black Doc Martins. Her fitted black turtle neck was tucked sharply into her waist line and secured there by a studded metal belt. Several long silver necklaces bounced buoyantly on her chest as she approached, gleaming like stars against a night sky.

"Isn't she just a little ray of pitch black," remarked Gus.

Feeling their eyes on her as she climbed the porch steps, Emily shot a challenging look in their direction. None of them said anything to her, but instead, regarded her with large curious eyes.

When Emily entered the store, Joan was tying an apron around her slender waist. Even in her senior years, it was still evident she must have been quite beautiful when she was Emily's age.

"Good morning dear," Joan greeted her. "Did you sleep ok?"

Emily nodded and scanned the store for something quick she could grab to eat. The smell of coffee mingled with baked goods was promising.

"I'm sorry again about Danny," Joan started. "I'm not sure if Ryan told you, but Danny has autism. His isn't as severe as some others on the spectrum, but routines are crucial for him. I should have known he would have seen the light on in the apartment and gone up to get Ryan for supper like he always does. Anything out of his routine is extremely upsetting, and I should have prepared him for that. He's thirty-three, but in many ways he's still a child. He will never be able to live on his own and relies greatly on us to keep his day to day life as predictable as possible. Like I said, I'm sorry. I should have…"

Emily put her hand on Joan's shoulder and stopped her.

"It's ok, Mrs. Corbin," said Emily. "You don't have to keep apologizing."

When Joan looked back at her, Emily could see the gratitude swelling in her eyes. She swept a lock of her hair off her forehead and breathed a sigh of relief.

"Thank you," Joan said.

Emily fidgeted nervously with one of her eyebrow piercings as she surveyed the store. She could feel Joan's eyes move from her face piercings down to the area below her belt. When she turned to ask Joan where the coffee was, she found her still staring curiously at that area. Joan recovered quickly when she realized Emily had caught her staring.

"Would you like a new muffin?" Joan asked.

She flushed profusely and searched the ceiling for the right words.

"I mean a fresh muffin? That is, we have fresh baked muffins if you're hungry."

Emily wondered if Joan may have forgotten to take her old people vitamins or something.

"Yeah, that sounds great, Mrs. Corbin."

Joan pointed to an area around the corner, and she was about to say something else but was distracted by Ryan bouncing through the door. Emily was so relieved to have someone else in the store to break up the awkward moment that she almost smiled.

"Hey, what time does that blue bus come back around?" Emily asked him.

"Good morning to you too," said Ryan.

"I said hey," Emily replied defensively.

"It could be twenty minutes. It could be three hours. There's really no set schedule," Ryan said with a shrug.

"Of course there isn't," said Emily. "I mean why would a bus have a schedule? That's just plain crazy, right?"

Suddenly, Ryan felt badly for Emily. Pine Ridge was nothing like Boston. She must feel a bit like Alice in Wonderland in this town. He decided he couldn't just let her fend for herself.

"I can probably give you a ride again, if you want?"

Joan pretended to be busy sweeping but smiled coyly at Ryan's offer.

"Don't you have work to do around here? I don't want to get you in trouble with your old man again," said Emily.

"Nah, we just got through the morning rush. They should be ok for a while. Hey Ma, do you mind if I give Emily a ride to see her sister again today?"

Joan looked up from her sweeping and pretended not to have been listening with interest.

"What?" Joan asked.

She looked at Emily as though she had forgotten she was there.

"Oh no, not at all. You kids run along,"

Ryan flushed at his mother's remark. He swore sometimes she thought he was still six.

The bells on the door chimed, drawing their attention to the front of the store. Susan appeared carrying an oversized purse and wearing dark sunglasses. Her blonde hair was pulled back into a tight bun. When she saw Emily talking with Ryan and Joan, she pulled her glasses down and looked at Emily as if she didn't quite believe what she was seeing.

"You're still here?" she asked incredulously.

The chill in the air could have put frost on the windows.

"Yeah, I'm not going anywhere until Lily gets better," Emily answered.

Susan just stared at her for a long moment. She always hoped Emily would come back one day but not in the middle of a crisis. How could she be so selfish? Then again, her daughter always had a knack for making a bad situation worse. Didn't she understand that her presence could be putting Lily's health in jeopardy?

"Do you really think your presence here is the best thing for Lily?" Susan said shortly.

"Yeah, I do," Emily answered defiantly.

"Well, I guess once again we fail to see eye to eye on what could be a matter of life or death," Susan answered.

Emily's breath caught in her throat and she began to tremble. Her mother's words had hit below the belt. How dare she bring that up now?

Susan absently picked up a stuffed puppy from a nearby table and examined it thoughtfully.

"I'll take this little guy," Susan said to Joan.

"Sure. I'll be right there," Joan answered.

"Lily needs something other than that hideous frog she drags around with her everywhere. That thing should have been taken away by a hazmat team the minute she brought it into the hospital."

Emily felt her face turn red and her jaw lock. She clenched her fists behind her back and glared at her mother. Oblivious to her daughter's rage, Susan turned and headed for the register.

Desperate to get out of the line of fire, Ryan turned to Emily.

"I'll meet you out front, ok?" Ryan said gently.

Emily nodded and trailed over to the coffee kiosk. She watched her mother pay for the stuffed animal and leave.

Outside, Harold, Max, and Gus were discussing Emily's more recently discovered peculiarities.

"She was shot *where* with a BB gun?" Gus asked.

"No dummy, there was no BB gun," Harold said. "She had *it* pierced."

"It? What the hell is it?" Gus barked.

Harold whistled and looked down at his crotch. Then he gave Max and Gus a pointed tell-all-look.

They both dropped their eyes to Harold's crotch and their mouths fell open simultaneously. Max was the first to collect himself.

"Her who-ha? What kind of freak pierces that? Boy, oh boy, that musta hurt somethin' fierce," Max remarked, and shifted uncomfortably in his pants.

Gus, who was having a more difficult time getting his head around this foreign idea, just nodded silently then instinctively put a protective hand over his own crotch.

"Oh settle down you two," said Harold. "It's not a big deal. It's like a new trend. Lots of young ladies are doing it now."

Feeling superior for educating his friends on the lifestyles of the young and hip, Harold sat up a little straighter on the bench. He pulled at his red suspenders and slapped them proudly across his crisp white shirt.

A hush fell over the men when Emily stepped out onto the porch. She regarded the old men warily as she watched their eyes move from her pierced nose, down to her lady bits, and back to her face. They all looked a little afraid, except Harold, who looked quite proud of himself.

She rolled her eyes and eagerly headed for the shelter of the small pavilion across the street. What the hell was wrong with everyone today, she wondered.

"She seems to have recovered nicely," Max said as he watched Emily bounce across the parking lot.

As Ryan's green pick up pulled up to the curb, Emily noticed Danny was sitting in the cab. Great, just when I thought a ride with Ryan couldn't get any more awkward, Emily thought.

Her mind flashed back to the previous night. It's not like she wasn't used to guys seeing her naked before, but the reactions were usually big smiles or hoots and hollers — not loud ear-popping screams. Seeing as she was fully dressed today, she assumed that Danny's reaction would be less... loud. She assumed wrong.

As Ryan's truck idled, Emily yanked on the door handle and started to climb in. Instead of Danny sliding over to the middle, he quickly rocked back and forth and started to chant.

"Danny's seat, Danny's seat!" he repeated.

Emily immediately stopped her ascent and shot Ryan a helpless, yet irritated look.

"Oh, sorry," began Ryan, "I forgot to tell you, Danny likes the window seat."

"Of course he does," she mumbled as she stepped back to allow Danny to switch places with her.

Once the seating arrangement was settled and the truck was rumbling up the road, Danny's smile returned as he happily gazed out the window. Emily watched as he rocked, hummed, and grinned. She noticed his neatly tucked in t-shirt which read, 'I HEART THE 80's'. It was impossible for Emily to be mad or irritated with this guy, despite him seeing *all of her.*

"Sorry again for Danny freaking you out yesterday. He really is harmless though," Ryan offered.

Danny acted as if he didn't hear Ryan and continued to roll his head from side to side.

"Everyone can stop apologizing really," Emily said. "It's getting annoying. Let's just forget it, ok?"

Ryan ignored her comment.

"He's pretty quiet until he gets to know you," said Ryan.

He looked at Danny, knowing he was listening to what was being said.

"Hey Danny, maybe you could try apologizing to Emily now, huh buddy?" Ryan coaxed.

Danny stopped rolling his head for a minute to give Ryan a pointed look. He wasn't going to apologize. If anyone should be apologizing here, it should be Emily apologizing to him. She was the one that tricked him by moving into Ryan's apartment before anyone could tell him, Danny thought. A moment later he went back into his own little zone and was smiling and singing.

"Emily was shot with a BB gun, do da, do da..."

Emily whipped her head around and stared at Danny. She looked to Ryan.

"What did he just say?" she asked incredulously.

"Nothing!" Ryan said quickly.

He assumed Danny would have forgotten that song by now, but apparently he was still on it.

"Nothing, just Danny being Danny," Ryan assured her.

Nothing? Shooting me with a BB gun is far from nothing, Emily thought. She had heard Mainers were obsessed with guns, but she didn't believe it until now. Emily rolled her eyes and looked out the window.

For the next ten minutes they listened to Danny chanting.

"Danny just being Danny. Danny just being Danny..."

Emily began to think the senior bus was looking more and more appealing. Then she remembered the smell and reconsidered.

Eager to push the unpleasant memory of the senior bus out of her mind, Emily let her thoughts travel to better places. She thought of another bus that her sister had taken.

Emily had just entered high school and was taking on more and more of the parental duties her mother could no longer perform. She was waiting for Lily to get off the bus so she could take her home. Some of Emily's friends had seen her and stopped to chat. Emily tried to push the conversation along quickly because she didn't want to be seen getting her little sister off the bus. Her friends had been excited about the band playing that night at the Speak Easy and had no intention of moving along without Emily.

So, when Lily climbed off the bus, Emily pretended not to know her. Being seen with a dorky fifth grader would be bad for her image, especially if any of her friends tied together they were sisters.

Having two different fathers, the girls didn't look anything alike. Emily was tall and curvy. She had thick lashes that lined her big deep green eyes. Her dark hair was long and full, and her flawless skin had a tinge of natural bronze.

Lily had the complete opposite characteristics as her sister. She was petite and frail looking. Her short, thin blonde hair hung limply around her shoulders. The color of her eyes were a cool shade of blue that hovered on the edge of gray. She had pale Irish skin with high cheek bones that were spackled with freckles.

It would be easy to hide the fact they were sisters, or at least that's what Emily had thought.

No sooner had Lily seen her sister look away from her excited glance, an older boy also getting off the bus, took advantage of Lily's distraction and tripped her. Lily didn't even have a chance to recover herself. She landed hard on the pavement, only able to catch herself at the last minute with one hand. Her other hand that had been carrying her books never lost its grip.

The moment Emily had looked over was when Lily was attempting to pick herself up with her books still clutched in her hand. Their eyes locked for a moment, Lily pleading and apologizing at the same time with her eyes.

Emily remembered thinking she'd be ok. That sort of thing happened to everyone at some point or another. Well, it never happened to her, but it happened to a lot of kids. Lily was tough and could handle herself, so Emily just casually watched her struggle to her feet.

Lily straightened her thin framed glasses and muttered an apology to the boy she had tripped over. Smart girl, now keep moving, Emily had thought. It turned out Lily was more naïve than smart that day. She truly believed she had been at fault for not looking where she was going.

She waited for the chunky boy to politely accept her apology.

"What are you looking at four eyes?" he had barked at her.

Lily caught on quickly then.

"Nothing," she said.

Lily turned quickly to get away from the boy, but she didn't move fast enough. Emily remembered the feeling of her jaw tightening when he grabbed Lily's arm and spun her back around.

"You dropped something," he said.

Poor Lily fell for it. When she looked down at the ground, he brought his fist down hard on top of her books and sent them tumbling out of her grasp.

Before she could bend down to collect them, Emily appeared at her side. She stopped her sister from getting on her knees to retrieve the fallen books.

"Why don't you be a gentleman and pick them up for her?" Emily had asked him coolly.

At the sound of her voice, the kid turned around excited to have another target to torment. When his dark eyes traveled up Emily's lean torso and reached her face, his excitement quickly dampened. She watched with pleasure as his chest deflated. She could see he recognized her.

"Or should I tell all the cheerleaders that you are nothing more than a cowardly punk?"

The boy just gaped at her and stammered.

"I was... I... I..."

"All it would take is for me to tell one of them, just one of them, what a tool you were and you'd be ruined. It would probably be safe to say you wouldn't get a date until you were at least half way through high school, maybe even college if I told the right girl."

Lily spun and stared at her sister in disbelief.

"It's ok, I'll get them," she had said.

"No you won't," Emily had told her firmly. "Jared here is going to get them for you. Aren't you Jared Baldwin?"

"Yes, yes," he had stammered.

A moment later he was handing Lily her books.

Emily put her arm around her sister and guided her to where her friends stood looking on in confusion. From that day forward, nobody picked on her sister.

If only saving her now was as easy, Emily thought, and let out a heavy sigh as she stared out the window.

Ryan heard Emily sigh and sensed her heavy mood. Even Danny glanced at her curiously.

"Hey, Danny, you should take Emily on some of the paths out in the woods sometime," Ryan suggested.

Emily shot Ryan a look that indicated she'd rather do anything else than be alone in the woods with Danny.

"You should give it a chance," Ryan said. "It's really beautiful out there. I bet you'd like it. You could probably get some good pictures there, especially along the river."

"I don't do nature shots," Emily said with distain.

Then again, she really didn't have a lot of opportunity to photograph nature in Boston. Usually she just stuck to candid shots of people. She loved taking photos of the girls dancing on stage. Sometimes it was something simpler that captured her interest, like the look on someone's face as they gazed out the window of the subway. Pets were always fun too. She imagined if she ever made a living as a photographer, she'd cover weddings or maybe find a job at a magazine or newspaper.

Ryan shook his head. He was approaching the conclusion that he was never going to engage Emily in a real conversation. He then remembered her Cure t-shirt and wondered if now would be a good time to play what he hoped was his ace in the hole. There's no time like the present, he decided.

"I noticed your Cure t-shirt last night. Disintegration was hands down their best album. Wouldn't you agree?"

Emily raised a skeptical eyebrow at him. She'd seen his music collection, and although she noticed there was some Cure in there, she doubted he was a *true* fan. He probably only liked the Disintegration album because of the top ten hit "Lovesong". She was also willing to bet he probably only bought their Wish album because of the pop hit "Friday, I'm in Love." While Emily thought those songs were 'just okay,' she preferred more of their darker stuff, especially their earlier albums. She decided to test her theory.

"I liked their older stuff better. Their Pornography album was my favorite," said Emily. "You have heard of that one, haven't you?"

She smiled smugly over at him with her poker face. She knew she was about to prove that she was the superior Cure fan.

Knowing that she was just testing him, Ryan offered his own smug comeback.

"You mean this one?" he said, pulling their Pornography disk out from his CD holder.

And just like that, her smugness was sucked out of the truck. Before Ryan could gloat, and before Emily could come up with a snide remark, their attention was turned to Danny.

A distressed moan sounded from his throat and his head was bobbing violently. Panic had taken over his face as he stared straight ahead out the windshield.

Emily followed Danny's gaze, trying to determine what the upset was all about, but all she saw was a tree lined country road. As they came around a sharp bend in the road, Danny's distressed cries became more urgent. Emily couldn't tell what was upsetting him, but a glance over at Ryan made it clear that he knew. Ryan's head was bent low in concentration, and he had a white knuckle grip on the steering wheel. Danny started flapping his hands at the wrists and shaking his head.

"No, no, no, bad tree, bad tree," he started repeating urgently.

Ryan usually made it a point to take a different route when Danny was in the car, but in his moment of distraction while talking to Emily, he had forgotten.

"Is he ok or what?" Emily asked.

Ryan looked at Danny with concern.

"It's ok buddy, the bad tree is gone. We passed it, ok?"

Danny's cries softened a little. He rocked harder against the seat to soothe himself. Ryan was right, they passed the tree. He knew they were safe now because they passed the tree.

"Yeah, he'll be ok," Ryan said to Emily.

The softer tone of his voice turned Emily's attention to Ryan. For the first time since they met, he looked somber and serious. What's the big deal about a stupid tree, Emily wondered. Mainers sure were a peculiar bunch.

***

Inside the hospital, Emily watched Lily run her pale white fingers self-consciously over her bald head.

"Remember when we used to play beauty parlor? We'd put makeup on and braid each other's hair? I guess we won't be doing that again anytime soon," Lily said, and laughed lightly at her own joke.

Emily nodded. She wasn't at the point where she could make jokes about Lily's condition. She doubted she ever would.

"Yeah, I remember, kiddo. It was one of the few times I actually paid attention to you."

Emily decided to use this moment to attempt to apologize for her past.

"I'm sorry I wasn't a very good big sister to you. I hope you didn't take me ignoring you as personal. It's just that…"

"It was just the age difference, I know. When I was into Barbie dolls, you were into boys."

Emily nodded sadly. That wasn't really it at all. She remembered getting up for school extra early because she'd have to make breakfast and pack a lunch for Lily. She wasn't just responsible for getting herself dressed and out the door, but she had to make sure Lily was also ready and out the door in time to catch the bus.

The truth was, Emily was hard-pressed to remember a time that she felt like a big sister and not a mother to Lily. Little sisters were supposed to be fun, not a chore. Maybe it wasn't too late to change that, Emily thought and smiled at an idea that took hold in her head.

"Trust me, I should have stuck with Barbie dolls," said Emily as she fished through her purse.

"What are you looking for?" Lily asked.

Emily pulled her makeup bag from her purse and grinned excitedly.

"We might not be able to braid each other's hair, but we can still play beauty parlor. You look too pale. Let's fix you up some, ok?"

Lily's eyes lit up and a grin stretched from ear to ear as she sat up eagerly in her bed. Emily moved closer.

"Close your eyes," she said softly.

Lily's eyes closed and Emily began to gently brush some of her dark gray eye shadow over Lily's pale fluttering lids.

"Stop fidgeting," Emily instructed.

"I can't help it! It tickles!" Lily said and started giggling.

Emily moved to her cheeks. She spread rose colored blush up her cheek bones, which the weight loss had left more pronounced than usual.

"Ok, what shade lipstick do you want?" Emily asked.

She held up two shades of lip stick.

"Scarlet or Sin?"

Lily studied the two shades and then moved her eyes to Emily's mouth.

"What shade are you wearing?"

Emily smiled.

"I'm wearing sin," she answered. "I think scarlet would look better on you though."

Even though she really wanted to wear the same shade as her sister, Lily nodded. She always wanted to be just like Emily. Her sister never had any trouble making friends. Lily knew Emily hated to be copied. She didn't understand why when she was younger, but now she was starting to see that Emily had always just wanted Lily to be her own person. Lily agreed to use the shade of scarlet to please her sister and show her she was ready to stand on her own.

As Emily applied the lipstick, Lily searched her face. She hadn't aged much in the seven years she'd been gone, but she looked different somehow. As Lily looked closer, she realized it was Emily's eyes. They looked deeper and wiser, but less bright than she remembered. There was a sadness there that hadn't existed before. Lily wondered what those seven years had been like for her sister. Had she been relieved to be out on her own with just herself to look out for? Or did part of her miss the family she had left behind? She knew very little about the lifestyle her sister led and nothing of how she felt about it.

Emily leaned back and looked pleased. She dabbed Lily's mouth with a tissue and took off the excess makeup until it looked just right.

"How did it come out?" Lily asked eagerly.

Emily reached into her bag and pulled out a mirror. She held it up for Lily to see. As Lily looked at her reflection, Emily read the emotions that flickered across her face. It was obvious her sister hadn't looked in a mirror for a while. As Emily saw the shock and sadness register on her sister's face, she cursed herself for such a stupid idea. However, the smile that followed made it all worthwhile.

Emily laughed as Lily puckered her lips and fluttered her eye lashes back at her reflection. Lily made kissing sounds with her lips and reached out her arms for Emily. Emily leaned in for a hug and let her sister plant a big scarlet kiss on her cheek.

For a moment, it felt like they were twelve and six again and the better part of ten years just disappeared. In that instance, they were sisters once more and Emily held Lily closely.

The embrace proved to be too much for Lily as she started coughing and gasping for breath. Emily let go and allowed Lily to fall back on the pillows of her bed. She reached to the table beside her bed and poured her a glass of water. Lily caught her breath and took the cup of water from her sister. She took one small, slow sip and then handed the cup back to Emily.

Lily's eyes began to water and the eye shadow was now smudged under her lashes. Emily diverted her eyes to the vase of flowers at her bedside.

"Who brought you the flowers?" she asked.

"Dad sent them yesterday," Lily answered in a voice just above a whisper.

Emily nodded.

"How is… Steve?" Emily asked politely.

It still felt strange to call him by his first name. Emily was six when her mother and Steve got married, and she had taken to calling him Dad right away. She was excited to have a father figure for the first time in her life and trying out the name Dad was fresh and exciting. She saw other kids at school with their fathers and knew that she was different because she didn't have one — not one that had ever been present anyway. Her mother got pregnant as a teenager, and when *the father* learned the news, he left town as quickly as possible. When Steve started dating her mother, it filled a void Emily hadn't even been aware was there.

Of course, all that changed eight years later when Steve decided his wife and two daughters weren't enough and started having affairs on the side. That was when he lost the privilege of being called Dad in Emily's eyes. From that point forward, he was just Steve.

"He's good. I saw him a few weeks ago. He's in Germany now on a business trip," Lily offered.

Emily huffed. She hated the term business trip because she always associated it with cheating. Lily saw the look on Emily's face and knew exactly what she was thinking. She politely changed the subject.

"So, how do you like living with the Corbin's? Aren't they wicked nice?" Lily asked.

"Nice?" Emily asked incredulously. "Sure they're nice, if you like freaks! Well Mrs. Corbin is pretty nice, but her husband and his old cronies are always giving me creepy looks. Oh, and last night I was getting out of the shower and their weirdo son was just standing there waiting for me!"

"If you're referring to Danny, Em, he's autistic," Lily corrected her.

Before Lily could set her sister straight further, Emily was already regretting her choice of words. She said that just for effect, but she felt terrible as soon as the word 'weirdo' came out of her mouth. She knew what it felt like to be on the receiving end of that kind of judgment. People often called her a weirdo or a freak just because she looked or acted different. The preconceived notions and condemning looks that were shot Danny's way were the very same ones Emily received daily.

Emily nodded.

"I know. I'm sorry I said that," Emily said. "If anyone's a weirdo, it's me."

"Wait…"

Emily watched as Lily started to piece together what she had said about the shower.

"So Danny saw you…"

"Naked? Um yeah!" Emily answered. "I screamed. He screamed…"

"You all screamed for ice cream?" Lily finished with a smirk.

"Now that I think about it, I should have gotten some damn ice cream! It certainly would have taken the sting out of the situation."

Both of them laughed. Emily didn't think she would be laughing about it so soon, but her sister had a way of taking a bad situation and making it better.

"What about Ryan? He's kinda cute, right?" Lily asked.

"You mean L.L. Bean boy?" Emily asked.

Lily nodded eagerly, anxious to hear if her sister found him as attractive as she did.

"Please! It's like the guy stepped right out of one of their catalogs. And he's always wearing that stupid Red Sox hat. I bet his whole world probably revolves around them winning the Super Bowl."

"The World Series," Lily corrected her.

"Whatever. He's just a little too straight edge for me, you know?"

Lily nodded and closed her eyes. She opened them for a moment but was forced to close them again. She sighed heavily against the exhaustion. She wished she wasn't so tired all the time, especially now. She wanted to spend more time with her sister, but she knew fighting off the fatigue would be a losing battle.

"I should probably get going so you can get some rest, Lily Pad," Emily said softly.

She reached over and rubbed her sister's bald head affectionately. Lily smiled up at her weakly.

"Are you jealous my hair style is finally cooler than yours?" Lily asked.

"Yeah, right," Emily said and then remembered. "Oh wait, I almost forgot. I want to show you something. You probably don't remember this but…"

Emily paused as she pulled out the old photo of her and Lily that she carried with her from Boston. When Lily saw it, her eyes grew wide with excitement.

"Oh my God! I totally remember that! It was taken on Easter when I was like five, right?"

Emily nodded.

"I'm not sure what's more shocking, that I look so sweet or that I am wearing a yellow dress!" Emily noted.

She stuck a finger down her throat to indicate how she felt about the dress her mother had made her wear for the photo that day.

"This was always one of Mom's favorite photos," said Lily. "She used to swear you took this with you just to spite her."

Emily shook her head sadly. She didn't take it to spite anyone. She remembered the exact moment she grabbed it off the mantle. She had packed her bags in a hot temper. Tears of hurt pride and disappointment were streaming down her face as she headed for the door. Even through her blurred vision, the photo had caught her eye and stopped her in her tracks. She stared at the photo and was torn for a moment. She was leaving because her mother made it clear she was no longer welcome, but Lily didn't deserve to be left behind. Emily remembered walking over to the photo and staring at her sister's smiling face.

Emily remembered thinking her mother was punishing Lily just as much as she was punishing Emily. First, Lily had been separated from her father and now her sister was being banished. Emily knew if she stayed, she would be doing Lily a huge injustice. She knew if she didn't leave, Lily, who idolized her, would end up walking in her foot steps and making the same bad choices she had made. The best thing Emily could do for her sister was to obey their mother and leave. Without such a screwed up role model in her life, Lily might just stand a chance. Maybe then, her mother could at least be proud of one of her daughters.

With that thought, Emily grabbed the photo from the mantle. She and Lily couldn't be together, so she had taken a piece of Lily with her. That photo was the only way she knew how to keep Lily close without tainting her.

"Despite that hideous yellow dress, that was my favorite picture too," Emily said. "If taking it pissed Mom off, that was just a bonus."

Lily smiled as she stared at the photo and traced her sister's face with her finger, but her eyes were getting heavy again. She closed them and found they were too heavy to reopen. With a deep sigh, she gave into the darkness that beckoned her. As she drifted off, she felt Emily take the photo from her hands and kiss her lightly on her forehead.

"I promise I'll make a copy of this for you," Emily whispered.

***

Once outside, Emily followed the sounds of Pearl Jam to the cab of the pine green pick-up truck. She watched Ryan and Danny taking turns playing their air guitar solos to each other. Ryan squinted and squished up his face as he rocked the air guitar. Danny bobbed his head lightly in a softened version of head banging.

She tapped on the window and Ryan dropped his "guitar" like it was on fire, but Danny kept on banging his head. She watched Ryan try to break Danny's concentration unsuccessfully. Nobody was going to pull Danny out of his jam session. Finally, Ryan turned off the stereo and Danny stopped. Ryan pointed over Danny's shoulder, and Danny looked to see Emily standing there smiling at them.

Danny smiled back at her. She looked pretty. Different, but pretty.

Emily opened the truck door, and remembering Danny's preference for the window seat, stepped back and allowed him to hop out so she could climb in beside Ryan.

As they pulled out of the hospital parking lot, Ryan pointed to a Styrofoam cup in a cup holder protruding from the dashboard.

"What's that?" Emily asked.

"It's Dunkin Donuts. I remembered they had one in downtown

Grafton Falls, so I stopped and got you one. I didn't know how you liked it, so I got the cream and sugar on the side." He handed her a small brown paper bag that apparently held the coffee amenities.

At first, Emily was confused, but then she remembered her snide comment the other day about the lack of Dunkin Donuts in the area. She didn't even care about Dunkin Donuts. She just made that comment to be a brat and make a point. Now that Ryan had gone out of his way to get her the coffee, she felt badly about her comment.

She recalled what she said to Lily about Ryan being too straight edge for her, and now she also felt badly about that. Why was she always going through such great lengths to distance herself from others? She sighed. Maybe straight edge wasn't so bad, she thought. Eric wouldn't have gone out of his way to say 'bless you' if she sneezed, never mind getting her a Dunkin Donuts' coffee because he thought she missed her familiar coffee shop.

Emily looked from the bag, to the coffee, to Ryan. She then said something she hardly ever had the opportunity to say.

"Thank you," she said softly.

"No problem," Ryan said with a shrug.

Emily took the cup in her hands but continued to stare at Ryan. She couldn't easily shake the unfamiliar feeling of gratitude. Ryan smiled at her uncertainty.

"You know you can drink it too?" he teased.

She sneered at him and took a sip. When she looked over at Danny, she noticed he was clutching some vinyl records in his lap. Was Maine so out of touch with the rest of the world that people still listened to vinyl here, she wondered? Her first instinct was to crack a joke about it and ask Danny if he had ever heard of this terrific invention called the CD, or better yet, the MP3? She smiled at her clever mockery and started to deliver her pun.

"Hey did you ever…"

Emily stopped herself. She was about to use sarcasm and mockery to drive a wedge between herself and others again. She thought maybe it was time for a different approach. She looked again at the vinyl album covers. One was Duran Duran.

"Did you know that Duran Duran was one of Princess Diana's favorite bands?" Emily asked in a kinder voice.

Danny didn't say anything, but he looked down and studied the cover of the album. Emily pressed on.

"I haven't seen a vinyl record in quite some time."

Danny still said nothing but continued to study his records.

"Yeah, my brother is quite the collector," Ryan offered. "They have a cool little store in one of the old mills just up the road. They sell all kinds of vintage stuff there."

"What else did you get, Danny?" Emily asked.

She leaned closer and looked curiously at the albums, but still, Danny remained silent. Just when she was about to give up, he slowly handed her his prize finds of the day.

Emily took them carefully and inspected them. She rattled off the bands as she flipped through them.

"Rolling Stones, Billy Idol, Heart, Bon Jovi. Wow, you really do love the 80s, huh?" she asked as she handed the albums back to Danny.

Danny nodded and smiled. His eyes were fixed on the band members of Heart emerging from a cloud of blue smoke on the cover of the Never/These Dreams album. They were all dressed in black, just like Emily.

9

Kiss You Where You Lay

"All I needed was to know
His kiss was more than just a kill
'Cause conquering me is never easy
And I fear nobody will"

The next few days Emily learned to adapt to the routine of small town life. Her lifestyle in Boston was that of a nocturnal animal, sleeping away the days and prowling the night. In Pine Ridge, she got up early and walked into town. There, she would get coffee and a muffin (a fresh one) at the Corbin's store. On most days, she took a few minutes to talk with Joan before heading out to explore her new surroundings. On other days, she would quietly join in doing chores around the store.

Emily was enchanted at the small residential streets of the town. Here, houses proudly displayed pumpkins or mums on their door steps, and scattered about in their yards were scarecrows and cornstalks beside their entrances. It was evident which houses had children, for they were clearly marked by abandoned bicycles in the yard, or clumsily carved Jack-o-lanterns, or posters of black cats wearing witches hats displayed on the front window panes.

She learned quickly to avoid the few public places in town because the stares she got from people passing by made her feel awkward and uncomfortable. It even made her paranoid enough to wonder if her mother had been warning the townspeople against her. She found herself seeking out the quiet corners of town, away from people and away from any chance of running into her mother again.

She discovered the park was spacious enough to provide a place of solitude. She would pick a bench up on the hill and look down at the children playing in the playground while she let her mind wander. Sometimes she would bring her camera and snap shots of people in the park. This usually lasted less than an hour before one of the children's parents noticed her and started shooting suspicious glances in her direction.

She also found part of the river Ryan had mentioned running along the train tracks. When she found it, she was immediately delighted at its remoteness. She shuffled her feet through the fallen leaves and kicked up the smell of the earth until her senses were overwhelmed.

However, it was the graveyard, with its looming oak trees that she liked best. There, amongst the grave stones, she didn't have to worry about hiding the tears in her eyes. When her sadness got the best of her, she could go there and cry. Most mornings, she could be found propped up against one of the massive trees that lined the pathways, writing in her journal as the fall leaves fluttered to the ground around her.

By late morning, she made her way back to the store knowing that the morning rush would be over. She'd sit on the bench across the street and wait, hoping to see the senior bus come bumping through town so she could go visit Lily.

She rarely ended up taking the bus, however. On most days, Ryan would come out of the store and approach her. He would say he had an errand to run in Grafton Falls and offer her a ride. She knew he didn't always have an errand to run and was just trying to be nice to her. She surmised it was probably because he pitied her.

Even though she appreciated it, she never made the effort to verbally express her gratitude. It was usually at the first sign of gratitude that men asserted themselves into a position of authority. She didn't need that kind of headache to add to her plate, so she just played it cool and pretended to be unaware he was going out of his way to do her a favor. She did make a minimal effort to be a little less sarcastic and even managed a sincere smile in his direction once or twice. More importantly, she refrained from making any more jokes about his taste in music. If that wasn't gratitude, then she didn't know what was.

By the time they got back, it was usually dinner time at the Corbin household. Joan never failed to extend an invitation for Emily to join them, but Emily always politely declined. Instead, she went back to her apartment to sketch in her art book.

Sometimes, while she would sit in the window seat sketching, she'd catch a glimpse of Danny emerging out of the woods. Shortly after spotting Danny, she knew she would be receiving a plate of leftovers from the Corbin dinner table. The leftovers never went to waste as Emily quickly rediscovered the magic of home-cooked meals. This was a simple pleasure she hadn't enjoyed since her early teens.

Emily wasn't sure if this familiar routine of small town life was comforting or boring. There were days she missed the spontaneous bustle of city life. She hadn't heard from Eric again, but Amanda and Chloe called a few times to check in on her. She assured them she would be home soon, but something else told her that might not be true. Lily wasn't getting better, and as the days went on, she grew paler and thinner than the day before.

Emily started to entertain the thought of finding a more permanent living situation. It wasn't that she thought "this is the way life should be", as the state logo suggested, but rather, Lily's recovery was taking longer than she had anticipated. She didn't want to walk out on her again without knowing she was going to be alright.

One morning, as Emily was crossing the Corbin's yard on her way into town, she noticed the entrance to the path in the woods that she sometimes saw Danny traveling. Curiosity got the better of her, and she decided to forgo her coffee and muffin for a walk through the woods.

She quickly discovered the well-worn foot path brought her to a section of the train tracks and the river she had found earlier in a different part of town. Pleased she had brought her camera with her, she couldn't resist snapping a few shots of the black iron tracks. Like her, the black tracks contrasted against the brightly colored fall leaves around them.

Emily felt the excited flutter in her chest when she knew she had captured a great shot. She hurried along, eager to see what other surprises the trail held. Eventually, the narrow path opened up into a clearing which exposed an old, rickety, wooden foot bridge crossing over the river.

When she saw it, Emily paused and approached it cautiously. She'd never seen anything like it before, and she didn't trust that it was structurally sound. She tested her weight carefully on one foot and then the other. The bridge gave no sign of distress under her weight, so she gingerly edged forward. Although the bridge creaked and groaned beneath her feet, the boards remained solid and stable.

She paused in the middle and peered over the railing at the rapids that ran over the rocks beneath it. She snapped a few more photos and then crossed the bridge taking a few more from the other side.

When she turned her attention back to the trail, she was struck at how different it looked from the other side of the bridge. Before she crossed, the trail was narrow but well-groomed and easily passable. One glance at the opening to this trail showed a practically non-existent path, crowded and darkened by heavy growth. The trees swallowed up the daylight and made the trail look more like a cave entrance than a path through the woods.

Emily hesitated, unsure whether she should continue down the forbidden looking path. She looked over her shoulder at the happily babbling brook and decided there was nothing to worry about in a place like this. What was the worst that could happen? She was dismayed by the answers her mind quickly provided. She could be eaten by a bear, bitten by a snake, trampled by a moose. She reminded herself that Danny fended for himself out here on almost a daily basis. Surely, if he could manage, so could she.

She pressed forward. Within three steps, the warmth of the sunlight and the happy sounds of the brook were swallowed by the heavy brush and trees. Still, she continued, telling herself the path would improve.

When it grew darker and quieter, Emily found herself wondering if it was hunting season. She laughed out loud at her own ignorance. This was Maine, every season was probably hunting season. She abruptly stopped laughing when she realized she had overlooked the possibility of getting shot by a drunken hunter. Wasn't she supposed to be wearing orange or something? She tried to picture how she would look wearing bright hunter orange. Orange is definitely *not* the new black , she laughed.

Emily quickened her pace as her mind circled back to the dangerous animals that could possibly be hunted in these woods. Sure there were probably deer, and rabbits, and wild fowl, but what about the other ones? Wasn't Maine known for its black bears? What would she do if she saw a black bear? She tried to recall the survival rhyme about bears. If it's brown, hit the ground. If it's black, run and don't look back? If it's black attack? Crap, what should she do, run and don't look back or attack? She scoffed at herself. How would she go about attacking a bear anyway? What the hell was wrong with this place? She couldn't believe she was actually walking through the woods wondering how to attack a bear.

As she was debating the best tactic for confronting a bear, she was unable to avoid confronting a large root that rose up from the path.

Her foot caught the top of it, and before she even realized what had thrown her, she was on the ground.

The first thing she did was check her camera. She whispered a sigh of relief when she saw it was still intact. After all, it was the most valuable thing she owned. She rubbed her throbbing ankle and glared angrily at the root that tripped her.

"Fucking root! This is why I don't do nature!" she snarled.

Just then, she was distracted by the sound of whistling behind her. She turned and saw Danny trudging up the trail. He was wearing another classic 80's t-shirt showcasing the band Journey, which was tucked neatly into his blue jeans. His red converse sneakers stopped abruptly in their tracks when he saw Emily on the ground.

"Oh crap. You're not going to start screaming again are ya?" she asked.

"You're hurt," he told her.

"Yeah, no shit Sherlock."

Danny stood there staring at her. He was unsure of what to do, so he began to rock back and forth nervously. Emily could sense Danny's anxiety, and she reminded herself to use a softer tone with him.

"I'm ok, Danny," she assured him.

She got to her feet to show him but winced when she tried to put weight on her ankle.

"You're hurt," Danny repeated.

"I just twisted it. It's fine."

After a moment of consideration, an idea took hold on Danny's face. He started beckoning Emily with his hand to follow him.

Without a better plan, Emily decided to follow. She limped behind Danny as he shuffled down the trail. Within minutes they were at the door of a small, rustic cabin.

With no indication of any vehicles or even a driveway, Emily assumed this was an old abandoned ski shed Danny had stumbled upon. Its sloped porch led to a thick wooden door with a round, rusted door knob. A mixture of pine needles and moss covered the roof and entrance way. The windows were frosted with decades of dust, blocking any glimpses of what might lay inside and lending an air of mystery to the tiny shack.

"Is this your secret fort?" Emily asked Danny.

Danny ignored her and rapped twice on the door before letting himself in. Emily wondered why anyone would knock on the entrance to their own secret fort, but she was learning not to waste too much time trying to figure out why Danny did most of the things he did. Instead, she followed him inside, feeling a bit like Goldie Locks.

The last thing she expected was for another living creature to be inside, and she nearly leaped out of her skin when a raspy old voice barked at her.

"Who the hell are you?"

Emily staggered backward when she saw an old man sitting in a rocking chair scowling at her. He wore heavy black boots, dark blue jeans, and a red flannel jacket. His thick, wavy, salt and pepper hair curled around his ears and fell loosely at his shoulders. His face was barely visible under a thick gray beard, but his pale blue eyes glared with fierce hostility at her from beneath a set of big thick bushy white eyebrows. His knotted old fingers were curled tightly around an empty bottle of Irish whiskey.

Emily drew in a sharp breath and looked to Danny for some help, but he was busy clearing a cluttered table for spot to put his bag. He obviously wasn't surprised to find this old man here. She took a second to gather her wits and reminded herself she had dealt with more intimidating men than this old hermit.

"Who the hell are you?" she asked.

The old man turned his angry glare toward Danny, who seemed oblivious to the tense situation unfolding in the cabin.

"Damn it, Danny! You know better than to bring strangers by here!"

"Emily hurt herself," he said.

His comment was more of a statement than an explanation. The old man looked from Danny to Emily. His eyes settled on her pierced eyebrows.

"It's not my fault she did that to her face!" the old man barked.

Emily rolled her eyes and watched Danny casually take a seat on an old couch that was losing its stuffing. He began to examine puzzle pieces that were scattered across an old coffee table in front of him.

The old man studied Emily carefully. He thought about tossing her out, but there was something different about her that intrigued him. The dark hooded jacket and heavily painted eyes lent her the appearance of a witch, but the boots suggested military. He couldn't help but wonder what kind of girl wore black combat boots with fishnet stockings?

"Doesn't your friend know that she's a little early for Halloween?" he asked Danny.

When Danny didn't look up from the puzzle to acknowledge him, he turned his attention back to Emily.

"Whatcha going as, the Wicked Witch of the West?"

"No, I was actually going to go as a drunk hillbilly, but it looks like you already got that one covered."

The old man looked surprised for a moment, and then he narrowed his eyes suspiciously at Emily. This young thing had a lot of nerve coming into his cabin and speaking to him like that, he thought.

"Your friend here has a quite the mouth on her, Danny Boy. Now what did you bring me today?"

Danny glanced up from the puzzle pieces and reached over to the table for the brown paper bag. The old man grabbed it from him and quickly pulled out several items. He cast the canned goods and newspaper aside without much interest. A scowl crawled over his face as he pulled out a bottle of apple juice. He held it up and looked at Danny disapprovingly and then returned to digging through the bag. His features brightened and his mustache twitched with something that resembled a smile when he pulled out a fresh bottle of whiskey.

"Atta boy, Danny!"

With a look of relief, his shaking hands twisted the cap off the bottle and took a long swig. Emily shook her head. People were the same no matter where you went, she thought. She looked pensively at a nearby chair. Her ankle was still sore, but she decided to risk taking a seat to give it some relief. The old man eyed her carefully as she limped over to the chair. Then, as if making up his mind about something, he extended the bottle to offer her a swig.

Emily shook her head no as she moved a pile of old newspapers off the chair. Once seated, she immediately began to rub her aching ankle. She was grateful for the boots. If she had been wearing anything else, she may have sprained it or worse. She loosened the laces and gave it some room to breathe.

"Why do you look so funny?" he asked.

"Why do you smell so funny?" she retorted.

He wondered if she was going to answer all of his questions with a question.

"Ooo wee! We got a live one here, Danny Boy!" he exclaimed.

He put down his bottle and rubbed his hands together excitedly. It had been a while since he had a conversation with anyone that had the wit of this girl. He liked Danny's company because Danny didn't talk to him or bother him much. He studied Emily, trying to figure out where this creature had come from.

"You're not from around here, are ya?" he implored.

"God, no," she scoffed. "From Boston."

"Ah, I should have guessed. You have Masshole written all over ya."

Emily glared at him. What was this guy's deal? She determined he must have some real serious issues to live out here in this tiny one room cabin. As she watched him pick up his bottle and take another long swig, she concluded what his main issue was. It was ten in the morning for crying out loud.

"I used to teach some classes in Boston… a long, long time ago," he told her.

His pale eyes flickered. Somewhere behind them, his mind traveled to another time.

"What did you teach, Wilderness Survival or Redneck 101?"

Frank tipped his bottle to her. He appreciated her witty response.

"Good question. A better question is, what's a Boston girl like yourself doing in Pine Ridge?"

"I'm just in town visiting my sister in the hospital."

"She sick or something?"

Emily looked at him in disbelief. Did the alcohol rot his common sense as well as his liver?

"No, she's there because she likes the food," Emily retorted.

Frank looked over at Danny, who was working the pieces of the puzzle diligently. He plugged one into place and gave his uncle a proud, happy smile.

"Who are your folks? If they live in Pine Ridge, I'm sure I know them," Frank asked, bringing his attention back to Emily.

"What's with all the questions? You writing a book or something?" Emily asked.

"Whoa! Looks like someone woke up on the wrong side of the coffin this morning," Frank said. "It's called conversation, Missy. Or don't they have that in Transylvania?"

Emily rolled her eyes. She didn't like anyone prying into her personal life. This is why she habitually answered questions with questions. That approach didn't seem to work as well in Pine Ridge as it did in Boston. People were annoyingly persistent here.

"If you must know, it's just my mother and sister who live here. You probably don't know them. They only moved up here a couple years ago."

He thought about insisting on getting her mother's name, but he knew Emily was right. He had been out of touch with town life for a while now. There had been a time, not so long ago, that he had known every face by name in Pine Ridge.

"Well, how do you know Danny then?" he asked.

"I'm sorta staying with the Corbin's while I'm here," Emily answered with a shrug.

Frank grimaced. There was something not quite right about this kid. Nothing about her made sense.

"I thought you just said your mother lives here?" he pressed.

Emily didn't like where this conversation was going. Why was everyone in Pine Ridge so damn nosey? Nobody asked questions in Boston and that's how she liked it. She looked at the door and thought about leaving, but her ankle still burned unhappily inside her boot.

Frank noted with interest that his question made Emily look like a trapped animal. He watched her eyes dart to the door, then to the window, and finally back to him.

"Let's just say we don't get along too well," Emily said dismissively.

She moved her eyes away from his face and shifted uncomfortably in her seat.

Frank leaned back in his chair and stroked his beard thoughtfully. It was clear to him the girl had issues. He wasn't surprised to hear she was disconnected from her mother.

"Hmm, imagine that. Hard to believe with you being so personable and all," he said sarcastically.

Emily glared at him. What a prick, she thought. She quickly

smiled, knowing that she was about to turn the table on this old fool.

"What about you?" she asked sweetly. "You some kind of hermit or something? No wife, no kids? No family?"

"I really don't see where that is any of your business," he snapped harshly.

The amusement that outlined his features earlier was quickly replaced with scorn.

"What? You're the only one that gets to ask questions?" Emily asked.

"That's right. This is my place, young lady. You don't come into my place and start asking me questions."

"Oh, I see. I hit a nerve," Emily said thoughtfully. "Your old lady kicked you out, huh? Shocking."

Frank began to tremble and shake. The golden whiskey in the bottle shook uneasily in his grasp. He leaned forward and gave her a look that sent shivers down her spine.

"I think it's time you leave," he said quietly.

Emily shrugged her shoulders and got up from her chair. Danny looked up from his puzzle. His eyes shot from Emily to his uncle.

"Both of you," he said to Danny.

Without a word, Danny got up and met Emily at the door. He turned and gave his uncle a friendly wave before they left.

Emily started down the path they had originally traveled to reach the cabin, but Danny stopped her. She looked at him and saw he was pointing in a different direction.

"We go this way," he told her.

With a shrug, she let Danny take the lead and followed him faithfully down another side trail. Eventually, the thick forest began to thin out, and they reached a much wider section of trail. By the two deep ruts on either side, Emily guessed it had once been a road. Her suspicions were confirmed when Danny hurried over to a section between two trees where several old rusted vehicles sank into the earth.

Danny looked over his shoulder and smiled excitedly at Emily. He waited impatiently for her to come over and discover his special treasures. Unable to resist his excitement, Emily joined him and inspected the old Cadillac he stood beside.

The car came to its final stop with its roof rolled down, which had allowed the elements to deteriorate the interior considerably. The windshield had been smashed out, and one of the front doors was missing. With its hinges rusted in place, the passenger side door stood permanently open. Danny swiped away a pile of dead leaves that had blown onto the seats. Their cushions and filling had long ago decayed or perhaps been destroyed by fire, and all that remained was the metal frames.

A closer look at the interior of the car indicated fire was quite possibly the reason the car had come to meet its demise as the steering wheel and dashboard were also stripped down to blackened metal.

Emily was a bit mortified when Danny climbed in the car and took a seat, but when she saw his huge smile and eyes beaming back at her, she couldn't resist joining him. She rounded the car to the driver's side, and she tentatively eased herself down behind the steering wheel.

When Emily gazed into the back seat she was surprised to find it mostly intact. She pretended to adjust the rearview and side mirrors, and then she reached for the place where she thought the radio might have been once.

"What station should we listen to Danny?" she asked.

"The 80s!" he answered urgently.

"Ah, of course. I should have known that, right?"

Danny nodded.

"Looks like they're playing a little Cinderella. How's that?"

Danny began to bang his head to the imaginary beat of the 80's hair band, Cinderella. It was clear the station had his approval.

"Better buckle up, Danny! I bet this baby can go pretty fast!" Emily said.

She reached for where the seat belt should have been. When she found none, she pretended to pull a strap around her and snap it into place.

"There, mine's on. Now it's your turn."

Danny smiled and mimicked what Emily had done.

"Good job! Now where should we go?" she asked.

Danny gave this question some serious consideration, and Emily waited patiently. Finally his face lit up with a destination in mind.

"Disney World!" he shouted gleefully.

"Ok! Disney World here we come! Woo Hoo!" Emily cried and pounded on the steering wheel.

The old Cadillac's horn blared out a strong toot and Danny and Emily both looked at each other in surprise. Emily burst into laughter and Danny joined in vigorously.

10

The House Next To The Drive-In

"I grew up in a house next to the Drive-In
We'd sit up on the roof and watch the cars roll in
And watch all the couples fog up their cars
And write on the windows their fingerprint hearts.
Then they slowly would drive home long after midnight"

Back at apartment above the Corbin garage, Ryan knocked on the door. He was wondering why Emily hadn't shown up to the store yet, and he was getting worried about her. When he didn't get an answer, he slowly opened the door.

"Emily?" he called. "Are you here?"

The silence of the apartment was the only thing that greeted him. Ryan stepped inside.

A pile of Emily's clothes lay in a heap on the living room floor. He smiled. He was not surprised they were all black. He peered around the corner to check if she had slept in but found the bed empty and made up neatly.

At the foot of the bed, a black backpack with various patches sewn onto it caught his eye. He approached it cautiously and inspected the patches. He chuckled under his breath when he saw the familiar band logos from The Cure, Depeche Mode, and Jesus & Mary Chain scattered across the bag.

He was about to turn and leave, but he saw a black, leather bound book resting on the nightstand. He stood there staring at the book, telling himself not to snoop. Even as he told himself to turn and leave, he reached out for the book. He held it for a moment, and then unable to resist his curiosity he opened it up.

Inside he found a collection of photographs she had taken with names and locations written underneath. Most of them were random shots in Boston; buildings, people, and lots of cemetery shots. He thought of Emily taking the photos, always on the outside looking in.

One photo in particular struck him. It was a black and white photo of an old Indian woman wearing a tunic. She was looking deeply into the camera. The lines of her mouth hinted at a smile, but it was the old woman's eyes that held him captive. The deep, dark brown pools gleamed with an untold story, a secret maybe. He studied the caption below and learned Emily had actually approached the woman and asked to take her photo. He could easily see why. The old woman had a mysterious beauty about her. Emily had seen that inner beauty and captured it perfectly.

Ryan went to put the book down and discovered there was another book beneath it. It was a tattered notebook with the words, 'Sketches and shit' written on the cover.

Curious as to what the 'shit' part was, he slowly opened it up. On the inside of the front cover, he found she had scribbled a quote. The words were surrounded by little black flowers that were connected by intricate black vines. Ryan read the quote out loud.

"All I needed, was to know his kiss was more than a just a kill, cause conquering me is never easy..."

He paused and let the weight of the words that followed fall over him. He shook his head as he read the rest softly.

"… and I fear nobody will."

The first six or seven pages of the notebook were filled with pencil sketches — really good ones.

He wanted to see what was inside, but he wasn't prepared for that initial quote or for the beautifully talented sketches. What did he expect, sad cat drawings? Of course, he knew Emily had more going on below the surface than what she led on. He expected to find more sarcasm and maybe some mean spirited opinions about the world but nothing that revealed she might have a vulnerable side.

It quickly became obvious to him what the 'and shit' part of the title meant. Mixed in with her sketches were random song quotes and pages of Emily's personal thoughts. Although extremely curious as to what made this girl tick, Ryan was very respectful and chose not to read any of her personal entries. He focused only on her drawings.

As he gazed at a sketch of a crow perched on an old gravestone, the sound of foot steps behind him startled him out of his thoughts.

"What the fuck are you doing?" Emily asked angrily.

She marched over to him and ripped the books from Ryan's hands and then looked at him accusingly. She couldn't believe he'd come in here and start going through her things. She thought Ryan respected her enough not to violate her privacy. Just like most guys, she was wrong about him.

"What is wrong with you people? Haven't you heard of privacy?"

"I was just..." Ryan started.

Emily cut him off.

"Get. Out. NOW!" she yelled.

She was shaking with rage. Ryan knew what he did was wrong, but he also knew better than to try and apologize now. Emily stood with her books clutched to her chest, and the look of hurt on her face instantly shamed him. He turned quietly and left without another word.

Once Emily heard the apartment door close, she let out the breath she had been holding. She stuffed her photo album and sketch book in her bag and chastised herself for being careless enough to leave them out.

She hugged herself and sat on the bed. Something about this town made her feel like she was an exhibit on display. They didn't think she was a real person. All they saw were the black clothes, the dark makeup and the piercings, and they figured she was just a spectacle to pick apart and dissect. She just wished everyone would leave her alone. A lump swelled up in her throat, and she tried to push it down along with her emotions.

She lay down on the bed and tried to calm herself. She closed her eyes and longed for the anonymity of the city where she was nothing more than part of a crowd.

She was soon pulled into the land of dreams, where she was chased by the angry faces. In the palace of her mind, she ran through the woods as she tried to escape her mother and the old man in the cabin. All the while, she tried to find her way back to Lily, who was lost somewhere in the heart of the forest.

***

Danny sat on the front porch of the Corbin farmhouse listening to music on his headphones. When Emily came over and sat down beside him, he took his headphones off and silently offered to let her listen.

"What? You want me to check out your music selection?" Emily asked.

Danny nodded. She took the headphones from him and put them up to her ear. The familiar sound of Axl Rose signing about Paradise City immediately grabbed her attention. She banged her head along to the tune and Danny smiled.

"Good one," she said.

She handed the headphones back to Danny and caught an intoxicating aroma drifting off from him.

"Hey, whoa! You got a hot date? You smell delicious," Emily remarked.

Danny smiled and shook his head no.

"I borrowed Ryan's man spray," he said shyly.

"Ahh, that explains it," said Emily. "Speaking of Ryan, do you know where he is?"

Danny nodded his head, and Emily realized she needed to be more specific.

"Where is he?"

Danny pointed up the road.

"He's in a tree?" she asked completely confused.

Danny turned his lips up in a half smile and shook his head.

"No!" he exclaimed. "He's at the drive-in!"

Emily remembered seeing the drive-in during one of her excursions of town. She recalled the image of the large wooden sign with flaking green paint which read: P ne R dg D ive In. Below it was an old faded sign, which had apparently falsely promised 'Reopening June 1997'.

"The drive-in?" Emily asked confused. "But that place looks like it's been closed for years. What is he doing there?"

Danny closed his eyes and began to play air guitar. Emily waited for Danny to stop, but instead, he put his headphones back on his head and began to jam harder.

Emily shook her head and got up. She started walking in the direction of the drive-in. Danny didn't even notice she was gone. He had already arrived back in Paradise City.

The drive-in was nestled in a clearing of pine trees not far from the Corbin's house. Rolling hills on one side of the clearing provided the perfect opportunity for the sky to display its pastel hues as the day faded into twilight.

In the last diminishing rays of sunlight, Emily found Ryan leaned up against the front of his truck strumming cords on his guitar. The old paint-peeled drive-in screen cast a large dark shadow that fell at his feet. Ryan paused to tug down the brim of his Red Sox hat to shield his eyes from the golden rays of light, which fell on him like a spotlight from above stage.

Emily sought him out to tell him she was over being pissed about finding him with her books. If the roles were reversed, she probably would have done the same thing.

Something about the scene she walked in on made her stop in her tracks. She reached into her back pack to retrieve her camera. In the shadows of the pines, she watched him as he addressed an imaginary crowd.

"Thank you, thank you," Ryan said. "Now this next one is called 'Outside of a Dream'. It's about the one that got away."

The chords of the guitar resonated inside the cove of trees and sank straight into Emily's heart. She knelt down on one knee and snapped a few shots. When Ryan began to sing, Emily forgot her camera and just listened. His voice was surprisingly smooth and nostalgic.

"We used to dance, but the best clubs in town are all closed down,
And all of the music sounds mean.
But what does it mean when the one thing I can't put down
Is the letter you wrote to me at twenty-three.
And dream, I'm on the outside of a dream,
Praying that you could salvage me.
Thy will be done.
No second chance was the last thing you told me,
And I was the fool who agreed.
Now I'm driving past all the places we went to,
Where the kisses flowed so easily from you to me.
And dream, I'm on the outside of a dream…"

Emily wasn't sure how long she would have stayed here in the shadows listening to Ryan's fluid voice move over the lyrics. If her cell phone hadn't started to ring, she may have sat there indefinitely.

The sound startled Ryan, and he spotted her immediately.

Emily's cheeks flushed. Now *she* felt like the one who had been caught spying. She made her way over to Ryan.

"Apparently, there's cell phone service here," Emily joked. "Sorry to interrupt. I was just walking by and I heard a crowd going nuts, so I had to see what all the cheering was about."

"Yeah," Ryan said sheepishly. "This crowd can get really amped up on a Friday night."

"So this is what you do for fun around here, huh? Go to an old abandoned drive-in and play songs to an imaginary crowd?"

Ryan shrugged. "I used to be in a band a while back, but now I just like coming out here and playing with myself."

Ryan's eyes grew wide when he heard the words come out of his mouth. He immediately corrected himself.

"Play *by* myself, that is."

Emily snickered.

"A band huh? Let me guess the name. Was it the Backwoods Boys? Or was it The New Hicks on the Block? That was it, wasn't it? The New Hicks on the Block?"

Ryan shook his head. Did everything have to be a sarcastic joke with her? He knew she had a serious side but why didn't she ever show it? He looked at Emily inquisitively as he wondered that very thing. She shifted uncomfortably under his scrutinizing look.

"So, that song you were singing, was it based on a real chick or was that just something musicians say to sound cool on stage?"

Ryan cast his eyes off into the sunset and nodded slightly. He braced himself for Emily's next jab.

"She dumped you, huh?"

"Actually, I guess I sorta dumped her. We dated for a few years in high school and then she went off to college at UMaine, and I…"

"Took over the family business?" Emily asked.

"God no," Ryan answered. "The last thing on my mind when I

graduated from high school was the general store. Of course, going off to college was about the next to last thing on my mind. Tanya was always more motivated than me, more career-orientated, more…"

"More mature?" Emily knowingly asked. "Girls usually are."

She paused for a moment to think about her last statement, which she realized really didn't apply to herself. She hadn't been anything like this girl Ryan was describing, or any of the girls she went to high school with for that matter.

"Don't get me wrong, I loved our relationship, but there were other things I was more focused on at the time."

Emily cocked her head to one side. She fought the urge to suggest Ryan was probably more focused on The Backstreet Boys. Instead, she found his choice of wording more interesting. He said he loved the relationship, not her.

Ryan paused to wait for one of Emily's zingers. He was surprised that she just looked at him curiously, waiting for him to continue. Her unusual behavior was making him a little uneasy.

"I guess I was more focused on my band and finding a way to get the hell out of Pine Ridge."

Emily nodded empathetically.

"I can understand why you'd want to do that. This place blows."

Ryan shot her a look, but she just shrugged it off.

"Anyway, the band and I had this plan... a master plan. We were going to move to New York, play in some local bars, get discovered, sign a big record deal, and live happily ever after."

"You lived in New York City?" Emily asked incredulously.

"Well, not exactly New York City. Do you know how damn expensive it is to live there? We got a place on the outskirts."

"So you lived in New Jersey?"

Ryan smirked at her joke.

"Something like that," he confessed.

"So what did your chick think about all of this?"

"Let's just say she wasn't a fan of my decisions and goals. I wasn't trying to break up with her by moving away. I really had no problem with doing a long distance relationship."

"Please," Emily scoffed, "Everyone knows they never work out."

"Yeah, that's what she said too. Eventually, it came down to her giving me an ultimatum: either quit the band and move back to Maine to get a real job, or..."

"And you picked the band," Emily concluded.

Ryan nodded. Emily knew this story all too well. The guys always picked the band, or the garage, or the drugs. They never picked the girl.

"She warned me there would be no second chances, but..."

"You figured you could get her back whenever you wanted, didn't you?"

Ryan hung his head in shame. Emily was good at figuring out how relationships went bad. She looked at him and shook her head in disappointment.

"Typical guy move," she concluded. "So, what happened next?"

"A reality check is what happened. Talk about a small fish in a big pond. We barely got any gigs, and when we did, they were places that record executives wouldn't be caught dead in. Actually, most normal people wouldn't be caught dead in the places we played. So long story short, my music career amounted to jack shit."

"So you just gave up?"

Ryan nodded his head sadly.

"Lame."

Ryan looked at her with wounded eyes, but he knew she was right, so he resigned with a nod.

"So why not just stay where you were? There must have been lots of other intriguing job opportunities. What made you come back to good ole Pine Ridge?"

When Ryan didn't offer any explanation, Emily drew her own

conclusion.

"Oh right, the girl. You came home to try and get her back, didn't you?. Let me guess, she had already moved on with someone else, right?"

Ryan fixed his eyes on the blank movie screen. He was beginning to regret that he had ever mentioned Tanya. He almost wished they could go back to their one sentence conversations because once Emily got started she really didn't know when to quit.

"What's with all the questions? You writing a book or something?" Ryan asked her.

Emily gave him a funny look and then smiled. Normally she hated it when people used her own lines on her, but this time it seemed fitting.

"Touché," she answered.

Emily followed Ryan's gaze to the old movie screen. A run-down wooden snack shack sat a few feet away. A sign still promising hot popcorn hung by a rusted wire next to the take out window. She tried to imagine what the place would have been like when it was open.

"I've never been to one of these places," said Emily.

Actually, that wasn't entirely true, she thought. A few years ago, she and Amanda decided to take a road trip down to Mendon, Massachusetts to the drive-in there. Emily remembered it was right around this time of year because they had stopped at some giant pumpkin patch farm. She also remembered them wandering around the intricate corn maze. The maze wasn't really that intricate, but their aimless wandering and uncontrollable laughter had more to do with their alcohol levels. There weren't too many things they did back then that didn't involve getting drunk or high first.

By the time they actually made it to Mendon and the drive-in, they were disappointed to find it had closed for the season a week earlier. A 1958 Chevy Apache was parked in one of the center rows, and next to the driver's side was one of those old drive-in speakers.

Considering drive-ins now use the car radio to transmit the sound, Emily deducted the truck and the speaker were just used as props.

Even back then, Emily had an eye for the perfect shot. As the dark, thunderous clouds gathered in the background, she began shooting. Emily thought the scene was quite poignant; the likeness of the antique truck with the fading popularity of the drive-in movie theatres. They were both two dying legends, sitting still beneath a stormy sky together.

She edited it over with a sepia tone to accentuate the historic significance of the photo. She remembered thinking at the time that she should try and contact the owner of the drive-in and see if they wanted to buy her photo. However, like most things in her life, she never followed through. Emily shook the thought away.

"So what's so special about this place anyway?" she asked.

Ryan wasn't sure if she was talking about the drive-in or Pine Ridge. After studying the curiosity on her face as she looked around her, he decided she meant the drive-in.

"We used to come here all the time when we were kids. Like most families around here, we couldn't afford to go on vacation, so this was it. There were two things we looked forward to every summer: Fourth of July fireworks over the river and coming here to the drive-in. If our parents had a really good year at the store, and if we were really lucky, they would take us down to the pier at Old Orchard Beach for a day or two. We'd hit the beach, the amusement park, and the arcade, but with the size of our family, even doing that got pretty expensive."

Ryan stared at a patch of dead grass and smiled nostalgically. He shook his head sadly and continued.

"It seems like yesterday we were all piling out of the station wagon and throwing our blankets down on the ground. Mom would make multiple trips to the snack shack, and Dad would complain the entire time about the mosquitos. Still to this day, I can't smell citronella candles without thinking of this place."

"So if this place was so popular, why did it go out of business?"

"I guess it got to be too tough to compete with the big Cineplex over in Grafton Falls. They could offer way more movies, not to mention, the whole 3D and surround sound crap."

"So this place has just been abandoned all these years?" asked Emily.

"Yeah, pretty much. On the weekends in the summer, they use it for the town flea market. For years now, they've been talking about putting a strip mall in here. Some say it would be better than an old, abandoned drive-in, but, well, I'm not so sure I feel the same."

The yellows, pinks and purples had faded into deeper shades of blue, and the first of the night stars became visible above their heads. Somewhere beside them in the grass, a cricket began to sing. Emily tilted her face up to the sky and let the breeze catch her hair. She liked listening to Ryan reminisce, mostly because she didn't have to answer any questions about herself.

Ryan followed Emily's gaze up into the sky and admired the stars with her for a moment before going on.

"I remember when I was a kid I'd sneak out of the house and cut through the woods to that hill right over there. From there, I had a pretty good view of the movie screen. Of course, I couldn't really hear much of anything, but I liked to make up the dialogue in my head as I watched the actors on the screen. Plus, I enjoyed the atmosphere. I was able to watch the families and the young couples enjoying themselves."

"You mean, you liked watching them make out, right?"

Ryan shook his head.

"It was more than that. It was like watching people's lives develop. It was seeing them fall in love, or grow up, or make a new friend. My parents had their first date here. As a matter of fact, I had my first date here too."

Emily smiled at the thought of a nervous, scrawny, teenage Ryan on his first date.

"Did you get lucky?" she asked.

"Ah, not quite," Ryan answered. "Not at all, actually. I spent what felt like an eternity fumbling around trying to undo her stupid bra, only to end up knocking my soda over in her lap. Of course, I found out later…"

Ryan trailed off, too embarrassed to continued. Emily wasn't too embarrassed to finish for him though.

"Her bra latched in the front and not the back?"

Ryan nodded and Emily released a whole-hearted belly laugh. It was the first sincere thing Ryan had heard from Emily since he met her. He looked at her in a pleasant amazement as if seeing her for the first time.

"Pfft. Rookie mistake," she said, and slapped him good naturedly on the back.

That's when he joined in with her, and they both leaned back on the hood of the truck and laughed up at the sky. When their laughter faded to silence, Ryan looked over at Emily. She was studying the night sky like it was the first time she'd seen it.

"Hey, I'm sorry about earlier… about looking through your stuff. I shouldn't have done that," Ryan offered.

Emily shrugged. Whatever anger she felt before was gone, but she was glad to hear him apologize.

"I just like my privacy, that's all. And it seems like ever since I got to town all anyone does is ask me questions and look at me funny. I just sorta like to keep to myself."

"Yeah, I've noticed," Ryan said. "And just so you know, I didn't read any of your… writing. I just looked at your photos and drawings, I swear."

Nine out of ten guys were fucking liars, thought Emily, but in this case, she knew Ryan spoke the truth.

"Your photographs were pretty amazing," he said. "I loved that one of the old woman wearing a tunic. And I was totally impressed with the details of your sketches. I mean, not like I am a good judge of art or anything. Heck, I can't even draw a good stick figure. I liked what I saw though. You've actually got talent, Emily."

Instead of looking pleased by Ryan's compliments, Emily had a scowl on her face and looked at him accusingly.

"Actually? What? I don't look like I could be talented? Oh, that's right, it's because pretty girls don't actually have brains, right?"

"What? No!" Ryan exclaimed urgently. "I didn't mean it that way at all! I was just trying to give you a compliment, that's all."

Emily felt herself relax. She always got defensive any time anyone brought up her artistic interests. She knew even if she did have talent, she was too much of a screw up to ever do anything with it, and that was a hard pill to swallow. When she looked at Ryan, she saw that he was being sincere.

"Oh, ok thanks," she replied in a softer tone.

"So, is that what you do back in Boston? Art and photography?"

Emily felt a pang of guilt. No wonder Ryan had been tempted to snoop earlier. She hadn't told him one thing about herself.

"Yeah right, I wish. I… um… I work at a club. Well, I *worked*, at a club. I sorta quit right before I came here."

"Oh, that's cool. What did you do? Wait tables? Bartend?"

"Something like that," Emily replied vaguely.

"Boston has some great clubs and bars. A friend of mine lives down there. We used to go clubbing down on Landsdown Street. It was crazy! Even crazier when the Sox are in town, am I right?"

Emily fought back a sarcastic comment regarding the Red Sox. Instead, she looked at Ryan's baseball hat and remembered the time her and Brian had gone to see the game.

"Yeah," she said softly.

Detecting a switch in her mood, Ryan let the sound of the crickets surround them. Why did she shut down any time the conversation steered toward her life?

Emily leaned back on her elbows and turned her face up to the night sky again. Ryan wondered what her fascination was with the stars. He looked up again, but he couldn't see what the big deal was. As if reading his mind, Emily offered up the explanation.

"The stars don't look like this in the city," she said.

"What do you mean? Sure they do."

"No, they don't. I mean, some of them look the same, but you can see so many more out here in the country. It's hard to believe I've been looking at these stars this whole time but never actually seeing them."

"Maybe sometimes you just need a different perspective to see what's truly in front of you," Ryan offered.

Emily wasn't sure if his statement was matter of fact or if he was specifically referring to her situation. Either way, she smiled. She absolutely loved its sentiment.

Ryan remembered living down in NYC (New Jersey) and how different the sky looked there, and he understood what Emily meant. The big lights of the city had a way of drowning out the ones in the sky. Only the brightest stars could be seen there while the less visible ones went unnoticed.

"Sometimes the hardest things to see are the ones right in front of you," Ryan said, referring to his own life.

Emily turned her head and gave him a funny little smile. He was totally referring to me, she thought. She sat up and wrapped her arms around herself as the night air settled around them.

"It's getting cold," she said. "I think I'm going to head back."

"I can give you a ride," he said.

"It's okay, I like walking."

Secretly, Ryan didn't want her to go. He kind of liked having someone his own age to talk to especially of the female variety.

"Ya know what," he said, "I could use a walk myself. I'll just leave my truck here and come by and get it in the morning. That is, if you don't mind me walking with you?" Ryan asked.

"It's a free country," she said.

"Ah, and just like that, the sarcasm is back," Ryan said with a chuckle.

As they walked back toward the house, Ryan recalled something his mother mentioned earlier that he meant to tell Emily.

"My mom told me today that Lacey, Claire, and Jake are all coming home for the weekend. It's my parent's anniversary and we are going to have a cookout and a small party for them."

"Am I getting kicked out?" Emily asked.

A few days ago she would have welcomed an excuse to find a motel somewhere, but the thought of leaving now left her unsettled.

"Nah, I don't think Jake's wife is coming, and seeing as Claire just got divorced and that Lacey is single, they'll probably all just crash in the house with the rest of us. Just like the good old days. It'll be like one great big Corbin slumber party."

Emily cringed when she thought about having more people around that would gawk at her and ask her tons of questions. A silence settled between them, and the only sound that could be heard was the gravel crunching under their feet as they walked up the driveway to the Corbin house.

"Well, good night, Emily," Ryan said as he turned toward the house.

Emily smiled and gave a slight nod of her chin before turning toward the apartment stairs.

"Hey, Emily?"

"Yeah?"

"I really am sorry for invading your space. But in a way, I'm glad I did because I got to see how talented you are. Your art work really is impressive."

"Thanks, Ryan. Your ability to fool people into believing what they want to believe most is also pretty impressive. It's no wonder you ended up in customer service."

Her words dropped the hopeful smile off Ryan's face. Immediately, Emily could see that once again, she had said the wrong thing. Her heart sank as she watched Ryan give a half-hearted wave before he disappeared around the corner.

She composed herself until she was inside her apartment. Once the door was closed, she let the condemnation of herself begin.

"Shit! Shit! Shit!" she cursed at herself.

She ripped her sweatshirt off and tossed it angrily onto the floor. She sat at the kitchen table and buried her face in her hands.

"Apology accepted Ryan, and thanks for the compliment," Emily said, practicing a better version of herself.

"Why couldn't I have just said that?" she asked.

11

F#*k It

"If anyone was wondering what's my philosophy
I can only tell you what it seems to be –
*Aw F#*k it!!*
Father time can just suck it. I'll keep my head in a bucket
So I can make my own sky"

Emily strolled through the one street that consisted of the 'downtown' area in Pine Ridge. She noted every other building appeared to be empty and most had a "For Lease" sign in the window. Some, however, apparently had given up on that idea altogether and just sat dark and vacant with layers of dust building up on the once active store front windows.

Curiosity got the better of her, and she paused along the sidewalk to peer through the dusty glass into the darkened interior of one store. She could clearly see the bright red leather covered stools and the chrome lining of a soda bar inside. There were tables with upside down chairs placed on top, and it looked as though somebody had just closed up shop one day and never came back.

Although the warm October sun beat fiercely onto her long sleeved black V-neck blouse, Emily warmed herself against a chill that ran down her spine. She found herself wondering what happened to this town to make it dry up like a river bed in a drought.

The colorful spinning red and white stripes of a barber shop ahead still spun cheerfully, promising that life still existed in scattered corners throughout town.

As Emily walked by, she saw an old man diligently working to trim the ear hairs from inside another equally old man's ear. She immediately thought of the general store porch trio, and she wondered what riveting life dilemmas they could be discussing at this very moment. The thought pulled her feet back in the direction of a place that was slowly beginning to feel familiar.

***

Back at the general store, Max, Gus,, and Harold were listening to an Akkord transistor radio. Elvis Presley's voice poured from the red and silver box pleading, "It's Now or Never." They all listened contently to Elvis promise that tomorrow would be too late, knowing at their age it was a likely possibility.

Gus shook his head in disbelief as they all watched a passer-through town leave the store. As he got into his car, Gus was the first to chime in.

"Can you believe that guy actually thought Paul Bunyan was from Minnesota? Everyone knows Bunyan is from right here in Maine," Gus said.

"Bangor to be exact," added Max. "And it took five giant storks to deliver him to his parent's house."

"His first bed was a lumber wagon pulled by a team of seven horses," Harold added. "And to rock him to sleep, his father had to drive the horses to the top of Maine and back."

"Just because Minnesota has a statue of Paul and his blue ox Babe, doesn't mean that's where he was from. People really ought to know their history before they go spouting off at the mouth," Gus said.

"Speaking of spouting off at the mouth," Max said nodding in the direction of Main Street.

They all craned their necks to see Emily strolling up the sidewalk in her black combat books and tight black jeans.

"Uh oh, here comes the Mistress of the Dark," Gus said.

Harold jabbed Gus in the ribs as they all snickered like school boys. When Emily climbed the porch steps, Gus had prepared a pop quiz for her.

"Hey Elvira, lemme ask you a question," Gus said.

Emily paused on the top stair with her hands on her hips, bracing herself for the onslaught of nonsense she was sure would follow. Her inquisitive stare was enough to encourage Gus to continue.

"Where is Paul Bunyan from?"

"Who the hell is that?" Emily asked.

She watched in bewilderment as all three jaws dropped simultaneously onto their flannel shirts and overalls. Harold was the first to recover.

"Surely, you jest?" he asked.

"Surely, you don't think I give a damn?" Emily countered.

The three men looked at each other in disbelief.

"Well I'll be a three pecker Billy goat!" Max exclaimed.

Emily recoiled at the image Max's term had left imprinted on her imagination. Mainers sure did have a lot of strange and disturbing expressions she had never heard of before.

"You've never heard of Paul Bunyan?" Harold asked.

"Sorry, I'm not into country music," Emily stated with a shrug.

The old men fell into an uncomfortable silence as they all eyed her suspiciously. Finally, Harold broke the spell.

"Paul Bunyan wasn't a country singer! He was the strongest lumber jack to ever swing an ax!! Ring a bell now?"

"Oh, is that the dude with the green ox?" Emily offered.

"BLUE OX!!" all three shouted in unison.

"Please don't tell me you old fools actually believe that old folklore story?" Emily asked.

Emily watched uneasily as all three faces turned a pastier shade of white. She thought she actually saw Gus's last patch of colored hair fade out to gray before her eyes.

"Folklore, my ass!" Gus shouted as he began to tremble with indignant anger.

"Easy there killer, you don't want to shake your dentures loose," Emily said.

"My great grandfather used to chop trees with Paul Bunyan!" Gus barked crossly. "He'd tell me stories about how Paul could cut a tree down with just one swipe of his ax!"

The other two men nodded solemnly while Emily rolled her eyes.

"Damn straight, Gussy!" Max added. "I heard he was so tough, he used to eat saw dust then crap out two by fours!"

Harold and Gus exchanged looks, and then nodded in serious agreement. They looked at Emily as if an important fact had just been proven. Emily threw her hands in the air and gave up.

"Is Danny here?" she asked.

Harold waved his hand absently toward the back of the store. Emily was quick to take the opportunity for dismissal and let herself into the store. She waved hello to Joan, who was ringing up a costumer, and followed the familiar pathways that led to the storage rooms out back.

When she found the rooms to be dark and quiet, she looked around slightly puzzled, wondering where Danny could be hiding. A loud metallic thud sounded from the back door. As Emily approached, she could hear the sound of kids jeering on the other side.

She opened the door just in time to see a rock whistle by and hit the dumpster above Danny's head. Danny dropped a bag of trash he had been carrying and ducked. He clutched his hands over his head and cowered down low behind the dumpster.

Two thirteen year old boys wearing striped shirts and blue jeans laughed at how they were able to make an autistic adult cringe with fear. One of them held a rock in his raised hand while the other yelled out insults.

"Hey look, it's Danny the re-re-retard!"

As Emily approached the dumpster undetected, she heard the other kid call out, "Hey Danny, shouldn't you be training for the Special Olympics?"

Another rock flew through the air and landed in front of Danny's face. He squeezed his eyes shut and hunkered down closer to the edge of the dumpster, rocking back and forth.

Emily's mind flashed back to a time when she was thirteen. She had always dressed differently and acted differently than the other girls at school. This often made her a target for teasing and torment. The girls would pick fights by calling her freak or punk slut, or worse. This had continued for only a few weeks before Emily decided to take a stand and stick up for herself.

The first time one of them put her hands on her, Emily punched so hard it knocked her off her feet. When the girl got up she was holding her nose and blood ran freely through her fingers. When she looked down to see her hands full of blood she began to scream and cry. Nobody at school picked fights with Emily after that.

"How the hell did you miss his fat over-sized head?" one of the boys asked the other.

The kid took the rock from his friend.

"Here, let me show you how it's done."

Just as he brought his arm back to launch the rock, a stinging pain seared his fist and he dropped it. He looked down at the rock that had hit his fist. When he looked up, he saw Emily step around the corner of the store. His face went white. She was dressed all in black with a belt made of studded leather and boots that were made for combat. Between her piercings and tattoos, her menacing appearance was frightening enough, but it was the look on her face, however, which left no doubt that she was something straight from their nightmares.

In her hand, Emily held two more rocks. She protectively stepped in front of Danny and crossed her arms over her chest. She dropped her chin and stood like a predator ready to strike.

"The next one will hit your tiny under-sized balls. Now beat it, you little douche canoes," she growled.

One of the boys put a protective hand over his balls, and Emily wondered if he pissed his pants. He absolutely would have if his friend hadn't grabbed him by the shoulder and spun him around. They both gaped at each other then looked back at Emily once more before they took off running.

Emily turned and saw Danny was still cowered behind her and still had his hands clutched firmly over the top of his head. He hummed loudly as he rocked back and forth. Emily recognized the tune. It was Survivor – "Eye of the Tiger".

Emily touched his shoulder.

"Danny, are you ok?" she asked.

Danny kept humming and rocking.

"Danny, it's ok. They're gone. The little douche canoes ran away like a couple of babies!"

Although Danny didn't look at her, he lowered his hands and stood up straight.

"It's alright. You're ok now. They won't be back," Emily said.

With his eyes cast down to the pavement, Danny nodded.

"Wait here. I'll go grab us a couple of drinks for our walk, ok? Us rebels got to stick together, right?"

Danny, still with downcast eyes, nodded once more.

As Emily reentered the store through the back door, the sound of her mother's voice stopped her in her tracks. Part of her wanted to see her mother again, but another part was afraid it would go just as badly as last time. Emily held back and tried to get a feel for her mother's current mood before entering the storefront. She listened as

Joan spoke to her kindly.

"Susan, how have you been?" asked Joan.

"I'm holding up alright," Susan said.

Her voice sounded tired and heavy with weight.

"How is Lily doing?"

"As best as can be expected, I guess. The chemo takes a lot out of her. I've got her on the church prayer list though. That's bound to help," Susan replied, trying to force hope into her tone.

Susan believed that a positive attitude was just as essential as the prayers from the church. If it weren't for the church, Susan may have given up hope a long time ago. It had been a life raft thrown out to her when she had been drowning in a sea of uncertainty. She now clung desperately to the services and the life of faith the church offered.

"We've been praying for her as well," Joan said.

There was a moment of silence, and Emily could feel the tension in the air from where she stood several feet away. Finally, Susan spoke on the subject both of them were now thinking about.

"I heard Emily is staying with you and Harold?"

"Umm, yes. She wanted to stay at a motel out of town, but I insisted she stay with us," Joan hesitantly offered.

Emily knew that Joan must have felt uncomfortable for being put in the middle of things and for offering her a place to stay. It was probably the same uncomfortable feeling her aunt Kay felt when she had Emily live with her at age seventeen.

Susan let out a heavy sigh.

"I tried my best with her, but somehow she still ended up just like me," said Susan. "At least with Lily, I still have a chance to get it right."

Her mother's words cut Emily straight to the core. Is that what her mother thought? She thought she failed her? Now her only chance at redeeming herself as a mother was to save Lily with the gospel and the power of prayer?

Emily didn't bother to listen to any more. She returned to the back lot without the drinks. Danny stood looking tentatively around the corner where the two boys had bolted around.

"Come on Danny," said Emily. "Let's blow this popsicle stand."

Danny looked anxiously around for the popsicle stand, but when he didn't find one, he figured Emily must just be confused.

***

Once again, Danny took the lead on the paths that wound through the forest. Emily struggled to keep up with his quick pace and made sure she kept a steady eye on the back of his Metallica t-shirt, which was tucked neatly into his black jeans and secured by a simple black leather belt.

No wonder the poor guy got picked on, Emily thought. She ran to catch up with him.

"Hey Danny. Danny, wait up!"

Danny paused on the path and turned back. When Emily caught up with him, she was a little winded. For a husky guy, he sure could move!

"A little fashion advice?" she asked.

Danny's face crumpled and he looked down in confusion at his outfit, which he thought really rocked. Emily detected his hurt pride and confusion, so she adjusted her approach a little.

"No, no, don't get me wrong. The t-shirt is bad ass. You got it going on there," she said.

Danny smiled a little and smoothed out the surface of his shirt so she could see it was from the "Ride the Lightning" album. Clearly, Emily was cool enough to appreciate that, Danny thought.

"Ride the Lightning, yeah one of their best, right?" Emily agreed. "No, see it's just that cool guys untuck."

Danny looked up at her, failing to understand what she was getting at.

"Cool dudes wear their t-shirts without tucking them into their pants. I mean, a shirt like that shouldn't be hidden or bunched up. We want to see the whole thing, ya know?"

Danny smiled a little and nodded. That made a lot of sense, he thought. He reached down and pulled clumsily at the fabric of his shirt. Emily watched as he wiggled the shirt free from his waist band. She reached over and helped him with the final pull and straightened out his shirt for him.

"There! Much better!" Emily said, feeling quite pleased with herself.

Danny seemed pleased too, and he pointed happily to a place within the trees. Emily didn't see anything at first and didn't understand. She was coming to realize that when it came to Danny, there was always a reason behind his strange behavior, so she followed him when he started making his own path. They wove around the trees in what felt like a jagged line until she caught a familiar sight.

From behind a white birch, she caught a glimpse of a rusted out fender and grill. Somehow, Danny had brought them back to the junk car lot from a different direction than they had taken the other day. Emily chuckled.

"You really love the classics, don't you?"

Danny glanced over his shoulder and smiled at her. He headed over to an old Jeep Wrangler. Its yellow paint had faded so much that it was hard to tell where the rust began and the paint ended. The windshield was covered in dead leaves and layers of forest dust, but its oversized tires still looked relatively new.

Emily pulled out her camera and snapped a few close ups of the rusted out fenders contrasting against the sturdy black tires. She circled around the back to get a shot of the red taillights, which still glowed brightly under a layer of dust and mud. When she came back around to the front, she found Danny had climbed into the passenger bucket seat.

He looked over at her, eagerly awaiting another road trip. Emily couldn't withstand the temptation and pulled herself into the driver's seat and took hold of the steering wheel.

"Pretty cool Jeep, huh?" she said.

Danny gave a full nod and stared straight ahead ready for a ride.

"Ever suppose this thing has been on safari?"

Danny gave her a look that told her he seriously doubted it had.

"Well, it's going now!" Emily cried.

Danny grinned and smacked his knee with excitement.

Emily feigned turning a key in the ignition and mimicked the sounds of the long dead engine roaring to life. She leaned out the driver's side and pretended to see something in the trees ahead of them.

"What's that?" she asked as she looked anxiously back at Danny.

Danny leaned his head around his side of the Jeep trying to see what Emily was talking about. When he didn't see anything, he looked back at her for an explanation.

Emily craned her head around the windshield once again.

"It looks like a giraffe!" she exclaimed.

Danny's eyes lit up with understanding. He peered around the side of the Jeep again. He looked back at her to confirm with a nod that he too had seen the giraffe.

Emily steered through the plains of Africa searching for more wildlife. Within minutes, she threw her foot down on the brakes and made the appropriate screeching noise. Danny looked over at her anxiously for an account of what was happening. Emily looked back at him with wide green eyes, full of surprise.

"It's a family of elephants crossing the road!!"

Danny looked eagerly and nodded excitedly.

"How many are there Danny?"

He looked again and appeared to be counting.

"Five!"

Emily smiled, thinking it had been a very successful safari.

***

Eventually, Danny led them back to the old cabin in the woods. Emily and Frank sat across from one another, eyeing each other warily while Danny worked tediously over the puzzle pieces on the table.

"Do you ever wear anything besides black, Missy?" he finally asked her.

"Do you ever wear anything besides the odor of stale booze?" Emily retorted.

Frank glared thoughtfully at her for a moment. He worked his jaw as he contemplated if he would tolerate this stranger in his home. Before he could decide, he had to learn more about her. He smacked his lips together decisively and then ventured out once more with an attempt at conversation.

"What did you say your mother's name was again?"

"I didn't," Emily replied.

She crossed her hands over her chest and looked at him hostilely. Wrong subject to bring up, old man, she thought. She tried to convey this with her angry glare, but the lost look in the old man's eyes made her relent.

"It's Susan. Susan McLoughlin."

Although the name didn't ring any bells in his memory bank, he still brightened at the information.

"McLoughlin, huh? So you're Irish?"

"Wow, no wonder you were a teacher. You're a friggin genius!"

Frank went back to working his jaw. Emily watched in mild

amusement as the wrinkles shifted and distorted his face.

"How long are you in town for?" he asked.

"Just until my sister gets to feeling better," Emily answered. "After that, I'm getting the hell out of this hole-in-the-wall town."

"Did you hear that, Danny Boy? Apparently, our quaint little town doesn't live up to Boston girl's standards."

Emily glared at Frank as he leaned back in his rocking chair and laughed. He howled at his own joke until he grew short of breath and began to cough violently. Emily waited silently while he regained his composure.

"So what does little Miss Big City Girl do for work?" Frank asked once he had his breath back.

Emily shrugged. She leaned over the coffee table and tried to work a puzzle piece into place. Frank began to chuckle condescendingly.

"Ahh, jobless. Doesn't surprise me," Frank said. "I mean, who's gonna hire you looking like that? Always dressed in black with all those piercings sticking out of your face everywhere. I sure as hell wouldn't hire you."

Emily stared at him hatefully, which gave him a small tingle of pleasure. It had been a long time since he evoked any emotion in anyone, and even if it was extreme distain, it felt pretty good.

"Like I'd work for you!" Emily retorted.

Emily tried to think of something more insulting to say, but her anger was boiling over making it impossible to focus. She shot up out of her seat and directed her attention to Danny.

"You know what, I really don't need this shit right now. Let's get outta here, Danny!"

Danny stood up slowly, still studying the puzzle pieces. Oblivious to how upset Emily was, he stood there unable to break his concentration.

"Danny!" Emily hissed urgently.

Danny looked up at her and then over at his uncle. As Emily headed for the door, he followed and paused to wave good-bye to the old man.

Once they were outside, it was Emily that took the lead with a marching stride, and it was now Danny who struggled to keep up with her. Danny watched from behind as Emily muttered loudly and made exaggerated hand gestures. He could only catch snippets of what she was saying.

"Who the hell does he think he is to talk to me that way? Maybe he should go talk to my mother. I bet those two would be able to talk for hours about how screwed up I am. And what the hell is wrong with the way I dress?!"

She fired a look back at Danny hoping for a response. Danny just shrugged and concentrated on keeping up with her pace. This was enough response for Emily to continue with her rant.

"It's like people look at you like you're pathetic, or broken… like you just don't belong. All because you look different. You know what I mean?"

She looked back at Danny and then slowed down long enough for him to catch up a little. When he was at her side, she looked at him again, more earnestly this time. She knew Danny didn't usually say much, but she needed to know there was somebody on this planet that understood her. Right now, she was willing to bet that one person was actually Danny, whether he could say so or not.

"Sometimes ya just gotta say fuck it! Yup, that's my philosophy. You know what I'm talking about, don't you, Danny? In a lot of ways we are in the same boat you and me. People think we are just a couple of misfits."

They continued walking in silence for a long while. When Danny finally spoke, Emily had almost forgotten what she had been talking about.

"Rudolph and the Island of Misfit Toys," Danny said.

Surprised that he had spoken, Emily whipped her head around to look at him. She wasn't exactly sure what he was talking about.

"What?" she asked.

"We're like Rudolph and the Island of Misfit Toys," Danny repeated.

Emily stopped in her tracks, and Danny nearly ran into her. Although it had been years since she'd seen Rudolph, she remembered how she always loved and related to the Island of Misfit Toys.

"That's right! That's exactly right, Danny! We're like a couple of misfit toys. Like the squirt gun that shoots jelly or the cowboy that rides an ostrich. Tell you what, you can be the train with square wheels, Danny."

Danny cast his eyes away shyly then turned back to Emily and smiled.

"And you can be the Charlie in the Box," he said.

Emily smiled sadly. The Charlie in the Box had always been her favorite misfit toy.

"Exactly, Danny," Emily agreed. "I'll be the Charlie in the Box… because no one ever wants to play with a Charlie in the Box."

Although they walked the rest of the way back to the general store in silence, inside Emily's head, there was an entire conversation going on as she analyzed what her mother said.

Emily felt horrible that she had turned out to be such a disappointment to her mother, but she never realized her mother blamed herself too. Emily was the one that screwed up and had done the unthinkable — not her mother. Until today, she never stopped to consider her mother might be just as disappointed in herself as she was in Emily, and that broke Emily's heart even more.

12

Symphonies Of Dirt And Dust

"As soon as I remember all the reasons I love you
Is as soon as I remember it's too late"

Ryan joined his mother as she was arranging items on the shelves in the middle of the store. As he grabbed cans of B&M Baked Beans from a box on the floor and added them to the empty space on the shelf, he looked at his mother curiously.

"Hey Ma, I understand why Dad always had to work here. His father worked here, and his father's father worked here, but how did you get sucked in?"

Joan looked at her son, a bit surprised by his question. She pushed a can into place on the shelf and wiped her hands on her apron.

"Well, when we first started dating, your grandfather had your dad working here seven long days a week. I hardly ever got to see him."

"So you started working here just so you could see him more?" Ryan asked bewildered.

He moved his puzzled gaze out the front window where his father, Max and Gus were challenging each other in a sunflower seed spitting contest. It was hard to imagine his father was once someone who had been able to capture the heart of a woman like his mother. Ryan looked back over at his mother, and they both shook their heads, knowing exactly what the other one was thinking.

"I can't believe out of all the jobs and all the men, you ended up in this old place just so you could spend more time with dad. It sounds kind of crazy if you ask me."

Before Joan could reply, Harold burst through the door with a crazed look on his face and a tape measure in his hand.

"Hot damn! You wouldn't believe what just happened! Max just spit a sunflower seed seventeen feet!!"

Ryan and Joan watched in quiet amusement as Harold marched over to the desk and started frantically searching for something.

"Harold, what on earth are you looking for?" Joan asked.

Without answering, Harold retrieved the most recent copy of "The Guinness Book of World Records". He held it like a prize over his head, and then he bolted back out the front door.

Ryan slowly turned to look at his mother and raised one eyebrow in her direction.

"Well, maybe it is a little crazy," she agreed.

***

Inside Grafton Falls Hospital, Susan sat by Lily's bed watching her sleep off a rough morning. The hours following her chemo treatment had been spent vomiting and shaking uncontrollably.

It was during these times Susan felt most helpless. The only thing she could do for her daughter was hold her head while she got sick and give her a cool face cloth for her forehead.

When Lily was well enough, Susan could guide her in prayer. Now she prayed alone while she watched her daughter fight for her life. The more time Lily spent sleeping, however, the more Susan felt like even her prayers weren't enough.

She promised herself back in the early stages that she would never cry in front of Lily. She didn't want her daughter wasting her precious energy worrying about anything besides getting better. As all these thoughts ran through her head, the tears she had swallowed down too many times burned in her throat. Despite her strongest efforts, Susan felt her eyes fill up, and she knew it was time for her to leave.

When she got up and grabbed her coat from the back of the chair, Lily's eyes fluttered open.

"Mom?" she squeaked out weakly.

Susan blinked back her tears.

"Yes sweetie, I'm here," said Susan. "Do you need anything? Some water maybe?"

Lily shook her head no and winced at the thought of anything in her stomach.

"Oh, okay. I was just leaving, but I can stay longer if you need me to?"

Lily's eyes began to sink with the weight of exhaustion as sleep threatened to reclaim her into the quiet darkness. Susan knew her daughter would only be awake for a few minutes, but these minutes were becoming fewer and further in between, so she took a seat and sat with her.

Susan closed her eyes and began to pray for strength for herself and her child. A moment later, Lily's voice interrupted the whispered prayers.

"Actually, there is something you could do."

"Of course dear, what do you need?"

"Can you just talk to Emily? Please?" Lily whispered.

"Um, yeah, sure, of course," Susan replied.

Susan's answer came too quickly and too easily to convince Lily.

"No, I mean like *really* talk to her. She's here, and she's making an effort to be back in our lives, ya know?"

"Oh honey, you shouldn't waste your energy worrying about things like that. You just need to focus on getting better."

Lily's brows furrowed and worry filled her pale blue eyes. She parted her lips and leaned forward to say something, but a violent coughing fit took her breath. Lily fell back onto her pillow and closed her eyes, her words temporarily forgotten.

"This is exactly why it is a bad idea for Emily to be here right now," Susan said with a heavy sigh.

Lily looked up at her mother with big wet eyes.

"If not now, when?" she croaked.

"Enough, Lily. I'm not getting into this with you. You shouldn't be wasting your strength on it either. Besides, I think we both know it's only a matter of time before she breezes out of town and back to wherever it is she's been living."

Lily closed her eyes. She was too weak to argue. In the fading light, she saw of all three of them playing in the park. It had been a cool autumn day, probably just like this one, she thought. Her mother had packed them a picnic, and they had played Frisbee until the sun went down. As the image faded to darkness, Lily wondered if she'd ever see another day when they were all together again.

"Get some rest, Lily. I'll check on you again later."

Once Susan was in the hospital corridor, she let the tears, which had been threatening to break loose, run freely down her pale cheeks. Too weak to stand against the flood of emotions that drove through her, Susan slid down the wall and held her head in her hands.

She struggled against the condemning voices that sounded inside her mind. The inner critic said she had failed to raise her first daughter properly, and now she couldn't even keep the youngest one alive. She couldn't help but agree.

Susan forced her mind back to a happier place; a place when she had been doing a good job as a mother — a place where all three of them where happy together.

She had taken the girls to the lake while Steve was away on a business trip. She and Emily were trying fruitlessly to teach Lily how to swim all summer. Now, in the late days of August, they were once again taking turns trying to teach Lily how to swim. Lily wore little pink floats on her arms but didn't have faith in their ability to keep her from sinking. She refused to let go of Susan's hands, and Susan wasn't tough enough to make her.

However, when it was Emily's turn, she took an unexpected step away from Lily as soon as she had her feet kicking in a good momentum. The look on Lily's face was unforgettable, shifting from shock, to worry, and then finally to amazement as she realized she was swimming. Emily paused and let her sister close the short gap between them.

"I swam, Mummy! Did you see me swam??" Lily had cried excitedly.

"I did sweetheart. You did so good!"

She and Emily shared a look of proud accomplishment. Later, on the ride home, Susan used the last of her pocket change to buy them ice cream. When Lily was fully engaged in licking her scoop of strawberry ice cream from her cone, Susan looked over at Emily, who gingerly scooped away at the contents of her hot fudge sundae.

"You did a really good job teaching Lily how to swim today," she said. "I'm so proud of both of you."

Emily looked up from her frozen treat and smiled at her mother, really smiled. As hard as Susan tried, she couldn't remember any time after that when Emily had smiled at her. It made Susan's heart ache for the daughter she had been missing for the last seven years.

She thought again about Lily's request. Her weak little voice rang in her head. *Can you just talk to her, please? If not now, when?*

Susan took a couple deep breaths and wiped the tears from her eyes. Then, somewhere inside her, she found the strength to stand up and walk through another day.

13

Black Sky Blue

"It don't matter where you go - It just matters where you stay
I would never claim to know - All the secret cards you hold
It's a case that leaves no clues - It's dangerous how I dream of you
Since you turned my black sky blue"

Later that afternoon, back at the Corbin residence, Ryan was exiting the house with his guitar in hand. Before he reached the bottom porch step, a voice from behind stopped him.

"You got another big concert at the drive-in tonight?" Emily asked.

She was catching the last rays of sun in a hammock on the far end of the porch. Her red and black plaid skirt flapped gently in the breeze as she rocked back and forth. Ryan wasn't sure what surprised him more, the fact that she wore another color besides solid black or that she was actually outside of her apartment.

"Yeah, something like that," Ryan chuckled. "You look comfy."

"Yeah, I guess I kinda am. It's like, so peaceful here. I can actually hear myself think, ya know?"

Emily moved her heavily ringed fingers over her forehead as if trying to touch her thoughts.

"And what do you think about when you can hear yourself think?" Ryan asked.

Emily was about to fire off a snarky sarcastic remark but just sighed. Before Ryan turned to go, his eyes focused on the book in

Emily's hand. It was the new Stephen King novel. Knowing she was busted, Emily smiled and guiltily shrugged.

"Ok, fine, I like Stephen King. Are you happy?"

Ryan smirked and gestured *a little bit* with his fingers.

"Well, don't let me interrupt your reading," Ryan said turning to leave.

"What's there to do for fun around here, anyway?" asked Emily.

Ryan stopped and turned back around.

"Here in Pine Ridge? Well, there's the Road House Tavern in town."

"Yeah, I saw that place, but it looks…"

Emily didn't want to say it looked like Hicksville Central, but the exterior of the tavern had sported picnic tables adorned with Budweiser umbrellas and a wooden statue of a lumberjack holding an ax. The sound of country music spilled out into a parking lot, which was filled with oversized mud splattered trucks. Most of which towed a four-wheeler inside its bed or behind it on a trailer. One glance told Emily she would feel a bit out of place there.

"Redneckish?" Ryan finished her sentence for her.

"You said it, not me!" Emily laughed. "Is that your hang out?"

"Nah, I'm actually not into the bar scene much anymore. Sometimes on Wednesday nights, Danny and I go bowling… or sometimes we just go to The Strand Theater in Grafton Falls. They show a lot of old classics."

Emily chuckled. How quaint, she thought.

"You're laughing at me aren't you?"

"I am totally laughing at you."

"Well, I would love to stick around and get made fun of, but I have a drive-in full of imaginary fans to play for."

"Knock 'em dead there, rock star!" Emily called after him.

Halfway down the driveway, Ryan paused and headed back.

"Hey, I just thought of something else to do around here.

Something you might actually like," he said.

Emily raised an eyebrow at him.

"Oh yeah? What's that? Bingo night at the community center with the clan from the Lakeview Retirement Home?"

"Just go get your camera and a jacket and I'll show you."

Emily was intrigued at the mention of being able to use her camera, so she put down her book and headed up to the apartment to gather her things. Ryan also headed back inside for a few last minute provisions.

"Oh, and put some pants on!" he shouted up to her as she disappeared into the apartment. Emily smiled at the irony. It was the first time a guy had told her to put her pants *on*.

***

With just a few hours of daylight left, they traveled down the back roads of Pine Ridge. The sun cast long dark shadows of the pine trees over the pavement. By the time the road turned to gravel, the sunlight was almost swallowed up completely. With the warmth of the sun gone, Emily pulled her bomber jacket tightly around her.

"Is this where you take all your victims before you kill them?" Emily asked.

"Kill them?" Ryan asked. "No, I just keep 'em locked up in a basement somewhere."

"Hey, you never know. After all, this is Stephen King country."

"Technically, Stephen King country is over in Bangor."

"Technically, I wasn't being technical," Emily remarked. "But seriously, where the hell are you taking me?"

Ryan eased the truck over onto the shoulder of the road. Emily looked around, but she couldn't see anything other than trees. Not even a single cabin was in sight.

"Ready?" Ryan asked as he reached for the cab door.

"Ready for what? Armageddon?"

"Just get out. We're almost there. We have to go the rest of the way on foot."

Emily got out of the truck and saw Ryan waiting for her at the head of an almost nonexistent trail.

"Gee, if I wanted to get this creeped out, I would have just stayed home and kept reading that Stephen King book," Emily muttered as she joined him.

Ryan just looked over his shoulder and smiled at her. He was too excited about what he was going to show her to counter her sarcasm.

After walking for about ten minutes, Emily began to wonder if the only thing this town had to offer was hidden paths in the woods. Finally, they came to a clearing that opened up onto a bog.

The sky opened up and Emily could see the first pastel hues of twilight starting to form along the horizon. Tall wheat colored grass swayed happily above patches of deep blue water that stretched out for miles around them. A great blue heron flew over their heads and landed in a nearby patch of marsh.

Ryan watched Emily's mouth drop open. Without taking her eyes off the bird, she silently grappled for her camera. Ryan slowly took a seat on a large fallen tree covered in moss. He watched Emily snapping shots rapidly all around them.

Eventually, she was satisfied and slowly walked over to where Ryan sat and joined him. They sat in a comfortable silence for a long moment before Emily started to fidget and grew a little anxious.

"So, now what?" she asked.

Ryan shrugged.

"We sit. Maybe talk. And wait for more nature to happen."

"You mean wait for nature to take its course?" Emily asked defensively. "If you think I came all the way out here so you could try to put the moves on me…"

"Whoa, chill out. I'm not gonna put the moves on you. Geesh.

Are you always this paranoid?"

"Well, why wouldn't I be paranoid?" Emily asked. "I'm deep in the woods, sitting on a dead tree and staring out over a swamp – an ominous swamp at that, and..."

"Technically, it's a bog, not a swamp," Ryan corrected.

Emily rolled her eyes but decided not to argue with Mr. Technically. Ryan unzipped his back pack and pulled out a thermos and two mugs.

"Coffee?" he asked.

Emily took one of the mugs hesitantly. She wasn't sure if she should be worried or grateful. Usually, when guys did something thoughtful, they wanted something in return, she thought. Either that, or they were up to no good.

"Did you roofie it?" she asked eyeing the thermos suspiciously.

He shrugged and smiled as he poured himself a mug and took a big sip. Emily held her own empty mug out tentatively. Pleased, Ryan filled her mug as well.

"How's Lily doing?" he asked.

"Okay, I guess. It's hard to tell. She looks so weak and fragile, but whenever I visit, a smile never leaves her face. She's like the sweetest, most upbeat person in the world. Her whole world could be falling apart and she would smile through it all."

"And you two are related?" Ryan asked incredulously.

"She's my half-sister," Emily offered.

"I was just kidding, but that actually makes more sense now."

"You're right, though. We are complete opposites. Just ask my mom."

"You and your mom really don't get along, do you?"

"Nope. Not in a long, long time."

"What happened to you two?"

Ryan could tell by the look on Emily's face he was treading into dangerous territory. He got the distinct impression she hadn't told anyone what happened. She just kept it to herself all this time and never opened up to anyone about it. Ryan knew what shouldering a burden like that alone did to a person.

"I really don't want to get into it, okay?"

Her response was better than what he braced himself for. At least his question was met with honesty and not a wall of defensive sarcasm. He nodded in quiet acknowledgement, and they sat in silence watching the sky slowly turn into varying shades of gold.

Ryan began to wonder if Emily's relationship with her father was any better. She never mentioned him, but that didn't necessarily mean there was bad blood there too. Surely, she must have someone that was close to her.

"So where does your dad live?" Ryan asked.

Emily shot him a warning look. She was trying to be social, but if he was going to keep prying into her personal life this little outing wasn't going to end well.

"Fine, I'll shut up," Ryan said, holding his hands up in a forfeiting gesture.

Satisfied with his answer, Emily nodded, but she still felt the need to put some distance between them. She got up and went to inspect the water's edge, hoping to catch a glimpse of some gleaming pebbles or maybe a fish passing by.

Instead, her attention was caught by some subtle movement on the water's surface. When she looked closer, she saw a family of turtles swimming toward her. She grabbed her camera and snapped some shots. Careful not to make any sudden movements or sounds, she waited patiently for them to approach. As the mother turtle crawled ashore with her babies in tow, Emily took a few more pictures.

She looked back at Ryan, who was smiling at her, and she decided to rejoin him on the log. She actually liked talking to him, but a conversation regarding personal information was something she was unaccustomed to. Even Amanda never really asked her any sensitive questions, but maybe that was just a stripper code of conduct. She figured if Ryan wanted to get personal, he would have to lead by example.

"So, whatever happened to that Tanya chick?" she asked as she sat down next to him.

Ryan shrugged and said, "We pretty much lost all contact when I left town. When I finally figured out my dreams weren't going to come true in New York, and moved back here to Pine Ridge, I decided to make it my mission to get her back."

"Oh, this ought to be good," Emily said as she leaned closer.

"A friend of mine told me she was living a few towns over in Hutchington, so I bought the biggest, most beautiful bouquet of flowers and drove over there. I was determined to find her and win her back. I even wore a tie."

"And you actually thought that would work?" Emily scoffed.

"What? Of course I did! It was a good plan... so I thought."

"You chose a band over her, and you thought flowers and a tie were going to win her back?" Emily asked with an arched eyebrow.

"Well, when you say it like that... yeah, I guess it sounds lame," Ryan admitted. "But I had a speech planned too! It was a really good speech... and the flowers, they were really expensive ones."

Emily couldn't help but smile at his naïve sincerity. *Small town boy thinks love happens in real life like it does on the big screen,* she thought. She almost said it out loud, but she kept it to herself.

"Go on," she coaxed.

"Well, I wasn't in Hutchington for more than five minutes when I spotted her walking down the sidewalk. Apparently, my idiot friend left out a couple of major details. First one being: the major rock on her finger. She was engaged. The second, and even more shocking detail, was..."

Unable to bring himself to say the words, Ryan held out is hands like he was cradling a ball in front of his stomach. Emily was never very good at charades, but she chanced a guess.

"She got fat?"

Ryan laughed. He should have known Emily wouldn't make it easy for him.

"No. She was pregnant. She was engaged and pregnant."

Emily's eyes popped wide at the double injury to poor Ryan's rock star pride.

"Yikes! So what did you say to her?" Emily asked.

"I didn't say anything. I didn't even get out of my car. She looked happy… like really happy. I knew then that I totally had blown it. I'd been chasing happiness in all the wrong places. I drove into Grafton Falls and stopped at the lookout point above the waterfalls. When I looked in the back seat, I saw the flowers still sitting there. I was so upset I got out and chucked them into the falls."

"I'm sorry. That sucks," Emily offered. "I mean, it was kinda your own fault, but it still sucks."

Ryan nodded solemnly.

A thick, heavy, fog began to creep across the bog like steam filling up a locker room. A silence settled over them. When Emily spoke again, her voice came in a hushed tone to match the change in atmosphere.

"That song you were playing the other night, is that the type of music your band played?"

"God no," Ryan answered. "We were more of a cross between The Pixies and Pantera. I guess most of our stuff was kinda loud and angry."

"My ex is in a band. Of course, his is a cross between loud feedback and utter shit."

Ryan chuckled.

"I like to think we weren't that bad."

"I'm sure you weren't. Five years is a pretty good run doing what you love."

"Technically, our band only lasted two and a half years before we fizzled out. And by fizzled out, I mean, we were at each other's throats. Two years of living off Mac & Cheese, Ramen Noodles, and Natty Light will do that to you."

Emily nodded and said, "Been there, done that."

"Not coincidentally, our last gig was also our lowest point. We played at this tiny, rundown shit-hole in Newark. Let's just say, our band outnumbered the audience. Of course, that didn't stop the three drunken idiots from requesting 'Freebird' seventeen times."

"Ah yes, the drunken bar crowd anthem."

"Yup. Anyway, a week later our lead singer moved to Cali with some chick he met. At first, we attempted to put ads out for a new singer, but it was pretty obvious that we were done. We all knew it, but none of us wanted to be the first to say it. We all had day jobs already to pay the bills, and those quickly turned into night jobs. Before we knew it, we had traded our dream for a time clock without ever really realizing it."

"At that point, why didn't you just come back home?" Emily asked. "Even Pine Ridge has to be better than Jersey."

"I guess I was just embarrassed, or maybe I was just too proud to admit I had failed."

"Ryan, a lot of great bands don't make it big. In fact, most don't."

"I know, I just thought we'd be different. I was actually so embarrassed about my failure, I continued bragging to my family about how well the band was doing. I made up stories and told them we had to turn down gigs because we were so popular. That's sounds pathetic, doesn't it?"

Ryan kicked at a tuft of grass at their feet.

Emily shrugged.

"It was like, the more I lied, and the longer I stayed away, the harder it was to come back home. Does that make any sense?" Ryan asked.

"Yeah, actually it does," Emily said quietly.

It made perfect sense to her. The first few months after she left home, she thought about going back often. However, the more time that went by where neither one of them made an effort to communicate, the distance between them just got bigger and harder to cover. Before she knew it, she stopped thinking about her mother altogether, Lily too. It was just easier to pretend they didn't exist than to admit she had made such a devastating mistake.

"Until a few months ago, I hadn't even picked up a guitar in four years. It's kinda cheesy, but when I picked it up again, it was like reuniting with an old friend. Except this time, it was different. I was no longer angry, or depressed, or looking to be the next big thing. I could just sit here and enjoy playing. I've actually been thinking about playing over at the Road House Tavern on Open Mic Night, but... well, I guess I'm just not there yet."

"So that's why you go down to the drive-in and pretend?"

"Yeah, pretty stupid, right?"

Before Emily could answer, she was startled by a loud shuffling coming from the bush a couple hundred feet away. The branches snapped and crunched under the weight of something enormous. Emily thought they were about to get run out by a group of angry land owners for trespassing. Then she remembered they were in bear country. She frantically tried to recite the brown bear black bear rule, but she couldn't concentrate. The longer she listened to the noise growing steadily louder, the more her mind raced. Was there really such a thing as Big Foot?

She grabbed Ryan's arm, terrified of whatever was approaching. He looked at her anxiously, but he wasn't afraid. He would have put his arm around her to comfort her, but she had a death lock on his bicep, so he just patted her leg in a manner he would have used to steady a frightened child. They both leaned forward on the log and focused their attention in the direction of the disturbance.

The first thing Emily saw was four long dark poles. She then looked up and saw they were legs attached to a moose. Her eyes widened and her merlot lips parted. She wasn't sure if she was going to faint or scream. Then Ryan smiled at her, and all her fear melted away.

"Holy shit balls! It's a moose! And he's fucking huge!" Emily cried.

They watched the moose walk gracefully through the bog. It paused and looked around but didn't seem to notice them on the log. A moment later, it lowered its massive antlers into the water and took a long drink. When it pulled its head up again, green swamp grass dangled from its antlers. Water ran from its face and rained into the pool below casting out ripples all around it.

"Emily, get your camera," Ryan said.

His voice snapped Emily out of her spell. She looked at him blankly as if she had forgotten the English language.

"Camera," Ryan said again, more urgently.

Emily blinked. Holy hell, he was right! She needed to get a picture of this, she thought. She quickly reached for her camera, and with shaking hands, she brought the camera up to look through the lens. Then, as a new thought took hold in her mind, she lowered the camera and looked at Ryan.

"Do moose eat people?" she asked in a frightened whisper.

Ryan grinned at her and whispered, "No more Stephen King for you."

She took a deep breath to steady herself and then she began snapping shots. She snapped the moose sniffing a water lily. Then she took more shots, as it carefully pulled off its leaves, making a snack out of them one by one. The moose periodically raised its head to look around, and when it looked in their direction, Emily was able to capture the perfect shot of him staring right at them. She lowered the camera and looked at Ryan in amazement.

"It just flared its nostrils at me!" she cried in an excited whisper.

When Ryan looked at her questioningly with a raised eyebrow, she demonstrated.

"Like this," she said.

Ryan watched in wonder as Emily flared her nostrils at him. He didn't even know people could do that. More than that, he didn't know Emily had a silly side. He laughed at her childlike demeanor.

When the moose had its fill of leaves and began to saunter back into the woods, Emily snapped one last shot. The moose glanced over its shoulder before disappearing into the bush.

After a short moment of silence, Emily turned to Ryan.

"That was amazing! I've never seen a moose before!" she whispered enthusiastically.

"Really? I couldn't tell." Ryan answered.

Emily gave him a playful slap on the arm.

"You mean they don't have those in Boston?" Ryan continued to chide her.

"Hey, I thought I was supposed to be the sarcastic one?"

"Well I can't let you have all the fun all the time," Ryan said.

The golden rays from the setting sun quickly faded into darker shades of pinks and blues. The fog continued to gather around them creating a chilling effect.

"Well, we should get going. It'll be pitch black out here soon."

Emily nodded in agreement. Ryan started to pack up the coffee, and Emily followed his lead by packing up her camera gear.

As they were walking back to the truck, Emily's cheeks began to ache. It took her a minute to realize her facial muscles were feeling the repercussions of smiling more in the last hour than she had the entire year.

On the bumpy truck ride home, Ryan and Emily shared a comfortable silence in the cab. Emily was grateful for this. She had a lot of thoughts running through her head that needed to be processed. Mostly, she was quite surprised at how much she enjoyed their little excursion. If Ryan had told her that he was taking her to a bog where they would sit on a log and watch nature, he probably would have had to drag her there kicking and screaming. She thought it was a clever play on his part for making it a surprise, but she was starting to feel Ryan, unlike most guys, didn't make clever plays. He was just an all-around sincere guy, who maybe just wanted to be her friend.

That was the other thing that surprised Emily. She had never hung out alone with a guy that didn't try to put the moves on her. She started to rethink her initial impression of Ryan being a typical college frat boy.

Maybe Ryan was just trying to be a friend to her all along. A wave of guilt washed over her as she realized the only thing she did in return was hold him off with a ten foot stick. He never once dodged any of her questions like she ducked and dodged almost all of his. In fact, he was nothing but sincere with her since day one. Emily bit her lip as she tried to bite back the feelings of culpability. How could she have been so aloof to the only people she had ever known that were actually trying to show her sincere kindness?

Sincere kindness. Was that actually a real thing or something that only existed in Disney movies? Emily shoved the last thought aside. She would save that one for later.

For now, she just wanted to try and show Ryan some of the same qualities he had shown her. She wanted to show him that she could let somebody get to know her and that she wasn't just a cold black hole. Before she knew what she was going to say, she heard the words coming from her mouth.

"I never knew my biological father. He bolted when my mom told him she was pregnant. All I know of him is age-wise he was five years older than my mother, but maturity-wise he was probably a lot younger."

Ryan looked over at her in shock. He couldn't believe she was actually divulging personal information without being prompted. He decided not to say anything but nodded his head to show he was listening.

"Between working so much and raising me, my mom didn't have much of a social life. Instead of going out with her friends on her twenty-first birthday, she spent the night cuddling with me on the couch. I was only three, but I totally remember that night. I had a fever. She didn't want to leave me with a sitter, so we watched The Little Mermaid and ate soup with crackers."

A thoughtful rumble sounded from Ryan's throat, but he didn't say anything. He felt if he stayed calm and quiet she would go on. He kept his eyes on the darkened road but listened intently.

"As bad as her social life was, her dating life was even worse. Don't get me wrong, she went on plenty of first dates – but not so many second ones. She always told me it was because she knew right away that they weren't right for her. When I got older, I figured out that had just been a nice way of saying none of them wanted to deal with a chick that came with a built in family."

Emily paused. She was thinking about all the sacrifices her mother had made for her. She wondered if she would have still made those sacrifices if she knew then what kind of failure Emily was going to turn out to be. She sighed heavily and stared out the passenger side window into the darkness.

Ryan's gentle voice brought her back to the conversation.

"But eventually she did meet someone, right? Lily's dad?"

Emily nodded and continued her story.

"When I was five, she went on her first date with Steve. Not only did the date go really well, but Steve was totally unfazed that she already had a kid. They were married a year later. Lily came soon after. I remember being so excited. I had always wanted a little sister.

In fact, I think I had even asked Santa for one the year before."

Ryan took his eyes off the road long enough to share a smile with Emily.

"Anyway, they ended up buying a house together, and not only did I have a baby sister, I had my very own bedroom all to myself. It was a pretty big deal not to have to have to sleep in the living room anymore. Another bonus was Steve had a good enough job that my mother could quit one of her two jobs, so she was around a lot more. In a lot of ways, Steve was the best thing that happened to us."

"It sounds pretty perfect," said Ryan.

"Yeah, that's what I thought too. Of course, it took me six years to realize the two big truths in life."

Ryan braced himself. He already knew Emily's idea of life truths was a little crooked, but he didn't want to know just how bad it was.

"There's no such thing as the Boogie Man, and the General Tso Chicken isn't always chicken?" Ryan asked hopefully.

Emily whipped her head around and looked at him. She was too worked up to even acknowledge his attempt at humor.

"What? No! The two big truths are: Nothing perfect or even remotely good ever lasts… and all guys are dick weasels."

Ryan winced. He knew it was going to sting, but he wasn't quite prepared for that last one. He concluded that Steve must have had an affair and things went south from there. Emily continued her story and validated his assumption.

"You know what the worst part was? It wasn't the fact that he cheated, it was my mother's reaction to it. She knew the whole time and never once called him out on it. As a matter of fact, it was Steve who finally approached her and informed her that not only had he been having an affair for the past year, but he was also leaving her."

"Wow, that's pretty harsh," Ryan said.

"I was only thirteen, but I remember being so fucking pissed at him… at what he did to my mother… to our whole family! The saddest part was I was the only one pissed at him for it. Lily was only six, so she really didn't understand what was going on."

"I'm sure your mother must have been rip-shit at him, no?"

"Not only was she not rip-shit at him, she begged him to stay. She literally begged him not to leave her."

Emily looked down at her hands and saw she was shaking. She paused long enough to take a deep breath and steady herself. When she continued, her voice had taken on a softer tone.

"Up until then, I thought she was the strongest most independent woman I knew. When I overheard her begging him to stay, I lost all respect for her. It's like I spent my whole life looking up to her only to find out she wasn't who I thought she was at all. She was just like all the other pathetic women out there that let men like him walk all over her."

As soon as she heard the words come out of her mouth, Emily felt like a hypocrite. She knew that she too had let plenty of men walk all over her. Sometimes standing up for yourself wasn't as easy as everyone else thought it should be. She thought of Chloe and Amanda urging her to leave Eric. She wondered if they thought she was weak and pathetic for staying with him for so long. Ryan's voice broke her thoughts.

"Maybe she didn't beg him to stay for her. Maybe she wanted him to stay for you and Lily. Sometimes, being strong means being selfless."

Emily slowly turned to look at Ryan. He couldn't tell by the dimly lit cab whether she was plotting his death or considering his words.

"Sorry, it's none of my business," he offered.

"No, it's okay. You're right. Unfortunately, I didn't realize until years later, but yeah, that's exactly why she did it. By that time, it didn't matter anymore. At the time it happened, I was thirteen and I thought I knew it all, but the truth was I was still just a stupid immature teenager."

Emily shook her head in self-disgust then continued.

"My mother knew things I didn't at the time. Like a divorce would have consequences. It would have been easier to stay in a loveless marriage than to be forced to move back into a small apartment that she had to work two jobs to afford. Most of all, it would mean risk losing Lily or maybe even both of us. Steve made way more money than she did, and if it got ugly and went to court, a judge might grant full custody to him."

"I can see why she would feel that way," Ryan said. "So did he? Get custody?"

"No," Emily quietly said. "She kept custody of us. But they ended up selling the house, and she was forced to move into a tiny two bedroom apartment. She was also forced to go back to working day and night. The worst part was my mother had the nerve to try and make me go with Lily on her weekend visits with Steve."

"Did you?" asked Ryan.

"Hell no!" Emily cried. "He wasn't my father. Besides, I looked at his offer to take me on weekends as a pity offering. It made me even more furious. I told him I would rather have no father at all than a piece of shit like him."

"You said that to him?" Ryan asked incredulously.

"Yeah, I did," Emily answered. "Obviously, my mom was just trying to keep us sisters together, but I was so mad I couldn't see the logic."

Emily paused, and when she spoke again, her voice was heavy with regret.

"I had no right being so mad though."

"Of course you did, that was the second time you got cheated out of a father. I would have been pissed too," Ryan offered.

Emily paused to consider Ryan's words. She had never looked at it like that before. His perspective made it a little easier to forgive herself.

"I shouldn't have directed all my anger at my mother. It wasn't her fault the douche cheated and left her. She was just trying to do the best she could in a shitty situation. Either way, that was the beginning of the end of our relationship. Everything just got worse from that point forward."

Ryan waited patiently for Emily to continue, but instead, she just looked out the window silently. He sensed there was a lot more to the story, but he accepted that this was where she apparently wanted to end it. If she wanted to tell him more, he knew it had to be on her own terms, so he didn't press for more.

The fact that she opened up and shared any personal information with him at all, left Ryan equally at a loss of words. He pulled the truck into the parking lot of The Road House Tavern and looked inquisitively at Emily.

Emily arched her eyebrow and shot him a disbelieving look.

"You've got to be kidding?" she asked.

"Come on, give it a chance! They've got wings to die for! You might just like it."

Unable to deny her stomach had begun rumbling ten minutes ago, Emily rolled her eyes and hopped out of the truck. She had no intention of ordering the wings though.

14

Feelings Without Weight

"I've been fading for so long I'm lost completely
I long to just get washed out in the waves
And feel the ocean floor fall out beneath me.
Feelings without weight"

In the midst of the fall weather, summer returned for one last appearance. People in town were throwing around the term *Indian Summer*, and the hum of window air conditioning units could be heard throughout town.

In the backyard of the Corbin residence, a gathering of family and friends had formed. Emily found a quiet place on the sidelines under the shade of a large oak tree. She watched Ryan's family members interact with each other while intermittently sketching in her sketch pad. She listened with interest to the pieces of various conversations that floated back to her.

Harold, Gus, and Max were huddled around the grill discussing the history of red hot dogs. Emily never heard of red hot dogs before, and she was skeptically curious about them.

"Everyone knows the red snapper hot dog was invented in Bangor Maine, but why do you suppose they made the casings red and not blue?" asked Harold.

"What kind of fool would eat blue meat?" Gus answered.

"I once ate a blueberry burger on a dare," Max said.

"You'd eat anything if it had ketchup on it," Harold said.

"All I know is they made the casing red to set them apart from all the other hot dog makers and it worked!" Max said.

Ryan and Jake were making small talk on the front porch steps. Even if Ryan hadn't told Emily that Jake was a lawyer, it wouldn't have been hard to guess by his appearance. Jake was the only one wearing neatly pressed khakis with a button up collar shirt tucked neatly into the waist. His hair was slicked back with gel, which kept every strand of his dark brown hair perfectly in place. However, it was his picture-perfect smile that gave away his profession. Only a lawyer could have a smile like that, Emily thought.

"Why didn't Beth come up with you?" Ryan asked him.

"She's actually working a flight to China as we speak."

"I could never be a flight attendant. I don't know how she does it," Ryan said.

"She loves it," said Jake. "Besides, it keeps her mind off Jake Jr. Even though he has one of the safest jobs in the army, she can't help but worry, especially with him being deployed to Iraq again."

Lacey, Claire, and Claire's teenage daughter, Jennifer, helped Joan set the picnic table. They were all being careful to avoid the subject of Claire's current divorce proceedings.

"How are you doing with your new students this year?" Joan asked Claire.

"Oh, they seem to be adapting well. There is always some initial confusion as they get used to the new building and new class structure, but they are all doing really well. Middle school is such a big shift from elementary school. It takes at least a month for the kids to fully get settled in. Routine is the key."

"That makes sense," said Lacey. "That's exactly what I tell the new waitresses I train at the restaurant. Once you have a routine then everything falls into place. I just wish dating was that easy!"

Joan and Claire laughed.

"Still no luck finding Mr. Right?" Joan asked her daughter.

"That's because she's too busy enjoying Mr. Right Now," said Claire playfully.

"There's no harm in playing the field a little," Lacey said defensively.

"There's a difference between playing the field a little and going to the championships," Claire said.

Emily's lips curled against a smile, and she made herself tune out of that conversation. She shifted her attention to Claire's twelve year old son, Adam, who was shooting hoops in the driveway with Danny. They were currently playing H-O-R-S-E and Danny was losing with a smile.

This was the first time in years she had attended a family event. She had never actually witnessed a family that was this close. She always thought families like this only existed in movies. Search as she might, she didn't find any arguments or ill feelings in any corner of the Corbin family.

"Horse!!" Adam shouted out.

Emily watched with an amused smile as he began a victory dance in circles around Danny. Danny waved him off and wandered over to where Ryan and Jake sat on the porch. Adam just shrugged and continued to shoot hoops by himself.

"So, tell me Ryan, does it feel weird on your pecker when you're doing it?" Jake asked with his eyes nailed onto Emily.

"What are you talking about?" Ryan asked.

"You know, I heard Goth Girl has her who-ha pierced," Jake explained.

"Emily got shot with a BB gun," Danny offered.

Jake looked at Danny in bewilderment then back to Ryan.

"She didn't get shot with a BB gun, Danny," Ryan said.

Danny looked over to Jake and smiled, "Shot with a BB gun."

"Look, I wouldn't know anything about her who-ha. We're just friends — and barely that, I think," Ryan explained.

"Brother, you should be tapping that every chance you get," said Jake. "She's a hottie. In a freakish kind of way, but definitely a hottie."

"Tap that? Hottie?" Ryan asked. "Seriously? When was the last time you got laid? 1988?"

"Hell no! It has been awhile though… at least a month now. Beth is like a damn sex camel."

"What?!" Ryan asked.

"You know, camels can go like a month without water. Beth is just like that… except with sex," Jake explained.

Ryan shook his head at his older brother. Danny laughed and started singing.

"Sex camel, sex camel, Beth is a sex camel."

Ryan and Jake exchanged a look of alarm and then both of them started laughing. Jake put his arm around Danny and pulled him in for a hug.

"I bet *you* don't have any trouble with the ladies, do ya Danny?" Jake asked. "Maybe you could give our little bro here some pointers. That is, unless, he likes beating off every night?"

Ryan was well-versed in Jake's relentless teasing, but he still found himself getting flushed with anger and embarrassment.

Danny noticed this and blurted out, "Don't…. don't be a douche canoe, Jake."

Ryan and Jake both gaped at Danny with open jaws. Ryan was the first to burst out laughing.

"Douche canoe??" he asked through tears. "Where did you learn that one?"

Danny just smiled and glanced at Emily.

Claire and Lacey noticed Emily sitting by herself and wandered over to keep her company. Lacey offered Emily a plastic cup filled with pink lemonade.

"Thanks," Emily said and accepted the drink.

Lacey and Claire each sat down on either side of Emily. Lacey peered over Emily's shoulder at her sketch pad and saw a detailed drawing of Ryan sitting on the porch steps.

"That's pretty good," Lacey said.

Emily looked down at her drawing but didn't say anything.

"Did he tell you he used to be in a band?" Lacey asked.

"Yeah. It was totally a boy band, wasn't it?" Emily asked.

"By the way he looks now, you would think so, but you should have seen him back in high school. He dressed in black every day of the week and even wore eye liner on special occasions!" Lacey said.

"Yeah, he looked like the poster child for Sad and Gothy," Claire added.

Emily looked down self-consciously at her long black skirt and black tank top. Claire immediately realized she had inserted her foot into her mouth.

"Oh, no offense, Emily," Claire said quickly. "On you, it looks very cool. On Ryan, not so much. You should have seen him when he was going through his Cure/Depeche Mode phase. His hair was all moussed up and drooping down over his eyes. He looked like an unwanted pound puppy."

They all laughed. Emily would have never guessed Ryan had ever strayed from his rugged prep boy look.

"Now look at him," said Lacey. "He looks like an L.L. Bean poster child."

They all stopped to watch Ryan swipe his shaggy long bangs out of his eyes. When he stood, his red and gray flannel button-up hung snuggly on his broad frame and laid perfectly over his faded blue jeans. They all let their eyes settle on the L.L. Bean hiking sneakers he wore. It was true, he looked like a walking L.L. Bean advertisement, Emily thought.

"Where is this L.L. Bean anyway?" Emily asked.

Both Claire and Lacey exchanged looks.

"We really need to do a shopping trip with you sometime, Emily," Lacey said.

Emily looked concerned.

"Don't worry, they have black clothes there," Lacey said and patted Emily's knee.

Just then, Joan called over to them.

"Girls, we are ready for the salads. Can you grab them from the fridge and bring them out now?"

"Okay Mom!" Lacey called.

"Let's go," Claire said to Lacey.

"We'll be right back," Lacey said to Emily.

Lacey and Claire disappeared inside the farmhouse leaving Emily free to return to her sketch book.

Ryan noticed a mischievous smirk on Lacey's face as her and Claire passed him on the porch, but he didn't think much of it. He was more interested in Jake's offer to take Danny out that night.

"I hear the old Strand Theater is showing 80's flicks all week, Danny, and guess what tonight's double feature is?"

"What?" Danny asked.

"Ferris Bueller and Say Anything!" Jake replied excitedly.

Danny looked down at his t-shirt, which depicted John Cusack holding a stereo over his head. A huge smile spread across his face.

"Really, Jake?? Can we go??" Danny asked.

"You bet, buddy!" Jake answered and slapped Danny on the shoulder.

Danny started to bounce happily on his toes.

"Bueller, Bueller Bueller!" Danny shouted in an imitation from the movie.

They all laughed and the girls clapped.

"Do another one," Jake prompted.

Danny paused for a moment and thought hard. Then his face lit up.

"I gave her my heart… and she gave me a pen," Danny recited, then fired off another Say Anything quote. "If you start out depressed, everything's a pleasant surprise."

"Ha! I've missed you and your movie quotes, Danny. You coming with us tonight?" Jake asked Ryan.

"Thanks, but I think I'll pass," answered Ryan.

"Ah, I get it. You're going to try and finally bag Vampira! I like the way you roll bro," said Jake.

"You like the way I roll? Bag Vampira?? How old are you exactly?" Ryan mocked.

Jake just winked at him in response.

Claire passed them carrying a bowl of various salads to the picnic table. Lacey followed close behind clutching a handful of photographs.

Once the salad bowls had been properly distributed across the picnic tables, Lacey grabbed Claire by the wrist and pulled her down to sit at one of the picnic tables next to Joan.

"Emily come on over," Lacey shouted.

Emily looked up from her sketch book to see Lacey waving her over to where the other women sat at the table. She set her sketch book aside and wandered over to join them.

"I grabbed some photos while we were inside," Lacey said excitedly.

She shuffled over on the picnic table bench and made room for Emily to sit beside her.

"This is Claire when she was in her Madonna phase," Lacey said.

From the top of the pile, she revealed a photo of sixteen year old Claire with curly blonde hair pulled back with a bandana. She was wearing a short skirt with fish net stocking, large sunglasses and about seventy-five bangle bracelets on each arm.

"Damn, I was hot!" Claire swooned over herself.

"Ok, calm down there Material Girl," Lacey warned.

"Here's one of me at one of my first dance recitals," Lacey said as she pulled a photo from of the pile.

Emily and Claire peered over Lacey's shoulder at the photo of a twelve year old girl striking a dramatic pose for the camera. She had the same shade of blonde hair as her sister, but instead of tight curls, her hair was pulled back into a neat bun.

"I think the actress in me was evident even then, don't you think?" Lacey asked proudly.

"All I see is a mouth full of metal. Nice braces, dorktard!" Claire said playfully.

"Oh you're just jealous because you weren't as cute as me when we were kids," Lacey retorted.

Unsure of what to say, Emily shifted uncomfortably on the bench. Joan shot her an apologetic look from across the table.

"Sisters will be sisters, I guess," Joan said.

Her comment sent an icy dagger of guilt through Emily's heart. She and Lily rarely had those moments of playful banter, primarily because Emily was always trying to put distance between them. She wished now that she and Lily were more like Claire and Lacey.

"Here's a classic picture of Ryan," Lacey announced.

Emily tried, but failed to stifle her laughter when she saw the photo of Ryan. His long greasy bangs hung over his eyes, which were marked up with black eye liner. He was trying to pull off the sad and disturbed look in his tight black pants and black leather jacket. But somehow, he missed the mark and ended up looking like a kid on Halloween.

The sound of their laughter drew Ryan over to the table. He leaned over their shoulders to see what all the commotion was about. When he saw the photo of him in his high school years, he felt the color leave his face.

"Oh God! You had to break out the pictures, didn't you?" he asked.

"Oh honey. I'm just glad you finally cut your hair," Joan said. "It was always drooping down and covering your face. My little boy's face is too handsome to be covered up."

Joan reached up and patted Ryan's cheek lovingly.

"Awwwww!" Lacey and Claire cried simultaneously.

"Ma!" Ryan protested and pulled away from her.

"What?" Joan asked defensively. "Can't a mother say her son's face is handsome?"

Claire and Lacey both reached out and grabbed Ryan. They pulled him closer and started mocking their mother by caressing and cooing over him.

"Yeah, you can't blame Mom for making such a handsome baby boy!" Lacey cried.

Ryan succumbed to their pawing and jeering and laughed. He reached over and ruffled Lacey's loose blonde hair.

"Well, somebody in this family had to be blessed with good looks. Why shouldn't it have been me?" Ryan replied.

Emily smirked. So this is how normal families acted, she thought. She wondered if any of them had ever done anything as stupid as she had done. And if they had, would they have been forgiven or shunned like she had been?

***

Later that night, Harold sat on the porch enjoying a cold beer in a long neck brown bottle. Ryan approached him quietly and sat down next to him. Before he could say anything, Jake and Danny came around the corner. Both Harold and Ryan immediately noticed something uncharacteristically different about Danny. His tee-shirt wasn't neatly tucked into the waist of his jeans. Instead, it hung loosely over his hips. Harold and Ryan exchanged looks, but Ryan was the first to speak.

"Hey Danny, what's with the new look?"

Danny looked down at his tee-shirt and then back up at Ryan with a smile. He was pleased his new style had brought some attention.

"Cool guys untuck," he said simply.

Ryan nodded thoughtfully and gave Danny a thumbs-up. Danny obviously had a new influence in his life, one that made up clever insults and had a keen fashion sense, Ryan thought.

"Don't wait up," Jake called to them. "We're probably going to go trolling for hotties after we get done at the theater."

Danny looked over his shoulder and waved happily at them as he followed Jake to his Lincoln.

"Trolling for hotties?" Harold repeated. "I take it Beth hasn't given him any lovin' in a while."

Ryan shook his head.

"I still can't believe he's actually a lawyer," Ryan mused.

"I still can't believe he actually found someone to marry him," Harold deliberated.

Ryan nodded in agreement and they joined each other in a good chuckle. After a moment of silence, Harold broke it with a more serious tone.

"It was good to have the whole family together again today… even Jake."

"Yeah, they all seem to be doing well in their careers," Ryan said.

Even though Ryan hadn't come right out and said it, Harold knew his son felt left behind on the successful career paths that his siblings had sought out and found. He looked over at Ryan, who was searching the stars above the tree line.

"Ya know, son, I might not have said it enough… or maybe not at all, but I am proud of you. The way you've been running the store is pretty impressive. You've really done a good job."

Ryan looked over and gave his father and look of appreciation.

"Not as good as when I was running it of course," Harold added.

"Right, I know, I know. I still haven't figured out how to work eight days a week twenty-five hours a day," Ryan recited.

Harold nodded solemnly.

"I know running the old general store isn't exactly the cool thing to do, but I'd like to think what we do matters," Harold continued. "I'm very proud of your brothers and sisters, but at the end of the day, it's not about fancy career titles. It all comes down to one thing and that's being able to look yourself in the mirror and knowing that you've put in an honest day of hard work. For nearly a hundred years now, our little store has provided a valuable service to this community. I think there's something to be said about that, don't you?"

Ryan shrugged and nodded slightly.

"How come you never put pressure on any of us kids to take over the store?" Ryan asked. "From what I heard, you and Grampa never had a choice in the matter. Your future was kind of predetermined for you."

Harold made a low rumble of agreement in his throat. He took a moment before answering Ryan's question.

"Growing up here, I watched all my friends do whatever they wanted. Parties, football games, drive-in movies, and when we graduated, most of them got to choose the jobs they wanted. Hell, some of them even got to travel around the country. Not me though, I was stuck at the Corbin's General Store. Now don't get me wrong, son, like I said, I'm very proud of the history behind our store. In a day and age where there's a damn Walmart popping up in every town, it's nice to know a little store like ours can still survive."

"Well, it doesn't hurt that the closest Walmart is nearly forty-five minutes away," Ryan said.

Harold smiled. He knew Ryan didn't quite understand yet what he was trying to say.

"No, no it doesn't. But I'd like to think, if it were only a minute away, people here would still choose Corbin's because we represent the community and provide a more personal experience than what can be found at a big box store."

The sound of Joan humming and the kitchen dishware clinking in the sink as she cleaned up drifted out of the open windows and spilled out onto the front porch.

"I still don't understand how Mom got sucked into working at the store all these years," Ryan wondered out loud.

Harold released a long heavy sigh.

"Between you and me, I hated that she got sucked into the store."

"Really?" Ryan asked.

"Don't get me wrong, I loved that we saw each other more, but I hated that she had to give up her own life. I hated it. I swore if I ever had kids I'd never force the store on them. To be honest, after your grandfather passed away, your mother and I actually considered selling it, but…"

Harold trailed off and left the conversation dangling in the silence between them.

"But what?" Ryan asked.

"You kids came along. The old general store never made anyone in our family rich, but it put food on the table and a roof over our heads. Once our family started growing, we couldn't afford to give it up to pursue more exciting careers."

Ryan pondered his father's words for a moment.

"If you could have, what would you guys have done?" he asked.

Harold smiled and chuckled softly.

"Did you know your mother was a brilliant dancer? She actually had an opportunity to go teach a dance class for young'uns back in the day."

Ryan was beginning to put the story line in perspective.

"So if it wasn't for us kids…"

He couldn't bring himself to finish the sentence, but he didn't have to. Harold knew what he was thinking.

"Oh son, it's nobody's fault. Life just happens."

Ryan nodded. This much he knew and understood.

"What about you? What would you have done?"

Harold smiled and took a long swig from his beer bottle.

"When I was younger, I had the notion that I wanted to be an architect."

"Really? Geez Dad, I never knew."

"I know you hate running the store and you only took it over because of my heart attack thingy. But your mother and I want you to know, you can walk away from it any time you want. We never want you to feel stuck there, son. You should be doing what you want to do."

Ryan gave his dad an appreciative smile then slowly shook his head as if in disbelief.

"You and Mom were always supportive of what us kids wanted to do. When I told you I wasn't gonna go to college and that I didn't want to work at our store, you and Ma never once tried to discourage me. I never really understood that, especially considering how much you hated the type of music we played."

Harold smiled and shook his head.

"I didn't hate your music, son. Your mother and I loved how passionate you were about it, just like we loved how passionate Lacey was about her acting. It's not our place to discourage you. Life has its own way of doing that to people. It's our job as parents to support you no matter what."

Ryan was a bit stunned. He'd known his father for twenty-eight years, yet, at that very moment, he felt like he was meeting him for the first time. He even looked like a completely different man sitting next to him.

"Thanks, Dad," Ryan said finally.

"No, thank you son, for stepping up to the plate when we needed you. But I meant it when I said you can walk away any time."

"No, I meant thanks for everything. I guess we all got so caught up in our own lives, we never even stopped to see how much you and Mom sacrificed your own dreams for us kids."

"Well, I'm not sure I would put it that way," Harold disputed.

"No?"

Harold started to fish around in the breast pocket of his old flannel shirt. With shaky, old, battered hands he pulled out a small corn cob pipe and a little yellow pouch of tobacco. He packed the pipe skillfully within seconds and then lit a match. The smell of sulfur drifted between them as Harold's face was momentarily illuminated in the glow of the flame. The sound of soft crackling was followed by the smell of sweet burning tobacco. Ryan watched a trail of blue smoke swirl up into the night air and disappear.

"Remember that game in Little League when you came up to bat in the last inning… bases were loaded with two outs?" Harold asked.

Ryan curiously nodded. The feeling his father was about to reveal some great secret hung in the air between them like the blue smoke trailing from the corncob pipe.

"Well, I was there with you," Harold said.

"I know Dad, you were at all my games."

"No, I mean I was right *there* with you - in the batter's box. I was as anxious and nervous as you musta been… and when that bat made contact with the ball, I swear I felt it in my own hands. And when the winning run crossed the plate, your excitement was my excitement."

Harold's lips curled as he saw understanding begin to dawn across his son's face. He continued to drive his point home.

"And remember when Lacey had her dance recital? Make no doubt about it, your mother was on stage with her that day. I could see it in her eyes… every jump, every twist, every turn… that was your mother up there on stage, son. That's how it is to be a parent. Every broken arm, every broken heart, every laugh, every smile, every victory is ours too. Your pain is our pain, and your joy is our joy. And if you're lucky like us, the good far outweighs the bad."

Harold paused a second to take a deep long pull from his pipe and then he continued.

"Did your mother and I have our own dreams before you kids came around? Of course we did. But it was because of you kids that we got to live so many more dreams... more dreams than we ever thought possible."

Two long trails of smoke streamed out of Harold's nostrils. Warmth that came from a source other than his pipe filled his chest when he saw Ryan smiling at him.

"For the record, I never said I hated running the store," Ryan said. "As a matter of fact, it's kinda growing on me. And you yourself even said I do a good job..."

Harold stopped his son short.

"Alright, son, don't push it now."

Ryan smiled and nodded. As Harold stood up to go back inside, Ryan stopped him.

"How about that time when I struck out on three straight pitches?" Ryan asked. "Were you in the batter's box then, too?"

Harold grinned.

"Nah, that was all you, kid," Harold replied and slapped Ryan on the shoulder.

Ryan chuckled and then asked his old man one final question.

"Hey Dad, be honest, you didn't really like the type of music I used to play, did you?"

Harold looked at his son with a mischievous twinkle in his old blue eyes.

"I hated that God-awful noise," he answered flatly.

And with that, Harold disappeared out of sight, leaving Ryan alone on the porch shaking his head.

***

After the talk with his father, Ryan had the urge to see Emily. He knocked on her apartment door, and she opened it dressed in sweat pants and a thin tee-shirt.

"Um hey, it's a great night for a walk," Ryan started. "I was wondering if you felt like joining me?"

Emily stared at him with a blank expression, and he suddenly felt like a fool for asking. Somehow, he just couldn't believe she preferred to be such a loner. Now, as she stood in front of him with her arms crossed over her chest, he doubted himself.

"Sure, let me just grab a jacket," she answered finally.

By the look on Ryan's face, her answer surprised him as much as it did her.

Within minutes, they found themselves strolling through the vacant grounds of the old drive-in. The clear night sky was ablaze with stars, and the sound of crickets all around them was almost deafening.

"It must have been a little overwhelming for you today to meet all my crazy family members at once, huh?" Ryan asked.

"It wasn't that bad. Your family is really sweet," Emily answered and then paused before she added, "Well, Jake kinda creeps me out a bit."

Ryan laughed out loud.

"He creeps everyone out. Just a warning, the whole shower thing with Danny was an accident... it won't be an accident with Jake. You might want to keep your apartment door locked."

Emily smirked painfully.

"I already do," she reminded him. "You never know whose gonna to come a wandering or snooping in."

Ryan grimaced.

"Yeah, I guess I earned that one," he confessed.

"I really like Lacey. She's such a free spirit," Emily said.

"She's always been like that," Ryan said fondly.

"I just think it's really cool how passionate she is about everything – especially doing theater."

"Yeah, she's been an aspiring actress for as long as I can remember. Secretly, I think she wants to be the next Anna Kendrick."

"Who?" Emily asked.

"The actress? From Portland?" Ryan asked incredulously. "She started out in theater and now she's a big time Hollywood star."

Emily just stared at him blankly.

"You must know who she is. She was in all the Twilight movies."

"And you just assumed because I wear black sometimes that I'm into vampire movies?"

"You dress in black all the time," Ryan corrected. "And I just assumed all chicks were into Twilight."

Emily fought the urge to tell him how wrong he was. Secretly, she knew exactly who Anna Kendrick was, but it wasn't for her role in Twilight. She actually never got into those movies. Emily loved Anna Kendrick for the role she played in Perfect Pitch. Emily had spent many drunken nights trying (and failing) to imitate the "Cups" song.

"Also, don't believe any of Jake's stories about me either — or my sisters for that matter. They tend to exaggerate."

Emily grinned. She already heard a few of Jake's stories.

"Like the time you went skinny dipping and got bit in the balls by a snapping turtle?" she asked.

"Oh God," Ryan protested. "First of all, I wasn't skinny dipping. I had underwear on."

"They were tightie whities, weren't they?" Emily chided.

"What?? No…"

Emily stopped him short with a disbelieving look.

"Ok, fine they were. And second of all, I did *not* get bit in the balls. It was on the inner thigh."

"Sure it was," Emily said doubtfully.

"It was! I still have the scar to prove it. Want me to show you?" Ryan challenged.

"Noooo! Keep your pants on there, Romeo!" Emily cried.

"I had to wade up to my neck for five minutes over at Turtle Pond," Ryan explained.

"Oh? You *had* to? How old were you?" Emily asked.

"I was twelve, and yes, I *had* to. My brother triple-dog-dared me!" Ryan justified.

"Jake or Danny?" she asked.

Before Ryan could answer, Emily drew her own conclusion.

"My first guess would be Jake, but now I'm kinda thinking Danny. He might have that innocent look going for him, but I'm definitely thinking he's a triple-dog-dare kinda guy."

Ryan's slight, yet sad smile was oddly out of place. If it hadn't been so dark, Emily might have caught the angst in his eyes and known something was wrong. Instead, she continued on with her train of thought.

"I'm not gonna lie," Emily started. "I'm kinda jealous of how close you are with your brothers and sisters."

"You're not close with Lily?"

Emily shrugged.

"Not really. Not like your siblings anyway. Our sweet sisterly moments were few and far between. There was always a big age gap between us. By the time she started first grade, I was already a teenager. It didn't help that I was out of the house and out of town by the time I was seventeen."

"Seventeen? Jesus." Ryan whistled.

"Yeah, I was what you might call a wild child. Anyway, I left Braintree and ended up moving in with my aunt and uncle in western

Mass for a little bit. I was only with them a few months before my uncle's job wanted him to relocate to Seattle."

Looking back on it now, Emily could see that had been a cross roads in her life. She had choices then, certainly more than she did now. She could have gone to Seattle with them, or she could have continued down the road she was already on; bouncing from guy to guy and place to place. She realized now, she had another option at that point she hadn't even considered at the time. She could have swallowed her pride and returned back home to try and make things right. She wondered what her life would be like now if she had. Finding the thought too difficult to process, she quickly shoved it from the forefront of her mind into the dark closet she kept the things she refused to think about.

"Why didn't you go with them?" Ryan asked.

"Looking back on it, I probably should have. But at that point in my life, I was done having adult supervision. I just wanted to be on my own. Besides, if I woulda went with them, I'm sure my aunt woulda forced me to go back and finish high school."

"You never finished high school?"

Emily felt her defenses rise like the hackles of a threatened animal.

"A lot of people don't finish school! It doesn't make me stupid!" she snapped.

"Whoa!" Ryan cried. "I didn't say it did!"

"I have more life experience than most adults!" Emily said hotly.

"Easy, I believe you," Ryan said softly.

His tone calmed her and made her realize she was being unnecessarily defensive. Still, she felt compelled to drive her point home.

"From the time I left home until I was twenty-two, I probably stayed with a dozen 'friends'. Sometimes it was even friends of friends. When you bounce around so much you see a lot of stuff. My friends used to call me a professional gypsy."

"What did you do for work? When you weren't being a gypsy that is?"

"Ha, what didn't I do? I was a barista, a waitress, a cook… I even played one of Santa's elves one year for Christmas."

Ryan snickered and started to say something, but Emily cut him off.

"Not one word," she said to him with a stern look.

Ryan put his hands up and made a zipper motion over his lips. Satisfied, Emily continued.

"It wasn't until a year, or so, ago that I got my first real apartment. It was a shit hole, but it was ours."

"Ours?" Ryan asked.

"Yeah, me and my boyfriend Eric rented it. My ex-boyfriend, I should say. Luckily for me, it's only his name on the lease. I'm sure now that I am gone, he'll probably be getting the boot soon. Besides dealing a few drugs here and there and playing in his God-awful punk band, he's pretty much unemployed – and by unemployed I mean he's a lazy, unmotivated idiot."

"Sounds like you picked a real winner."

"I always do," Emily said with a heavy sigh.

"Can I ask you a question?"

"Why not, you always do."

"Since you left home, how many times have you seen your family?"

"My mom and Lily?"

Ryan nodded and quietly wondered what part of 'family' hadn't implicated them specifically.

"Not counting the last few weeks?"

"Right."

"Not once," Emily said remorsefully.

"Really?" Ryan asked incredulously.

He couldn't imagine being so disconnected from his own family.

He wondered again what had happened to bring Emily to this point. He searched her face for some clue, but all he found there was a distant sadness.

"The only person I stayed in contact with was Aunt Kay, and that was only because I needed to borrow money once or three, times."

Her answer didn't make sense to him. He knew that Lily had been in the hospital more than once. Wouldn't Emily have gone to see her before now?

"I overheard my mom say this was Lily's second time going through this type of cancer."

Emily nodded with regret filling her eyes.

"The first time they were still living down in Braintree. She went through her treatment over in Boston, but…"

Emily was overcome by a swelling sense of guilt. She didn't even want to say the words that would follow.

"But what?" Ryan urged.

"But I never visited her. Not even once," Emily confessed.

The words spoken out loud were like a blow to Emily's chest. She sucked the crisp night air sharply into her lungs, but she still felt like she was fighting for oxygen. She made up false reasons why it had been better for Lily if she didn't visit. Like stocks on a hot market, she had invested belief in those reasons because it was easier than owning the truth. She looked at the shock and disbelief on Ryan's face and felt herself shrinking in her shoes. She just wanted to disappear.

"Why not?" Ryan asked.

Those false reasons for not visiting Lily were well-rehearsed in her head, and she was tempted to feed them to Ryan. A few of Emily's "reasons" were: *Lily was too sick to even know who was there and who wasn't…* or *She didn't visit because she didn't want the drama between her and her mother to upset Lily…* or *Lily's condition really wasn't that serious.*

As Emily recited them in her head, she realized they were just excuses and not legitimate reasons. Ryan's simple question presented her with the opportunity to face the truth or just keep investing in those falsehoods she had bought into to save herself from reality. She searched for the truthful answers to see what they might actually sound like. Emily recalled the first time Lily was in the hospital back in Boston and what she had been doing with her life at the time. What had she been thinking?

The honest answer came more quickly than she expected. The only thing that was important to her back then was finding the next high that would take her mind away from reality. She'd been so consumed with guilt over what she had done, she was desperate to block out anything that would make her remember. In the process, she forgot the one thing that mattered. The truth burned her up with self-loathing, but she wasn't going to lie to herself or anyone else any longer.

"I know, I know, I'm a horrible sister… and daughter. The truth is, at that point in my life, I was just a fucked up, selfish little bitch. I couldn't even look into the mirror without seeing a big, black, fucking hole."

Ryan wondered if this was purely self-inflicted or if someone else had helped her achieve such a poor view of herself. Either way, he felt badly for her, but he didn't know what to say. He searched for the right words to comfort her, but without knowing the whole story, he came up short.

In Ryan's silence, Emily's self-loathing grew. She regretted saying anything to him about that. He was probably judging her right now, thinking about how screwed up she was. A guy like him, from a good family, educated, and managing the family business wouldn't know a thing about the kind of heartache she had been through. She felt like an idiot for thinking he might.

"You know what, forget it. You wouldn't understand anyway," she said dismissively.

"What's that supposed to mean?" Ryan asked.

"I'm just saying, you don't look like the type that would understand my kind of problems, that's all. I mean, you've got like the perfect family… with the perfect life…"

Ryan cut her off.

"You don't know anything about my life," Ryan said.

He could take Emily's sarcasm and her off-handed remarks, but he wouldn't stand for her judging and labeling him into something he wasn't. He wanted to make her understand he hadn't always had it easy either, but she was too stubborn to see anything that wasn't already a preconceived notion about him.

Emily recoiled at Ryan's harsh tone. She wanted to say she knew enough about his life, but she just shrugged her shoulders and rolled her eyes. Her response only aggravated Ryan more.

"You don't have the market cornered on depression, ya know?" Ryan said angrily. "And you're not the only one that's ever had to live with regret."

The last word he spoke stood between them like a brick wall.

"Ah yes, the tragic ex-girlfriend story," Emily recalled. "And oh, how could I forget — the poor, depressed boy-in-black phase."

"Ohhh, I see. For me it was a phase, but for you it's an emotional statement," Ryan countered. "Aww, poor, poor Emily. She wears black on the outside because she's a black fucking hole on the inside."

Ryan's words seared through her. She couldn't believe he just used her own words against her. This is exactly why she didn't talk to people, she thought. She covered her wounded feelings with a sarcastic smirk.

"Aww, that's so cute," she exclaimed cynically. "You actually thought I cared what you thought?"

Ryan felt his face get hot. He actually thought for a minute that maybe she had cared about something other than herself. He hated being wrong about people.

"You know what, Emily, you've been nothing but sarcastic and judgmental from day one. And from day one, I've always given you the benefit of the doubt. Now I can see what a waste that was."

"I never asked for the benefit of your fuckin' doubt!" Emily yelled.

"No Emily, you didn't. I did it because once in a while, once in a great while, you have these moments... these moments when you act cool or even normal. It's in those moments where I catch a glimpse of this sweet, caring person inside you, but then you open your mouth and say something stupid like tonight. Like I said, you don't have the market cornered on sadness and regret. We all have dark moments in our lives."

"Oh really? What's yours, L.L. Bean Boy?" Emily jeered.

Ryan squeezed his eyes shut against his own dark moment that hovered just below the surface. He had no desire to enter Emily's contest where the biggest regret won an award. He turned sharply away from Emily and began walking in the opposite direction.

Emily laughed. She wasn't surprised by his reaction. That's exactly what men did when things got difficult. They disappeared. She should have known Ryan was no different, but why did she think he was? Her disappointment quickly moved to anger.

"No seriously, what was your darkest moment, Ryan? Was it when your favorite signer got voted off American Idol? Or was it when Michael Jackson bit the big one?" she called after him.

She smiled at her own clever remark, proud that she had one upped him. She waited eagerly for him to respond, so she could fire another one off at him. Ryan didn't even turn around. He just kept walking until he was out of sight.

As she stood in the abandoned drive-in, the wind rocked the tops of the pine trees, which loomed over her, making her feel small. She wrapped her arms around herself, and in the silence, she realized she had never felt so alone. A chill crept over her as an old and familiar emotion settled in to keep her company. How did she manage to make sure every relationship left her alone with regret?

"Shit, shit, shit!" she whispered at herself.

She crumbled under the truth of Ryan's words. She always managed to say the stupidest things. She always said and did exactly the wrong thing every time. Why did she do that with him, though? He was practically the only one that had ever thought to give her the benefit of the doubt and tried to get to know her. Now, she had successfully pushed him away just like she had with everyone else that mattered in her life. She let her back slide down the cold steel pole that supported the deteriorating movie screen. With the long empty movie screen towering over her, she hugged her knees to her chest.

15
Here All Along

"You scratched all your suffering. You tattooed the scars.
So no one sees, you reckoning, what was a lifetime ago.
You let go of your truest friends to hold on to your high"
But no one knows, how slow it goes.
When you're falling down from the sky"

The next day at the general store, Emily tried to keep a low profile as she made herself a cup of coffee. However, as she was shaking the seventh package of sugar into her cup, she felt the heaviness of eyes settled upon her. When she looked up, she was met with a glare from Ryan. Their eyes locked for a moment before he turned and retreated into the back room.

He couldn't believe she had the nerve to show up looking for a ride after being such a jerk to him last night. He was about to tell her as much, but the look of remorse on her face caught him off guard. He ran his hand through his bangs as he struggled with the decision on whether he should offer her a ride or to tell her she was out of line last night.

He turned to go face her and tell her not to expect any more favors from him, but when he went to the front of the store, he found she was already gone. He looked out the window just in time to see Emily climbing aboard the little blue old folk's bus. He thought the sight of seeing her riding the bus would make him feel better, but it didn't.

When he turned around, he found his mother watching him with interest. Although she didn't say anything about it, the look she gave him screamed - *Why didn't you give that poor girl a ride?*

Why should I feel guilty, he thought. Ryan wanted to defend himself to his mother, telling her it was Emily who started it... but he decided to simply keep his mouth shut and go back to work.

***

At the Grafton Falls Hospital, Emily pulled open the shades in Lily's room.

"There, is that better?" Emily asked.

"Yeah, I love the feeling of the sun on my face," Lily answered.

Emily quietly gazed out the window for a moment before walking over to Lily's bedside. Even then, she stared blankly toward the window.

"Are you okay, Em?" Lily asked.

Emily looked over at her sister in surprise.

"Yeah, of course. Why do you ask?"

"You just seem a little off today, that's all."

Emily released a heavy sigh. She was never very good at hiding things from Lily. The girl had an uncanny sense of what was going on around her without anyone saying anything.

"It's nothing. I just went and put my foot in my mouth again," Emily admitted. "I think I might have really hurt Ryan's feelings in the process."

"Oh no! What happened?" Lily asked with concern.

"I don't even know. One minute we were talking, and the next thing I know, I was shouting at him and basically accusing him of being shallow."

"Shallow? Ryan doesn't really strike me as the shallow type."

"He's not, but that didn't stop me from suggesting the biggest emotional crisis he ever had to face was when his favorite singer got voted off American Idol."

"Emily! That's just mean!" Lily scolded.

Emily looked over at her sister guiltily. Then Lily laughed lightly.

"Funny, but mean!" she rebuked.

"I know," Emily answered glumly.

"Why would you say something like that?"

Emily buried her face in her hands.

"I know, I know! My mouth is like a loose cannon. He's been really sweet to me too. The whole family has actually."

Lily patted Emily's shoulder empathetically.

"What are we going to do with you, Em?"

Emily shook her head. She couldn't speak because a ball of tears had formed in her throat and she was desperately trying to swallow them down. Every single person who had ever cared for her always ended up a causality of her carelessness. Even when she wasn't hurting people with her words, she was hurting people with the lack of them. How could she let so much time pass without even a phone call to her sister? Her sister, who had never been anything but sweet and loving to Emily, was left forgotten on the side lines of Emily's horror show. And now, here Lily was comforting her when it was Lily who needed comforting.

Emily was furious at herself, and she couldn't understand how Lily could possibly be anything but disgusted with her. Finally, after years of pent up guilt, Emily let it all out.

"How come you're not pissed at me?" Emily blurted out.

Lily looked at her sister with round eyes full of surprise. Before she could answer, Emily continued.

"I've been such a shitty sister to you over the years," Emily chastised herself with tears brimming in her eyes.

Lily grabbed Emily by the hand.

"It's okay, Em," she said softly.

"No, it's not okay, Lily! I swear I wanted to call you or visit you so many times. When I found out you had cancer and was in the hospital the first time... my heart absolutely broke."

The tears she had tried to hold back, finally broke free.

"You need to know I wanted to come see you! I even made it as far as the hospital parking lot once, but I was just so... embarrassed."

"Embarrassed?" Lily asked.

"Embarrassed for how everything played out with Mom. Embarrassed for not being in contact with you sooner, but most of all, I was embarrassed at what kind of person I had become. I was so screwed up back then. I didn't know up from down, never mind wrong from right. I know that's not an excuse. There is no excuse."

"Emily, it really is okay. You're here now, and that's all that matters to me."

"Seriously, how are we even related?" Emily asked.

As she forced a smile through her tears, Emily swiped at the hot trail running down her cheek.

"We're all allowed second chances, Em. It's obvious that you're not that same person you were a few years ago."

Deep down, Emily knew there was some truth to that statement. She *had* been trying to change and be a better version of herself, and even she had noticed some small improvements. Although she'd kicked the drugs and alcohol, she knew facing the demons that had driven her so far away from her family would be much more difficult.

"It's because of you, you know?" said Emily. "If I'm a better person now, it's because of you, Lily Pad."

"Me?" Lily asked doubtfully.

"Do you realize how happy I was when I saw your friend request last year? I mean, I'm not gonna lie, I also felt nervous and unworthy... but I was so happy because I knew that there was still a chance to make things right. After all the years of being a shitty sister to you, you still reached out to me. You totally gave me the motivation to be a better person."

"Ha! I think you're giving me way too much credit," Lily said dismissively.

Emily clutched her sister's hand and adamantly shook her head no. After a moment, Lily spoke again.

"You know Mom misses you, right?" Lily asked.

Emily released a sarcastic snort.

"Well, she has a funny way of showing it," Emily replied. "I swear I've tried to be civil to her, but she just has a way of pushing my buttons…"

"That's because you two are so much alike," Lily pointed out.

Emily shot her sister a glare. The last thing she wanted was to be like her mother.

"It's true," Lily insisted. "You both have a hard time expressing your feelings, and you're both as stubborn as a mule. But underneath it all, you both have big hearts. She'll come around, Em. Don't give up on her."

Emily got up and walked over to the window. She gazed out at the cars in the parking lot. Noticeably absent was the sight of the big green pick-up truck, which usually sat in the front lot waiting for her.

"Sometimes while I was on Facebook with you, I'd catch Mom looking over my shoulder at your pictures. Trust me, Em, she feels just as guilty as you do."

"Guilty for what?" Emily asked. "For me being such a disappointment?"

"She still feels embarrassed and guilty about her breakdown. She hasn't forgiven herself for putting you in a situation where you were forced to be the mother."

Emily didn't say anything. She just shrugged and continued to stare out the window.

"You were only fourteen, Em. You shouldn't have had to deal with all that responsibility. She probably thinks that's what drove you away."

"Trust me, she doesn't think that," Emily said flatly. "And besides, that wasn't it… that's not why I left."

"I know," Lily admitted.

"You do?!"

Emily turned around in surprise. She didn't think anyone knew why she really left except for her mother and her aunt.

Lily nodded. She dropped her eyes to her lap. She knew one day she would have to own up to her part in Emily's departure.

"I was such a brat to you, always clinging onto you and following you everywhere you went. You never had a chance to be a normal teenager because of me. When you weren't taking care of me, I was always pestering you to play with me or to let me hang out with you and your friends. You probably lost more friends because of me than I will ever know. If I was you, I probably would have left too."

Emily's heart shattered into a thousand pieces at her sister's confession. She couldn't believe Lily could think for one second she had been the reason that she left. Knowing that Lily had been carrying that around all these years just about brought Emily to her knees. She rushed to Lily's bedside and grabbed both of her hands.

"Oh Lily, no!" Emily cried. "That wasn't it at all! It wasn't because of you! It wasn't even because of Mom. It was all me. I was the one that screwed up. I was too much of a coward to own up to my own mistakes, so I just did the easy thing and ran away."

Lily looked at her sister with tears welling up in her eyes.

"Well, maybe I wasn't the only reason you left, but I'm sure I played a part in it." Lily whimpered.

"That's just not true, Lily!" Emily sobbed. "It was never you! In fact, you were the only reason I should have stayed."

"I missed you, Emily," Lily said weakly.

"I know. I missed you too, Lily Pad." Emily whispered.

16
Kids To Chase

"I never, never did what I wished I did,
but I lived every wish through my little kids"

The entire Corbin family was gathered at the Grafton Falls VFW with all their closest friends to celebrate Joan and Harold's 40th wedding anniversary. A hush spread throughout the crowd as Claire stood up and raised her glass indicating she was about to make a toast.

"It's always nice to get together with the whole family, but this weekend is particularly special because it's Mom and Dad's anniversary. You guys have set the bar so high when it comes to marriage, that I think I speak for all of us when I say; we should all be so lucky to be as happy as you two still are today after forty years of marriage."

An approving murmur swept through the crowd as party goers raised their glasses.

"A toast… to Mom and Dad," Claire proclaimed.

A cheer arose from the crowd as people turn to one another and clinked their plastic champagne glasses in the air.

"Seeing as it's your fortieth, we all pitched in and got you something big," Claire continued. "Like really big."

Right on cue, Danny stood up and walked over to them with a huge smile. He sheepishly handed Harold a large envelope.

"Whoa, look at this Ma, the big spenders got us an oversized card," Harold exclaimed.

"It's not a card, it's a…"

Claire put her hand on Danny's bicep and squeezed as she shook her head no, but her subtle signal was lost on him.

"… boat trip," he finished.

Harold and Joan exchanged curious glances and then looked anxiously inside the envelope. Harold's hands started to shake as he pulled out a brochure for a cruise ship. When the two tickets slipped out, Harold caught them in his other hand and showed them to Joan. They both gaped speechlessly at the tickets.

"It's a cruise to the Caribbean," Joan beamed.

"Ah, for Christ sake, the last time I was on a boat I got seasick," Harold said.

"Dad, that was a fishing boat," Ryan explained.

"And you were wicked hammered," Jake added.

All the brothers and sisters exchanged worried looks.

"I think what your father means, is you shouldn't have spent all that money on us," Joan explained.

"No, I meant, I'm worried about getting seasick!" Harold declared.

"Dad, you won't even know you're on a boat because it's so big and there is so much to do!" Claire urged.

"They have all you can eat buffets and there is even a casino," Lacey encouraged.

Harold's eyebrows shot up at the mention of a casino. A smile spread over Joan's face as she began to examine the brochure.

"Honey, they even have putting greens and shuffleboard," she said pointing excitedly at the brochure.

Again, Harold's eyebrows shot up. He looked across the room at Max and Gus and yelled, "Did ya hear that, boys? They have shuffleboard!"

"Dad! Your old crony friends aren't invited. It's a romantic getaway for you and Mom," Lacey said.

Harold's face crumpled in confusion at the thought of spending a day without his two best friends. Max and Gus' faces crumpled as well. They sure did love shuffleboard.

Joan continued to read through the brochure. She pointed eagerly at the pages and exclaimed, "Look Harold! They have a ballroom where we can dance!"

Jake tried to stifle a laugh at the thought of his old man dancing.

"What's so funny, smartass?" Harold demanded. "You don't think your old man still has his dance moves?"

Jake could no longer contain himself and started laughing hard enough to form tears at the corner of his eyes.

"That's what I'm afraid of!" Jake managed between bursts of laughter.

Joan ignored him and looked at Harold with stars in her eyes.

"Remember how we danced all night on our honeymoon, Harold?"

"Like it was yesterday, dear," Harold said warmly.

As he looked at his wife with memories sparkling in his eyes, he reached out and grabbed her hand.

"I say we do this cruise! And I say we dance all night again… and maybe afterwards I'll see if I still have some of my other moves from our honeymoon," he said with a wink.

"I guess we shoulda got you some of them little blue pills then," Jake joked.

Joan began to blush as all their children either gaped with open mouths or cringed painfully. Eager to change the focus of discussion, Ryan grabbed his guitar and made his way front and center.

"I sorta wrote a song for you guys," Ryan announced.

Joan beamed proudly at him, but Harold just stared at Ryan with a raised eyebrow and bemused interest. Harold wasn't sure if his new ticker could handle Ryan's loud, raucous music. He was tempted to crank down his hearing aid but decided to give his son's song a chance. Danny settled in between his two sisters, and the family eagerly awaited Ryan's song.

Ryan cleared his throat.

"This song is called Kids to Chase," he announced.

After a few chords on his guitar, he began to sing.

"Old Man Gray in polyester every day,
Arms like the hands on a watch,
Watch as he goes driving home through snow,
Thinking 'I never, never did what I wished I did,
But I lived every wish through my kids', I say,
And Old Lady May in the backyard today,
Hangs his few clothes on the line,
She remembers the time,
So many clothes almost made her cry,
She's thinking, 'I never, never did what I wished I did,
But I lived every wish through my kids'.
Well no regrets and no mistakes,
In fact, there's no turning back,
We're running ten steps ahead of the silver bullet on the tracks,
Seems like I'm busy all the time
Being put on hold and standing in line
But these are the times that I think of you,
And I'm able to smile for the two of you,
You gave me all my style and all my grace,
And my only a mother could love face,
For Old Man Gray and Old Lady May never had no time to waste,
They had kids to chase, kids to chase, kids to chase."

When the last chord on the guitar strummed into silence, the small crowd broke out in applause. As Ryan set his guitar aside, Joan rushed to his side and pulled him into her arms for a big hug and kiss. Ryan glanced over his mother's shoulder and made eye contact with his father, who smiled approvingly at Ryan.

About halfway through Ryan's song, Emily had quietly entered the lodge. She stood in a vacant spot on the far side of the room where she leaned up against the wall and watched Ryan play.

When Ryan's song was finished, Danny was the first one to spot her. He smiled at her and waved. When everyone turned to see who Danny was waving at, a murmur fell over the crowd. Being a new person in a small town was like being a fox in a hen house. A nervous, curious vibe fell over the room. Joan was the first to break the tension by walking over to her and giving her a big hug.

"Emily, I'm so glad you could make it," Joan said warmly.

"I don't wanna interrupt, I just came by to give you and Mr. C this," Emily said quietly.

She handed Joan two wrapped presents. Joan looked at them in surprise and then looked at Emily inquisitively.

"I just wanted to show my appreciation for you guys letting me stay with you," Emily explained. "Trust me. It's really not much of anything."

Joan smiled affectionately at Emily.

"We should take this over to Harold and let him help me open it, don't you think?" she asked.

Emily glanced anxiously at the exit. She didn't intend on staying, but Joan already had her by the hand and was leading her to where Harold and the other family members were gathered.

"Look who stopped by?" Joan announced.

"Didn't someone explain to her that it was an anniversary party and not a funeral," Jake murmured as he drank in Emily's black attire.

"Give me a minute, and it could be yours," Emily growled.

With raised hands, Jake backed off.

"She brought us something," Joan continued.

Joan handed the first package to Harold then began to open the second one. Inside the wrapping paper was a framed pencil sketch of the Corbin General Store. Sitting on the front steps of the store, Emily had sketched six people; Joan, Harold, Harold's parents, and Harold's grandparents.

"Oh Emily! You drew this?" Joan asked incredulously.

"Yeah, with a little help from your daughters," Emily said.

"We dug up old pictures of all of them for her," Lacey explained.

Joan handed the sketch to Harold. He stared silently at the photo for a long moment. Seeing the sketch made him realize just how significant the family business had been through the generations. He set it down carefully and looked at Emily with gratitude in his eyes. There were no words to express what he was feeling, so he wrapped an arm around Emily's waist and pulled her in for a hug.

Seeing as Harold had forgotten about the other gift, Joan carefully began to open it. It was a photograph of Joan and Harold sitting on the bench on the general store's porch holding hands and smiling at each other. Joan put her hand to her mouth and gasped. She smiled widely as she proudly showed it off to her children and husband.

"I took that picture the other day," Emily explained.

Claire looked at the photo with a puzzled look.

"Huh, that's weird," she remarked.

"What's weird? That your mother and I still hold hands?" Harold asked defensively.

"No, it's weird that Max and Gus aren't there sitting between you," Claire replied.

Everyone except Harold thought her remark was funny and chuckled good naturedly. Harold just sneered at Claire and nodded.

"I suppose you think that's pretty funny?" he asked.

Claire nodded proudly.

"Thank you, Emily. These were very sweet of you," Joan said.

"Christ! We get them a cruise, and yet they go gaga over a sketch and a photo? Unbelieveable!" Jake exclaimed.

Claire and Lacey, who were both standing on either side of Jake, smacked him simultaneously on each shoulder.

Ryan met Emily's eyes for a moment. He was still upset with her for the remarks she made the other night, but he managed a slight nod of approval. Embarrassed and pleased at the same time, Emily quickly cast her eyes down to the floor. A slow smile spread across her face and warmed places in her that had been cold for a very long time.

17
Search Inside

"Hey, we're all lost in the forest
Searching for signs from the sky
When every map down here is useless
You better start searching inside"

Emily and Danny trudged through the woods, and the soft autumn sunlight filtered through the colorful leaves above them creating kaleidoscope colors above them. The wind occasionally swept up a handful of forest debris and formed swirling wind tunnels in front of them on the beaten path. Their steps were softened on a blanket of pine needles, and Emily spoke to Danny in hushed tones.

"I can see why you like it out here, Danny," she said. "It's so quiet and peaceful. I can actually hear myself think clearly here."

Emily had grown accustomed to Danny's silence and lack of response, but she knew he was listening.

A moment later, Danny darted off the path and started making his own way through the trees. This was also something Emily had grown used to, and she no longer doubted that he knew exactly where he was going. She followed him faithfully as he wove between the trees at a steady pace. She wasn't surprised when they came upon a familiar clearing where the old junk cars lined the forest floor.

Emily spotted an old Cadillac Deville with its grill press up against a thick oak tree. She climbed inside the driver's seat and waited for Danny to ride shot gun as he normally did. However, instead of joining her in the car, he stood next to the driver's side door looking a bit uncomfortable.

"What's the matter Danny?" Emily asked.

Danny didn't respond, but just stood like a statue looking at the ground. Emily usually didn't have a hard time understanding Danny, but this time she was a bit confused. He loved this game and she couldn't understand why he didn't want to play. Then it occurred to her. She slid over into the passenger seat.

"You want to drive this time Danny?" she asked.

He glanced over at her curiously but made no effort to move.

"Well, actually, I think you'll have to drive, buddy, because my license just got revoked," Emily coaxed.

This time when he looked at her, she held her hands up helplessly in the air and Danny smiled. Hesitantly, he opened the driver's side door and climbed in.

It was hard to see through the spider-webbed cracks in the windshield, which was covered in layers of dead leaves and branches. However, Emily was willing to play navigator.

"We have to make a pizza delivery across town, Danny," she said playfully. "We better take a short cut on the left because the customer was promised his pizza twenty minutes ago."

Danny grabbed the steering wheel and jerked it hard to the left. Emily pretended to brace herself in her seat. Her hands wrapped around the edge of the faded and cracked leather interior. Danny laughed at her antics and pulled the wheel harder to the right.

"Woot! Woot!" Emily cheered. "Faster, Danny! Pizza is gettin' cold!"

Danny grinned impishly and threw his foot down on the rusted out gas pedal. The back of Emily's head hit what was left of the head rest, and she braced herself against the sunken dashboard.

"Danny, you're going too fast! It's too fast!" Emily cried out.

Danny laughed and swung the steering wheel again to the left.

"Look out! Look out! You're going to hit that tree!!" Emily yelled.

Danny froze and looked at Emily with a panic stricken face. Pleased that he was playing along, Emily slapped her palms together hard.

"WHAM!! We're dead!" she shouted.

She dropped limply back in her seat, closed her eyes, and let her mouth fall open. A moment later, a gut-wrenching wail that was barely human filled the interior of the car. Emily shot up in her seat with a jolt and saw Danny screaming with his eyes fixed on the tree. His face was red and contorted, and his hands had a white-knuckled grip on the steering wheel.

"Danny! Danny! It's ok! It's ok! I'm not really dead!!" Emily cried.

Danny moved his eyes from the tree to her face, but his screams only intensified. Emily read the fear and agony in his eyes and knew whatever set him off was more than just her fake death. As her eyes shifted from his face to the tree, she recalled his reaction to the 'bad tree' they had passed in the road on their way to Grafton Falls.

"Danny," she said softly in an urgent tone.

Danny continued to wail loudly.

"Danny, it's ok," Emily pleaded. "We didn't hit the bad tree."

There was a break in Danny's cries as he paused to consider her words. He looked back at the tree and resumed his terrible wails as tears streaked his face. Emily took his hands gently off the steering wheel and turned him in his seat to look at her. He tried to pull his hands out of her grasp, but she held onto them firmly.

"It wasn't a bad tree," she repeated again. "It wasn't a bad tree."

His cries slowly subsided to whimpering, but the tears still flowed fiercely from his eyes. When he began to rock back and forth, Emily wasn't sure if that was a good thing or not.

Unsure what to do, Emily hesitantly reached out and put her hand on Danny's shoulder. She knew there was a distinct possibility this could cause him to spaz out even more, but she needed to do something.

As she soothingly patted his shoulder, she started to softly hum random 80's songs. After a few moments, Danny quieted and slowly lowered his head onto her shoulder. Emily put her arm around him and then rested her head on top of his. They both sat there dazed and motionless looking at their reflections in the spider webbed glass.

***

Harold, Max, and Gus sat in their usual spots on the bench of the general store. When Gus saw Emily walking down the road toward them, he made the sign of the cross with his fingers.

"Oh boy, here comes Night of the Livin' Dead," Gus warned his friends.

"Witchy-poo is probably coming to stock up on broomsticks," Max replied.

"She has a name you know!" Harold retorted gruffly.

His two friends spun their heads around in unison to stare at Harold like he was a complete stranger.

As Emily climbed the porch steps to the general store, she noticed the three old men gaping at her as they did every morning. Gus in particular, was fixated on her tattooed arms. Due to the unusually warm fall weather, she wore a black spaghetti-strapped top, which allowed her tattoos to be fully visible.

Gus' eyes slightly bulged out when he spotted the brunette pin-up with her breasts exposed.

"Who the hell gave you that graffiti?" exclaimed Gus.

"Graffiti? You mean my tattoos?" she questioned.

Gus scoffed and slowly pulled his sleeve up. Very slowly. When his forearm was finally exposed, he proudly showed off his tattoo to Emily. It was a small version of the Air Force emblem.

"Now that's a tattoo," boasted Gus. "All that stuff you got going on there is nothing more than graffiti. I hope they caught the hoodlum that did that to ya," he concluded.

There were no words for Emily to say. She was sure this old dude had completely lost his marbles. Before moving on and heading inside, she noticed Gus' cane had fallen from its usual propped up position against the bench arm. It lay just out of his reach on the porch floor. Emily decided to do her good deed for the day by bending over and retrieving it for him.

Gus watched as Emily's tight black jeans slid down her backside, exposing a lacy black thong as she bent over.

"Jumping Jesus on a pogo stick! Could your pants be any lower?" Gus asked. "Ya bend over and I got ass crack staring me smack dab in the face!"

Emily stood up promptly, tugging at her waist band as she did. She glared at Gus as she propped his cane up on the bench next to him.

"Could your pants be any higher?" she retorted. "It's called a waist band, not a tit band!"

Gus grabbed his cane and struggled to his feet with the intent of showing Emily she was sadly mistaken. However, when he peered down at his chest, he could see his belt was indeed lodged just below his breast line.

Emily shook her head and gave Gus a smug look and then peered around him to give a friendly smile and wave to Harold. Grumbling unintelligible words of protest, Gus reclaimed his seat.

"Your Dickies are pulled up pretty high," Harold remarked sensibly.

"Ayuh, pretty high alright," Max agreed.

Inside, Emily found Ryan stocking shelves in the back of the store. She could tell he was pretending not to notice her. She still felt terrible about the things she said, and she had made up her mind to try and set things right between them. She certainly wasn't good at apologies, but she figured now might be a good time to start. She took a deep breath and walked straight up to him.

"Hey, I'm sorry about the other night. What can I say, you're right, I'm a judgmental, sarcastic bitch."

Ryan turned and looked at her, searching her face to see if he could find an ounce of sincerity behind her words. He was surprised to see all he found was pure authenticity. There was no sarcasm or defensiveness, just Emily apologizing.

"Well, you got two out of three right. I never called you a bitch though," said Ryan.

Emily chuckled softly.

"Yeah, but you wanted to," she said. "And if you had, you woulda been right."

She held up three tickets.

"I picked these up when I was visiting Lily yesterday. I was hoping you'd let me make it up to you by taking you and Danny to The Strand tonight. I know how much he likes 80's movies. They're showing Sixteen Candles tonight. I'm not sure if he likes that one or not, but…"

The sound of Danny's loud voice imitating one of the movie quotes from Sixteen Candles stopped Emily in mid-sentence.

"Wot's a happenin' hot stuff… No more yanky my wanky…"

Ryan and Emily started to laugh.

"Yeah, I think he's a big fan," Ryan confirmed. "I don't see how we could let him down."

***

The crisp October night air hit Emily's face as she and Danny and Ryan exited The Strand Theater. It was hot inside the small theater, and Emily welcomed the breeze tossing her hair gently back from her face. Danny marched ahead of her and Ryan, happily reciting lines from the movie.

"You sure made his day," Ryan commented.

"What can I say? I have my moments," Emily answered.

They both smiled at each other and walked on in silence.

"I think Danny really likes it when you go for walks with him in the woods too. Not many people know how to relate to him, but you make it seem easy."

"Yeah, we have fun together," Emily said nonchalantly. "Speaking of the woods, what's the deal with that old drunk dude in the cabin?"

"Drunk?" Ryan asked and then it dawned on him. "Aww man, Danny knows better than to sneak Uncle Frank alcohol."

"That guy is your uncle?" Emily laughed.

"Yeah," Ryan answered. "Technically, it's my parent's cabin. It came with the land when they bought it. They never really used it much though. My uncle has been living out there about a year now."

"Let me guess, his wife kicked him to the curb for drinking too much?" Emily guessed.

"Uh, no," Ryan answered carefully. "His wife, my dad's sister, passed away last year from cancer."

Emily swallowed hard. There she went again, putting her foot in her mouth. Couldn't she ever say anything right?

"When Aunt Jenny passed away, Uncle Frank just lost it and sunk into a huge depression. He didn't even go to the funeral. And not only did he completely shut down, but he started shutting everyone out, including his own daughter, Leah. She lives out in Vermont with her husband and son.

For weeks, he never left his house and nobody was allowed in... except for my dad. For some reason he always let my dad in. My dad said most days all he did was just sit there staring at Aunt Jenny's photo. He wouldn't talk or do anything at all. He just kept staring at that photograph all day, every day."

"He wouldn't even talk to his own daughter?" Emily asked.

"Nope," Ryan confirmed. "After a couple of weeks of her unsuccessfully trying to get him to come around, my parents convinced Leah to go back to Vermont. They said he just needed more time to grieve. I felt so badly for her. Not only had she lost her mother, but in a sense, she had lost her father too."

Emily nodded. She understood all too well what it was like to lose a parent that was still alive.

"They promised Leah they'd watch over him. They were sure in time he'd come around, but he only got worse. What we didn't know was Uncle Frank had to refinance their home in order to pay for Aunt Jenny's medical treatments. After a few months, the bank started sending foreclosure notices."

Emily listened intently as Ryan continued.

"And to make matters worse, the townspeople were starting to gossip that Uncle Frank had gone mad. Kids started to egg the house and shout nasty things as they rode by on their bikes. It turned into a nightmare. I'm not sure Uncle Frank was even aware of how bad things were getting, but my parents were. It really upset my folks, especially my dad."

"People can be so cruel," said Emily. "So your dad let him stay in his cabin?"

"Yup. Now my family and Leah are the only ones that know where he is."

"So everyone else still thinks he's in his house?" Emily asked.

"It depends on who you ask. There are definitely a lot of rumors floating around out there."

"Has Leah been to the cabin?" Emily asked.

"No," Ryan answered. "I'm sure it killed my cousin to see her dad like that, and I know she wanted to come see him, but she knew that he had to find his way back to her on his own terms."

"She must be crushed," Emily said.

"For the past year, she's been writing him a letter every week. She sends it to my folks, and they make sure Danny brings it with the groceries. I have no idea if he's read any of them, but..."

Emily was filled with empathy for Frank. Never in a million years would she have guessed they would have something in common. Suddenly, his hostility and defensiveness echoed with something familiar inside her.

18

Hanging By A Thread

"And it seemed too clear when it beckoned me
To leave my home and my family
But the woods were dark and the river ran wild
And the city called to the desolate child"

Ryan pulled his truck into the hospital's parking lot. Emily began to fidget uncomfortably in her seat.

"Are you ok?" Ryan asked.

"What? Oh yeah, I'm fine," Emily replied half-heartedly.

She didn't look at Ryan, but instead, looked distractedly out the window.

"Look, I can tell something is wrong. What is it?" Ryan asked.

Emily took a deep breath. That morning, Joan mentioned to Emily that one of the nurses from the hospital had stopped into the store as she was coming off her night shift. Being such a small town where everyone knew everyone's business, she informed Joan that Lily seemed to have taken a turn for the worse. The news turned Emily's stomach inside out, and she'd been a nervous wreck since. Now that they were at the hospital, she wasn't sure she had the courage to go in and see her sister. She didn't know if she could handle what she might see.

The last thing she wanted to do was let Ryan know she was scared, but looking at the concern on his face, she didn't have the heart to lie.

"I heard Lily wasn't doing so well," Emily confessed.

The worry on Ryan's face deepened. He seemed lost in thought for a moment and then he brightened.

"You know what? She's put up a hell of a fight up to this point. She's not going to give up now. She probably just needs some encouragement from her big sister."

Emily's eyes fell to her lap. A voice inside her head reminded her that she was a pathetic big sister and suggested she wasn't fit for the task. She clenched her hands into balled fists. Her blood red nails dug deeply into the palms of her hands. She shook her head no and pushed the thought from her head. It was time to face her demons and show them she was stronger.

When she looked back up at Ryan, he saw determination mingled with hope within her eyes.

"Do you want to come in?" she asked quietly.

Ryan leaned back in surprise.

"If you want me to, I will," he said.

Emily gave him a slight smile and a nod.

Inside, they found Lily lying in her bed with her eyes closed. Unsure if she should enter, Emily hesitated at the door. Ryan put his hand on her shoulder to steady her, or perhaps to keep her from leaving.

Lily sensed another presence in the room and her eyes fluttered open. She looked around and when she saw her sister, she smiled weakly.

Emily approached her bedside and put her hand on Lily's bald head. It was hot to the touch.

"Hey kiddo, I heard you had a rough night. How are ya feeling now?" Emily asked hopefully.

Lily cast her eyes down to her lap where she held the worn stuffed frog Emily had given her so long ago. She stroked its head absently.

"Better now," she answered in barely a whisper.

She reached up and grabbed Emily's hand and squeezed it as tightly as she could. Then she shifted her attention to Ryan.

"You know Ryan, right?" Emily asked.

Lily smiled sheepishly and nodded.

"Otherwise known as the hottie who runs the general store," Lily confirmed.

Ryan looked over questioningly at Emily.

"What?!" Emily cried indignantly. "Don't look at me. I never said that!"

"My friends Chelsey and Ann have a major crush on you," Lily explained. "They hit the store every day after school to check you out."

"Ahh yes, Red Bull and candy bar girls?" Ryan asked.

"That would be them. You'll have to embarrass them for me some time," Lily weakly smiled.

Ryan smiled broadly and gave Lily a wink and a nod.

"Does that make you feel better?" Emily asked "Teenage girls that think you're cute?"

Ryan gave Emily's question serious consideration then shrugged and nodded.

"Don't worry, Ryan, Emily thinks you're cute too," Lily said.

Excitement and curiosity danced behind Ryan's brilliant blue eyes as he raised an eyebrow at Emily. Her face squished up as if she had just encountered something unpleasant.

"I totally never said that," she declared.

"Don't let her tough girl appearance fool ya," Lily whispered. "Behind all of her walls is an amazingly beautiful person."

Emily gave her eyes a sarcastic roll and laughed off Lily's compliment. When Lily tried to laugh too, her breath caught in rasping gasps. She grabbed her sheets and balled them up in her fists as she started to cough violently.

"You okay, Lily? Want me to go get you a drink or something?"

Emily asked concerned.

"I'll get her something," Ryan offered.

As Ryan turned to leave, Emily caught his eyes and gave him a warm smile. She felt better having him here. Lily noticed their exchange as her coughing subsided.

"I see he got over your American Idol comment?" Lily asked in a whisper.

"Yeah, but why do I always have to go and act like a bitch? I swear I don't intend to be."

"It's just your defense mechanism," Lily explained.

Emily looked at her with surprise. When did her little sister grow up and learn terms like defense mechanism? Her comment made Emily realize just how much time she had missed with her sister. She covered her guilt with a sarcastic question.

"Oh is that so, Dr. Phil?"

"Think about it, you've basically been on your own since you were seventeen. You've been through a lot. You were kinda forced to have thick skin, and it's only understandable that you built walls up to protect yourself," Lily continued.

"Listen to you. Here you are in the hospital going through one Chemo treatment after another, and you tell me I had it rough?" Emily asked incredulously. "You never cease to amaze me, Lily Pad."

"You're the amazing one," insisted Lily. "When Mom was in her depression, you stepped up and became the parent and took care of us... especially me."

"Until I didn't," Emily added darkly. "I just can't shake the guilt I feel for leaving you when you needed me so much. Things happened that I didn't know how to deal with and... and... I'm just sorry we lost touch for so long because of it."

Somewhere inside, Emily knew she was trying to tell her sister everything that had happened. She needed her to understand, but at the same time she didn't want to place any more stress on her while she was sick. Emily held back, telling herself when Lily fully recovered, she'd tell her everything then.

"We've already been over this, Emily. There is nothing to feel guilty about. I'm not mad at you – at either one of you. If there's one thing I've learned, it's that life is too short for resentment. I only hope that you and Mom can realize that one day."

Instead of answering, Emily absently picked up a cool wash cloth that was sitting on Lily's bedside table. She placed it gently on her forehead to soak up the beads of sweat that had formed there.

Just then, Ryan entered the room carrying a pitcher of water and a cup. He poured her a cup and placed it by the bedside table. Lily gave him a beaming smile of appreciation, but before she could thank him, Susan stepped through the door.

It had been seven years since Susan had seen both her daughters in the same room. The sight was jarring and put an icy grip on her stomach, clenching it until she couldn't breathe.

Part of her wanted to wrap them both up in her arms and hold them tight. Another part needed to protect herself, and Lily, from the damage she knew Emily was capable of inflicting. When Emily left, the heartache was even worse than when Steve left them. Susan's heart had been broken all over again, but Lily had been absolutely devastated.

As much as she missed Emily, she had to think about Lily now. She'd do anything to shield Lily from the heartache she had felt when Emily walked out on them. She might not be able to protect Lily's body from cancer, but she could still protect her heart.

Emily stared at her mother like a deer frozen in headlights as she held a cool face cloth to Lily's feverish forehead. When Susan noticed Emily tending to her baby, it brought feelings of guilt and shame to the surface. It was bad enough that she was back in town threatening to shake things up again, but now she was playing caretaker again? It wasn't Emily's job to take care of Lily now. It was hers. It had always been hers. There was a time when she wasn't able to do that job, but she could now, and she didn't want Emily stepping up in her absence as she had to before. The thought that Emily felt she needed to now, filled Susan with a self-defensive rage.

"Emily, you shouldn't be bringing your boyfriends by here. This isn't a dorm room. It's a hospital and Lily needs her rest," said Susan. "No offense, Ryan, but you really don't belong here. It's for family only."

Ryan looked up at Susan in surprise, but before he could say anything, Emily jumped to his defense.

"Don't you talk to him like that! He's treated me more like family in the last few weeks than you have in seven years. And besides, since when are your stupid church friends considered family?"

Susan stood there fuming, unable to formulate a response, but the heat from her glare could be felt by everyone in the room. Ryan held his hands up in a defensive gesture and slowly started to back out of the line of fire.

"I think I'll just wait outside," he said.

Emily felt her heart sink as Ryan left the room. She hadn't intended to put him in the middle of a family argument. She shot her mother an accusing look.

"Great job, Mom! You really know how to scare off the opposite sex, don't you?"

"You watch your mouth young lady! And for your information, my friends from church have been…"

"Enough!" Lily shouted.

Susan and Emily both turned their attention to Lily, who was trembling with fright and rage. Big fat tears welled up in her eyes as she stared at them both disbelievingly.

"Great, see what you did?" Susan asked. "This is exactly why I don't want you here."

Her mother's words stung deeply, mostly because Emily knew she had a right to feel that way.

"Both of you, enough already! This fighting has got to stop. It's about time you and Emily get past your… issues … or whatever it is. All three of us are family here, and if I don't make it, all you'll have is each other."

The tears spilled over her cheeks and landed on the hospital blanket beneath her. She bit nervously on her lower lip to keep it from trembling and looked anxiously from her sister to her mother, desperately hoping one of them would have the courage to make the first move.

"Oh honey, don't talk that way," Susan said as she rushed to scoop Lily up into her arms.

Susan held Lily's head close to her chest and rocked her back and forth. Lily, too weak to protest, let herself collapse into her mother's embrace. As Lily closed her eyes, Susan shot Emily an accusing look.

"We've all been praying extra hard for you, Lily. It's all going to get better, you'll see," Susan said softly.

Yeah, because praying cures everything, Emily thought sarcastically. She wanted to fire those words at her mother, but she kept her comment to herself, for Lily's sake. Her mother might be delusional about some things, but she was right about Emily making a bad situation worse. After all, that's what she did best. Defeated, Emily cast her eyes to the cold hospital tile and then got up to leave.

She was too upset to even say good-bye to Lily, but as she gazed over her shoulder on the way out, she caught Lily's eyes pleading with her not to go. Emily just shrugged her shoulders helplessly and shook her head no.

As Lily closed her eyes again, a single tear ran down her cheek. She knew Emily would be leaving town soon.

19

These Mistakes

"I swore if I left here I would never come back
Now my pockets are both empty and my arms all scratched
Drove the wrong way down a one way street
'Cause feeling free costs too much for me."

After Ryan dropped Emily back off in Pine Ridge, she headed straight for the woods. As she trudged through the paths, her thoughts turned to Boston. After the latest incident with her mother, her heart was torn between staying in Pine Ridge for Lily or returning home to her familiar lifestyle.

The words of her mother echoed in her head — 'This is exactly why I don't want you here'. Emily felt like a fool for allowing a small part of her to hope by coming home she could start to mend the broken fences in her family. How could she mend fences when she always managed to say and do the wrong things? She did it with her mother just like she did it with Ryan. It would only be a matter of time before she did it again. Maybe she should just leave now before she did any more damage. Lily was better off without her now just like she was better off without her then. Nothing had changed at all. She hadn't changed at all.

Emily kicked her feet through the dead crackling leaves on the forest floor. The scent of earth drifted upward and filled her senses. She would miss that smell.

Without fully realizing where her feet were leading her, she found herself at Frank's cabin. She hesitantly knocked on the door but got no answer. She stood outside for a moment and debated whether or not to go in. Finally, worry got the best of her, and she decided try the door to see if he was alright.

When she entered, she immediately saw Frank passed out in his favorite chair. She also noticed the wood stove was burning low and the cabin was chilly. Emily found a tattered wool blanket and placed it over Frank's slumped body. His head jerked up for a moment, and he muttered an angry snarl. Then his gnarled fingers curled around the edge of the blanket and he returned to his deep slumber.

Emily picked up an unfinished bottle of Gunpowder Rye Whiskey sitting on the arm of his chair. She shook her head and then set it aside on a book shelf next to the stove. Emily looked around and started to place the other scattered bottles she found in a brown paper bag. She wondered how long he'd been making Danny sneak him alcohol. She also reminded herself that she was certainly in no position to judge how others handle their pain.

Under a pile of newspapers, she found a half-eaten meal of chicken and rice crusted onto a paper plate. She tossed them both into the bag and mumbled her disgust. As she cleared the floor around Frank's chair, her eye caught on a stack of mail stuffed under his chair. She scooped up a handful of envelopes and saw they weren't just junk mail, but handwritten letters. Her mind quickly recalled her conversation with Ryan about all the letters Frank's daughter, Leah, sent regularly.

She started filing through them absently, hoping she might find one that had been opened. None of them had so much as a torn corner. She wondered why he would keep all these letters but never open them? She looked curiously at Frank and shook her head softly.

Emily was reminded of her own letter writing days. Over the past seven years, she had written dozens of letters to Lily and to her mother. Of course, she never found the courage to actually mail them, and at one point, during a drug induced haze, she lit them all on fire. Emily knew how much courage it took for Leah to write and mail her father all these letters, and it broke Emily's heart to see them unopened.

Sensing a disturbance in his normally vacant environment, Frank awoke. Emily quickly hid the letters behind her back and held her breath. As Frank came to, he reached for the whiskey bottle that was no longer there. When he discovered it was gone, he jolted straight up and scanned the cabin for another. He noticed the clutter around him was gone, and he scanned the cabin for any other violators of his privacy. Finding none, he narrowed his eyes on Emily.

"What the hell is going on here?" Frank demanded furiously.

"I was just…" Emily started.

"You were just what? Stealing my booze? Who the hell do you think you are, sneaking into my place and helping yourself to whatever you find?" Frank barked.

"I didn't steal anything!" Emily cried.

"No, of course not. A girl like you probably never stole anything in her life, right? What kind of fool do you take me for?"

Emily's cheeks burned. She clenched her fists around the letters she held behind her back.

"Who are you to judge me?" Emily shot back. "This isn't even your cabin, and I really don't think the Corbin's would approve of you using Danny to bring you booze so you can spend your afternoons passed out drunk."

Emily watched Frank's jaw tremble as he tried to work out the words he wanted to say, but no words came. Finally he threw the blanket Emily had put over him onto the floor and leaned forward in his chair. When he spoke, his voice came out in a low growl.

"Is that so?" he challenged.

Emily already regretted her words.

"Look, I'm sorry. I get it. Ryan told me about your wife. I know it must be hard on you…"

"What the hell do you know?" Frank shouted. "You're just a God damn kid!"

"I'm just saying… I can only imagine what was like to…" Emily stammered.

"You have NO idea what it was like!" Frank bellowed loudly.

Emily knew the harder she tried to console Frank, the angrier he would become, so she stood her ground silently, hoping he would calm down. With the letters still clutched tightly behind her back, leaving wasn't an option. She had to wait for an opportunity to discreetly put them down. She slowly began to back up toward the book shelf.

Frank seemed slightly appeased by Emily's silence, and he began to scout his eyes around the room looking for his bottle. He spotted the Gunpowder Rye on the book shelf and grabbed it. He twisted off the cap with shaky hands and took a long pull. Relieved she hadn't stolen his whiskey, he continued in a softer tone.

"You have no God damn idea what it was like… to watch someone in so much pain… and to know there's not a God damn thing you can do about it."

Emily's mind flashed back to Lily, lying small and helpless in her hospital bed. She knew it would be unwise to argue with him, so she remained silent. Frank looked at her and shook his head no, answering his own question.

"Do you have any idea what it's like to sit in an empty house?" he continued. "A house that was once filled with her voice, her cooking, her laughter. Her stupid, obnoxious… beautiful… laughter."

Frank took another swallow of whiskey and stared nostalgically out the window before speaking again.

"I used to think when she yelled at me for doing something stupid, it was the loudest sound I'd ever heard… but I was wrong."

Frank shook his head and squeezed his eyes shut, deepening the wrinkles in his face.

"You know what the loudest sound I've ever heard is?" he asked.

Emily carefully shook her head no.

"It's the silence. In my house… in my head — the silence. That's the loudest God damn sound I've ever heard," he said softly.

When he turned back to look at Emily, he had tears glistening in his old faded blue eyes. But seeing the sympathy in Emily's eyes only brought back the rage, and a scowl quickly replaced the momentary remorse on his face.

"So until you experience something like that, I suggest you keep those God-awful pierced lips of yours shut and mind your own damn business!" Frank snarled.

Unsure what to say, Emily cast her eyes to the cabin floor. Two more feet and she could slip the letters on the shelf and leave.

"Just because you dress like you're in mourning doesn't mean you know anything about what it's like," Frank continued to berate her. "You walk around with a chip on your shoulder, like the world owes you something. Lemme clue you in, Missy, life owes you shit!"

He glared at her with disgust. How dare she presume to know grief at her tender young age? How dare she even suggest she could understand?

"You don't need to be so mean. I was just trying to help," Emily said softly.

"I don't need your damn help! I just wanna be left alone!!" Frank screamed. "Can't you get that through your stupid self-centered head?"

Emily grasped the letters behind her back tighter, trying to keep herself from shaking with rage. If she wanted to be called stupid and put down she never would have left home in the first place. She didn't tolerate that from her mother and she sure as hell wasn't going to tolerate it from this guy.

"And to think, I almost felt bad for you!" Emily spat. "Why your daughter keeps writing you letters is beyond me, but the least you could do is read them instead of punishing her!"

Emily threw the letters at him. The envelopes scattered in various directions and fluttered to the floor. Frank's eyes grew wide as one landed in his lap. He stared at his daughter's handwriting on the seal. She had scribbled the words: Please read. He picked it up and stared at it as if it were on fire. He dropped it on the floor and pulled himself onto his feet. He pointed an angry finger less than an inch from Emily's face.

"You little shit! Who gave you the right to go through my things? Get out! And I don't ever wanna see your studded metal face around here ever again!"

Emily didn't flinch. Instead she swallowed her anger and quietly turned to leave. She knew exactly what Frank was doing because she had been doing the same thing to other people most of her life. Her calm reaction infuriated Frank even further.

"It's pretty clear to me why your own mother doesn't want you around," Frank shouted after her. "You should take a hint and leave town. You don't belong here."

Emily turned and shot an angry glare at him before she reached the door. Out of the corner of her eye, she caught him trying to take another haul off his now empty bottle. Just as she slammed the door behind her, she heard him yell, and the sound of shattered glass hit the door behind her.

As silence settled in around him, Frank stared down at the letters scattered across his cabin floor. Each one was a reminder of the bad decisions he had made.

Emily walked briskly through the forest trails, clenching and unclenching her fists as she headed back to the Corbin residence. She only slowed down when a chime sounded from her pocket. She retrieved her phone and saw she had a message from Amanda. She paused beneath a towering maple tree to listen to it. The sound of

Amanda's voice calmed her slightly.

"Hey Em, I haven't heard from you in a while, so I thought I'd call and check in to see how things are going with Lily… and your mom. Well anyway, let me know when you're planning on coming back. I could really use the company of an adult. Sarah is great, but there is just only so much toddler-talk one person can stand without going completely bonkers. Hope to hear from you soon! Bye!"

Emily hesitated. The serenity of the forest was broken by the voices in her head. 'You don't belong here. I don't want you here. Then you open your mouth and say something stupid. You should take a hint and leave town.'

The voices circled around in her mind and urged her to make the phone call that part of her had wanted to make for weeks. She dialed Amanda's number. When Amanda's voicemail picked up, Emily left her message.

"Hey Amanda, thanks for checking in. Sorry I haven't been in touch. Reception here isn't the greatest. Yeah, I'll be home by the end of the week. See you soon, girl."

When she ended the call, she felt a sense of relief. Finally, she would be leaving this nightmare town and returning to civilization. She was looking forward to being back in Boston where people didn't want to know your story, didn't care where you came from, and most of all, didn't care what you did or said.

She walked with a lighter step the rest of the way back to the Corbin residence. Her only burden now – how was she going to tell Lily that she was leaving… again? She knew by her bolting back to Boston, it would fulfill her mother's prediction. Emily hated that. She hated that her mother would be right.

When she reached the Corbin's, she found Danny and Ryan shooting hoops in the driveway. She gathered they were playing a modified version of H-O-R-S-E when she heard Danny shout out his victory.

"Douche Canoe! I win!" Danny yelled.

When he saw Emily, he ran up to her.

"I just won Douche Canoe, Emily!" he said proudly.

"Good job, buddy," Emily laughed.

Ryan was also laughing, but he gave Emily and Danny a moment alone as he made his way towards the front yard to play fetch with Riley.

Danny puffed his chest out proudly and beamed at her. Then his face brightened as he remembered something. He reached in his back pocket and pulled out tickets for The Strand Theatre. He showed them to Emily and she read the name of the movie title out loud.

"Stand By Me on this Saturday night?" she asked.

Danny nodded shyly.

"Who are you going to take?" Emily asked.

"My new friend!" Danny exclaimed.

Emily's brows furrowed as she tried to think of who that might be. Coming up with no guesses she had to ask for the answer.

"And who would that be?"

"You, silly!" Danny said with a big smile. "Can we go?"

Emily's breath caught in her throat. She knew it would be difficult telling Lily that she was leaving town, but she didn't realize it would be equally tough telling Danny.

Emily planned to take the bus back to Boston on Friday. Looking at Danny's hopeful smile and shining eyes, she dreaded telling him no. She looked down sadly at the tickets. When she didn't say anything, Danny tried to entice her with a movie quote.

"Friends come and go like busboys at a restaurant," Danny recited.

His choice of quotes from the movie cut her to the bone. She told herself she would inevitably let Danny down just like she did with everyone else. It was better for him to be let down by her now rather than later. She handed the tickets back to him.

"I'm sorry. I don't think I can make it," she said.

Danny's face fell and his shoulders slumped. Before she could register the disappointment in his eyes, Emily did what she did best, she ran away from the situation. She turned and hurried up the stairs into the apartment and threw herself on the bed, and for the thousandth time in her life, she cried herself to sleep.

20
EXTRAORDINARY

"This life is a short sprint
Gone before you know it despite your plans
And you looked extraordinary, and you lived through the hard times
And you loved with an ever open, ever hopeful mind"

The next morning, Joan sat on the front porch cradling a cup of tea in her hands. When she saw Emily sitting on the steps looking glumly at the ground, she motioned for her to sit down next to her. Emily complied and silently sat down next to Joan.

"Day off today?" Emily quietly asked.

"Just the morning," Joan smiled. "My friend Betty and her daughter are working a couple of shifts a week to give Ryan and I a little breather."

Emily nodded, but it was obvious that she didn't really hear Joan's answer. Noticing this, Joan cut right to the chase.

"What's on your mind, kiddo?"

Emily released a deep sigh and shrugged.

"Do you think my mom is right... about me being a bad seed? Be honest."

"Of course I don't. And I'm sure she didn't really mean it either," Joan answered.

"Yes she did," Emily said. "It makes me sick what kinda religious fanatic she's turned into. No offense. I know you go to the same church and all, but you don't act anything like her. You're open-minded and so easy to talk to. She's just so closed-minded, so unemotional, and… cold."

"No offense taken," Joan assured her.

"She wasn't always like that, ya know?' Emily explained. "She used to be the life of the party. She was actually a lot of fun, and she had a great sense of humor too. Of course, all that changed when Steve left us."

"Steve is your stepfather?" Joan asked.

"Not anymore," Emily huffed. "It's not like he was ever around much anyways. Apparently his 'business trips' were more pleasure than business. I was thirteen when they got divorced. He moved to California about a year after. I haven't talked to him since. I guess some people just aren't meant to be fathers… or husbands for that matter."

"That must have been tough on all of you," Joan remarked.

"My mom took it pretty hard. She just slowly started shutting down. She barely left the house or her room, for that matter. I was pretty much forced to take care of Lily myself. Not only did I resent my mother for that, I kinda held it against Lily too. Ya know, for not being able to take care of herself and all. God, that sounds horrible, doesn't it?"

"You were still a kid and you needed taking care of too," said Joan. Emily shrugged as Joan continued, "But she eventually snapped out of it, right?"

"Yeah, one day out of the blue, she decided she was going to go to church. The next thing, ya know, she was *reborn!*"

Emily paused to dramatically shake her hands in the air and roll her eyes. She understood the term 'reborn' meant exactly that. The mother she knew was replaced by a completely different personality.

"I suppose I should have been grateful. I mean, it did get her back on her feet and living again. But… she was never the same after that. She may have found God, but she never found the closure she needed with Steve leaving."

Joan nodded thoughtfully.

"Then she started forcing the whole church thing on Lily and me. Lily was only six or seven, so she really didn't mind, but I was just hitting my teenage years. There was no way she was forcing me to do anything. I refused to go to church. I refused to listen to her. I basically started to rebel against everything she said."

"Emily, that's what every teenager does."

Emily shrugged.

"I guess I just took it to more of an extreme than most teenagers do. About that same time, I started hanging out with the 'cool' crowd. The wrong crowd, but the cool crowd, ya know? I started drinking and smoking. Cigarettes and... other stuff. I basically did whatever I knew would piss her off the most."

"We all made some bad choices when we were teenagers," Joan said.

"Yeah, but not every teenager has a church-crazed mother that thinks she can *save* her daughter through faith. For the next few years, she tried everything short of exorcism to get me to be the good church-going daughter that she thought I should be."

"I'm sure your mother was just trying to guide you in the best way she knew how," Joan reasoned.

Emily scoffed.

"The only thing I was guided to was bad grades and poor choices. By the time I was sixteen, I was failing all my classes, and we both had about enough of each other. It was around that time, I started dating Kyle Walker. He was like the king of the wrong crowd. So, naturally I was attracted to him. I guess you really couldn't call it dating because all we ever did was... well, you know. And you certainly couldn't even call it a long term thing because within a month, he had grown bored with me and moved on to some other chick."

Emily looked up from the rings she had been fidgeting with on her fingers, and Joan could see the sorrow swimming in her eyes.

"I was totally heart broken. It sounds pretty ridiculous and silly now," Emily admitted.

"It's neither silly nor ridiculous, Emily. We've all had our hearts broken, especially by someone who didn't deserve it in the first place. Let's just say I dated my share of losers before I met my Harold."

"Really?" Emily asked.

"Leonard Pearson. AKA the biggest jack ass in New England, which is probably what attracted me to him in the first place," Joan confessed.

Emily smiled. The thought of Joan being attracted to a bad boy was a welcomed surprise.

"On our two week anniversary, I caught him at the A&W sharing a milkshake with Sally Jenison – with just one straw! The bastard! I cried myself to sleep for weeks. My point is, Emily, it got better. It always gets better."

Emily's smile faded.

"Not in my case, it didn't," she confided.

Joan tilted her head and looked at her inquisitively.

"A month after he dumped me, I… I found out I was pregnant. I was so scared. I had no idea what to do. I didn't really have any close friends to confide in; not any real friends anyway. And I certainly wasn't going to tell my mother. I had to work up the nerve, but… the only person I told was Kyle. What a big mistake that was! The asshole claimed it could be anyone's baby, seeing as I slept with half the school."

Joan sucked in sharply. She was already putting the pieces of Emily's story together and knew the inevitable outcome. Emily mistook Joan's reaction of surprise and was quick to defend herself.

"I mighta drank and did some drugs, and I know I had a wild streak, but I swear Mrs. Corbin, I did NOT sleep with half the school! As a matter of fact, Kyle was my first! I swear to you!" Emily pleaded.

"Oh Emily, you don't have to defend yourself to me," Joan said.

"I just don't want you to think what he said was true. I was a lot of things, but I wasn't a slut."

Joan patted Emily gently on her knee, and Emily eased back into the fidgeting of her rings as she continued her story. She imagined when she was done, Joan would agree with her mother with regards of her being a bad seed, but part of her dared to hope for a different outcome.

"I had no idea what to do. I couldn't even take care of myself, never mind a baby…"

Emily paused to fight the lump of tears that had formed in her throat. Although very curious as to what happened next, Joan patiently sat back, waiting for Emily to continue on her own terms. After a few moments, Emily slowly began to speak again.

"The one thing I definitely knew was I couldn't tell my mom. Being newly 'reborn' and all, she woulda shit a brick. So finally, after days of debating and crying, I decided to go to the clinic and… well, you know, take care of it."

Emily moved her gaze from the ground, up to Joan's face, fully expecting a look of disappointment. Strangely, Emily's look was met with one of kindness and sympathy.

Joan thought for a moment then gave Emily a quizzical look.

"How old did you say you were again?"

Emily knew exactly what Joan was getting at. If she was under eighteen, she would have needed a parent or guardian with her.

"I was almost seventeen. I ended up paying some random man outside of a 7-11 to pose as my guardian. The clinic was kinda shady, so it really wasn't that difficult. I never felt so alone in my entire life. Ever."

Defeated in her battle against the tears, Emily's cheeks glistened under the hot trails that ran from her eyes. In the silence, she turned to Joan.

"You must think I'm a horrible person," Emily said.

"Emily, you were a teenager. You made the best decision you knew how. A decision, I might add, that I wouldn't wish on any woman, never mind a sixteen year old girl."

Emily took a deep breath and prepared to tell the hardest part of her story.

"Apparently, one of my mom's church friends saw me enter the clinic, and of course, she had to report back to my mom. She confronted me as soon as I got home. At that point, I was so broken down that I didn't even bother trying to lie about it. We must have yelled at each other for an hour straight. She kept calling me a sinner and told me I would go to hell for what I did. She said the only way I could do something so horrible was if I had the devil inside me. I lashed back by telling her it was her fault that Steve cheated on her and left us. I also went as far as to say if it wasn't for her lack of parenting skills, I wouldn't have been put in the situation I was in."

Emily paused and stopped fidgeting with her rings long enough to look up despondently into Joan's searching eyes.

"Everyone at some point or another has said things they didn't mean when they were upset," Joan said.

"I shouldn't have said it... any of it. It absolutely wasn't her fault that Steve cheated on her. And it wasn't her fault she went into that severe depression. I shoulda just kept my big mouth shut. She was still too fragile to hear something like that."

Emily collected herself and continued.

"So that's when she snapped and told me to get out. She said she wouldn't have the devil living under her roof. I was so embarrassed and ashamed at what I had done. I knew I didn't deserve her forgiveness, so I packed my things and left. Lily was at her friend's house, so luckily she didn't have to witness any of this, but... but I never got the chance to say goodbye to her. And after I packed my things and left, I never turned back."

"Where did you go?" Joan asked cautiously.

"I moved in with my aunt and uncle for a while. At first, I told myself that my mom and I just needed some time apart. You know, to cool off. There were so many times I wanted to tell her I was sorry and that I didn't really mean all the things I said. Sometimes I think my only talent in life is being able to say the meanest things at the most inappropriate times."

"Why didn't you? Why didn't you ever go back and tell her how you really felt?" Joan asked.

"I don't know," shrugged Emily. "I guess the longer I put it off, the harder it seemed. Does that makes any sense?"

Joan nodded and Emily continued.

"If truth be told, Mrs. Corbin, I… I was scared. Just because I didn't mean what I had said to her, maybe she meant what she said to me. Maybe she really meant every word she said about me. Worse yet, maybe it was true. Do you think some people are just bad at the core?"

The tears flowed freely down Emily's cheeks now. She didn't bother trying to hold them back. She had been holding them back for too long now, and their release gave her a sense of liberation she hadn't been expecting.

Joan wrapped her arm around Emily's shoulder and pulled her close. Emily didn't resist, but instead allowed her head to fall limply on her shoulder.

"I don't know whether some people are just bad at the core, but I know you're not, and I know your mother doesn't think you are either, Emily. I think you're a much better person than you give yourself credit for. Don't you ever forget that," Joan said softly.

Having cried herself dry, Emily swatted away the last few tears from her cheeks. She and Joan sat in silence, watching the leaves on the branches of the old maple tree test their fading grasp in the brisk October wind.

"I think I'm gonna go visit Lily," Emily said finally. "I kinda owe her an apology for leaving so abruptly yesterday – and for fighting with Mom in front of her. She always ends up getting caught in the middle and that's not fair."

Emily also knew it was long overdue to tell Lily everything. Her confession to Joan was just a warm-up for telling her sister. She needed to finally tell Lily why she really left home. Emily knew Lily loved her unconditionally, but she was still scared to death of telling her how she had sinned all those years ago.

"I also wanna give her this," Emily said pulling something from her backpack.

It was an 8x10 inch framed copy of the photo Emily had been carrying with her for years; the Easter photo from she and Lily were kids.

"Aww, she'll love it," Joan said.

Emily smiled and then glanced over her shoulder at the front door.

"Do you mind giving me a ride, Ryan?" she asked out loud. "He's been eavesdropping this whole time," Emily pointed out to Joan.

Joan nodded, and by the look on her face, Emily concluded Joan already knew.

"I wasn't eavesdropping!" Ryan said defensively as he stepped out onto the porch. "Not the whole time, anyway. Wait, how did you know?"

"All that man spray you've been wearing lately is kind of a dead giveaway," Joan answered.

"I don't wear that much," Ryan argued.

Emily and Joan chuckled, and Joan got up to head back inside.

"Hey Mrs. Corbin… thanks for…" Emily started.

"Any time dear. Any time," Joan answered.

As Ryan and Emily stepped off the porch, side by side, Ryan paused to take a whiff of himself. Emily looked at him with a raised eyebrow waiting for him to validate Joan's claim. He just shrugged and kept walking.

***

An uncomfortable silence filled the truck on the ride to the hospital. Ryan felt badly about eavesdropping and felt even worse about everything Emily had gone through with her mother.

Surprisingly, Emily was a little less uncomfortable than Ryan. Even though she wasn't one for wearing her heart on her sleeve, or for opening up to people, it felt good to get some of that off her chest. Emily really didn't mind that Ryan overheard her conversation with Joan. She was embarrassed, for sure, but the truth was, there were a few occasions in the last week that she found herself almost confiding in Ryan regarding her and her mother.

Emily knew full-well that Ryan's silence was due to him feeling guilty about eavesdropping, so she let the poor guy off the hook by initiating some small talk.

"So, what's the deal with your dad and his old cronies?" she asked.

"Who? Max and Gus?"

"No, Fat Albert and the Cosby kids," Emily answered sarcastically.

Ryan shot her a look from the driver's seat.

"Oh, those guys go way, way back. They all went to school together. Gus did a stint in the Air Force, but he eventually came back home and joined his brother Max at the shoe factory in Grafton Falls. That was before the corporate giants bought it out and shut it down. They used to stop in the store every morning for their coffee and pastries. I guess when the factory closed down, part of them still needed to maintain the routine of everyday life. Every morning they wake up and hit the general store just like they did when they were working. A lot of people moved when they lost their jobs, but Max and Gus were a few of the lucky ones that were offered an early retirement package."

"That's so sad," Emily said softly. "Why would a corporation buy a factory just to shut it down?"

"Easy. Eliminate the competition and outsource their jobs overseas where the labor is cheaper," Ryan answered. "In fact, that's the old factory right over there."

Emily stared out the window at an abandoned brick warehouse on the riverside. The cold black windows offered no glimpse of what still might be inside. She wondered if the old work stations were still intact, maybe even with people's names still written on them. Were there still barrels of old inventory that never got assembled sitting in the aisles? A chill crept over her skin thinking about it, and she was filled with an inexplicable feeling of emptiness.

When Ryan pulled into the Grafton Falls hospital parking lot, he didn't wait for Emily to ask him to come inside.

"I think I'll wait out here today," Ryan said.

They both smiled at each other, and Emily hopped out of the truck. She turned back and grabbed the framed photo of her and Lily. She held it up proudly for Ryan to see and was pleased when she saw his face light up.

"She's gonna love it, Em," Ryan said.

Emily beamed up at him and without another word, she shut the truck door and headed into the hospital.

Upon entering the third floor wing, Emily recognized one of Lily's nurses on the phone at the reception desk. Emily nodded a friendly hello to her and continued past the desk and down to Lily's room. She had already reached Lily's door when she heard the nurse running down the corridor after her.

"Wait!" the nurse called.

Emily saw the empty hospital bed and assumed the nurse was coming to let her know Lily had been moved to another room. It wasn't until Emily saw her mother standing with her back to her and looking out the window that her stomach began to tighten.

"Mom?" Emily asked tentatively.

Susan cringed at the sound of Emily's voice. It was usually so full of confidence, but now sounded like a small lost child. She couldn't answer.

"Mom, where's Lily?" Emily asked.

The nurse finally caught up to Emily. When Emily turned to her, the look on the nurse's face said everything.

"I'm... I'm so sorry, Emily," she said softly.

Emily shook her head no. Her mind already raced with reasoning and bargaining, trying to find a way where it was all just a mistake.

"I figured somebody would have called you, but when I saw you just now I knew that you hadn't heard..." the nurse's voice trailed off.

Emily was no longer listening. She walked over to her mother and tentatively put a hand on her shoulder. She needed her mother to tell her it wasn't true.

"Mom?" Emily pleaded.

She needed to hear her mother's voice. She needed to hear her say something, anything. But she just continued to stare silently out the window.

Susan started to reach for Emily's hand, but her entire body felt as heavy as lead. Her hand stopped just short of Emily's and then she turned around. For a brief moment, she looked into Emily's eyes searching for something to say, but there were no words to speak. Instead, she headed for the door.

As her mother reached the door, Emily called out to her once more. She was unable to hide the desperation in her voice this time.

"Mom?!"

Emily's voice cracked under the weight of sorrow and her hopeless denial. The sound tore at Susan's heart. A mother never wants to hear their child in pain. She searched desperately for something to say to her daughter, but her chest was heavy with grief.

"I'll be sure to inform the Corbin's of the funeral arrangements," Susan said softly.

Emily gaped at her mother, unable to comprehend the words she had just spoken. Susan didn't have the strength to say out loud that her youngest daughter had died that morning, so she turned and left her eldest daughter standing alone in the vacant hospital room.

As the emptiness settled in around her, Emily looked down at the framed photo of her and Lily she was still holding. A tear fell from her cheek and splashed on the glass surface blurring Lily's smile. She couldn't believe she would never get the chance to give her sister the gift. She looked up hoping to see Lily back in her bed, but all she found was Lily's stuffed frog sitting in the chair next to the empty hospital bed. Tony's dark beaded eyes looked blankly at her.

She wandered absently over to it. She reached out for it with shaking fingertips, but before she could grasp it, her legs gave out and she crumpled to her knees. She lowered her face down and pressed her wet cheek to Tony's back. She couldn't help thinking Lily had just been clutching that frog yesterday. She wondered what was to become of the frog now that it no longer had purpose and it was no longer loved by anyone. She concluded it would likely be cast into the dumpster and never thought of again.

The image of Lily's winter blue eyes pleading from her hospital bed for Emily to stay, pushed into her mind. When Emily realized that would be her last memory of Lily, she thought about how selfishly she had behaved yesterday. She hadn't been there for Lily when she needed her and now there would be no more chances to make it right. There would be no more opportunities for Emily to show up with a stupid gift and say she was sorry. All she was left with now was the memory of walking out on Lily when she needed her to stay. The thought destroyed what little strength she had been trying to hold onto. It pressed down heavily on her heart until she let herself become lost in the grief.

Emily knelt in front of the chair, clutching Tony and crying onto his balding back. She cried until she had no more tears left to cry. Emotionally exhausted, Emily had no will to move. Moments later, she felt a warm hand on her shoulder and turned to see the nurse standing behind her.

"Is there someone you'd like us to call for you?" she asked.

Emily stared blankly at her and then she swiped the tears off her cheek. She shook her head no. She knew she was being asked to leave, so she took a deep, shaky breath and pulled herself to her feet. She clutched the frog and her framed photograph to her chest.

"I have someone waiting for me in the parking lot," she whispered.

The nurse nodded.

"Do you want me to walk with you?" she asked.

Emily shook her head no and left quietly.

***

When Ryan returned to the hospital parking lot after running errands for his folks, he found Emily sitting on the curb waiting for him. When she lifted her head at the sound of the pickup truck's distinctive rattle, he could see she had been crying. It wasn't until she stood, and he saw the stuffed frog and the framed photo still in her grasp, that he knew why.

Ryan's heart dropped to the bottom of his stomach as Emily climbed wordlessly inside the cab. He didn't have to try to imagine how she felt. He already knew what it felt like to lose somebody that close. He also knew, in a situation like that, there were no words that would bring comfort or relief from such a devastating blow. Still he tried.

"Are you okay?" he asked softly.

Emily looked at him with eyes that were heavy with exhaustion and grief. She looked like she had aged ten years in the last hour.

"No," she whispered, "I'm not."

Considering the matter closed, she cast her eyes out the window and leaned her head limply against the glass. The cold surface felt good against her burning skin. She closed her eyes, but she could still feel the weight of Ryan's gaze. Whether he was waiting for her to say something more, or simply trying to size up just how bad off she was, it didn't matter. Nothing mattered anymore.

***

That night at the Corbin residence, Ryan broke the news to his family. He watched Emily's apartment tentatively, but as darkness fell, no lights or movement could be detected behind the apartment windows. As he sat on the front porch swing, he debated on whether or not he should go check on her. He knew how dark things could get when faced with such overwhelming shock and grief. He hadn't seen or heard from her mother, and he could only imagine how alone she must be feeling.

As if to answer his unspoken question, Joan stepped out onto the porch holding a tray with a plate and a cup of tea.

"She might not feel like eating, but I'd feel better if you could at least try and get her to take some tea," she said.

"Me?" Ryan asked.

Joan nodded solemnly, and Ryan dutifully took the tray and crossed the driveway to Emily's apartment.

When she didn't answer his knocks, he hesitantly tried the door knob. Finding it unlocked, he let himself in and called her name.

Although he got no answer, he was able to follow the sound of her weeping to the bedroom. There, he found Emily curled into fetal position clutching the stuffed frog to her chest.

"Emily?" he called.

She looked up from her tear-streaked pillow. When she saw Ryan standing there with a tray, she rolled over onto her back, but she was unable to muster up the strength to acknowledge him.

He walked cautiously over to her bed and set the tray down on her nightstand.

"Mom made you some tea and something to eat if you're hungry."

Emily shook her head no.

"She always said there was a tea for every ailment. I'm not sure if they make one for a broken heart, but if they do, I'm sure this is it," Ryan coaxed.

Ryan tried to hand her the mug, but Emily shook her head no again. He set the mug aside.

"Ok, well I'm not here to push tea remedies on you. I just wanted to check to see if you needed anything," Ryan said gently.

Emily stared at the ceiling. She wished he wasn't being so nice. It made her heart hurt more. A single tear escaped down her cheek and disappeared into her dark hair line, but she shook her head no again.

"Ok, then. I'll go," Ryan resigned.

When he reached the doorway to her bedroom, her voice stopped him cold.

"Ryan?" she asked.

He turned to see her looking at him with pools of emotion swimming in her eyes. The look nearly brought him to his knees. He waited for what seemed to be an eternity for her to say what she needed from him.

"Stay?" she asked finally with searching eyes.

Part of her didn't want to ask because she didn't want to know if he would stay, or if he would walk out on her like her mother had earlier. She didn't think she could stand to be left alone again, but she didn't think she could stand the emptiness any longer either.

Her request caught Ryan off guard. For a moment, he didn't move, and she thought he would leave. But then, he moved quietly over to her bedside and sat down. He didn't try to talk to her and she appreciated that. Instead, he just silently handed her the mug of tea again. She took it this time and scooted over to sit on the bed next to him.

As she gingerly sipped from the mug, he reached over and took her other hand. She didn't pull away like he half expected, but she didn't return his grasp either. Instead, she looked down at their hands. Then, slowly, he felt her fingers curl into his.

They sat like that, in silence, until she finished her tea. Ryan took the empty mug from her hand and placed it carefully back on the tray. When he looked at her, she still looked dazed, but much calmer.

The tea helped soothe her throat that was raw from tears. She pushed the hair back from her eyes and exhaled slowly. She looked at Ryan tentatively and then lowered her head gently into his lap.

Ryan rested his hand on her shoulder and waited for the sleep he knew would inevitably come. Within minutes, her breathing had taken on a slow, steady rhythm. He held her a few minutes more to ensure she was soundly asleep before he shifted his legs out from under her head.

She only stirred slightly when he lifted her head and placed a pillow beneath her cheek. The words that escaped her sleep-soaked lips shattered his heart.

"I'm sorry... Lily Pad," she murmured.

He swiped a tear from his own face before he tucked a strand of her dark hair behind her ear. Before he left, he pulled a blanket over her and placed Tony under her arm.

21
GOD IN EVERY CLOUD

"Life is a joyful music
Turn it up nice and loud
You used to tell me you could see God in every cloud"

A silence settled over Pine Ridge as a thick fog rolled in and blanketed the earth. The skies were a deep shade of gray, and the vibrant colors of fall were muted beneath nature's veil. Nothing stirred in the wind, nothing gleamed in the sun, and no children played outside in their yards.

At noon on a Tuesday, a sign hung at the Corbin's store entrance. The black hand-painted letters reading: CLOSED, served as an ominous statement that all was not well in Pine Ridge.

A crowd of people stood outside on the sidewalk in front of the small church in the center of town. A majority of them were teenagers huddled together to form a battalion against a kind of sadness many of them had never known. Their dark clothes were paled only by the sorrow that darkened their faces.

Slowly, they began to filter in through the church doors to pay their last respects to Lily and her family. Ryan, Danny, Joan, and Harold shuffled their way through the crowd and found an empty pew toward the back of the church.

In the front row, Lily's parents sat with Lily's aunt Kay between them. They did not speak to each other, but instead, stared helplessly at the arrangement of white lilies that stood in contrast to the black casket before them. A low murmur of hushed tones drifted through the church aisle. When the minister cleared his voice, an immediate silence fell over the assembly.

"My friends, I thank you, and the family of Lily McLoughlin thanks you for coming today to celebrate the life that was cut short too soon…" the minister began.

Ryan hadn't seen Emily in days, and her absence at her own sister's funeral caused him to look to his mother with concern. Joan knew exactly what was on her son's mind, and she quickly reassured him.

"Don't worry, sweetie, she'll be here. She'll be here," Joan whispered.

Ryan nodded and turned his attention back to the minister's speech.

"There will be disbelief and sadness in the hearts of many of us who are in this room as we are confronted with feelings of loss and uncertainty…" the minister continued.

A blast of cold air followed the sound of the church doors opening. The minister paused in his eulogy as heads turned to the back of the church. Emily stood at the entrance dressed in a long black dress that blew around her in the October wind. The scent of lilies was overpowering, drawing her attention immediately to the casket adorned in the white flowers.

She took a deep breath and scanned the crowd for a familiar face. She spotted the Corbin's sitting near the back, and Ryan offered her a sympathetic, yet relieved smile. Emily continued to scan the crowd until she found her aunt Kay. She smiled at Emily and motioned for her to sit with them. Susan didn't look at Emily. She remained emotionless and in perfect posture with eyes straight ahead. Susan's oblivion wasn't out of spite or out of anger towards Emily. In truth, Susan was so lost that she hadn't a clue who was or wasn't around her. Emily hesitantly made her way to the front of the church.

Emily paused as she drew near enough to see Lily's shaved head peeking out of the casket. She had makeup on, lots of it. Emily's mind flashed back to the beauty session she and Lily had only a short time ago in her hospital room. She clenched and unclenched her fists as she fought to keep the tears back, but it was useless. The tears spilled free and Emily had to force herself to look away. With all eyes on her, she quickly found a seat at the far end of the family pew.

The minister resumed his eulogy, but his words sounded like they were in a foreign language to Emily. As her eyes fixated on the white lilies, a collage of memories played through her mind.

The flood of memories was too much for Emily to endure. Without even realizing it, she had stood up and made her way to the front of Lily's casket. As tears poured from her darkly lined eyes, she clutched her sister's hand. Lily was no longer hot with fever. The feeling of her cold, pale, skin sent Emily to her knees. Emily hung her head and let herself become consumed by her grief.

Ryan's first impulse was to get up and go to her, but his mother held him back. She knew Emily needed to deal with this in her own way.

Somewhere deep within Susan, she was also tempted to go to her daughter's side, but she didn't. Her body was frozen still, and although no tears fell from her eyes, her heart was broken in a million pieces.

The minister finished his sermon, but all eyes were emotionally focused on Emily sobbing at her sister's casket. Slowly, people filed out of the church with somber faces. The Corbin family huddled together on the sidewalk waiting to say their condolences to the family. They saw Steve exit the church first, but he had his head down, and he was headed to the parking lot with a determined stride. Shortly after, Susan, Kay, and Kay's family followed. They lingered and made polite nods and handshakes to people that were also waiting to offer their condolences before leaving.

Worry washed over Ryan's face when he didn't see Emily exit the church with them. He was about to go inside to check on her when he saw her appear on the front steps of the church. She looked lost and dazed as she scanned the crowd with uncertainty. Nobody approached her or offered her their condolences. She was an outsider here and she knew it.

Ryan excused himself while Susan and Kay made their way closer to where his family waited for them. He walked over to Emily. She looked surprised, yet grateful, to see him there.

"How are you holding up?" Ryan asked and immediately regretted it. "I'm sorry, I just never know the right words to say in situations like this."

"It's okay," Emily said politely.

She glanced behind her shoulder at the now empty church.

"I... I just, didn't want to leave her," she offered with a cracked voice.

"I know," Ryan said empathetically as he guided her over to his family.

When Kay saw Emily approaching, she closed the gap and gathered her into a warm embrace. Emily surrendered easily into her aunt's arms. Emily gazed over her aunt's shoulder and her eyes settled on her mother. Susan was surrounded by people offering their condolences, but it was obvious to Emily that her mother was completely zoned out and drowning in her sadness. It had been many, many years, but it was a look Emily was all-too familiar with.

Kay followed Emily's gaze and knew exactly what Emily was thinking.

"She'll be okay, Emily. She just needs some time," said Kay. "And when she does come around, she'll find her way back to you. I promise."

Emily was never one to believe that time heals old wounds or even that time makes the heart grow fonder. When it came to her mother, Emily just assumed that time made it easier for the heart to forget.

"I promise you, Emily, she'll come around," Kay reiterated.

How could she pretend to be so sure of that? Emily wondered. Instead of speaking her mind, Emily politely changed the subject.

"How long will you be in town for?"

Her aunt seemed grateful for the distraction.

"Another day or so," she answered. "We'll definitely get together before I go, okay? You do know you can call me anytime if you ever need someone to talk to, right? And you know you'll always have a place to stay if you want?"

Emily nodded and gave her aunt another hug.

She turned her attention back to Ryan, who had been waiting for her patiently. He placed his hand on the small of her back and continued to steer her gently toward his family.

When Joan saw Emily, she wiped a fresh tear from her eye and pulled Emily in for a tight embrace. The gesture brought the ball of tears Emily had been holding in her throat closer to the surface. When she pulled back, she saw Harold looking down at her with watery eyes.

The sight of the big, tall man nearly in tears pulled at Emily's heart. She gave him a small encouraging smile to show him she was alright. He outstretched an arm and pulled her to him, planting a kiss on her forehead as he gave her a squeeze. Max and Gus stood on either side of them, and both nodded their condolences to her. Gus, who had removed his aviator cap for the occasion, reached out and squeezed her arm affectionately.

Before Emily could say anything to any of them, Danny stepped up to her and began chanting softly.

"Danny has a new favorite toy, Danny has a new favorite toy…"

His voice grew more urgent with every repeat.

"Not now," Ryan gently scolded Danny.

Emily smiled warmly at Danny.

"It's okay, Danny. What's your new favorite toy?" she asked.

Danny looked down at his feet and shifted nervously in his shoes. Without looking up at her he answered.

"It's a Charlie in the Box. A Charlie in the Box from the Island of Misfit Toys," he told her.

Ryan didn't know what Danny was talking about, but he could clearly see by the look on Emily's face that she did. Unable to contain the tears any longer, Emily let them spill down her cheeks as she gathered Danny in her arms. Danny, who usually didn't respond to hugs and tended to shy away from human touch, actually leaned into Emily. He lifted his arm limply in an attempt to return the embrace as his family looked on in amazement.

"Emily loves her train with square wheels, too," she whispered in Danny's ear.

***

Out in the cabin, Frank leafed through the newspapers that Danny dropped off earlier in the week. He let his eyes settle on the obituaries. It was a guilty pleasure of his to see who else might have lost a loved one. Somehow, if he saw a family name he recognized, it made him feel less alone in his grief. Knowing someone else out there was suffering from heartache too made him feel slightly better. He recognized the name as soon as he saw it, and he read the print out loud.

"Lily Ann McLaughlin, 17, of Pine Ridge, died early Tuesday morning in Grafton Falls Hospital..."

His voice trailed off into a whisper. He pulled his hand down over his face in a subconscious effort to remove what he had seen. Seeing that name certainly didn't make him feel better. Mourning the loss of a child was a heartache he wouldn't wish upon even his worst enemy. His mind flashed back to the last conversation he had with Emily. His own words came back to haunt him and echoed around him in the silence of the cabin.

"You have no God damn idea what it was like... to watch someone in so much pain... and to know there's not a God damn thing you can do about it."

Those were the words he shouted at her in anger. He remembered Emily telling him that her sister was in the hospital, but he never bothered to ask why. He just assumed it was something simple.

He shook his head in regret. He had been wrong about that. He had been wrong about a lot of things lately. He looked down at the pile of letters at his feet and stared at them for a very long time. His wife had always told him, it was never too late to try and set things right. For as hard as he tried, he could never think of a time she had been wrong.

With a trembling hand, he reached down to his feet where the letters lay next to a half-finished bottle of whiskey. His hand hovered over the whiskey bottle, wanting to numb the pain. Instead, he found himself picking up one of the letters. Maybe rather than numbing the pain, he could try to heal it, he thought for the first time. With shaking hands, he opened the envelope and pulled out the first of many, many unread letters.

22
INTO THE BRIGHT LIGHTS

"Soar from the moonlight straight to the sunrise
This will be our time to free-fall and nosedive
Out of the black night into the bright lights
With the whole world in our sight
Like a miniature paradise"

When the dismal days had finally passed, Emily awoke early and made her way outside. It was a bright, clear fall morning, and she noticed Ryan sitting on the front porch leisurely leafing through the Sunday paper.

"I haven't seen you around lately. Are you avoiding me or something?" she joked lightly.

"No. Not at all. I just figured you could use some space," Ryan answered. "And like I told you before, I'm horrible at knowing what to say in situations like this."

Emily smiled in appreciation.

"So, you heading to work soon?" she asked.

"Nope. I actually have the entire day off."

"Wow! How will they survive?" Emily teased.

Ryan playfully sneered at her. Emily just smiled and began searching for something else to say. However, no words came to either of them and they fell into an awkward silence.

Ryan sensed Emily wanted to say something more, but didn't.

"Well, I'll let you get back to enjoying your day off then," she said reluctantly.

As she walked away, Ryan was hit with an idea.

"Hey, Emily?" he called after her.

She turned around quickly with curiosity dancing behind her eyes.

"I was actually thinking about taking a drive out to the coast today… if you wanna… join me?"

Emily's face lit up and she instantaneously said, "I would love that."

"Just a warning," Ryan added, "it's a long drive, so you'll be stuck in the truck with me all day."

"As long as you leave your Backstreet Boys CD at home, we'll be all set."

"Ha, ha," he responded. "I told you before, that CD is Lacey's. I don't know how it got thrown in with mine."

"Uh huh," Emily smiled.

"Just go grab your camera," Ryan said shaking his head.

***

It took nearly two hours to trek across Maine to its coast. If this was a few weeks earlier, Emily would have dreaded being stuck in a truck with him for that long. The feeling would have been mutual for Ryan as well, but today was different. There were no uncomfortable silences, no overly sarcastic remarks, and no avoiding basic questions. The conversations were kept simple, but each of them seemed to have plenty say. They talked about movies, music, and all things pop culture.

About an hour in, Ryan took the exit towards Bangor.

"I thought we were going to the coast?" asked Emily.

"We are, but I thought you'd enjoy a little side trip."

Less than ten minutes later, they were standing in front of a thirty-one foot statue of Paul Bunyan.

"You've got to be shitting me," Emily laughed as she pulled out her camera. "We should get the smelly blue bus to do a field trip here. Your dad and his two sidekicks would love it."

"Oh trust me, once a year those three make a pilgrimage here, and they spend hours bantering and worshipping this thing."

The imagery of that made both of them crack up laughing.

"Well, that was quite the side trip," Emily said as they got back into the truck.

"Oh that wasn't the side trip I had in mind. I actually forgot about that statue until we drove by it."

"So what's this other side trip then?" she asked.

Ryan didn't say a word. He simply smiled and drove on.

Moments later, he pulled into a neighborhood and parked on one of the side streets.

Emily gave him a suspicious look and said, "Please tell me we're not visiting one of your crazy relatives or something,"

Again, he simply smiled without saying a word. He exited the truck and motioned for her to follow. Up ahead, there were a handful of people snapping pictures of a house. It was a nice, well-maintained house, but just a house nonetheless.

They walked closer, and before Emily could ask who lived there, she saw the front gate. It was made of iron and was in the design of a spider web. At the top of the gates were perched two iron bats. All at once it hit her.

"Holy shit balls! Is this Stephen King's house?" she whispered loudly to Ryan. He smiled and nodded.

***

By late morning, they arrived at the picturesque coastal town of Camden. The vibrant, well-maintained store fronts on Main Street were a direct contrast to that of Pine Ridge. Although most of the stores were closed, it was only due to it being off-season. The scent of pine, which Emily had become accustomed to, was replaced by the ever-present scent of salt air.

To Emily's delight, a few of the stores that were open were photography and art galleries. Ryan stood by and watched Emily's eager eyes go from one picture to the next, and although she never said a word, he knew she would do anything to one day have her own artwork hanging in a place like this.

After taking a walk along the waterfront, they got back into Ryan's truck and made their way further down the coast. Leisurely, they headed south on Route 1, stopping frequently for Emily to get plenty of beautiful shots of the Maine coast. From rocky beaches, to fishing boats, to lighthouses, and even to the giant pyramid of lobster traps in Rockport, Emily was in photography heaven.

When they passed over the bridge into Wiscasset, Ryan made it a point to stop at Maine's famous takeout stand, Red's Eats. Unfortunately, the iconic little takeout stand was also closed for the season, so his craving for a lobster roll would have to wait.

As the sun fell from the sky, Ryan's truck rumbled into the mid-coast area and the town of Boothbay Harbor. Boothbay, like Camden, was another quintessential coastal Maine town. And also like its counterpart, most of the shops and restaurants were closed for the season. One of the places that was still open was the Tugboat Inn and restaurant. Built around a real tugboat, and located directly on the water, this proved to be the perfect spot for dinner.

Ryan made it a point throughout the day not to talk about Lily or even about Emily's mother. It was obvious that both of these topics weighed heavily on Emily's mind. Ryan made sure to keep their conversations simple. It wouldn't be until after dinner that Emily finally said what was on her mind all day.

After leaving the restaurant, they made their way down one of the many piers and sat on its edge. Behind them, the sun made its final descent beneath the horizon with its fiery red blaze leaving a trail of shifting pastel hues in its wake.

As they sat quietly, thoughts crashed through Emily's head like the waves on the rocks beneath them. Finally, she broke the silence with a heavy sigh.

"The last few days I've been waking up thinking it was all just a bad dream. I'm just so pissed at myself. I never should have let all that time go by. You always think there is going to be another tomorrow… until there isn't."

Ryan knew there were no words of comfort he could offer her, so he reached over and took her hand. She looked down at their fingers intertwined but did not pull away. Instead, she gave his hand an appreciative squeeze.

"I can't help but to feel so guilty for not seeing or talking to her more over the last seven years – especially when she was in the hospital the first time. I wanted to, I really did, but… I was in no condition to. Everything about me then was a mess. There was no way I could face her… or my mother, not with the type of person I had become. The longer I put off visiting her, the more regretful I became. And the more regretful I became, the more pissed off at myself I became. It was like this sick, vicious circle. Eventually, I found myself sinking into this hole… this dark, deep hole of depression."

Emily paused and reminded herself who she was talking to. Ryan had never been through something like that, and he certainly didn't need to be brought down by her feelings of self-hatred and remorse.

"You know what, forget it. I'm sure you don't…"

"Don't what? Understand?" Ryan asked.

"Well, I'm sure you understand. I'm just not sure how well you can relate," Emily offered.

Ryan looked at her in a way that suggested she was off base. Emily mistook the look for a warning not to tread into territory that had brought them to their argument.

"No, it's not a put down, I swear. Everyone should be so lucky to have a life and a family that is as perfect as yours," Emily said softly. "It's just that not everybody is."

Ryan's silence made Emily start to feel self-conscious. She decided to stop talking before she said something stupid again. When she looked over at Ryan he seemed to be a million miles away.

"Are you ok?" she asked.

Ryan nodded and shook off his reverie. He looked at her like he had forgotten she was there. Then he slapped her knee playfully as he prepared to change the subject.

"So, my mom tells me you're headed back to the big city tomorrow?" he asked.

Emily nodded half-heartedly.

"You don't seem very enthused," Ryan said and then paused to ponder something. "Aww, don't tell me you're gonna miss it here in… what did you call it… East Bumfuck?"

Emily smiled guiltily.

"Do you have a place to stay? You mentioned that you broke up with your boyfriend and moved out. Are you having a change of heart about that?"

Emily looked at Ryan like he had two heads.

"Not a chance! I'm totally done with that. For now, I'm gonna crash on my friend Amanda's couch until I can find a place. Hopefully that will be sooner rather than later. She lives with her four year old daughter, so it's not exactly an ideal situation, but then again, none of my situations have ever been ideal. I also have to find a new place to work."

"What happened to that club you worked at?"

Emily shrugged her shoulders. She knew she could probably get her job back at the club. Part of her wanted something different, but another part of her said she couldn't do any better.

"Well, I'm sure there are hundreds of clubs or restaurants in Boston you can waitress or bartend in. Maybe if I get some time off, I could come down and we could hang out sometime. Rumor has it, there is more to Boston than just the Red Sox."

Emily forced a smile and looked away.

"You okay? Did I say something wrong?" Ryan asked.

Emily shook her head no. This wasn't the way she had hoped this conversation would go.

"Look, the club I worked at isn't the type of club you think. I'm not a waitress or even a bartender there. I'm kind of a... dancer.... kind of."

Ryan looked confused. When he originally asked her about what she did, he just assumed it was one of those cool Boston dance clubs. What other kind of club was there, he thought? His eyes quickly lit up with the answer.

"Holy crap! You're a stripper?"

Emily shook her head. Ryan's amusement only made her feel more ashamed.

"Exotic dancer," she corrected. "But just so you know, I only dance. I don't do anything on the side or in the back room or whatever."

Ryan was about to crack a joke, but the look of shame on Emily's face stopped the words from leaving his mouth. He quickly found himself reformulating his answer.

"Why didn't you just tell me? It's just a job, Em. And, hell, I'm sure it pays pretty good too."

"Try really good. That's the only reason I did it so long. I just don't know if I can keep doing it though. All the rude comments, the pathetic come on lines, all the pervy stares."

Ryan tried to take his amusement down a notch and aimed for a more sympathetic approach. He put his hand on her knee to show her he didn't look at her any differently. Before she continued, Emily took a deep breath and seemed to relax a little under his touch.

"The ironic thing is, when I first started, I loved it. I absolutely loved all the attention, but now... now I'd just settle for thirty seconds of real eye contact."

Emily hadn't been able to look at Ryan since she said the word dancer, but she forced her gaze back to his. She was both relieved and annoyed to see his goofy grin.

"Go ahead, get your jokes out of the way," Emily said.

"No jokes. It's just... I've never known a real strip... exotic dancer before. As in, be friends with one... outside the club. Not for lack of trying though."

Emily shook her head and rolled her eyes at him as he continued to smirk sheepishly at her.

"Sooo, what was it?" he asked eagerly.

"What was what?"

"What was your stage name? Mercedes? Savannah? Wait, wait, you look more like a Raven!"

"Really?" Emily asked.

Ryan just threw his palms up helplessly and shrugged his shoulders.

"If you must know, I just used my middle name, Rose."

"Rose, huh? It's not Bambi or Cinnamon, but it's not bad I guess."

Ryan seemed a little disappointed.

"Gee, thanks for your approval," Emily said sarcastically. "Do you wanna hear something else embarrassing?"

"Well, I wouldn't want to stop you while you were on a roll," Ryan said with a smirk.

"When I first started, I actually got a tattoo on my ass of the nickname they gave me."

Ryan raised an intrigued eyebrow at her and she turned away in embarrassment.

"I guess they thought Rose was a little on the plain side too, so they started calling me the Wild Irish Rose. I liked it so much I had it written under a small black rose on my left cheek."

"Right on your ass?" Ryan asked incredulously.

"Right on my ass," Emily confirmed. "The sad thing is, I was actually proud of it; the nickname, the tattoo, the attention. But now it makes me feel so…"

"It's just a tattoo, Em. It doesn't define who you are. Neither does a job or how you dress. They're all a reflection of you, but they don't define you."

Emily gave him a warm smile of appreciation. That was a kind thing for him to say, but she wasn't really sure how much of it he truly meant. As the last rays of sunlight disappeared beneath the horizon, the wind from the ocean picked up. Emily wrapped her arms around herself to protect against the onset of a chill.

"You wanna walk on the beach for a bit?" Ryan asked.

Emily looked at him skeptically.

"It will warm you up," Ryan offered.

Emily shrugged her shoulders, but she didn't resist when Ryan pulled her to her feet. They followed the sidewalk down to a set of steps that lead them onto the beach. Emily welcomed the feeling of the soft sand shifting beneath the soles of her shoes.

The air was still moist and chilly, but Ryan was right, now that she was moving, she felt warmer. They walked along the water's edge for a long while before Emily finally broke the silence.

"Believe it or not, I really am going to miss this place. The whole small-town thing has kinda grown on me – especially you and your family. It was one thing to open your house up to me, but you also made me feel at home when you did. It's a feeling I've been missing for a long time. I know it sounds corny, but I really think this place kinda saved me from me."

"How so?" Ryan asked.

"Remember I told you when Lily first got sick that I couldn't bring myself to go visit her?"

"Yeah?"

"I wasn't exaggerating when I said I was a mess. Emotionally and physically, I was a total fucking mess. I was drinking a lot and experimenting with different drugs. Well, not really experimenting in the conventional sense, but more like experimenting with which ones dulled my sense of reality the best. I had just started at the club, and with all the attention I was getting there, I totally thought I was a hot shit… but I wasn't. I was just a hot mess."

"Yeah, but that's not who you are anymore," Ryan offered.

To an extent he was right, but she could still feel the person she had been lingering just beneath the surface, ready to pop back into action at the drop of a hat. It was easier being that person, but she could see now, that person had also been missing out on a lot of important stuff life had to offer.

"I'd like to think I'm a better person than before, but… as soon as I heard Lily was gone, I had this overwhelming desire to fall back into my old habits."

"But you didn't," Ryan reminded her.

Guiltily, she looked over at Ryan and said, "I kinda did. Well, at least I started to. I actually caught a ride on that stupid little blue bus in hopes of taking a bigger bus back to Boston. I even called my douchebag ex. Of course, he answered the phone by saying *'I knew you'd come to your senses eventually. When are you coming back? The rent was due two days ago'*. That was a real wake up call."

"Please tell me you reamed him out?"

Emily shook her head no.

"I didn't have the energy to deal with him. I just hung up. That's when I told the bus driver to stop so I could get off the bus. I knew then that I didn't want to keep running away from my problems. I had so much regret about all the times I didn't talk or visit Lily while she was alive. I sure as hell needed to be there for her funeral."

Ryan wrapped his arms around her shoulders and pulled her in for a hug. She fell into his arms easily and welcomed the affection. They stood in each other's embrace at the base of some old sea-weathered steps that led up to another pier. Then, a moment later, Ryan guided her wordlessly up the steps. The wide wooden planks creaked softly under their footsteps. They both draped their arms across the top of the railing at the end of the pier and gazed down at the waves swirling beneath them.

For a long moment, no words were spoken between them and they both got lost in their own thoughts as they listened to the sound of the crashing waves surround them. Finally, it was Ryan who broke the silence.

"It wasn't Danny or Jake," he stated.

Emily was shaken out of her own thoughts at Ryan's seemingly random comment. She had no idea what he was talking about, but she could see by the look on his face it was serious.

"What?" she asked.

Ryan shook his head when he realized he had been thinking out loud. He watched her eyes turn a deeper shade of green as concern filtered through them, and he knew he couldn't hold back what he had wanted to tell her all along.

"The whole Turtle Pond thing... it wasn't Danny or Jake who dared me. It was my other brother, Thomas... my twin."

Emily looked relieved and somewhat amused.

"You have a twin?" she asked smiling widely at him.

"I did. He, umm... passed way."

The smile fell off Emily's face and was replaced with shock.

"Oh my God, Ryan. I never knew..."

Her words trailed off as she began to realize how wrong she had been about him not being able to relate to her.

"My family doesn't really talk about it much. You've actually never been in our house, have you?" he asked.

Emily shook her head no and answered, "Not really. Just the foyer and the kitchen."

"There are some pictures of him in the living room and on the wall heading upstairs."

Ryan paused a moment before continuing.

"We all get together every year on the anniversary and go the cemetery."

After a long moment of silence, Emily hesitantly began to ask, "How did he…"

Unsure if she was overstepping her boundaries, her words trailed off. Ryan's kind blue eyes assured her that her question was fine.

"I was still living down in New York at the time. He went to a Labor Day party at one of our friend's house. It was like an annual thing. You know, a huge bonfire, live band, the whole works. Thomas lived for those sorta things. He was always the life of any party. Actually, he was the life of wherever he went; a party, a classroom, our dinner table. It didn't matter where he was, he could tell a story like nobody's business. The guy had a story for everything, and he could take the worst joke in the world and make it the funniest thing you've ever heard."

Ryan shook his head and smiled at the memories running through his head while Emily listened carefully.

"Even though Thomas was a huge party animal, he never drove drunk, and he never ever forgot to wear his seat belt." Ryan paused then continued, "Unfortunately, on that night he did both. He ended up wrapping his car around a tree on Huckins Road."

Emily immediately remembered the sharp turn in the road that first day Danny had driven with them to the hospital and how Danny had wailed at the sight of the "bad tree". With a shaking hand, Emily immediately covered her mouth and uttered, "Bad tree… that's the bad tree Danny was talking about."

Ryan nodded his head and pulled his gaze from the swirling tide below and looked at the pools gathered in Emily's eyes.

"I got the call from my dad a little after 3 A.M. that morning. The funny thing is, I knew what he was gonna say before I even answered the phone. Thomas and I were always so opposite. I never really believed in the whole 'mental connection' between twins… not until that night anyway. About an hour before my dad called me, I woke suddenly with this sharp pain in my chest and a splitting headache. I've had headaches before, but this one wasn't like any I'd ever had before. I can't really explain it, and I know it sounds crazy, but I just knew something terrible had happened to him."

"I've heard about things like that happening before with twins," Emily whispered.

"Yeah, I just never thought it would happen with us, not like that anyway. We might have been identical, but in every other aspect we were pretty opposite. We listened to different types of music, we had totally different tastes in women, and we sure as hell weren't the type of twins to finish each other's sentences, ya know?"

Emily nodded and placed a hand on his shoulder. Ryan turned his gaze out over the horizon and continued.

"After the funeral, I never ended up going back to New York. As a matter of fact, I stopped playing music all together. I just lost all motivation for it. Or maybe it was my passion that I lost because I just gave up on everything that used to mean anything to me."

Emily nodded. She knew all too well what it was like to give up on living even when your heart still pumped blood.

"So that deep, dark hole of depression that you mentioned… yeah, I know exactly what you were talking about. Over the next few weeks, I found myself sinking deeper and deeper into it – and every time I tried to climb out…"

"An avalanche of more shit would fall on you?" Emily finished his thought for him.

Ryan looked at her in surprise for a moment and then nodded in agreement.

"I barely left my room, never mind the house, and I started drinking more and more."

"Your parents must have been worried sick about you?"

"Normally, my dad woulda given me a swift kick in the ass and my mom woulda hired a team of therapists for me, but I'm not sure they even knew I was there. They both took the accident pretty hard, like really hard actually. Being the responsible adults, they forced themselves back to work, but they were definitely still in a haze of denial and grief. The last thing on their minds was my depression and drinking. Rightly so, they had enough to deal with."

"I'm so sorry, Ryan... for everything."

Emily felt terrible for being so judgmental of Ryan and assuming that he had never experienced real sorrow. She needed him to know she wasn't just saying she was offering him her condolences, but that she was sincerely sorry for labeling him without even giving him the benefit of the doubt. She took his hand in hers and squeezed it until he looked at her again.

"For everything," she repeated.

Ryan gave her a small smile that said he understood and nodded his appreciation. They stood watching the ocean in silence while Emily digested everything he had just told her.

"So how did you finally climb out of it?" Emily asked.

Ryan slowly pulled his hand from her grasp and stuffed them in the pockets of his denim jacket. He knew if he continued, the story was about to take a turn for the worse. He would have been content to let it end there, but Emily was searching his face with those intent green eyes. He sighed heavily and continued.

"On the one month anniversary of the accident, I went up to the cemetery and got absolutely wrecked by Thomas' grave. When I finally ran out of alcohol, I proceeded to drive drunk back to my parent's house to get more booze."

Emily sucked her breath in sharply. It caught in her throat and she had to mentally command herself to release it again. It came out in a small white vapor cloud that hovered between them for a second before flashing off into the crisp fall night.

"I know, I know. Trust me, even in my condition the irony wasn't lost on me. Luckily, our house was only two miles away. My parents were still at work when I got home, so I raided their liquor cabinet. The next thing I knew, I was in my parent's bedroom with a bottle of vodka, and I was going through shoeboxes of old photographs."

Emily found her muscles tensing as she braced herself for what she knew was going to be hard to hear.

"I actually turned it into a drinking game. Every time I would come across a picture of Thomas I would have another drink."

Ryan laughed a hard, cynical laugh, one that Emily had never heard him use before. She cringed at the sound.

"I started going through more and more boxes. For some stupid reason, I was determined to find this old Halloween picture of me and Thomas dressed as Batman and Robin."

Again, his laugh cut the air between them, but this time, Emily didn't flinch. Instead, she shifted her body closer to his until their arms were touching as they stood side by side.

"While I was searching, I came across another box... the box my dad kept his revolver in. Ironically, the combination was our birthdate. At the time, it felt like a sign that I should..."

Ryan trailed off. He had to pause to take a deep breath and steady himself before he could continue. His blue eyes searched the night sky which was bright with stars above them. He could feel her eyes on his mouth as she quietly waited for him to find the words.

"The next thing I knew, I was sitting on their bed with the bottle of vodka in one hand and the gun in the other. I had no idea if it was even loaded, but at that point it didn't matter. Nothing mattered. I just remember there were so many thoughts going through my mind... about how my music career was a giant failure... about how I totally fucked up my relationship with Tanya... and that I was going to be stuck in Pine Ridge for the rest of my life as a fuckin' nobody. And of course, I thought about my brother and how I was never gonna see his face again or hear one of his stupid jokes."

Again, Ryan took a long pause before continuing.

"I just remember closing my eyes and feeling the cold steel of the barrel against my temple."

Emily could feel Ryan's body begin to tremble next to hers. She slipped her hand between his arm and his body to try and steady him. Ryan welcomed her touch and took his clenched fist out of his pocket and grabbed hold of her hand. He looked down at her small fingers locked inside of his.

"Then it happened. For some reason I opened my eyes, and there, standing in front of me was Danny. I'll never forget that look of fear, of utter fear and helplessness on his face. I've never seen him look that way before. People can say what they will about Danny and his autism, but he knows what's going on around him. And on that day, he knew exactly what was about to go down."

Emily's heart tightened as she pictured Danny walking in on Ryan in that state. Anyone would have been horrified, but she knew Danny felt and processed things much more intensely than others. She couldn't even imagine what must have been going through his head.

"Oh my God, what did he do?" Emily gasped.

"Before I could do or say anything, he came over and sat down next to me. He seemed to be taking careful inventory of everything that I had scattered across their bed. Finally, he rested his eyes on that Halloween picture of me and Thomas. He picked it up and just sat there staring at it for what seemed like forever. By that time, I had lowered the gun and forgotten all about it. I was too worried about Danny and how he was going to react. Then, all of a sudden, a smile broke out across his face and he started singing the stupid theme song from the old Batman TV show."

Emily smiled in relief through her tears and saw Ryan was doing the same as he shook his head, still in disbelief.

"The next thing I know, we were both singing that stupid, friggin song. It's not even a song, just a bunch of dunnah nunna nunnas!"

Emily smirked at the image of Ryan and Danny singing the Batman song together. She pictured Ryan slurring and Danny a little off beat.

"Needless to say, that whole situation sobered me up pretty fast. That day was the last time I got drunk. I still have an occasional beer now and again, but I haven't had so much as a buzz-on since that day."

Ryan shifted his gaze back to the ocean waves, his eyes taking on a distant look as he did.

"A day doesn't go by without me thinking about that look on Danny's face. I mean, what if I had... and Danny was the first to find me... and my poor parents... right in their bedroom."

A single tear escaped from Ryan's eye and traveled quickly in a jagged trail down his cheek. Emily tightened her grip on his hand and rested her head on his shoulder. Danny already had a special place in her heart, but now she cherished him a little more because he had saved Ryan.

Without another word spoken, they made their way back to Ryan's truck and began their long ride back to Pine Ridge. Emily's thoughts turned towards the Corbin's. She really was going to miss them. In such a short time, Ryan's family had begun to feel like her family too.

A few miles down the road, Ryan asked, "Are you in a hurry to get back to Pine Ridge tonight?"

"Why, what do you have in mind?" she curiously answered.

"I thought we could maybe swing by L.L. Bean," smirked Ryan.

"At this hour?" she incredulously asked.

"It's open 24 hours a day, 365 days a year."

"Of course it is," she smiled. "Fine. We can stop at your little L.L. Bean store."

It was exactly midnight when they arrived at the store in Freeport. Not only was Emily impressed with how big it was, but she was shocked at how many people were actually there shopping at this hour. By now, Emily felt comfortable enough around Ryan to let her guard down and enjoy the whole L.L. Bean experience.

Inside the store, Emily made Ryan pose with the many stuffed wooded animals. She even asked a stranger to take a picture of her and Ryan in front of a huge moose. Emily also allowed herself to be photographed doing the ultimate touristy thing; posing in front of the famous, giant L.L Bean boot outside the entrance. What amused Ryan the most was when he caught Emily eyeing and admiring a cute outfit. A cute, all-black outfit, but an L.L. Bean one nonetheless.

Nothing much was said on the long, dark ride back to Pine Ridge. Emily thought about her return to Boston later that day. She was excited to see Amanda and Chloe again, but the more she thought about it, that's pretty much where her excitement ended. What was she really going back there for anyway? And if not Boston, where else would she go, she thought? From there, Emily began thinking about Pine Ridge, more specifically, the Corbin's.

With Lily gone, and her mother still shutting her out, they were like her only family now. Emily shook her head. Honestly, who was she kidding? They would probably be relieved when she was gone. She knew she had been a burden on them and they were just too kind-hearted to ever tell her that. No, she thought, it was time stop being sentimental and move on.

She tried to come back and make things right with her own family and the only thing she managed to do is prove to herself that she hadn't changed at all. Learning about Ryan's twin proved again just how judgmental and self-centered she had been since she got here. She would continue to make the same mistakes she had always made and end up hurting the people she loved the most. The best thing she could do now was ignore the selfish part of her that wanted to stay, and just return to Boston.

***

It was nearly 3 A.M. when they pulled into the gravel driveway of the Corbin residence. Nervously, Emily began to fidget with her camera strap.

"Thanks for today," she said quietly. "I really needed it."

Ryan didn't say anything, not because he didn't want to, but because he couldn't find the right words. He just looked at her face, dimly lit up by the soft glow of the porch lights and nodded.

Emily hesitated a moment before reaching for the handle of the truck. When she jumped out of the truck, a pang of anxiety rushed through Ryan as he realized this was one of the last moments he was going to spend with Emily. He wanted to say something memorable to let her know exactly how he felt. The thought of her leaving and forgetting all about him made him cringe. He jumped out of the truck and circled around to the front after her.

"Hey Em," he called to her as she reached the stairs to her apartment.

Emily turned around. The urgency in his voice suggested he wanted to tell her something important. She blushed when she realized what she wanted to hear him say.

Ryan let his eyes drop to her dark red lips, which were slightly parted, and he lost his focus.

"Um... I'll see you tomorrow," he mumbled.

Even from the softly lit driveway, he could see the slight shadow of disappointment filter across Emily's face. She gave him a small nod and let her eyes fall to her feet.

Ryan watched her disappear up the stairs, and he knew right then and there that he had let the moment pass. Life gives us little windows of opportunity and if we don't jump through them when they open for us, we might find ourselves locked out. Ryan watched the light in Emily's apartment flick off and realized he had just missed his window.

The late fall winds grew restless that night in Pine Ridge, and with them, an uncertain energy settled over the town. Some felt the energy as a tug at matters left unfinished. Others felt it as an internal shifting towards a new perspective, but one thing was certain - change was in the air.

As the winds rattled the thin window panes of Emily's apartment, she pulled Lily's old stuffed frog protectively under her arm. She flipped through an album filled with photos she had collected since she arrived in Pine Ridge, and she wished for a reason to stay longer.

She smiled at the many images of the Corbin family she collected at the barbecue, the reunion party, and at the general store. She paused at some photos she had taken of Danny on one of their many walks through the woods. Her favorite was of him peering over the railing of the bridge into the rushing water below. He never said very much, but all it took was one close look at his face to know there was a lot going on behind those eyes. Danny was a lot like that brook, Emily thought, there was so much more to it than what appeared on the surface.

Her smile froze when a photo she had taken of Ryan at the barbeque caught her eye. She had been taking candid shots of the family that day and Ryan must have felt her watching him through the camera lens because he had looked up unexpectedly. In that moment, she had snapped the shot and captured Ryan looking straight at her. He hadn't been expecting the camera on him, so he wasn't smiling. The look on his face was serious and intense. Looking into his bluish grey eyes now, she felt he was looking right into her soul. She shivered at the thought.

It was a long, emotional day and night, but after Ryan dropped Emily off, he wasn't the least bit tired. He grabbed his guitar and went for a long late night walk. The wind blew against Ryan's back as he walked through the quiet streets of Pine Ridge alone. He paused outside the darkened porch of the Corbin General Store. The windows that usually offered a view of life's activities within were now dark and unyielding.

From town, he headed back towards home, stopping when he reached the cove of the old drive in theater. He settled against the east side of the concession stand and took shelter from the wind. It was there that he spent the rest of the night strumming chords on his guitar as he worked out the lyrics to a new song. He remained at the drive in until the sun came up.

23
WILD IRISH ROSE

"And every time I see you dance, my Wild Irish Rose,
I want to jump up on stage with you and give you my clothes.
And may the devil take my soul"

When Emily woke up that morning, she found Danny sitting out on the porch looking through his newest vinyl purchases. It didn't take much coaxing to get him to show them to her. It also didn't take much coaxing to get him to take one last walk down the beaten forest trails.

This time, they didn't stop when they reached the collection of abandoned cars. Instead, they played another game where Emily tried to guess the name of that 80's tune Danny hummed.

"I Want to Know What Love Is by Foreigner?" Emily guessed.

Danny grinned and shook his head no. He liked being able to stump Emily.

"She's Like the Wind by Patrick Swayze?"

Danny turned and placed his index finger on the tip of his nose. That meant she guessed correctly. Emily beamed proudly.

"I'm gonna miss you, Danny," she said.

Danny didn't respond, but his smile faded and he slowed his pace. She knew he understood she was leaving, and by reading the subtle changes in his body language, she knew he was feeling sad about it.

"Lately, I've been thinking a lot about taking chances," said Emily.

"Taking chances is really nothing more than overcoming your fears, ya know?"

Danny looked over at her with interest.

"I took a chance on coming here," she continued. "Just like you took a chance on letting me be your friend."

Danny seemed to give her words careful consideration.

"Every time you take a big risk in your life, no matter how it ends up, you're always glad you took it because if you didn't, you'd have regret. I've learned regret is always worse than not taking a chance, Danny."

They trudged on in silence. The only sound was the wind rustling the few remaining leaves in the tree tops. Emily was relieved that Danny didn't feel the need to stop and visit his uncle in the cabin. It wasn't that she was still angry at him, because she wasn't, not at all. It took losing her sister to realize just how lonely and empty he must be without his wife. Emily held no animosity towards Frank, but she assumed he was still furious at her for invading his privacy.

***

If Danny and Emily did stop to visit Frank, they would have been surprised to find the cabin was empty. Apparently, Ryan wasn't the only one who couldn't sleep that previous night. The late fall wind seemed to draw Frank out of his old cabin and towards town.

When the sun finally poked its head over the horizon, and when the wind had settled, Frank found himself at the gates of the Pine Ridge Cemetery. Although his tired old legs ached from the long walk, his heart ached more.

He pulled his coat closer to his body and cradled the flowers he carried protectively in his arms. A playful breeze nearly swept his hat right off his head, and without thinking, his feet began to carry him without demand in the direction of his wife.

Although he never attended the funeral, they had visited the cemetery once shortly after her diagnosis. Jenny was never one to be caught unprepared. She told Frank she already had a spot picked out in the family plot and had even spoken to their pastor about her funeral.

At the time, Frank didn't want to hear this, and he just shook his head and told her she was overreacting as usual. When she tried to tell him what she wanted at her funeral, he stubbornly refused to listen.

Now, as he stood looking at her name on the headstone, he removed his hat from his head. He hadn't listened to her then, but he hoped it wasn't too late to start a new conversation now.

"I didn't want to listen to you talk about planning your own funeral, Jenny," said Frank. "I know I didn't listen to everything you had to say, but it wasn't because I didn't care. It was because I just wasn't ready to face the idea of living without you."

With a shaking hand, he reached down and placed the pale pink roses on her grave. He didn't have to listen to her back then to know her favorite flowers were pink roses.

"I'm ready now," he told her.

Over the next hour, he sat and talked to his wife. He reminisced about their good ole days and even found himself laughing out loud. He reminisced about the first time they met, their first date, their first kiss… their first everything.

Inevitably his conversation turned to their daughter, Leah. Frank took a long pause then began apologizing for his lack of communication with her.

"I'm so sorry, Jenny. I'm so sorry for how I've treated our daughter since you… left. I know you must be disappointed in the man that I've become this past year, but I promise I'll make things right. I swear. It was just so hard being in that house without you… and even harder being around Leah. She's always been a spitting image of you; her eyes, her dimples… even her laugh. It was just too hard to look at her… to be around her, ya know?"

Frank carefully traced the engraved letters of her name on the headstone.

"I know, I know, that's no excuse for how I treated her. But you'll be happy to know that I read all of her letters the other night, and I even wrote one back," he said, shakily holding up an envelope. "I'll make things right, I promise."

***

Later that day, Emily appeared at the Corbin General Store with her bags packed. The old men were too entrenched in conversation to even notice her walk up the steps. From what she gathered, they were trying to count fireflies in the gathering dusk.

"You already counted that one, numb nuts," Harold said.

"How would you know? You're as blind as a bat!" Max countered.

"He's deaf, not blind!" Gus argued.

"What?!!" Harold yelled.

Emily shook her head and smiled. She knew full-well she was going to miss the inane banter of the three ole stooges. Once inside the store, she was greeted by Joan, who raised an eyebrow at her packed bags. She wasn't surprised that Emily was leaving, but secretly, she hoped she would have maybe found a reason to stay.

"Rumor has it, there will be a bus passing this way soon," Emily said lightly.

Joan looked at her watch and nodded.

"Passing through here on their way back from the Oxford casino, I suppose," she answered. "Those old folks sure do love their nickel slots."

Joan knew she was in the same age bracket as those on the casino bound bus, but she liked to think of herself as younger and hipper.

Emily chuckled at her observation. Without notice, Joan approached Emily and wrapped her up in a big hug.

"We're sure gonna miss you, Emily."

Emily gave Joan a big squeeze and a warm smile.

"Thank you, Joan... for everything. I don't think I can ever repay you for all of your kindness. I..."

With a finger to her lips, Joan stopped her right there.

"You always have a home here. Do you understand?"

Emily smiled and nodded.

"Can you say goodbye to Danny again for me?" she asked.

"Of course, sweetie," Joan said as she watched Emily scan the store. It was obvious she was looking for Ryan.

"I think he's over at the drive-in practicing for tonight," Joan said.

"For tonight?" Emily asked.

"I think he's planning on playing at the open-mic night at the tavern."

Emily smiled in approval. She was happy to learn Ryan was finally taking some chances of his own.

"I think he goes on around seven," she specified. "You know, just in case you miss your bus," Joan winked.

Emily opened her mouth to protest, but no words came out. Joan smiled and returned to the back of the store to continue stocking shelves.

Emily tried to shake off Joan's comment by fixing herself one last cup of Corbin's coffee. As she sipped it, she wandered out to the front porch where she found Harold, Max, and Gus sitting on their bench. Their conversation had moved onto something more... amusing. Emily stood quietly and observed.

"Why have I never heard of this douche canoe?" Gus questioned.

Harold shrugged and said, "I've never heard of it either, but Danny keeps talking about it."

"What the hell is the difference between a regular canoe and a douche canoe?" Gus persisted.

"How am I supposed to know!" snapped Harold. "I just got done telling you I've never heard of the damn thing!"

"And where the hell do they sell these douche canoes?" Gus inquired.

Harold let out an irritated sigh and shot him a glare. Before he could tell Gus just how stupid he was, he was interrupted by Max.

"I think it's one of them limited edition canoes from L.L Bean," Max pointed out.

As Harold and Gus pondered Max's theory, they finally noticed Emily standing there staring at them. She did her best to fight back her laughter.

"What do you think there, Missy? Have you ever heard of these new douche canoe thingys?" Gus asked.

Emily's insides felt like they were about to burst. She again fought back her laughter and matter-of-factly said, "I think Max is right. I think they're a new L.L. Bean thing."

Max slapped his leg triumphantly and gloated, "I knew it!"

Slowly, Harold and Gus nodded their heads and in unison said, "Ayah, good ole L.L. Bean."

Once the douche canoe mystery was finally solved, Harold noticed the suitcase by Emily's side and knew that she was headed out for good. Without a word, he pushed himself up off the bench and approached Emily.

"Come here, kiddo," he said softly with open arms.

Emily pressed her small frame into his and placed her head on his chest.

"Don't you be a stranger now," Harold said.

"I don't see how she could *get* any stranger!" Max exclaimed loudly.

Emily playfully sneered at him then gave a polite nod to Gus. She turned and headed down the steps but turned back before she reached the bottom.

"By the way, nice pants, Gus," she said with an approving smile.

Gus looked down at his Dickies, which he had pulled down to a normal level. He looked back up at Emily and gave her a proud smile.

"Now all you have to do is work on that nose hair of yours," she added with a smirk.

The smile on Gus' face quickly vanished as he lifted his hand self-consciously up to his nose. Emily laughed and waved over her shoulder. She could hear Harold as she walked down to the sidewalk.

"Don't look at me," said Harold. "I would have said something sooner, but I thought you were trying to catch flies or something with that situation."

"You do have a lot going on in there, Gussy," Max agreed.

"Well at least I don't have hair growing out of my ears like you do Max," Gus retorted.

"Yeah you do," Harold argued.

***

Later that evening, inside the Roadhouse Tavern, locals filled the tables and lined the bar. The scent of beer and fried food mingled with sweat and cheap perfume. In this part of the world, dressing up for a night out meant putting on your best pair of Carhartts and a clean flannel, or for the ladies, putting on a tight pair of jeans and maybe a little makeup.

At the back of the bar, several men gathered around a dimly lit pool table. They all wore expressions of serious concentration as they studied the layout beneath them. A gold and red glass chandelier advertising Coors Light swung unsteadily on its chains above them.

At the front of the bar, a makeshift stage was set-up near the large stone fireplace. On one side of the crackling fire there was a microphone placed in front of a wood carving of a moose standing on its hind legs. On the other side, an acoustic guitar leaned up against the stone surface of the fireplace. Between the two, Ryan sat on a stool studying the pages of music he had created at the drive-in.

Once he had arranged the pages in order, he placed them carefully on the stand in front of him and reached for his guitar. He strapped the instrument across his shoulder and took the microphone.

"Evening. It's been a while since I've played in front of anyone so forgive me if I'm a bit rusty... or nervous."

With the exception of one or two curious patrons, the crowd ignored him and continued their conversations or watching the game that played on the televisions above the bar. Standing in the back of the tavern, Emily was one the patrons whose attention was directed to the stage.

She remained unnoticed as she leaned against the wall, which was decorated by various Maine license plates. Some of the license plates sported the Maine state bird, the chickadee, sitting on a pine tree branch with Vacationland stamped underneath. Others had a red lobster in the background, or Support Wildlife with a picture of a moose and a fish.

The other curious patron held a lighter in the air with one hand and a raised beer over his head in the other.

"Free Bird!!!!" he yelled with a little too much enthusiasm.

Ryan laughed it off. There was always the one guy in the crowd, he thought.

"A lot of things were going through my head when I wrote this song last night. My life, my family, and..." Ryan trailed off as an image of Emily filtered through his mind.

She was probably looking out a darkened bus window right now, he thought. Ryan cleared his throat and shook the image away before he continued.

"Well anyway, the lyrics probably won't make much sense to you guys, but they mean something to me, and..."

"Sing the damn song already!!" shouted the Free Bird fan.

"Right," said Ryan. "This one is called Wild Irish Rose."

Emily felt her eyes widen and her breath quicken. She shook her head. No, he didn't, she told herself.

"They're closing down the farmers market,
And traffic's building down the lane.
I'm an angry taxi driver's target,
But that's okay, it's just the way he shakes his pain.
Some days my lover can't complete me.
Sometimes my work cannot be done…"

The loud voices of the bar slowly began to quiet as the attention of the patrons was won over by Ryan's smooth melodic voice and the rich tones of the guitar.

"Some days I see my sun as setting,
And I don't know, I don't know which way to run.
And every time I see you dance - my Wild Irish Rose,
I want to jump up on stage with you,
I want to give you my clothes,
And let the devil take my soul…"

Emily felt a single tear burn a path down her cheek and she quickly swiped it away as Ryan continued to sing.

"The sign said Live Exotic Dancers,
Not surprised to find myself inside.
It's like I'm looking for some answers,
For why my spirit's dead inside.
And every time I see you dance - my Wild Irish Rose,
I want to jump on stage with you,

I want to give you my clothes,
And let the devil take my soul…"

A complete hush had fallen over the bar and all eyes were on Ryan.

"And I never met my great grandfather,
But I swear I saw his ghost last night.
He looked just like he looked in pictures,
Except he was not black and white.
But every time I see you dance my Wild Irish Rose,
I want to jump on stage with you,
I want to give you my clothes,
And let the devil take my soul."

When the song ended, the bar was filled with the sound of applause. Ryan ducked his head down bashfully and set his guitar aside. However, the weight of a stare from across the room pulled his gaze upward again. The gravity of Emily's eyes pulled his look directly to her. When she smiled at him and saw his face light up, Emily knew she had finally done the right thing. Satisfied, she smiled at him and turned and exited through the back door.

Ryan followed her with his heart in his throat. She was the last person he expected to see in the crowd, and now she was the only one that mattered. Outside, he found Emily waiting for him under a large maple tree in the dusty dirt parking lot.

"Emily? I thought you left?" Ryan asked incredulously.

Emily smiled shyly and shrugged.

"I… kinda missed my bus," she confessed.

Ryan chuckled softly and took her hand.

"Well that's good, because it just happens to be a great night for a walk," said Ryan. "Shall we?"

Emily grinned and nodded.

As they walked down the sidewalk, the October wind licked at Emily's dark locks. One strand was tossed over her eyes, temporarily blinding her, but she swept it away gracefully. She wondered if she misread the vibes she had picked up from Ryan the night before.

"Sooo, a little birdie told me that you wanted to beg me to stay a little longer?" Emily asked.

Ryan stopped in his tracks. His face flushed several shades of red before he could find the words to answer.

"My mother has such a big mouth," he muttered.

Emily giggled at his embarrassment.

"And just so you know, I never said *beg*, but I might have mentioned that I liked having you around. That's all," Ryan clarified.

"You do know you're an idiot, right? Do you know how badly I wanted you to ask me to stay last night?"

"Really?" Ryan looked over at her in surprise. "But if you wanted to stay, why didn't you just…"

"Because I wanted *you* to want me to stay," Emily explained

Ryan shook his head, realizing he still had a lot to learn about women.

"You'd really stay here? In Maine? In Pine Ridge? As you know, it's not very exciting around here - especially compared to Boston. I mean, you'll probably get bored… in which case, I totally wouldn't hold it against you if you wanted to leave."

"Are you done yet?" Emily asked with her hands on her hips.

"I'm just surprised, that's all," said Ryan. "Lots of people leave small town Maine for the big city, but rarely does the big city ever come to the small town."

Emily looked around and shrugged.

"I can't promise how I'll feel in a year, or a month, or even a week from now, but as far as right now is concerned, this place just feels like home to me… and a lot of that has to do with you."

Ryan felt his heart leap inside his chest, but he continued walking to mask his reaction.

"I know a lot of the time I can be…" Emily started.

"Judgmental? Sarcastic? Rough around the edges?" Ryan finished.

"Um. I was just going to say a pain in the ass, but thanks for specifying."

"I'm just kidding. Lily was right, ya know? Those are just walls you put up. Because behind all the walls, and behind all the black clothes, and the black eyeliner, and the black…"

"Okay, okay, I get the point," Emily huffed.

"What I'm trying to say is… behind all that stuff there is a really sweet, caring, and talented chick. And she's even funny, in a dark, sarcastic, judgmental sorta way."

"I guess I'll take that as a compliment," Emily resigned.

She wasn't surprised when they rounded the corner to the drive-in and Ryan guided her inside the wooded cove. They sat on a large flat boulder in the corner of the abandoned parking lot.

"I really do appreciate your friendship the past few weeks. I know I don't always make it easy for people to get to know me, but thanks for putting up with me," Emily said.

Ryan gave her a warm smile and remembered the words he saw scribbled on one of her pads: *'Conquering me is never easy, and I fear nobody will'*.

"Now, about this Wild Irish Rose song of yours," she said with a playful spark in her eyes.

"I know, I know. You're probably pissed that I used that name, and it probably wasn't as Goth or as punk as you'd like…" Ryan said.

Emily slipped her hands around his bicep and pulled him to her.

"It was the most beautiful song I've ever heard," she whispered.

This time, as Ryan looked into her eyes, he knew he wasn't going to let the window close. He placed his hand on her chin and pulled her mouth to his. Her lips were warm and welcoming, and it felt like coming home. After a long, lingering moment, they parted. When Emily looked up at him she was smirking.

"What?" he asked defensively.

"You've sooo wanted to do that since the first time you saw me," she declared.

"Pahleeeease. You probably put some kind of black magic spell on me. I didn't even stand a chance," Ryan replied.

Emily giggled and pulled Ryan to his feet as she slid off the rock. He put his arm around her waist as they exited the drive-in.

"Just for future reference, does your bra unhook in the front or the back?" Ryan joked.

"Who says I wear one?" Emily asked with an arched eyebrow.

Ryan gaped at her, but quickly recovered with another pressing question.

"So, when do I get to see this Wild Irish Rose tattoo of yours?" he asked eagerly.

"Settle down, L.L. Bean Boy. Baby steps," Emily chided playfully.

As they reached the driveway of the Corbin residence, Emily was struck with a realization that left her feeling distraught. Sensing a shift in her mood, Ryan gave her an inquisitive look.

"What the hell am I going to do for work around here?" Emily asked.

Her question put a huge smile on Ryan's face.

"Ohh no! I am sooo not gonna work with you at the general store!" Emily protested.

"Nah. My idea for you is way cooler than that. I've actually been thinking about this for a while now. My idea is borderline genius."

"Well? What is it?"

"Settle down, Goth girl. Baby steps," Ryan teased.

They both laughed as they reached the steps to Emily's apartment. Emily turned to Ryan and tucked the red streak that ran through her dark hair behind her ear. He wondered if she would kiss him again, but instead, she took his hand and led him up the stairs and into the apartment.

From the small window overlooking the Corbin front porch, Joan smiled and shut out the porch light.

24
TIME TO FORGIVE

*"It's time to forgive these sins
It's time to forgive..."*

(Six months later)

Ryan exited the general store with a coffee and a small brown paper bag. He nodded to his father, who was entrenched in one of his famous sunflower seed spitting contests with Max and Gus.

Moments later, he arrived at one of the newly rented storefronts in town. The fresh paint on the building brought a renewed energy to the downtown area. Ryan looked up at the sign above the door and smiled as he read it:

THE LILY PAD, and in small caps beneath it: EMILY'S PHOTOGRAPHY & ART STUDIO.

As he stepped inside the brightly lit space, he admired the many pieces of Emily's artwork that lined the walls. Although she still had many candid shots of characters she caught in daily routines, her style had expanded to include many nature scenes as well. There were images of the river, the railroad tracks, rolling hills, faded old farmhouses, the church, and of course, the Corbin General Store.

Ryan's favorite was one she took of the old, abandoned drive-in at sunset. The large dark clouds that hovered ominously behind the blank looming movie screen gave the photo gripping emotion.

Ryan found Emily hanging new artwork on the back wall. He set the coffee and bag down on the counter next to her. Emily glanced down at them and smiled.

"From my mom," Ryan said.

"She didn't have to do that," Emily replied.

Ryan shrugged it off, just as he knew his mother would.

"How's business?" he asked.

"Pretty good, actually. Now that I have the website up and running, I'm getting more sales. Plus, the Miller's just asked me to do their daughter's wedding."

"See? I told you my idea was borderline genius," Ryan bragged.

Emily was about to whip off a remark to put Ryan's ego back in check, but the ringing of the phone stopped her short.

"That's probably Mrs. Miller now," Emily said excitedly.

Not wanting to hold up progress, Ryan gave her a quick kiss and headed out.

Just as Emily was finishing up with the phone call from Mrs. Miller, she heard the bells on the front door of the shop ring again. She figured it was Ryan coming back to get his truck keys. He was always forgetting them someplace.

"I swear you'd forget your head if it wasn't…" Emily stopped in mid-sentence. When she came around the corner, she saw her mother standing at the counter with a framed photo in her hands.

When Susan placed it on the counter to pay for it, Emily saw she had selected the childhood photo of Emily and Lily in their Easter dresses.

"This was always my favorite picture… of my two beautiful girls," Susan said carefully.

When they both looked up from the photo, each of them had tears brimming in their eyes. Emily smiled and nodded. A giant lump formed in Emily's throat, blocking the passage of words.

For seven long years, they had tirelessly rehearsed the right words to say to one another… the perfect words to make everything forgiven. When it came right down to it, however, no words were needed, for their looks said all that was needed to be said.

Emily still didn't believe in fairy tales or happily ever afters. She'd experienced too much sadness and heartache for that. But day by day, she was slowly starting to see that there was not only true beauty in this world but within herself as well.

Outside the store window, Emily caught a glimpse of Frank walking by with his daughter and grandson. He smiled through the window at Emily and tipped his hat in her direction. It was then Emily knew she was finally home.

The End

About The Authors

Jody Clark

Jody grew up in the Kittery/York area of southern Maine. He originally started out as a screenwriter. As of now, he has written nine feature-length screenplays ranging from dramas, to dramedies, to comedies. Not only did Jody grow up in Maine, but he makes it a point to utilize and represent his state as much as possible. From Maine's scenic rocky coast, to its remotely pristine backwoods, to its eclectic characters; all serve as backdrops and pay homage to his beloved state. His ultimate goal is not to just sell his scripts, but to have them filmed right here in the great state of Maine.

Unfortunately, searching for the proper financing has been a long, tiring, and at times, disheartening process. Feeling helpless in the whole 'funding' process, Jody decided to reverse the typical Hollywood blueprint. That blueprint being: It's almost ALWAYS a novel that gets turned into a screenplay and not a screenplay which gets turned into a novel. Jody's thought process was simple: It's much easier to self-publish a book rather than self-finance a movie, and who knows, maybe, just maybe, this will be a screenplay that gets turned into a book only to eventually get turned back into a movie! But even if this wild idea never comes to fruition, at least by turning it into a novel, the *stories* themselves will be able to be enjoyed by the public. Whether it's two or two million people who buy his books, Jody is just happy that they are no longer collecting dust in a desk drawer.

About The Authors

Jessie Taylor

Jessie Taylor first gained writing experience working as a newspaper reporter for Seacoast Media Group. She went on to write a history book of Berwick, Maine, which was released as part of the Images of America series by Arcadia Publishing. "The Wild Irish Rose" is the first published fiction project she has worked on to date.

Other books by Jody Clark

"The Empty Beach"
The Soundtrack to My Life Trilogy-Book One

"Livin' on a Prayer – The Untold Tommy & Gina Story"

Available at
www.vacationlandbooks.com

I do most of my posting & promoting via my FB profile
Feel free to friend me!!
Jody Clark (vacationland books)